Praise for *The*

M000034668

"Funny, poignant, unputdownable… Fast-paced, plotty and beautifully written, taking me to worlds I've never been to but now feel like I know."

– Sarah Laing, author of *Mansfield and Me*

"A ripping read… Once started I couldn't put it down… Billy and Sasha had such a complex yet simple relationship that holds you enthralled all the way through."

– Shane Dangerfield

"I loved this novel… The two protagonists have been written with a clear-eyed love. They are real & complex, and weeks after finishing the novel, they are still resonating with me."

– Susan Pearce, author of *Acts of Love*

"Vivid storytelling, engaging characters, great visual descriptions, suspense and interesting character development make this book a must-read. Check out this well crafted first novel."

– Andrew D Deppe

"Lively, engaging, witty and 'out there', *The End of Billy Knight* manages to be both hilarious and poignant in its depiction of the (highly dysfunctional) relationship between an aging drag queen and a hot young wannabe porn star. It's also a fascinating portrait of the US gay scene and the porn industry."

– Caren Wilton, author of *The Heart Sutra*

"A complex, poignant love story set in the intriguing (lost) world of 80s porn stars. Great, sympathetic characters and a compelling story."

– Bianca Zander, author of The Predictions

"In his literary debut, Ty Jacob's The End of Billy Knight takes readers on a rocky tale of unrequited desire, desperate quests for fulfillment, and everyday struggles for people working in nightlife and porn... But what makes it worth following goes beyond the steamy sex scenes and carnal gazes Jacob pens in vivid detail. At the heart of the novel lies an empathy with people typically seen as shallow, cold and unlovable."

– Windy City Times

THE END OF BILLY KNIGHT

TY JACOB

Copyright: © 2014 by Ty Jacob

ISBN: 978-0-473-28833-4

Publisher: Lucky Pony Press

Cover Design by James, GoOnWrite.com

Formatting by Hynek Palatin

Proofreading by Misti L. McCloud

Contents

PART ONE

RUNAWAYS

1
The Rifle

MIKE DIDN'T KNOW how old he was when it happened, but he was young enough to be sitting on his mom's knee when the man rushed into the back room with a mask over his face, carrying a rifle. It was his happiest boyhood memory.

They had just finished eating dinner and the room still smelled of warm roast beef. The dingy peach walls were lit with the soft light of the daisy lamp that hung above the table. The dishes had not yet been cleared. The blue-white fluorescence of the shop out front spilled in, framing the man's thick body in the doorway, an angry silhouette in a bright rectangle of light.

Mike felt his mom's arms wrap around him. She screamed and turned so that her body hid him from the gun. For a moment he couldn't see. His mom's arm was across his face, her chest heaving. He could feel her trembling. She was holding him so tightly that it hurt.

When she reached out to grab his sister, Lisa, and pull her close, he saw that Lisa was crying. Lisa's long brown hair jolted to the side as his mom pulled hard and fast.

Then all at once his mom was standing up, directed by the man with the rifle. She was setting Mike down and moving into the corner, one of her hands holding each child on either side. His dad was standing in front of the man with his hands in the air, yelling. "Please don't hurt my family, just please don't hurt my family!"

The pale skin around the man's eyes stuck out against the dark mask. Mike grabbed the floral print of his mom's skirt and hid. She kept her hand down in front of him, as if it were enough to protect him. The man came close. Mike saw the mud on his shoes, the dirty grey denim of his jeans. Looking up he saw the nearness of the rifle, the dusky black metal. He heard his mom screaming.

His dad shouted, "Abby, don't move!" and ran out into the shop. Mike could see him through the doorway, opening the cash register, pulling out all the money and putting it in one of the white plastic grocery bags they used for the fruits and vegetables. Then he came back into the room, the bag in one hand and the other hand up in the air, empty.

The man grabbed the bag of money and pushed past. Then he turned back and said, "Don't call the police. I have men outside all around you. If you pick up the phone they will kill you." He ran through the doorway and into the shop, past the tomatoes and carrots, beyond the eggplants and bananas, and he disappeared into the heavy darkness of summer night.

What Mike loved about the memory, what would make him cling to it throughout the rest of his life, was not the man with the rifle, not the soft peach room turning suddenly dangerous. It was the way his mom had held him, the way his dad had begged for their safety as though he really cared, the way both his parents, in that horrible moment, did everything they could to protect him. He was someone who was cared for, cherished. There were people in the world who wanted to keep him safe.

It would be years before he'd have that feeling again.

2
Silver Lamé Solves Everything

DALE'S HAPPIEST BOYHOOD memory wasn't until he was sixteen. That was the day he wore a dress to school.

He had planned it for nearly a year, ever since the silver lamé evening gown caught his eye at a secondhand shop. He was a plump boy. The dress hugged him across the stomach, a small dimple at his belly button, but it would do. Before then it had always been a secret – trying on his mother's dresses when nobody else was home, staring at himself in the full length mirror on the back of his parents' bedroom door.

Now Halloween was his excuse to do it in public. Unbeknownst to his parents, on Halloween day he stood in the boys' bathroom before first hour applying Sapphire Dream eye shadow, heavy rouge, and thick mascara – all of which he'd stolen from a drug store near his house. The blond wig he actually bought, with money from mowing the neighbor's lawn. An old pair of socks gave the silver dress some much-needed cleavage. Black pumps, a little too small, finished off his look. When he stepped out of that bathroom and into the wide institutional hallway of Lincoln, Nebraska's Fletcher J. Morgan High School, he was transformed. He was no longer timid and withdrawn. He was proud, bold. The wig was a helmet, the makeup a mask. The silver lamé was like armor.

Everyone who saw him laughed. He didn't care. He laughed with them. That was, in part, the point. People should laugh. It was fun. He smiled and even pretended to flirt with the boys, who then laughed louder. It was Halloween, and it was all a game. Doug Kohler – who was dressed in his varsity football uniform, blue and orange from head to toe, broad shoulder pads and Kohler 10 across his back – actually walked up to Dale and put his arm around him, saying, "Hey babe, you look good. Wanna see a movie after the game?" Doug's friends snickered and someone shouted. "She's as good as you're ever gonna get, Kohler!"

Dale was normally overlooked at school, and he loved the attention. His dress sparkled. Girls who'd never seen him before came up to him and cried out, "Oh I love what you've done with your hair!"

"Thank you, darling," he'd say, and flip his blond coif to the left, everybody smiling. He was a star.

It was only the next day when it turned sour, when several of Doug Kohler's football friends repeatedly collided into him in the hallway, pushing him hard with thrusting shoulders, knocking his books out of his hand and calling him *queer* under their breath as they continued on. The enchantment of Halloween was over, and Dale was once again just an odd, chubby boy with very few friends. He was convinced then that the dress the previous day had shielded him, as if the farce of wearing it had somehow created a spell of protection around him, for as long as he kept it on. He wanted that play, that safety, the happy attention he found in that dress, every day.

3
Good Looking Kid

TWO MONTHS AFTER Mike turned sixteen, he thought of the robbery as he slipped into the dark shop late at night, a large bump already turning purple on his forehead. It was the summer of 1981. His mom and Lisa were both gone, each departed in their own separate ways. His dad was passed out upstairs.

Throughout the shop, the vegetables were lumps of shadow and faint color in the dark. He had heard over and over the story of how this shop would be his some day. His dad used to stand behind him and make him wait on customers when he got home from school. "Math is the only thing you need to learn," his dad would say. "You need to know how to give change, count vegetables, pay the farmers at the market." He would place his hand on the back of Mike's neck, take another sip of the bottle he kept on the shelf below the register. Golden brown liquid sloshed behind clear glass as he tipped it back. A loud smack of his lips followed as he screwed the cap on and put it away.

Mike didn't want to own a pathetic little fruit and vegetable shop. He didn't want to become his dad.

He reached up and touched his forehead, wincing as he did. He walked over to the apples and filled his backpack, zipped it shut, and then stood behind the counter. The register was at least as old as he was. His dad had made sloppy repairs to it many times over the years. After the robbery he put a lock on the drawer and hid the key next to his bottle.

Mike was never sure how long after that robbery his mom had died, but it couldn't have been long. His childhood was a hazy country, the landscape hidden by fog and shadow. He couldn't quite see the edges of things. When people asked, as they inevitably did, he just said, "She died when I was a kid," and if they pressed him for an age the answer was, "I was little." Then he started talking about something else. They usually stopped asking.

He took the key from behind the bottle, still there after all these years, and reached out in the darkness, feeling for the small opening on the register's left side. He didn't think it would wake his dad, but he wanted to be sure. The bell in his fingers was smooth and cold. When he opened the drawer the only sound was a click, the feeble thump of the captive bell, the metal track sliding open, and there was the money. His dad hadn't made a deposit in three days. Mike remembered the man in the dark mask, and he took everything.

When he stepped out the front door, the night air smelled of freshly cut grass and pine trees. He walked toward the highway, his backpack heavy with apples and money. Eventually he saw the headlights of the highway through the trees, and his stomach tightened. He was this close to getting away from small-town Brewerton. He thought about all the things he was happy to leave behind, the things he hated: school, that pathetic little shop, his dad. Mostly his dad. Of course there were things he knew he would miss. Lying in the sun on the banks of the river, skinny-dipping with the other boys. The hay bales in the Thompson's hay shed. Charlie, who he fooled around with from time to time.

8

At the edge of the highway, he put out his thumb. It was just past midnight and there weren't that many cars. Sporadic headlights glared into his eyes and passed him by. He walked along. After a while a big four-door sedan stopped at the side of the road. He couldn't see who was inside. He walked up to the car, opened the door and saw a beard hiding most of a face, a Green Bay Packers baseball cap low over the eyes.

"Where you headed?" the man asked. He was big. He sat tall in the seat.

"Cincinnati, wherever."

"I'm going as far as Hillsboro. Hop in."

"Where?"

"Just outside Cincinnati."

Mike's side hurt as he got into the car.

The man said his name was Jerry, and he pulled into the empty stream of highway. Mike said his name was Charlie.

"Where'd you get that bang on your forehead there?" Jerry asked.

"Fell down," Mike answered. There was no way he was going to tell this man what had really happened. He was still reeling, still scared. He was amazed he didn't get shot.

"Okay. So, what's in Cincinnati?"

"Nothing much. Just going. What's in Hillsboro?"

"My wife and kids."

As they drove along, Mike felt Jerry staring at him in the dim light of the car, oncoming traffic sometimes illuminating the front seat.

"You're a good looking kid," Jerry said.

Mike turned toward him, meeting his gaze head on but smiling and speaking warmly. "You wanna watch the road?"

Jerry turned away.

Charlie used to say, "You could be a movie star, man." At school the girls were constantly trying to flirt with Mike – something he found annoying and flattering at the same time. Although his sandy brown hair was slightly disheveled, he kept it short enough so people could see his face. Still, he never quite saw in himself what others said was there. It felt like being color blind, having to ask somebody else, *What color is my shirt?* He could only trust that what they said was true. What he did know, what he learned at an early age, was that when he smiled and gave people all his attention, it changed them somehow, made them easier to deal with.

"How old are you?" Jerry asked.

"Eighteen." Mike turned his body in the seat so he was completely facing Jerry, his back against the door. Jerry was big and broad. Mike was only five foot eight, with a slim build.

Jerry scratched his beard. "You look young for eighteen."

"How old are you?" Mike said.

A slight pause. "Thirty."

"You look young for thirty."

"Well," Jerry said, then fell quiet and stayed that way for the rest of the drive.

After a while, Mike felt the heavy weight of sleep. His head nodded forward and jerked back up again as he tried to stay awake. In the end he gave in, tipped his head back on the headrest, and slept.

When he woke up the car was stopped and Jerry was sitting in the driver's seat, watching him. They were in an empty parking lot somewhere. To his right there was a large, unlit building. It looked abandoned. The night was thick and there were no stars. He wondered how long they'd been parked there.

Jerry said nothing. His eyes peered out from just under the rim of the cap.

Mike reached for his bag, which he'd kept at his feet. "Is this Hillsboro?"

"Yes. This is Hillsboro."

"How long have we been parked here?"

"A little while."

"So this is as far as you go?"

There was no response.

"Well, uh, how about the bus station?" Mike said. "Can you drop me off there?"

Jerry looked down, then turned and stared out the window, toward some traffic lights. He lifted his hand and slowly scratched the back of his neck, pushing his cap forward as he did, then straightening it out again. There was a long pause while Mike watched him, wondering what would happen next. It was probably three in the morning. The parking lot spread out in all directions in the darkness. Jerry kept staring out the window.

Mike was tired and suddenly afraid. He leaned forward and tilted his head, pretending to be more sure of himself than he really was. He smiled. "Tell me about Hillsboro."

"What?"

"Tell me about it."

Jerry looked confused. "It's all right."

"What's your wife's name?"

"Why?"

"Just curious."

"You don't need to know."

"Well, how many kids do you have?"

"Two girls."

"How old?"

11

"What is this, twenty questions?"

"You have pictures?"

Only when Mike leaned in further did Jerry reach into his back pocket for his wallet.

"This is Michelle," he said. "She's eight." Already his voice was changing, becoming softer. "This is Jenny." There, in Jerry's hands, were two cute girls, both with blond hair and braids, smiling brightly.

"Jenny," Mike said. "Sounds like Jerry."

"She was supposed to be a boy, Jerry Junior, so we settled on calling her Jenny."

"They look happy. You're a lucky dad."

Jerry nodded slowly.

Mike leaned back now. "So, what about the bus station. Would you take me there?"

Jerry put the pictures away, tucked his wallet into his back pocket again, and let out a deep sigh. "Yeah, sure kid," he said, looking out the window. He reached forward and started the car.

4
The Lucky Pony

BY THE SUMMER of 1981, Dale had been living in Los Angeles for almost fourteen years. He stood backstage at the Lucky Pony getting ready, and he remembered that Halloween when he was sixteen, that silver lamé. He was thankful Nebraska was long ago and far away. He'd always felt like a strange, alien creature back there, living on a planet where the air was just a little too thin for him. He'd escaped as soon as he could.

He stepped out of the dressing room, not yet fully made up, and peeked through the silver streamers that hung down behind the stage. He was scanning the audience in the bar. The disco ball turned above the dance floor, throwing stars around the room. A small group of muscular young men standing in front of the stage were calling out, "Sasha! Sasha!" These were his fans, and he loved them. There was magic in the fact these young men were calling out so eagerly for a fat, ugly, prematurely balding man in a skirt. Dale was thirty-two, but when those who didn't know it was uncouth to ask a drag queen her age actually did the unthinkable, he would give them a brazen smile and say, "Why, I'm nineteen, of course." Sometimes he'd bat his eyes shamelessly and add, "Barely legal." It always made them smile.

He went back into the dressing room, with its stuffed chair smelling of spilled beer and cigarette smoke, and sat in front of the cracked mirror. He did the last fixes to his makeup and then – finally, always the last touch – he put on his wig.

Tonight it was a beautiful set of brunette curls. Suddenly Dale was no longer Dale. He was Sasha. Sasha Zahore. Glamorous and truly fabulous.

As Sasha stepped out onto the stage, the rhinestones on her Western-style blouse sparkled like diamonds. The very short denim skirt she wore was her own handiwork, and she'd given considerable thought to the mother-of-pearl snaps that went up the back. Her plaid scarf was tied charmingly at the side of her throat (carefully obscuring her double chin), and her red cowgirl boots were graced with an expensive pair of comet-shaped spurs in iridescent blued steel, which jingled every time she took a step. She'd saved for those boots for months, and wore them proudly. Her red cowgirl hat was tipped at a jaunty angle. As Patsy Cline crooned "Crazy" over the cheap sound system, Sasha lip-synched in perfect time, gesturing melodramatically, twirling her finger around her ear and rolling her eyes each time the word "crazy" passed through her pouting, perfectly lipsticked mouth.

The audience ate it up, as they did every Wednesday, laughing and smiling, some singing along. This was her art, her way of giving people pleasure, and she took it seriously, forever sewing costumes, combing the thrift shops in her tireless hunt for new inspiration, and diligently preparing for the next week by practicing what she called her 'choreography' in the tiny kitchen of her West Hollywood apartment. She lived, she hated to admit, in a shabby two-bedroom place, which she shared with a bartender who wanted to be an actor and a waiter who was a selfish, coke-snorting ass. The waiter slept on the couch. More than once she'd stumbled across him *in flagrante* with a guest. But none of that mattered in this moment. The bright spotlight followed her across the stage, shimmering in the waves of her synthetic hair, and every unglamorous thing outside the glow of that blue-white circle faded from view. She mouthed along with Patsy about feeling lonesome and so terribly blue.

* * *

When Sasha wasn't on stage at the Lucky Pony, she worked at Stacked & Hung on Hollywood Boulevard. From noon until nine, five days a week, she poised herself in full drag behind a display case laden with dildos and fur-lined handcuffs, ringing up sales and taking five dollars from each customer who wanted to go into the video booths to watch the wide selection of gay and straight porn. They were almost always men alone, sometimes a couple, straight or gay. Once there was a dyke who said something about inverting the masculine paradigm as she handed over a five, but women alone were rare. It didn't matter. Sasha didn't care who came in. The job was easy. It allowed her to pay rent and buy clothes, and it didn't exhaust her the way her first job in LA had, when she was frantically waiting tables at a Mexican restaurant. The only slightly unpleasant task about working at Stacked & Hung was mopping up the gooey spunk the men left behind. Yet even that wasn't so bad if you thought about it, since it was just cum after all.

Between stage and work, Sasha made little videos, something she'd been doing ever since that day two years ago when she marched into Menken Electronics on Santa Monica Boulevard and rented a video portapak. It was a big machine, but you could carry it. There was a hand-held color video camera that connected to a portable videocassette recorder with a shoulder strap. The technology was amazing. She could record up to 30 minutes of video.

That day she drove her green Plymouth to Venice Beach, the heavy portapak on the passenger seat beside her like a newfound friend. There, wearing a provocative white dress with a slit up the side, she stood near the beachside gym and filmed men in their shorts and tank tops as they lifted weights and sweated spectacularly in the bright California sun. She knew they didn't believe she was a real woman. She was too fat in a mannish way, too large. But it didn't matter. She had a newfangled video camera, and it made her desirable. Eventually she managed to coax one of the men home to film him working out. It took five or six guys and several months of trying before she finally found one who agreed to jack off on camera. What a fantastic day that was!

After that she began branching out with her video experiments, making her first hardcore shorts. She couldn't really pay her models much, but there was usually someone willing to do it for fifty bucks. When she could find hot guys, it was so much fun. They were amateur productions, but she didn't mind. She loved watching men having sex together, unashamed and unafraid.

* * *

Now Sasha spun on stage, ready for Patsy Cline to start the big wrap up. All through the song Sasha had been trying to find exactly the right young man. She loved the effect she had on them – not all of them, but some. She liked to find a slightly shy one, as cute as possible, and make him squirm as she heaped the last lines of the song directly on him.

And there was the one – purple polo shirt and blond hair, adorable grin, standing right up front with a plain looking girl, obviously just a friend. Sasha didn't know who this young man was, but it didn't matter. There would be a different one the next time.

She walked over to him, smiling lewdly, staring him down and mouthing the final words of the song, as though she really did love this particular stranger in the crowd. She bent over and pointed dead at him, smoldering all the sex she had, all the intimacy and desire and lust she held in the round folds of her abundant body. As the song ended she moved closer, held his head in her hands, and kissed him on the cheek. She took it as a mark of her success that his face turned several shades of pink.

5
Bees to Honey

IT WAS A Sunday afternoon, 1984. Mike sat at the bar at Thunderbird Bowling Lanes and looked at the clock on the wall. They usually started showing up around one.

At the entryway from the bowling alley, a neon sign read, "Spares 'n' Strikes Bar," one bright bowling pin blinking back and forth, perpetually falling and becoming upright again, ready for another fall. Below the neon a white piece of paper with large black handwriting stated, "Under 21 not admitted."

Mike was nineteen now, but that didn't stop him. He wore jeans and a white T-shirt, his black Converse tennis shoes. It was what he always worked in.

Along the wall behind the bar, a series of large plaster bowling pins rose up from the counter to the ceiling like a row of Greek columns. A menu on the wall listed drinks like "The 300 Game" and "Strike-a-roo!" The bar was always noisy, with the sound of rolling balls and crashing pins coming in through the entry to the bowling alley, the video games in the corner beeping and chiming, the music over the speakers, country western and rock mostly. Throughout the bar the carpet was grey and dirty, dotted with black spots from cigarette burns or chewing gum. The round Formica tabletops were like white lily pads, floating over the muck of floor.

The bartender walked over to Mike and said, "Hi, Bill."

"Hey, Frieda," Mike answered.

"The usual?" Frieda was a large-breasted older woman with a dyed red beehive hairdo and a smoker's voice. She pretended not to notice what happened in the bar, as long as the customers tipped her well.

"Yeah, thanks," he said. He'd shown Frieda his drivers' license only once, when she asked him for ID his first time in the bar. She'd never forgotten his name. She had looked at it and said, "That picture don't do you justice, Bill," then handed it back with a wink.

Mike had gotten the license when he picked up a guy named Bill in Clepper Park, solely because the guy was over twenty-one and they looked a bit alike. Mike went home with him and got him drunk by making a show of waiting on him, mixing drink after drink, gin and tonics – lots of gin in Bill's and water in his own. He was hoping Bill would pass out quickly, but he didn't. In the end Mike had to wear Bill out with sex until the guy finally collapsed. Mike didn't mind. He liked sex. He found Bill's wallet in the jeans on the floor, took his driver's license and slipped out the front door.

"There ya be, Bill." Frieda set down a bottle of Miller Lite in front of him. "That'll be a buck twenty five."

He paid and took a long drink, then looked around the bar. Ralph had come in and was sitting at a table in the corner. Mike hadn't yet met Ralph, but Toby had talked about him. Mike had heard about the costume hidden in a suitcase in the back of Ralph's car. He was old, but at least he wasn't fat. That would be an easy one, he thought.

When he'd first arrived in Cincinnati, Mike had gotten a bed at the Y.M.C.A. and began spending the money he'd stolen from his dad. He took taxicabs and bought expensive running shoes. The cash didn't last as long as he thought it would. All of a sudden he realized he couldn't even pay for his bed. The only person he could turn to for help was his sister, who'd left Brewerton herself years earlier, ending up in Cleveland. He called her from a pay phone on the street.

When he said, "Hey sis," she screamed "Mikey!" She was incredibly happy to hear from him. She started rambling on about this and that, the way she always had when they were kids. She tried to get him to go back to their dad, back to Brewerton, but he said, "No. No way."

"What happened the night you left home?" she asked. "Dad won't talk about it."

"Nothing. Nothing happened. I just left."

She didn't ask again. In the end she sent him $200 because, she said, "I don't want you living on the street." Before they hung up she added, "If you won't go home, then get a job," and he did.

He started washing dishes at Luigi's Tavern, and he worked there for over two years until one night a man approached him on McFarland Street, between 3rd and 4th, after the bars closed. He was walking down the sidewalk when the man pulled up next to him in a BMW and said, "How much?"

"What for?" Mike asked, although not entirely naïve.

"Blow job."

Mike paused, looked directly at the man. "You tell me. How much?"

"Fifty."

At the time Mike was making minimum wage, $3.35 an hour. Although he was never very good at math, he later calculated that the money he made in twenty minutes in that deluxe BMW would have taken him over fourteen hours to make in the terrible heat of the tavern's back kitchen. Plus it was cash in hand, no tax. He began walking down McFarland

Street more regularly. Eventually he quit the tavern altogether.

Mike stood now at his usual spot at the bar in the Spares 'n' Strikes. His back was to the room, one leg up on the footrest to show off the curve of his ass. His jeans were tight. One of his regulars once told him, "Your customers are like bees to honey when it comes to that rear end of yours, boy. Bees to honey."

Two straight couples walked in. They'd just finished bowling and didn't seem to notice the number of men in the bar, drinking alone. Then an older, fat guy came in and started staring at Mike. Mike turned away. He didn't like old, fat guys. Not if he didn't have to. The problem was that in Cincinnati there were a lot of old, fat guys.

A guy who called himself Tuck walked up to Mike and said, "Hi, Bill. Mind if I buy you a drink?"

"No," he answered, "I'm fine with this one."

"What's wrong with you?" Tuck was stocky, with thick wrists.

Mike turned and looked at him. "Last time, you gave me bruises. I don't like bruises."

"Come on, don't be sore." Tuck nudged his arm.

Mike turned his back on him and walked over to the jukebox. He stood staring at the song titles until he was sure Tuck wasn't following him, then he walked over to Ralph's table.

"Hi," he said. "Mind if I join you?"

Ralph looked up nervously. "Oh, no. Not at all. Please do sit down." He was almost entirely bald, with a grey comb over and a very shiny gold pinky ring.

Mike smiled. "I thought you looked like you could use a little company."

"Why, yes, yes. I could. I can. Yes."

"I'm Bill," Mike said.

"Well, nice to meet you Bill. My name is Ralph. I've seen you here before, yes I have."

"Yeah, I think you know my friend Toby."

"Ah, yes Toby. I do. I have been acquainted with Toby. Toby's not here today, is he?"

"Nope. He's not." Mike finished his beer and set the empty bottle down on the table.

"Oh, may I buy you another drink?"

"Sure. Thanks."

Ralph walked up to the bar and got them each another drink, then came back to the table. Tuck was watching them. They made small talk about the weather and the Red Sox and the plans to convert Union Terminal Station into a museum. Mike kept the conversation going. "So, what do you do, Ralph?" he asked.

"Well, I sell insurance, you see. Home, auto, life, income protection. Yes. You see, I sell all kinds."

"Ah, that's nice."

Ralph didn't ask what Mike did.

"Yes," Ralph continued. "It's very important to be insured."

Mike began looking around the room. He didn't know if this was going anywhere. He looked over at Tuck, then at the old, fat guy.

"Um," Ralph said in a quiet voice. "I wonder, if you had the time just now, could you and I go someplace together?"

Here it is, Mike thought, then asked, "What do you like to do?"

"Oh, there's that motel across the road. And, do you like costumes?"

"What do you mean?"

"Well, I have a costume in my car, and I'd like to put it on."

"Hmm." Mike said. "I don't do kinky." He was lying, driving up the price.

"Oh, it's not so bad, not really."

"I don't know. What kind of costume is it?"

"Promise you won't laugh."

"Of course not." Mike smiled. "I'm a professional."

"It's a bunny costume. Pink with big fluffy ears. I take off all my clothes, put it on, and you spank me. There's a little powder-puff tail. It's not kinky. It's very cute. Then you leave me alone and I take care of myself."

"Hmm. I don't know."

"I'll pay you eighty."

"To spank you and leave you?"

"Yes, in the bunny costume. Leave me lying on the bed in the bunny costume."

"I don't know."

"Okay, one hundred."

"Oh, well. Okay."

Ralph smiled, and they left the bar together.

6
Cougar Studios

SASHA'S THIGH-HIGH, green, vinyl go-go boots were heavy and her legs inside them were hot and sticky. She could feel the sweat trickling down her calves and gathering in pools between her toes as she walked down La Cienega Boulevard. She had made a very big mistake. This was no day to be wearing vinyl go-go boots.

She should have worn her open-toed, platform sandals with the roman straps instead. She felt a blister coming on, so she stepped lightly with her right foot. The California sun made her scalp itch under her long blond wig, and she could feel her makeup actually starting to melt. Her appointment was at noon, and as usual, she was running late. She'd had to park over on Huntley and she'd just walked four blocks – no small task in these boots. She was afraid she'd be a wilted mess by the time she arrived, and if there was one thing she knew in this world it was that nobody, but nobody would hire a sweaty, overweight drag queen with runny mascara and a limp. She had to pull it together.

As she turned the corner she saw the old warehouse building on a side street. It didn't look much like a glamorous movie studio, but there was the name, Cougar Studios, in large red letters above the door. She stepped into an alley and opened her enormous green vinyl handbag. She pushed aside her promotional tape – scenes from the short films she'd made, guys from Venice Beach working out and jacking off, guys she'd met around town having fabulous sex – and she found her compact. She opened it up and checked her makeup, powdered her nose, and wiped the beads of sweat off her brow with her large, mannish hands. Then she closed her eyes and said a tiny prayer. God, she was certain, was the most fabulous drag queen of all.

Sasha wanted to be a big, famous director – not of Hollywood slop, but of beautiful, sexy, gay porn. Not just directing the small-time, low-budget shorts she'd been doing, but top-quality feature films with one of the big studios: Hard Bodies or Magnum Man or Cougar.

She was painfully aware of the two main facts of her life. 1) Lip-synching to Patsy Cline and Cher would only take her so far. 2) There was really no future in working behind a counter full of someone else's dildos.

Sasha wanted to call the shots, and there was money to be made in gay porn. Besides, she loved it. So now she held her head high and knocked on the front door of Cougar Studios, her faux diamond tennis bracelet sparking in the hot midday sun.

A young man in a blue mesh tank top opened the door. He had startlingly white teeth, bleached blond hair, and biceps like melons. "Hi," he said. "Can I help you?"

She looked him up and down. "Doll, I've got a long list of ways you could help me, but unfortunately I'm late for an appointment. Twelve o'clock with Steve Logan. Be a dear and take me to him, won't you?"

"And your name is…"

"Sasha, baby. Sasha Zahore. Don't you know me? I do a show down at the Lucky Pony. Perhaps you've seen it?"

"Just a moment please." He shut the door, leaving Sasha outside in the heat. She curled her lip and cursed him under her breath, but a moment later the door opened again and he invited her in.

"Why, thank you, doll. A girl could die out there in that scorching sun. Makes me want to take off all my clothes. Don't you feel the same?"

He led her down a carpeted hallway, past doors that said "Studio C" and "Studio B." A young man wearing nothing but a towel passed them in the hallway. "Oh dear," Sasha yelled out after him, "if you're looking for a shower I can take you back to my place after I'm done here!"

The one with the melons for biceps told her to sit in a white room with a desk and a sofa. He sat down at the desk and began typing something on a typewriter. He was probably in his late twenties, and had a chest so smooth it had to be waxed. The desktop was a mess, piled with papers, gay magazines and videotapes. A gold plaque on the door behind him said simply "Steve." Sasha sat on the sofa facing the gold plaque and waited for her future to start.

After five minutes she became impatient. "What's your name, doll," she said to the young man behind the desk.

He looked up and answered quickly, "Günter," then turned back to his typewriter.

"Günter?" She hadn't noticed any accent. "Is that your real name, or assumed?"

He looked at her and said, "I'm from Frankfurt." There it was, a light German inflection.

"So, tell me, Günter. Is Steve a nice guy?"

He gave a wry smile. "Steve can be real nice. If he likes you." He looked briefly down at her body from across the room. His mouth slipped into a subtle frown, as if to imply Steve wouldn't like her at all.

After about twenty minutes the door finally opened and out walked Steve Logan. Sasha had seen him around but never before at such close range. Her immediate thought was that he was trying very hard to remain well preserved. He had to be in his early fifties. He was still a bit buff from working out, very well tanned, kept his thinning hair in an army-style brush cut, and had a large brown mustache and sideburns that looked like they'd come straight out of a 1970s beer commercial. He wore jeans with a rip in the knee, construction boots, and a red flannel shirt unbuttoned just enough to show off a patch of thick chest hair. Sasha immediately understood. Here was a man in *man-drag*. He presented himself more as the *idea* of a man than as an actual man.

"You must be Sasha," he said, and shook her hand with such an unnecessarily strong grip that she winced.

"Charmed, I'm sure." She said, and gave a small curtsey.

He turned to Günter. "If Matt calls, put him through." Then he quickly led Sasha into his office.

The walls were hung with poster-sized video covers of the latest Cougar releases. They showed tanned, muscular men – much younger than Steve – in various states of undress, posed under porn titles. *The Bigger They Are. Jock Cock. Construction Worker Bang Gang.*

"Oh!" Sasha squealed loudly as she sat down, "I just loved *Construction Worker Gang Bang*. It's *so* unfair you didn't win Best Gay Group Scene at the Adult Entertainment Awards. Really, *Danny's Dildo Party* had nothing on your film, nothing at all. It was criminal."

"Thank you. We put a lot of work into that movie." Steve gave a sad, resigned smile.

"I'm sure you did." Sasha reached out and touched Steve's desk. "And we know the boys *love* their work."

"What can I do for you?"

"Well, first of all, thank you so much for taking the time to meet with me."

"You were very insistent on the phone."

"Well, yes. I put that same determination and drive into all my work." She took a deep breath and explained how she wanted to make top quality porn, with excellent production values, using skilled sound and lighting technicians. This, she knew, was the most important sales job of her life so far – more important than any double-headed dildo she'd ever sold over the counter.

"I want to make porn that's so good it'll make even your mama proud," she said. "I don't need to tell you about today's gay porn consumers. I mean, really. It's 1984, for fuck's sake. They're out there marching in gay pride parades and demanding equality in human rights. You know as well as I do that they don't want sloppy, poor-quality porn that makes them feel they're doing something *wrong*. That's why I like what you do here at Cougar. It's top-notch stuff. And that's why I want to direct Cougar's next big feature."

Steve laughed. "Whoa. What makes you think you're going to walk in off the street and start directing?"

"That's a very good question, Steve. But Sasha Zahore is not just in off the street with no experience. I've been directing my own low-budget projects for years now." She pulled out the promotional tape from the depths of her bag and set it on Steve's desk.

The previous year, Sasha bought the very first consumer camcorder ever made, the Sony Betamovie BMC-100, which was both a video camera and a video recorder in one unit. It was lightweight, could record up to three and a half hours of footage, and most importantly had a beautiful rainbow-colored carrying strap. Of course, the $1,500 price tag had completely exhausted the rainy day funds that she'd stashed under her mattress, but she didn't mind. What was money for if not for spending? She'd been making videos at a furious pace ever since.

"I call this cute, little videocassette here my Sin Sampler," Sasha said. "I've done workout, jack-off, and short hardcore. Now, these are not up to your excellent production values, I'm sure, but they do show my skills as a director. I pride myself in bringing out the best in my models. Whatever you do, watch all of it, start to finish. You don't want to miss what I've got them doing in the last scene with the orange traffic cone. It's pure genius, if I do say so myself."

She paused and waited for Steve to respond. She wanted desperately for him to just say, *Yes*, to lean forward in his chair and say, *Of course I'll let you do what you've always wanted to do. I know how important it is to you, and because you've had the courage to ask for it, I'll give it to you. Here. It's yours.*

Steve did lean forward, and for a moment she almost believed he was going to say exactly what she wanted, but then he sighed. It was a long, slow sigh, followed by a subtle, yet meaningful, headshake. "Listen, Sasha," he said. "Let me lay it on the line. Look around you." He gestured to the posters on the walls. "Look at these guys. Cougar sells masculinity, Sasha. These are strong, straight-acting guys. It's what sells. Now, look at yourself. Honestly, you're just not right for us at all."

"I'm not asking to be *in* the videos, just to direct."

"I'm afraid it doesn't matter." He was not being unkind. He almost seemed sad to have to break the news to her, like a stranger who was being forced into telling a child he'd just met that there was no Santa Claus. "Sasha, you see, there's a certain philosophy here at Cougar, at all the big-name gay studios, really. They'll all tell you the same thing. You can sum up our business in one word: masculine. That's all. That's all we care about. We're dealing with an audience that's been called sissy all their lives and they want to feel butch. Our directors have names like Mitch Braun, Phil Steele, and Adam Rockford, not Sasha... What is it?

"Zahore. Sasha Zahore."

"Not Sasha Zahore. I'm sorry, but drag queens don't direct porn, at least not *our* porn. Why don't you just stick to what you do best? I'm sure your show is great. Just keep doing drag and leave the directing to the big boys." He stroked his mustache and then pushed the videotape toward her side of the desk.

"Come on now, Steve." Sasha leaned one shoulder in and touched her fingertips to her collarbone. "Don't you think you're being just a little bit, oh, *narrow-minded*?" She knew she shouldn't have said it. She was trying to win him over, not make an enemy.

"Narrow-minded? I'm trying to let you down lightly and you call me narrow-minded? I could be a mother fucking asshole and have you thrown out of here right now. Do you understand that?"

"Oh, Jesus. There I go again." She leaned back and smiled. "I've got a terrible mouth and it always gets me in trouble. Sometimes I think the only way to keep this mouth shut is to stick a dick in it." She watched him to make sure he smiled. He did. "I'm sorry, Steve," she continued. "Really, you're a smart, hunky man. You obviously know what you're doing. You wouldn't have your own successful studio if that weren't the case. But just let me prove myself to you. I love porn. Love it. I want to work with it in any way I can. There must be something around here that you can let me do. Anything. For the past four years I've been working in a sex shop mopping up cum, so it can't get much worse than that."

"I don't know."

"Steve, come on. You know the drag queens were there at Stonewall in 1969, throwing beer bottles at those crooked cops right next to all the butch gay boys. We're in this together. And I promise you, I will work for you harder than *any* of the pretty little muscle boys you've got skipping around here. Nobody has my stamina, my commitment, and hell yes, my *enthusiasm*."

He smiled again. "Yes, I can see you're very enthusiastic. Okay, look. I might regret this, but we do need some people in Marketing and Distribution."

Sasha pointed at Steve energetically. "There it is! I'm your gal!" Then she paused and tipped her head. "What's that mean, exactly?"

"It's easy. You call the video shops around the country to tell them how great our newest release is. You find out how many copies they want, and you try and get them to order more. I think you could sell."

"Sell?! I could talk the hind leg off a donkey. When I was nine I sold so much lemonade at a stand in front of my house that the neighbors reported me to the IRS. I kid you not."

"Can you can start Monday? Ten o'clock."

"Yes! You *won't* regret it, Steve. I swear you won't. Thank you. Thank you." She picked up her bag, wanting to leave before he changed his mind. She paused and touched the videotape on the desk. "Now, are you sure you don't want to see what these strapping young men do with that traffic cone?"

"Hmm," Steve said.

"Listen, doll. I'll leave it with you." She tapped it twice and winked. Then she stood up, shook his hand, and walked proudly out of the room.

7
Pinned

THE GUY HAD been fucking him for almost an hour before the trouble started. It was 1989, and Mike had been living in Cincinnati almost eight years, turning tricks for six. He thought he was experienced, thought he knew all the warning signs, but this one took him entirely by surprise.

At first the guy just started slapping his ass, and Mike didn't mind. But then the slaps got harder, and more frequent. The guy was powerfully built and hairy, which Mike liked, and he'd paid well, up front, so Mike let the slaps go on for longer than he would have normally, but finally he said, "Hey, ease off. Hurts too much."

It got worse then. Suddenly the guy pulled his dick out of Mike's ass and punched him hard in the small of the back with a solid fist. Mike struggled to get air into his lungs. His small size put him at a disadvantage as the big guy pinned him down. When he finally caught his breath he yelled, "Fuck you! Get off me!" but it was too late. He knew he was in trouble.

The blows kept coming, again and again, each to the small of his back. The guy was vicious. Mike had never seen him before that night, and he felt vaguely, as each fist came down on his back, that he should have known better. It was a mistake. Maybe he'd gotten complacent after too many years. Maybe his judgment had been thrown off by too much beer, by this guy's masculine allure. He tried to get away now but couldn't. He turned on his side, covered his head with his arms and hoped it would be over soon. The impact of the guy's large fist on his face nearly knocked him out.

When the guy started fucking him again, at first Mike didn't know what was happening. Even after he saw the condom lying like a dead jellyfish at the side of his head, it took a moment before he realized the guy was fucking him without protection. Mike heaved and twisted. He screamed. He would rather be beat to within an inch of his life than be fucked this way.

Mike was always careful. He didn't do it without condoms, never ate cum. Sometimes guys offered to pay more if he would, but he said no. He followed the rules. *No glove no love. Come on me not in me.* He didn't want to get sick. He thought of Freddy, one of his old johns. He didn't want what happened to Freddy to happen to him.

When the big guy came inside him, Mike was crying.

Afterwards, the guy got up and got dressed without a word, leaving Mike alone there, covered in blood and tears on the hotel bed, right across the road from the Spares 'n' Strikes, where Frieda was probably closing up at that very moment. Mike could barely move, but he forced himself to get up and go into the bathroom. He wanted to get the guy's cum out of his ass. He knew that it was too late, that it didn't matter. If the guy was positive Mike probably would be now, too. He prayed the guy was healthy.

He decided that moment – bent over on the toilet, shaking, crying, and bleeding – that he would do something different. He no longer wanted to risk picking up strangers on the street and in bars. He didn't want to be alone with these men, who were too often desperate, with secret lives, and who seemed to be filled alternatively with sadness or

34

anger – it was never clear which one until you were alone with them.

The next day he lay in bed in his tiny apartment on St. Clair Avenue and his entire body ached. Each time he moved, pain shot up his back. He called Toby and told him what had happened, but Toby's voice came back flat over the phone. "Hey, man, sorry to hear it. You'll be okay. Listen, I gotta go."

Mike hung up and wondered if he hadn't made it clear how bad it was, or if Toby didn't want to talk about it because he was afraid it could happen to him too. Mike started to curl into a ball in his bed but it hurt, so he lay still. The room was cold. He pulled his old green blanket up to his chin. His left eye was swollen completely shut, but he stared at the ceiling with his good eye until eventually the light outside started to fade and the sounds of the bar downstairs came up to his closed window, music and people laughing.

In the middle of the night he got up, went to his freezer, and pulled out a bag of frozen peas. There was a tear in the plastic and he put his hand inside, pulling out the money he'd been stashing away. The bills were covered with frost, and they crinkled in his hands. He laid the money out across the bottom of his bathtub, so that it would defrost and dry. Icy peas rolled into the corners of the tub. He counted four hundred and fifty dollars. This was all he had from eight years of work. He was only twenty-three, but he already felt old.

Back in bed, he held the half-empty bag of peas against his swollen eye until he fell asleep.

Two days later he was sitting behind the wheel of his 1979 Chevy Nova. It was blue and shining in the bright winter sun. The tank was full and he turned on the radio and drove southwest on I-71, toward Louisville. There was a map under his left leg. He was still sore. He had packed his clothes and cassette tapes in his grey duffel bag and put everything worth taking into the back seat and the hatchback. The money was split between his wallet and the glove box.

It was only in leaving Cincinnati that he realized there was no one to say goodbye to. He wondered how he could spend so long in one place and have nobody. There must be something wrong with him. Most of his time was spent alone, and when he was with somebody he was usually being paid. Sometimes guys wanted more than sex. Some wanted to go out to dinner beforehand, or see a movie together. They wanted companionship. So did Mike.

The only people he could think of who would miss him were his regulars. A couple of them were a little in love with him. They said nice things and bought him presents. He thought again about Freddy, the only john he'd ever stopped charging for his time. He wished Freddy was still around.

Toby might miss him. Or at least he'd wonder why Mike wasn't showing up at the Spares 'n' Strikes. Maybe he'd call Mike's place to find the line disconnected. Mike had left what second-hand furniture he owned in the apartment. The landlord could have it.

Driving past a wheat farm with three grey silos in a row, he began to wonder: if he had died alone in his apartment, how long would it have taken for someone to figure it out? Who would come looking for him? Would anyone realize he was dead before a neighbor noticed the smell?

In the past eight years he'd called his sister in Cleveland once a year or so, usually around Christmas, and never again to ask for money. The last time they talked she was dating a guy from work and talking about getting married. Mike had moved quite a few times in Cincinnati, each time a new phone number, so she was never really able to call him back. He hadn't spoken to his dad since leaving Brewerton.

He leaned to the right and looked at his eye in the rearview mirror. Although it was no longer swollen shut, it was still bulging and purple. It looked like a rotten, bruised fruit. He tried to concentrate on the road. It was January and the fields were brown, but there was no snow.

Forty miles outside Cincinnati he saw a hitchhiker – boots, jeans, a down jacket. He thought he should pick the guy up. He owed it to somebody. But he was afraid, and he kept driving.

It took almost two hours to get to Louisville. He stopped at a McDonald's just off the interstate to eat lunch, then hopped right back in the car and followed I-64 west across Indiana and Illinois. It was snowing when he pulled into a K-Mart parking lot in St. Louis that night. He flipped up the collar of the black wool pea coat he'd bought at the Army Navy Surplus, then curled up under the same green blanket he'd had on his bed back in Cincinnati.

In the morning his breath came out like grey feathers in the cold air. He stopped at a gas station to fill up, use the bathroom and get hot coffee. He had to make the money last. He went to a tiny grocery store and stocked up on food. The fruits and vegetables in wooden bins made him think of his dad, and he quickly looked away. It was still early when he pulled onto I-70 and began driving across Missouri. It felt good to have distance behind him, like waking up from a kind of bad dream. He put in his favorite cassette tape, The Pretenders, turned up the volume and sang along to "Stop Your Sobbing" in such a loud voice that he was almost yelling. Things were going to be different now.

He ate lunch and dinner as he was driving – ham and cheese sandwiches he made when he stopped for gas. He snacked on potato chips and apples. The flatlands and rolling prairies of Kansas were filled with wind and snow. He drove all day and into evening to get to Denver, where he stopped the car in a dark parking lot in front of the Mile High Motor Lodge. The room was twenty-five bucks. He took it, happy to have a warm bed and a bathroom and to be nowhere. It was good to be out of the car.

He showered right away. Drops of water were still clinging to his shoulders when he jumped naked onto the bed and turned on the TV. There was an adult pay channel, but it was all straight. It didn't matter. He used the remote to order a movie and jacked off to a hairy-chested guy fucking a brunette from behind. He pushed away thoughts of what had happened. He imagined being there, taking that brunette's place.

This was what he had decided to do. He would do gay porn. It was such an obvious next step that he wondered why he hadn't thought of it years ago. The only thing he was really good at was sex. He knew how to fuck, knew how to please people, and knew how to look like he was having a good time even if he wasn't, which was rare because he liked it so much. There were times when sex felt like real work, but only when he was hard up for money and had to suck off the old, fat guys. But in porn all the guys were hot, so the sex would be easy and fun all the time. And he'd never have to be alone with a guy he didn't know and couldn't trust. There would be other people around him, looking after him, directors and cameramen. It would feel safe.

The vision in his head was clear. He would be famous – not just some anonymous porn star. He'd be on the cover of the box. Gay guys would recognize him on the street and smile knowingly. They would want him.

He'd watched a lot of porn over the years and knew the names of all the big gay superstars like Jonathan Branch, Chris Dakota. His all-time favorite was Luke Champion, and his dream was to do a scene with him. That was what he wanted more than anything. If he could just do that, he would know he had made it.

Mike understood that the big stars were all tops – strong, aggressive men that dominated their partners. Guys who were bottoms were never famous. They just came and went, like interchangeable parts to a car. Mike had heard some of the gay superstars were in fact total bottoms off camera. They loved being fucked. But the studios paid them big money to pretend they were rugged, straight-acting tops. If they ever took it up the ass on screen it was a sure sign that they were at the end of their career, like a big Hollywood movie star doing a soap commercial.

Mike himself was a bottom, but he didn't care. He wasn't afraid to admit he liked to be fucked. Even with Charlie, years ago, back in the Thompson's hay shed, he'd always let Charlie do whatever he wanted. Now, on the bed in the Mile High Motor Lodge, he watched the hairy-chested guy shoot his load all over the brunette's back, and he thought about how the women in straight porn were often the big-name stars, and got paid more. There were some notable exceptions, but in many cases the guys just provided the dick. Why couldn't it be like that in gay porn? What was wrong with guys getting fucked? Mike suddenly became even more determined to make it big as a bottom, to become as legendary as all those tough, famous gay tops. He would be as popular as Luke Champion.

The next morning he felt good for the first time in nearly a week. His body was a little stiff from driving, but it was no longer so sore. His eye was back to its normal shape. A dark bruise still circled it. In the light of day the Rocky Mountains were amazing. He'd spent his entire life in the flat plains of the Midwest, and had never seen anything like these jagged ridges topped with snow. At the motel gift shop he bought a small Rocky Mountain pocket calendar with pictures. He marked down the day it happened, then counted out three months, to April 21st. There was a three-month period before the virus showed up, so he would have to wait until then to be tested. In spite of the beautiful images the calendar contained – Longs Peak, Shadow Mountain Lake – the pages between now and April 21st seemed to hold a kind of blank and empty terror.

He got back on I-70 and drove up into the Rockies and toward Utah. Big white snowflakes turned clear when they hit the windshield, melting into nothing. The road was full of curves and drop-offs. There were ramps for runaway trucks. He kept his eyes ahead of him and stopped only once, in Utah for gas and food. By nightfall he was driving into Las Vegas. He took off his pea coat and threw it on the back seat. Driving down the Vegas strip, he looked at all the bright neon signs he'd seen only in photographs and on TV.

Money was starting to worry him. Gas was expensive. If he ran out of cash before he got his first porn job, he'd have to work the street, but he really didn't want to. He spent an hour walking up and down the strip but then went back to his car and slept there.

At around three in the morning he woke to a terrible banging sound, a machine-gun-like repetition of fists on the roof of his car. He sat up quickly and looked around. His heart was pounding. A few dark shapes were running off down the street, laughing.

In the morning he headed out early. He drove for four hours and then, finally, on a bright Saturday afternoon, he was headed down the San Bernardino Freeway and into Los Angeles. He stopped to get gas and a local map, and then he went straight to West Hollywood, where he heard the gay guys lived, and where all the gay porn studios were. Driving along Santa Monica Boulevard, he saw one good-looking man after another. He thought every single one must be a porn star.

The sky was blue and there were palm trees and he imagined that even in the middle of LA he could smell the sea. There was something bright and shining about the place to him, so it wasn't that hard to ignore the trash in the streets, and the graffiti. He looked only at the beautiful people, the stores full of fashionable clothes, the expensive cars. He was going to be a star.

8
Under the Disco Ball

AN ENORMOUS BRIGHT blue bouffant wig sat in the dressing room at the Lucky Pony. Dale looked at it as though it had just fallen out of the sky and he didn't quite know what to do with it. Tonight he did not want to perform. He was tired. He'd had way too much to drink the night before. But Sasha was supposed to do three numbers, and Carl, the manager of the bar, was counting on her. She always brought in crowds.

There were evenings when Dale, sitting alone at home and sipping Chardonnay, wished he could do it himself, wished he could do everything that Sasha did. He wanted to stand, as himself, at Venice Beach and film the men working out, wanted to invite them home – as Dale, as a man – but he couldn't. It felt too dangerous. Without the dress people wouldn't think it was funny. A man doing that would be threatening, or pathetic. A drag queen was amusing. When Sasha went out she got attention from everyone in the room. Dale got nothing.

He looked in the dressing room mirror, at the lines growing deeper around his eyes, at his bald head, and he wondered if he was doing it all wrong. He was thirty-nine years old. In his weaker moments, he thought he should stop the drag, work out, lose weight, go to the tanning booth, grow a mustache, get a hair transplant, and change his name to some testosterone-induced absurdity. Maybe then Steve Logan would decide he fit the mold. But it would never feel right. It would never feel as natural as being Sasha. It would feel like a costume.

In the mirror he saw Carl dart into the room behind him.

"You're on in ten. Are you okay?"

He talked to Carl's reflection. "Now, Carl, since when has Sasha *ever* been on time?"

"It's just that there's that new girl doing a quick number before Sasha. I'm not sure if I should stall her. She's really anxious to go."

"Uh!" Dale waved his hand in the air dismissively, like Sasha. "Who cares. Nobody's here to see her. They're all here to see *Sasha*." He said the name with special panache.

"Of course they are. But this girl's in the other room practically peeing her pants."

Dale smiled. There were two dressing rooms at the Lucky Pony. One for Sasha, and one for everybody else.

"So please," Carl said. "Get Sasha ready, would you?"

Carl left the room, and Dale picked up the foundation and began applying it, evening it out, hiding the shadow of his beard. He couldn't help smiling a little, thinking about Sasha on stage. She was fearless, and he loved her for that. Underneath an occasional and fleeting jealousy, there was something deeper. He had to admit that he admired and respected Sasha. He was happy to be the one inside her.

As he put on the blush, the eye shadow, the eyeliner, the mascara and the lipstick, the fake nails, he slowly warmed inside. Here she was, peeking out at him, that old friend. He stood up and put on the padded bra, then the short, blue gingham dress which he'd made himself, with the bibbed front and the small, white, puffed sleeves. He picked up a pair of small, feathered wings. They were blue and sprinkled with silver glitter. He slid his arms through the two straps, so that the wings were suddenly sprouting from his back, and then he put his feet into the size twelve pumps covered with red sequins. Finally he sat down on the front edge of the chair, careful not to crush his wings, and reached over for the huge wig, pulling it down over his head like a new sovereign crowning herself.

Sasha positively beamed. She winked at the mirror and whispered in an airy voice, "You're beautiful and I love you."

When the silly new girl was done with the opening act, Sasha stepped out on stage and scanned the crowd, waiting for the spotlight to illuminate her. She was always looking for new talent, guys she could ask to be in her videos. She refused to let Steve get her down. He'd had the balls to steal her traffic cone idea and use it in *Construction Worker Gang Bang 2*, but even after years of hard work in Marketing and Distribution he still wouldn't let her direct for Cougar.

She continued to direct her own films, on the side. She didn't have the money for the production quality she dreamed of, but she did her best. She'd talked to her contacts at other leading studios about directing – Joe Butch over at Hard Bodies and Gavin Kennedy at Magnum Man – but nobody was interested in her. Still, even if her own videos just sat in a pile on her bedroom floor, she refused to stop making them. It was the thing she wanted to do more than anything else. How could she stop?

Nevertheless, sometimes even the mighty Sasha Zahore doubted herself. As she waited for the spotlight, she stood in the dark thinking about how quickly time was passing. The 1980s were almost over, and what had she really accomplished? What had she done with the decade? She would be forty soon.

A feeling rose up in her then. She couldn't explain where it came from, but she felt it deeply. This year was going to be her year. 1989 would be fabulous. She was going to become the director she dreamed of, even if it killed her. She would have to double her efforts, but it could happen. She could make it happen. Couldn't she? After all, it was only January, and the entire year lay in front of her like a wide-open road. She could do it before the decade was over.

Suddenly it seemed anything was possible. She might even find the love of her life this year. For all she knew, he was out there right now, waiting for her in the crowd, waiting for the spotlight to come up and illuminate her, for Sasha Zahore to come sashaying directly into his life. He could be here tonight. Couldn't he?

Finally that bright circle of light came up and lit her face. "Oy!" she yelled. "A girl could grow old just waiting for a spotlight around here! Hello, boys and girls. Are you feeling good tonight?"

There was a faint murmur from the crowd.

"Oh my god, did that first tramp put you to sleep? Hello?! I said, 'Are We Feeling Good Tonight?!'" She shouted out each word with a bounce and an increase in volume.

The audience yelled "Yes!" and some people whistled and hollered. Sasha loved it when they made noise.

"As many of you know, I'm Sasha Zahore." She paused for some clapping. "You've probably heard a lot about me. But you know what they say. You should never believe what you read on the bathroom walls."

She nodded to the DJ and the music started, an older Judy Garland singing "Somewhere Over the Rainbow,' a raspy voice mellowed by drugs and age. Sasha gestured theatrically and sashayed around. She was a fat, comic Dorothy. She

45

turned her back and flipped up her short skirt, showing the ruffles of her large white panties to the crowd. She jumped up and flapped her hands, tripped and stumbled like a tragic, elephantine bluebird trying to fly. Then, on the last word of the song, she pushed up her fake boobs to the sky, until they almost hit her chin, and she wiggled them around in circles. The audience cheered.

Carl came out on stage and did some raffle for an AIDS charity while Sasha changed into her Cher costume backstage – a long black wig and a black dress, a sparkling silver boa for her neck. It was while doing "Gypsies, Tramps and Thieves" that she first noticed the exceptional young man standing directly under the disco ball. All the bright stars of the room seemed to revolve around him. There was a light shining down on him, and she could see him clearly. He had to be in his early twenties, wearing jeans and a white T-shirt. She was struck by the masculine line of his nose, his tousled hair, the way that T-shirt was clinging to his lean, slim body. She'd never seen him before. As she performed, he sipped a beer and watched her intently. Sometimes, she noticed, he nodded as if in agreement. She liked him. He had relaxed posture and a gentle smile. He seemed very much at ease.

For her last number, she pulled out her old standby, Patsy Cline. Putting on her red cowgirl boots in the dressing room, this time with a white cowgirl hat, she already knew who she'd target for the last line of the song.

Out on stage, she couldn't help herself. She performed almost the entire number in his direction, twirling her finger at the word 'crazy' with a smile for him every time. She had a new denim skirt, which was long and spun out when she turned. She felt fantastic. It was only another silly performance, she knew, but there was something deep and strong twisting inside her as she mouthed the words.

In the middle of the number she realized that he was too far away from the stage to kiss him on the last line, so she pointed to him and gestured him forward. A couple of older guys and some straight girls turned around to see who she was pointing at. The crowd parted, and he stepped forward into the brightness that spilled out from the stage.

He was even more attractive up close. He could be a movie star. She reached down and held his chin in her hand. His dark brown eyes looked up at her. She suddenly knew that this one was different. This one was special. She wiggled his face back and forth gently, like he was a little boy, and people laughed.

She winked at him and delivered the last few lines directly to him, as though they were the only two people in the room. This time the words in the song felt like they were true. It didn't feel like a game. It really did feel like she was mad for loving this young man in the crowd. She'd never felt that way before. Who was he? She had to know. She would have to come out immediately after her performance and meet him, talk to him. She hoped he wouldn't run away.

When the song was over, she leaned over and kissed him on the forehead, pressing hard, wanting to mark him with a big red lipstick kiss. It would be easier to find him later. She noted, as she pulled away, that he didn't blush. Instead he looked back up at her directly, confidently, as if those brown eyes could see right through all her layers of makeup, and he smiled.

Beneath her large padded bra, Sasha's heart did a tiny flip.

PART TWO

WORKING BOYS

9
Lipstick Emergency

MIKE FELT TERRIBLY lost his first few days in Los Angeles. His initial high upon arriving faded quickly, and he had no idea what to do next.

He got a room at the Gold Coast Motel, just at the edge of West Hollywood, forty bucks a night. Then he spent two days wandering around alone. He went into stores and tried on clothes he couldn't afford. He bought food at a grocery store and ate in his motel room. During the evenings he had drinks in dark bars. At a place called Buck's Saloon, he watched a group of biker men playing pool. They wore black leather, looked tough and dangerous. When they came up to the bar to order more beer, they were talking about antiques.

By his third night he was very low on money. It was a Wednesday, and he stood outside a place called the Lucky Pony. There was music coming from inside, and laughter. He smiled and chatted with the guy at the door until he got in for free.

He ordered just one beer, with the plan to make it last the entire night. When a drag show started, the first queen looked nervous, but the second one was big, fat, and hilarious, kind of charming. Mike liked that she didn't seem to care how fat she was. She just got up there and did it anyway.

It felt good when she pointed at him to come up closer to the stage, singing in his direction, kissing him on the forehead with everybody watching. Afterward she curtseyed to the crowd, and then once more to him. Just before she disappeared behind the silver streamers at the back of the stage, she turned to take one last look in his direction. He saw her do it. Drag queens turned him off, but he liked it when people were into him, even if he didn't feel the same way back. It made him feel like he held some kind of power, like he was special.

After the show was over, he walked to the opposite side of the bar and leaned against a black wall. The Lucky Pony was run down, but it was good to see all the people laughing and talking. On the wall behind him hung large glossy photos of various drag queens, each one signed as if they were celebrities. The DJ began playing music, and people danced in front of the empty stage. A mirrored disco ball reflected points of light across the floor and walls. A couple guys climbed up on stage and began dancing shirtless, showing off their gym-toned chests and arms.

He turned his back to the room and counted the money in his wallet. He had only twenty dollars left. He knew the glove box was empty. Tonight he'd have to sleep in the car, although he wasn't sure where it was safe. Tomorrow he'd need more money for food. There was no way around it. He was going to have to turn a trick tonight. He hadn't had sex with anyone since the guy who came inside him, and he was scared.

He faced the room again and examined the crowd. This wasn't the right place. Most of the guys here weren't going to pay for sex. They'd just expect it for free. He had to figure out where the hustlers go.

"Hey, doll. Thanks for being such a willing victim."

He turned and there was the big drag queen. She'd put on a long, blond wig and some kind of burgundy evening gown.

She was tall, over six feet probably. Everything about her was enormous – her head, her hands, her hair, her body. Along the edges of the dress he could see her protruding stomach, the rolls at her side, all of it covered in a layer of material that shimmered in the light.

"No problem," he said.

"Let me get you a drink. To thank you. What'll it be?"

"Thanks, but that's all right. I'm about to go."

"Go?!" She looked horrified. "I won't have it! Surely you have time for just *one* little drink before you go running out of here like Cinderella at the stroke of midnight? Another one of those?" She pointed to the beer in his hands. "Good, now come with Sasha." She grabbed his wrist firmly and began walking toward the bar.

He allowed her to lead him. He would have one more beer, then go.

"Ross," she said to the bartender, "be a dear and get this hot little package a Miller Lite, would you? And a Gin and Tonic for me, a double." As the bartender turned away, she lowered her voice and said, "You want a shot too? I'll set you up."

"No, that's cool." Mike said.

"Listen, doll. I don't *pay*. It's on the house. I'm Queen Sasha, and all you see is my domain." She made a great, sweeping gesture which took in the entire bar, all the beat up tables and chairs, the walls painted black and the raised wooden stage, the glossy photos across the room and the disco ball above the dance floor. "Let me give you the royal treatment." she said. "Tequila? Top shelf? Okay, we'll do a shot together."

They did the shots there at the bar, side by side, before she even asked his name. When their empty glasses hit the bar, she squealed.

"Oh! Look what I've done to you!" She held him by the shoulders and moved him into a stream of light shining down from the ceiling. "You poor, darling boy." She turned to the bartender. "Ross, we've got a lipstick emergency here. Can you get me a glass of water and a napkin, pronto?"

The bartender stopped in the middle of mixing a drink for someone else, and he got Sasha what she wanted.

She turned back to Mike and said, "Doll, I have left my big, sloppy lips all over your dear, sweet forehead. Oh, what would your wife say when you got home?! How would you ever explain lips that *large*?" She was already dipping the white bar napkin in the glass of water and dabbing Mike's forehead. "Hold still, dear," she said, and held his chin with her hand for the second time that night. He felt her long plastic nails against his face. "Mommy's made a mess of you," she said, and stuck out her tongue, dabbing the napkin with her saliva, using it to wipe off his skin.

By then Mike was laughing. She was too much. She was gross. She was funny. He liked her. He had the odd feeling that everything in his life had instantly become less serious. He was, in that moment, suddenly less sad. It was good. Mike was tired of being sad.

"Thanks," he said. "I'll never find a trick tonight if I go around looking like an idiot." He didn't care what she knew. It seemed like it was okay to be honest with her.

"Oh," she said, nodding slowly. "I see. You're a working boy. Of course you are. With looks like that, you'd be a fool not to. I tried it once. Didn't make a dime. What's your name?"

"Bill," Mike said. "Your show was great."

"Thanks, Bill. But that Patsy Cline number of mine is as old as the hills."

"It was good. You're good. Drag queens in Cincinnati, they're not so good."

"Ah, corn-fed Midwestern boy, are we?" She looked at him up and down. "So tell me, at what point did LA become suddenly more beautiful with your presence?"

"I got here a couple days ago."

"Oh! Fresh off the boat, and looking for a little money, eh? Fantastic." She began to say something, and then paused. "Me, I'm from Nebraska originally, but I've been here over twenty years now. Just love it."

"Do they pay you? To sing? Or to pretend to sing?"

"A little. Not much. Mostly it's the free booze, you know. And the glory, the *fame*, of course. You know this isn't a working boy's bar, right?"

"I got in free, thought it would be fun."

"Excellent. All work and no play makes Bill a dull boy. Do you know where the working boys go?"

Mike shook his head.

"Pinky's Boy Bar or the Green Carnation," she said. "Pink and green, those are the colors for you. Or of course, there's Griffith Park, but that's strictly A-Y-O-R. Don't go there, doll. I've heard bad things. At Your Own Risk, you know."

"No, nothing risky."

"Well, between the two bars, I recommend Pinky's. More johns. I'll show it to you later." She raised her gin and tonic and clinked it against Mike's beer.

"Where is it?" he said. "This Pinky's."

"Oh, you really are in a hurry to get to work, aren't you? Why the rush? Stay here and talk to me."

"I'd like to, but I really do need to make some money tonight."

"Who says you're not going to make it with me?"

He looked at her. The only thing worse than having to suck off an old, fat guy, was having to suck off an old, fat guy in a dress. "Sorry. No," he said.

She visibly winced. "Where are you staying?"

"I was at the Gold Coast."

"Ack! Horrible place. Cum-stained sheets."

"Well, I'm sort of running out of money, so tonight, if I don't stay with somebody, I'll just sleep in my car."

"Oh, please, doll. You can't do that in LA. God only knows what will happen to you." She paused. "Listen. I have a proposition for you."

"No," he said firmly. Then, to soften it, he added, "I'm really sorry, but no."

"You don't even know what I'm about to say."

"I need to go." He reached out to set his half-finished beer down on the bar. He didn't want to end up having sex with this overweight queen.

"Well, that's too bad, because Sasha knows a way you can make a little money, get a place to sleep, and you won't have to hop in bed with a *soul*."

Mike froze.

Sasha looked off into the crowd. "But you've got places to go, people to do..."

"No, what is it?"

She turned and looked back at him, pretending to be surprised. "Are you still here? I thought you were off to find yourself some shriveled old dick to suck."

"Okay, alright. Tell me what it is."

"Have you ever done video?"

"Ah, sure."

"Well, you see, I have this little hobby. I direct jack-off videos. Now here's my proposition. You come home with me, smile for the camera, take off your clothes like a good boy, and jack off while I tape it. Easy-peasy. Fifty bucks in your hot, sticky little hand."

"Yeah?"

"When we're done you can sleep on Sasha's sofa, and if you're real sweet you might even get breakfast in the morning. I make nice pancakes, just like my momma made back in Nebraska."

Mike looked down at her body.

"Don't worry, doll. I won't lay a *hand* on you. Scouts honor." She held up her hand. "Fifty bucks and a place to sleep tonight."

"You do hardcore too, or just jack-off?"

"I direct some hardcore. I work for Cougar Studios. Why? Are you interested in doing hardcore?"

"Fuck yeah." He couldn't believe his good luck.

"You're fast. From jack-off to hard-core in fifty seconds flat. Wait a minute. How old are you?"

"Twenty-three."

"Seriously?"

"Yeah."

"Okay. You're legal. Are you a top or a bottom, or versatile?"

"Bottom. Total bottom."

"Have you ever topped?"

"Yeah, sure. If I have to, but I'd rather bottom."

"Well, Bill. If you're real nice to Sasha, maybe she'll consider your first little jack-off movie as a screen test." She winked and gave him a devilish smile.

10
A Natural

WHEN SHE GOT Bill home she was a little shaky – something that hadn't happened since her very first shoot. This boy was gorgeous.

As she opened the door, she remembered with relief that she'd cleaned the day before. Normally she didn't care what her models thought, but for some reason with Bill she wanted to make a good impression.

She'd moved to this little place on Orlando Avenue shortly after starting at Cougar. It wasn't much. The building was run down, but at least she had no roommates. There was one bedroom, a tiny kitchen, and a living room that was big enough to hold not only her large video collection, but a small bookcase full of books, her pink sewing machine and a large, faux black leather sofa. She was proud of this living room. The walls, which she herself had painted deep red, were covered with her collection of feathered masks, blue and green and yellow and orange, some with eyes outlined in sequins, some with noses like large beaks. She told Bill to sit down, and she pulled out her video camera.

Sasha had upgraded to a shiny new VHS camcorder two years earlier. It was even lighter than her old Betamovie. The moment she pointed it at Bill, she knew he was a natural. He had an intense, piercing way of looking at the camera, as though he was thinking of all the dirty little things he would do with you, if he could just get you alone. The fact that

Sasha was, in reality, alone with him, that she was so near to him as he took off his clothes, made her hard.

He did everything she told him to, exactly as she said. He got down on his knees and arched his back, spread his cheeks, squatted over the camera and played with himself. His body was beautiful – tanned and nicely toned – but far and away the most amazing thing about him was his ass. It was the perkiest, most fuckable bubble butt Sasha had ever seen. If there was an ass that could launch a thousand ships, this was it.

He never complained about the positions she asked him to get into, never grew impatient and, unlike most guys, he came precisely when she told him to, like it was a switch he could flick. He was in total control of his body, even if he was a little drunk. She was very impressed. She gave him his fifty bucks, slapped his ass lightly, and tucked him into bed on the sofa.

When she finally stepped into the bathroom to get ready for bed, she was exhausted. She'd worn the evening gown throughout the shoot because it was so glamorous. She'd wanted to look good for Bill even if she wasn't allowed to touch him. Standing at the bathroom mirror now, she put one hand at the front of her wig and slid it off slowly, with a long deep sigh, until it was Dale looking back, holding Sasha's hair in his hand.

Dale turned and placed the wig on a mannequin head that sat on the shelf behind him, then unzipped the back of the dress and let it slide down off his shoulders. It became a burgundy ring at his feet. Picking it up, he hung it carefully on a hanger on the back of the bathroom door. He took off the fake nails. Then slowly he unclasped the padded bra, damp and sweaty, and dropped it on the floor. He began removing the makeup with cold cream, rubbing gently in circles as he'd once read in his mother's beauty magazine when he was thirteen, clockwise first, then counter-clockwise, trying to keep his skin toned. Finally he stepped into the shower and felt the hot water fall down around his waxed and hairless body. He thought of Bill out on the sofa, of the video they'd just made and – safe in the noise of the splashing water – he jacked off vigorously.

When he stepped out of the shower, he put on a green silk robe and opened the door, moving silently into the living room. He stood behind the couch until his eyes adjusted. The light above the stove in the kitchen passed through the doorway and into the room, causing a faint glow off the red walls.

Bill was already fast asleep. He had kicked back the sheets and was sleeping in his underwear – simple white briefs like a boy would wear.

Dale watched the smooth skin of Bill's chest slowly rise up and down. Such perfect skin. He wanted desperately to reach out and touch it. In the darkness he could just make out the shadow of hair on Bill's legs. This somehow felt more intimate, just standing here and watching Bill sleep, than it had the entire time Bill was jacking off in front of the camera. Here was this young man, twenty-three if he was telling the truth, and there was so much ahead of him. Dale knew logically that there were things ahead for himself as well, but certainly not as much.

It seemed lately, as he moved through his days, that he was walking down a long hallway that became increasingly narrow with every step. It was impossible to undo things, to choose a different direction. There were fewer and fewer doors. Decisions he'd made years ago had led him to where he was today, this lonely man with a green silk robe and a stack of videos in the corner, staring at the tender, astonishing beauty of this boy. If it weren't for Sasha's steadfast optimism, he was certain he would fall into despair.

He looked carefully at the line of Bill's jaw. He wanted to help him. He wanted to use him. He walked toward his bedroom door and went in, shutting it tightly behind him in the dark.

11
Staying for Breakfast

MIKE WOKE UP the next morning not entirely sure where he was. Then he remembered the Lucky Pony, Sasha getting him drink after drink. He remembered making the video, remembered how fantastically naked he'd felt in front of the black camera, more naked than ever, but also powerful and good. Sasha had oo-ed and ah-ed in her evening dress as she filmed, and the masks on the red walls had felt like a crowd of eager strangers, watching him.

He got up off the couch to pee now, and when he came back into the room he was surprised to find a fat man in a green robe sitting there.

"Hi Bill," the man said, smiling.

"Ah, hi." Mike noticed the eyebrows. They were Sasha's, slender and neatly curved.

"I'm Dale." The man stood up and shook Mike's hand. "Hungry?"

Mike nodded. "Have any coffee?"

"Coming right up."

Dale moved into the kitchen and started making coffee. Mike didn't bother getting dressed. He walked into the kitchen in his underwear, leaned against the counter and looked at Dale from behind. The man's ass was a giant blob of extra fat. His head was completely bald, except for a laurel wreath of stubble around the edges. His body was shaped like an avocado. His green robe came down around an increasingly wide trunk and stopped just above his knees.

The legs below the robe were hairless, white, and plump. Mike thought of a mermaid. But instead of a fishtail this man had been cursed with a body that ended in two enormous blind, albino worms. His stomach churned.

Dale turned around and said, "Did you sleep well?"

Mike saw Dale stare at his crotch. He didn't mind. His body was what he had, what he offered. Although he would never allow Dale to touch him, it was okay to look. He needed Dale to be into him.

"Slept like a log," he answered, reaching up and stretching the sleep out of his arms, pretending not to notice that Dale's eyes were on him the entire time. He looked away and absentmindedly rubbed his crotch.

Behind Dale, the coffee maker was starting to steam and drip. "Well," Dale said. "How about those pancakes I promised you?"

"Thanks for letting me sleep here last night."

"You worked hard for it, boy." Dale winked. "Orange juice?"

"Yes, please."

Dale poured the juice in a tall glass with pink flamingos on the side. Mike pushed himself up onto the countertop and set the glass next to his leg.

"You can stay longer if you'd like," Dale said. He was getting out flour and eggs and a large silver bowl.

Mike looked out at the black couch. "That would be great."

Dale started mixing the batter, pouring it into the pan on the stove. Mike found the conversation easy. They talked about where they were from, about Brewerton and Lincoln, Ohio and Nebraska, and Dale seemed to understand exactly what Mike meant when he said, "I had to leave." That was all the explanation Dale needed. Mike was happy that Dale didn't ask the annoying questions some people asked – not johns but other people, normal people – questions like "Do you miss home?" or "Do you miss your family?" They were leading questions. You were supposed to say yes. If you said no, people's heads turned a little to the side, and they looked at you strangely, as though you had just admitted to smothering a small kitten. Brewerton, Mike felt, was where he was from, but it wasn't *home*, hadn't been *home* since his mother died. As of right now, home was here in Dale's kitchen.

When the pancakes were ready he sat across from Dale at a small white table in the corner, next to the refrigerator. The coffee was good and strong. Dale drank tea.

"There's syrup for you," Dale said. "Or jelly if you'd rather, and here's some honey. That can be nice too. Can I get you anything else?"

"No, this is great. Thanks."

"Oh, how about some strawberries? I have some in the fridge." Dale was already standing up and pulling them out, rinsing them and cutting them at the sink. "More orange juice?"

"I'm good for now. These pancakes are fantastic."

"Well, I made a lot so eat up. Nobody likes a skinny rent boy." Dale laughed. "What am I saying? No doubt there are those who go for that."

"Tell me about the porn you do for Cougar." Mike said.

Dale stood at the counter cutting strawberries, but he didn't answer. Eventually he set a bowl of sliced strawberries on the table and sat back down, looking at the floor. When he looked back up he gave Mike the warmest, most caring smile that Mike had received in a long time. It seemed there was nothing sexual behind it at all – no leer, no suggestive grin – just a gentle kindness. For a moment Mike forgot all about the albino worms hiding underneath the table.

"Okay," Dale said. "I have a confession to make. I can't lie to you, my charming Midwestern boy. You'll find out sooner or later anyway. I don't actually make movies for Cougar."

Mike's heart sank. He should have known better than to believe this guy. He felt like an idiot. He'd jacked off for him. At least he'd made fifty bucks. He set down his fork and leaned back in the white wooden chair. "You said you did."

"Well, technically speaking, I didn't say that. But I admit I led you to believe it. The truth is I work at Cougar in Marketing and Distribution. I call up the video shops and push the new releases, and lately I've been trying to get the gay porn mags to run shots of Cougar stars on their covers. I don't direct for Cougar, not yet, but I hope to. Some day. The hardcore films I do are on my own time, and I'm afraid they're very low-budget productions. I've never had a proper film crew. Just me."

Mike felt a little bit relieved. This could be a start. He picked up his fork and took another bite.

"Here. Take some more." Dale picked up three pancakes from a platter and dropped them on Mike's plate.

Mike spooned some strawberries on top. He couldn't remember the last time he'd had homemade pancakes.

"But you see," Dale continued, "I think you've got talent. There's something about you. Last night, when you got in front of that camera, you looked like you were born to be there."

Mike looked up. "Yeah? Was I good?"

"Billy boy, you were great. We can watch it later."

"Good. I want to," Mike said. "I really want to be a big porn star."

"Well, I want to be a big porn director, doing top notch stuff. The problem for me has always been money. But with someone like you on my side, I might be able to get somebody to loan me some money, as an investment. As soon as they lay eyes on you, they'll know we would make a hot movie together. Sasha can charm them, do a bit of a sales pitch, give them some of my films and your jack-off video as a sampler. Listen, how about you and I make a full-length movie, top quality? Of course you would be the star. You would be in almost every scene. It would be all about you."

"You'd put me with hot guys?" Mike asked.

"I'd have hunky tops fuck you silly."

Mike smiled. "Count me in." He shoved another forkful of pancake into his mouth and said, "Totally safe sex, right?" He knew all the major studios used condoms now. He just wanted to make sure about Dale.

"Of course. I'll keep you safe."

Mike tried not to think about April 21st, when he had to get his HIV test. It wasn't simply his own safety he was concerned about.

Dale took a sip of his tea and said, "We'll have to think of a porn name for you. You wouldn't want to use your real name, of course. That can get complicated. Stalkers, relatives, you know. It's a shame though. Billy suits you."

"I have a confession too," Mike said. "Don't be angry."

"Angry? How could I be angry at a hot young man sitting at my kitchen table, eating breakfast in his underwear?"

"My name's not Bill. It's Mike."

"Mike? Huh. Well, that's easy then. Billy can be your porn name. Perfect. Any other confessions? What about being twenty-three? Don't tell me you're really jail bait."

"No. I'm really twenty-three. I'll be twenty-four at the end of April. Honest. I was born in 1965."

"Oy! The year you were born was the year I first wore a dress in public. On Halloween. I wore it to school. I was sixteen years old, and I looked *fabulous*."

Mike wasn't really listening. He was wondering what would happen between now and the end of April. He was going to have to get tested a week before his birthday.

"And Ohio?" Dale asked.

"Huh?"

"Are you really from Ohio?"

"Oh, yeah. Everything I said was true. Just my name. It's Mike Dudley."

"Dudley? Oh, sorry but what a dreary name. Almost as bad as mine. Dale Smith. Sorry, but Dudley's going to have to go."

"It's not so bad. Rhymes with studly."

Dale smiled. "Well, yes. There is that. But that won't do either. Don't worry. I'll think of something. A nice last name to go with Billy. In the meantime, *Mike*, I'm very, very pleased to meet you." Dale put out his hand like a lady, palm down and fingers dangling.

Mike looked at it.

"Go on," Dale said, and jiggled his arm.

Mike reached out in a playfully gentleman-like manner, leaning forward and placing one light kiss on the soft skin that covered the back of Dale's hand.

12
Working Boy Needs Job

SASHA KICKED INTO overdrive. She needed money fast. Her rainy day fund had never really recovered since she'd started buying video equipment. However, she knew a drug dealer named Fabio who had connections, customers with money, and very soon she had several meetings lined up. There was one particularly successful dinner meeting where she displayed her darling Billy at her side. The elderly gentleman they dined with that night agreed to be a silent partner, and he offered her a thousand dollars on the spot. All he wanted in return was another dinner with Billy.

The only problem was that a thousand dollars wasn't enough for the kind of quality production she wanted to do. Nevertheless, not being one to pass up good deal, Sasha said yes immediately.

By then Billy was sleeping on her couch and going out with her almost every night. She loved walking into bars with him, loved seeing heads turn in their direction – the big, glamorous queen and the hot, young guy at her side – but she was worried. Soon word would get out that there was a hot new bottom in town, looking for work in porn, and the vultures would descend. She knew that if it took too long to get the money for the kind of production she wanted, Billy would be tempted to go. She told him not to talk to anybody about their plans, to keep his desire to do porn to himself, because it would be better for him to simply come out with a movie and surprise them all.

She took him to Pinky's Boy Bar. The interior had become a bit shabby, she realized, but it was still the busiest bar for working boys in LA. Billy insisted on wearing his jeans and a white T-shirt, and she'd put on a white dress so they would match. They stood at the long, wooden bar waiting for drinks. The walls everywhere were pink stucco, and there were year-round Christmas lights strung up over a pool table nearby, imbuing the room with a pastel glow. When she introduced Billy to Dave, the bartender, Billy seemed withdrawn.

"How are you doing there, kiddo?" Dave said. He was in his fifties, balding, and with an open collar that displayed two silver chains against tanned skin.

Billy didn't respond. He simply turned away.

"Billy, don't be so *rude*," Sasha said. "So sorry, Dave. The boy's a bit nervous, I suppose."

"No problem, Sasha."

Dave gave them their drinks and Sasha led Billy to a table in the corner, where they had a good view of the door.

"Billy," Sasha said. "You *have* turned tricks before, right?"

"Yeah, sure."

She looked at him closely "I don't know why you're so nervous then."

Billy shrugged.

"Are you okay?" She reached out and patted his hand.

"Yeah. I'm fine."

Sasha turned and took in the room. For the untrained eye, it would it would be difficult to tell who was buying and who was selling, but Sasha knew. There was a wide range of working boys present – from the cute twinks fresh as daisies to the rugged veterans, covered in muscle. The buyers were mostly middle-aged men with a bit of padding around the middle, but not always. Some were handsome enough that at first glance it looked like they could be selling, but the look in their eyes gave them away.

She glanced back over at Billy. He looked almost sullen, like a working boy who didn't want to work at all.

"My darling Billy," she said. "The movie we're going to make is something we're doing *together*. It's going to be good for both of us. But I need your help. We need to get the money to make it. I've been able to line up our one investor, and just this afternoon I finished the script, but we want this production to be top quality, don't we? That takes a lot of cash."

Billy said, "Why can't we just do it with the money we already got?"

"Trust me, doll. If you want to be a big star, you've got a lot to learn. You know the cards are already stacked against a sweet little bottom boy like you. This too we shall overcome. However, one thing's for sure. Big stars don't do low budget. We need professional cameramen, sound and lighting crew, an editor, the works. Top notch. You want to enter the porn world looking like a professional. To do that, we need money."

"I don't know, Sasha."

"You were certainly eager to turn a trick that first night I met you."

"I was desperate."

"Oh, you were desperate *then* but now that you have Sasha's sofa and Sasha's food and Sasha's booze at the Lucky Pony, you're fine?"

"I was hoping I could just get work in porn, stop turning tricks." He paused. "I had some trouble before I came to LA."

"What was it?"

"Doesn't matter. Look, I'm just tired of street and bar hustling. Back in Cincinnati, I decided I didn't want to do it anymore."

"Well, isn't that *nice*? And perhaps you've also decided that soon the Angel Gabriel will pop out from behind a pumpkin patch and give you a box full of gold doubloons? Listen, don't make me chain you to the bed with your ass in the air. 'Cause I *will* and I'll be the one taking money at the door."

"Sasha, it's not that I don't want to work. I just want it to be safer. Don't be such a bitch."

He'd never called her that before, and it felt like a physical slap. "Excuse me," she said, then stood abruptly and walked to the women's bathroom, which was always empty at Pinky's. She pulled up her dress, pulled down her nylons just enough to get her dick out, and peed standing up in the stall. Afterward she looked in the mirror and checked her makeup. The last thing she wanted was to put Billy in harm's way. She knew bar and street hustling were the lowest rung of the ladder, the most dangerous and poorly paid work.

When she got back to the table, she didn't even sit down. "We'll figure something out," she said.

Billy stared up at her. Sitting there alone he seemed like a little boy who was too shy and afraid to make friends with the other kids at the playground.

Sasha nodded toward the door. "Let's go."

Within twenty-four hours she had a solution. She knew someone who knew one of the bouncers at Exposé – a high-end West Hollywood strip club owned by Pascal of Montreal. The clientele were better off than the ones who just wandered into Pinky's off the street. At Exposé, Pascal and his burly bouncers knew *all* the clients, and they turned away anybody who gave the strippers trouble. Pascal, it was said, also paid off the cops to keep them out of his hair. All in all, it was a more controlled environment. Billy could ply his trade without the danger that existed in typical bar and street hustling. Most importantly, she was certain the money would be better than at Pinky's. Her one concern was throwing Billy in with all those sexy strippers. What if he fell for one of them? She pushed the thought away.

"You'll have to dance," she explained to him when she first came up with the idea. "But of course I'll help you with costumes and choreography. You'll be fabulous."

Billy said that he'd give it a try, and she immediately made some phone calls and got him an audition. She helped him put together a routine and even drove him there on the big day. He looked wonderful in his sailor hat. Of course they hired him. Who could say no to Billy?

When he finally started bringing home cash, she was thrilled. She took fistfuls of it from him, saying "For the movie, doll," but she always left him a few bills for spending. He didn't seem to mind, or if he did he didn't say so. When he came home one night strung out on crystal meth, she said, "Honey, you get hooked on that and you'll burn right through our money. Do you want your porn career to be over before it starts? Back off the crystal or my home is no longer yours." She never saw a sign of it again.

In her small apartment, she and Billy developed simple habits that soothed her and pushed away the loneliness. She would leave every morning at 10:00 to go to work, and if Billy hadn't been out late with a trick the night before, she would whisper softly, "Rise and shine, sleepyhead." She'd place a cup of coffee on the table by the sofa and lean over to stroke his hair. "Don't waste your day," she'd say, before slipping out the door.

At work she interspersed her legitimate business for Cougar with calls attending to her own affairs, lining up the film crew, getting someone ready to help her edit the final cut, looking for a guy who could take care of the sound. She never told Steve what she was up to.

Sasha and Steve had developed an amicable relationship, full of a playfulness that sometimes bordered on cruelty. "Looking a little wider around the edges there, Sasha," Steve would say with a smile. "Oh, Steve," she'd snap back. "Just look at that shine on your head. It glows so nicely against the subtle orange hue of your simulated tan." She saw how he promised porn stardom to so many young guys, but never delivered. He strung them along with false hope in return for good sex. She knew it took work to make a gay porn superstar, time and investment, getting their image out into as many magazines as possible, planning their movies right so fans didn't forget them or lose interest due to overexposure. She had to keep Billy away from men like Steve.

When she came home each evening, Billy was usually trying to make dinner. He wasn't a very good cook, but she was teaching him. He could already make a half-decent stir fry, and of course there was always spaghetti. The first time she cut into one of his chicken breasts, she found the center almost raw. "Doll, you have to cook chicken all the way through," she said. "Otherwise it will make you sick." When she taught him to steam asparagus, it was like a revelation for him, and they ate bright green stalks almost every night for two weeks. She would laugh and say, "Oh! Steamed asparagus again, honey? You shouldn't have!"

They would sit down at the small kitchen table to eat, and sometimes they'd open a bottle of wine. She'd ask if he worked out that day. She bought him a set of weights and Billy took to it well, doing curls and squats in the middle of the living room, bench presses lying lengthwise across the wooden coffee table. She said that if their careers took off he could get a gym membership, and she teased him about bodybuilders in the showers.

She made it very clear that just hanging out in the apartment all day and watching bad television was not acceptable. She set out rules, gave lessons and assignments for the following day. "First, exercise for one hour, then practice your new dance routines. After that, watch 'Frisky Summer' and take note of Brent Cole's excellent blow job technique. He gets good length. That's the term in the industry for really going up and down on the dick. Makes it look hotter when you're just watching. And Brent's face communicates how much he's enjoying himself, which is the Golden Rule of porn. Look like you're having fun. Don't forget that. Then you can do whatever you want for the rest of the day."

She loved Billy most when he needed her, when he would ask her the best way to drive to Silverlake, or where he could go to buy some new clothes. She always helped him with his choreography, and sometimes she'd show up at Exposé and sit in the back, watching as he stripped in front of all the whistling men. She thanked the goddess, the great drag queen in the sky, for giving her this, for bringing Billy into her life, for finally, or at least almost, answering her prayers.

When they were out at a dance club one night, Sasha suggested that he pick up a guy and bring him home, so that she could watch. He found a guy named Greg, dark sideburns and a goatee. Just as the three of them were about to leave the club together, Greg turned to Billy and said loudly, "I don't want a fat queen watching. Come back to my place alone."

Sasha thought it was awfully bad manners.

Billy answered plainly. "If Sasha can't watch, you can't have me."

Greg and Billy had sex on Sasha's bed that night, as Sasha stood in the corner and imagined that she were Greg, who was doing everything to Billy that she wanted to do. At one point she walked over to Billy, as his head was hanging back over the edge of the mattress, his eyes closed, and she touched his hair. He looked up at her, surprised, and gently pushed her hand away. She went back to the corner, pulled up her dress, and jacked off.

After three weeks of work she'd obtained a second silent partner for the film, had secured several locations, and had finalized deals with the last of the technical people she needed. She didn't have much money, only two thousand dollars in total. She wasn't entirely sure that it was enough, but she knew she had to get started. One evening after dinner she sat Billy down and opened her copy of the Gay Video Guide. "Choose the talent you want to do scenes with," she said.

"Just look at all these hot actors."

"Models, doll. In the business we call the porn actors 'models.'"

Billy smiled and began pointing at all the pictures of brawny, hairy men. "I want that one, and that one, and that one," he said, like a child choosing toys.

"Sorry, that one died last year," she had to explain. "Overdose. Crystal meth and Lord knows what else. I told you that stuff is bad. And that one's on an exclusive contract with Stallion Studios."

"What about Luke Champion? My dream is to do a scene with him. Can I?"

"Oh, I'm afraid Luke Champion is too much of an A-list gay superstar for us to be able to afford him. He'd take our entire budget. Besides, we're nobodies. He'd never stoop so low as to do a scene with us. If we succeed and make it big – if you do really well in this film – you'll perhaps be able to work with him some day. But now these three, I can talk to them."

Mike had never heard of them, but they were hot. "You really think I could work with them?"

"Why not? We might not be able to afford them, but we can ask. Doll, I have two rules in life. The first one is, 'You ain't gonna get it if you don't try.'"

"And the second?"

"When all else fails, never underestimate the power of a glue gun."

"I've been thinking of my porn name," he said. "Why *not* Billy Studly?"

"Ah, well… No. Sorry. 'Billy' needs to be balanced by something strong but romantic. I've already decided your last name should be 'Knight.' It works. 'Billy Knight.'"

"Yeah," Billy nodded enthusiastically. "That's good."

She dipped her fingertips into the glass of Chardonnay in front of her. "My child, I hereby christen you, Billy Knight, model and porn star *extraordinaire*." They laughed together, and Sasha watched as a drop of wine rolled slowly down the smooth, tanned skin of Mike's forehead.

13
Banging Billy

THEY SHOT THE movie over two weekends, because most of the people involved had other jobs. Sasha's script was about a young guy who'd just moved to LA from Nebraska. The opening shots were of Billy Knight driving down the San Bernardino Freeway in his blue Chevy Nova, getting out of the car on Santa Monica Boulevard, and walking down the street in a cowboy hat and boots. By the end of the movie he'd traded in the cowboy gear for muscle tees, had been fucked by several guys he'd met in saunas and bars, was abducted and forced to service three men simultaneously in an old warehouse, and was then dumped in front of a gas station where he was helped by a surprisingly attractive mechanic who not only had a big heart, but a dick that matched.

Mike was nervous the morning of each shoot. His stomach felt tight and uncomfortable. Yet as soon as the cameras started rolling and the sex started, his fear fell away.

He couldn't believe that he was the star – that he was in every scene, was actually being paid, and there was no risk of losing control or being in any *real* danger. There was a guy who stood on the side and kept giving them condoms and lube. The feeling on the set was jokey and easygoing, like they were all friends. Sasha put everyone at ease, made everybody laugh. Mike loved that all the sex was with guys he'd chosen, rather than the other way around. It seemed impossible that he could in any way be grouped together with those people, who were so handsome, so beautiful. And it felt great to be naked and having sex in front of the other people with clothes on, everybody looking at him – the cameraman, the sound guy, a couple of others. Sasha could only afford to pay him a hundred dollars altogether, which was less than he gave her toward the movie anyway, but he didn't mind. The other models and the guys in the crew had to be paid too, and anyway Mike wasn't doing this film for the money. It was for the exposure. He was going to become a star.

He was careful, much more so than he used to be. When he was ready for his cum shot with the mechanic, Sasha said, "Shoot your donut glaze on his face." Mike acted like he was going to, but at the last minute shifted left, and he shot his load across the guy's chest instead. What if some accidentally went into the guy's mouth? And what if he found out on April 21st that he was positive? He would have to tell the guy. He'd be just as guilty as that guy who punched his back and came inside him, just as responsible for filling somebody with all that fear. Mike couldn't handle that. He wouldn't take the risk.

After the scene was over, Sasha walked over to him. He was still standing beside the mechanic in front of the tool bench where they'd just had sex. They were filming in the garage of a gas station that Sasha had found through a friend. She looked at Mike sternly and said "Billy?" Then she reached over and thumped the mechanic's sturdy chest, still covered in Mike's cum. "Does this look like somebody's face?"

"Sorry Sasha," Mike said, and looked away. He hated disappointing her, after she'd done so much for him.

As soon as filming was over, he became impatient. He just couldn't wait to become a star. Sasha arranged a photo shoot for him with a friend of hers who was a professional photographer. Mike posed on her fake black leather couch. Another friend, a DJ who wanted to become a musician, agreed to do the music for free. He composed thumping techno beats on a synthesizer in his bedroom.

Music and rough footage in hand, Sasha called in sick to work one day and Mike drove her to a basement studio in Long Beach so she could review the footage with an editor named Hanif. She said she could drive herself, in her own car, but Mike insisted. "I want to help," he said. He liked to drive, and besides, he didn't want to stay at home while his future was being made.

At first Mike sat with Sasha and Hanif, thinking the review would be fun, but he soon realized it was dreary and monotonous. He became bored and left, wandering off to hang out at Shoreline Park, where he heard men had sex in the bushes.

Heading back up the San Diego Freeway on the way home, he asked her, "Is the movie done?"

"You can't rush perfection, doll. In a week I'll get a rough cut, then I'll review it again and make suggestions."

"When will it be on the shelves?"

"I've already spoken with several people at small studios about marketing and distribution. A company called Stunning Productions said they might be interested in releasing it, depending on how it turns out."

Mike felt a pang of worry. "Depending on how it turns out?"

Sasha looked over from the passenger seat. "Oh, don't you trouble your pretty little head. You are one hell of a sexual performer, Billy Knight. Every time the camera lands on you, you're on fire. And that heavenly bubble butt of yours looks so good, even straight men will want it. In fact, I'd have to say that your ass is even more photogenic than your face, and that's saying something." She leaned over and grabbed his earlobe. "You make your mama so proud!"

He felt good. She liked it.

When the post-production work was finally done, Sasha asked him to get a sign made for her front door. He ran off to the copy shop and asked for a large blue poster with black letters. Then he brought it home and unrolled it on the kitchen table for Sasha to see.

"Oh, it's perfect!" she said. There, in big, bold letters, were the words 'Banging Billy: World Premiere.'

The invitation-only party was a huge success, and Sasha's apartment was packed. She had to be very selective about who she invited, given the size of her place. Ross from the Lucky Pony mixed Martinis in the kitchen. There were two lesser drag queens there, the film crew, the models, and just three or four others she knew. At midnight she put the movie on and everybody crowded around to watch, jockeying for a place to see the TV screen. Even the people who were doing coke in the bathroom came out to watch. Mike sat to the right of Sasha on the couch. Tom, from Stunning Productions, sat on Sasha's left. He'd already seen the film and had agreed to take on distribution. Mike liked it that all of the tops were sitting down on the floor in front of the couch, and he was up next to Sasha. Everyone else stood behind the couch or along the walls on either side. Ross stood in the kitchen doorway on a chair. Mike noticed that Sasha hadn't invited her boss from Cougar, or anyone from any of the large studios who hadn't been interested in letting her direct. "It's my silent *Fuck You*," she told him. He wasn't totally sure he believed her.

As the movie played that night, Mike noticed that people talked here and there, but every time Billy was in front of the camera, they all kept their eyes on the screen. Sometimes, between the scenes, Sasha interrupted with funny stories about the filming, like when an unexpected shipment arrived at the warehouse just as Billy was down on all fours. Mike knew it wasn't the best-made film he'd ever seen. Some of it was a little amateurish, he knew. But there was nothing he could do about that. He'd done his part well, and it was just a start, after all. At the end the credits rolled and everybody clapped. Several people, inspired by the film, had already disappeared into Sasha's bedroom.

For the rest of the evening, people came up to Mike and slapped him on the back, told him he was great. He liked the attention. One guy with a paunch and a fat gold watch put a hand on his shoulder and said, "You look good in a cowboy hat, Billy." Someone nearby quipped, "He looks better with a dick in his mouth." Another guy reached out and pinched his ass, and Mike turned with a jump. "That's the best lookin' back end I've seen in years," the guy said.

Mike noticed that some of the older guys, ones he hadn't met before, looked at him differently when the movie was over, as though the film had given them some kind of permission. He pretended not to notice they were staring. There was more power in being watched than in watching. This was his skill. It felt good to command so much attention.

One woman, a friend of Sasha's who had starred in straight porn for years, came up to him with a camaraderie that surprised him. She had big, curly brown hair and a blouse with large shoulder pads. "You're great," she said. "It's not easy, I know." She gave him a long, tight hug.

Banging Billy began appearing in adult video shops across the country at the beginning of April. Although Stunning Productions distributed it, Sasha herself did everything she could to make sure people took notice.

She got her friends to go into the LA video shops even before the movie was available and ask for it by name, saying how good they'd heard it was. She made sure the movie was an option for selection in the video booths at Stacked & Hung, and that it was prominently displayed at the front of the store. She told Mike that she'd even called friends who worked at gay magazines and newspapers across the country – Gay Chicago Magazine, Houston's Lambda News, Atlanta's Gay Times – to make sure it got good reviews.

The first time Mike walked into a random video shop and saw it on the shelf, he felt something like an electric spark inside. The box cover showed Billy Knight lying on his stomach, naked on a black leather couch, his head turned over his shoulder toward the camera behind him, his butt arching up into the air.

Mike stood back and watched as several guys looked at the box, picking it up to get a better look. The clerk who worked at the shop came up to him and pointed over to the video, saying, "Hey, man. Is that you? That video's hot. You're hot." Then he looked around and gestured to the back room. "You busy?"

Mike smiled a bit flirtatiously, not because he was being propositioned, and not because he found the guy attractive – he was skinny and had horrible teeth – but because some-times, if there was no real risk of anything happening, that was just what Mike did. There were times, even when simply paying for his groceries, if the check-out girl kept looking up at him as she scanned his milk, his cereal, his apples, when he would offer her a seductive smile just to give her a little thrill, just to see if she would smile back, or blush. He did it partly out of a desire to feel his specific kind of power, but also out of something like an instinct for generosity. He imagined that the check-out girl, or the video store clerk, would go home feeling a little bit sexier, feeling attractive and good, because a young man that day had smiled at them in a particular way.

"Sorry," Mike said now, sounding genuinely disappointed. "I'd love to, but I'm on my way somewhere." He smiled again, then nodded and walked away, happy to feel the clerk's hungry eyes burning holes in the back of his head, happy to turn and catch him still staring as he walked out the door.

Sasha came home that night with good news. She'd been slipping in mentions of *Banging Billy* while doing her marketing calls for Cougar, and she'd managed to get Billy Knight a profile in the April issue of *Rod & Shaft* magazine.

When it came out, Mike bought seven copies – even though he didn't have anyone except Sasha to give them to. The profile was limited to only half a page, toward the back. Mike ripped it out and put it on the refrigerator, under a Marilyn Monroe magnet. It showed the photo of Billy Knight from the box cover. There was only one small paragraph of text and a few headings. Star sign: Taurus. Position: Bottom. Those were all the words he had. Mike felt like there should be more.

"How do I get on the cover of the magazine?" he asked Sasha. "And how do I get a huge interview?"

"We have to make more movies," she said. "And fast."

"And when can I do a scene with Luke Champion?"

Sasha smiled. "In time, Billy. In time."

14
Sick

DALE NEVER MENTIONED to Mike that he was disappointed with *Banging Billy*. There was nothing wrong with Mike's performance; it was flawless. Billy Knight was the best thing about the film. The problem, Dale feared, was with himself.

He knew it wasn't quite an A-list movie, and he felt a little sad. He had expected so much. It didn't look as polished as the movies from Cougar, or Magnum Man, or Hard Bodies, or even any of the second-tier professional studios for that matter. The sound, in places, was bad. One of the scenes had atrocious shadows on the wall, and at one point you could just see the edge of the cameraman's leg in a mirror. He tried hard to listen to Sasha's voice in his head, which told him that it was okay, that he was an artist in the process of development. It would get better. He was still learning his craft. "Be gentle with yourself," she said.

On a balmy Friday night toward the middle of April, Dale and Mike got dressed up and went out the door as Sasha and Billy. Sasha wore a black, knee-length dress with a rhinestone necklace and earrings to match, and Billy wore a pair of tight black pants and a white dress shirt, the sleeves rolled up and a smooth V of skin trailing down from his neck. They went to the Boom Boom Room together and danced to silly 70s music. One of the bartenders recognized Billy.

"Hey, I saw *Banging Billy*. Great stuff."

"Thanks," Billy said, and gestured to Sasha. "She directed it."

Sasha gave a strained smile. Had this bartender noticed the shadows on the wall, the leg of the cameraman?

"Wow, that's cool," the bartender said. "You're great. Hey, these drinks are on the house."

"Thanks, doll. The next film's going to be even better." She put her arm around Billy and walked with him to the edge of the dance floor, where they stood sipping their drinks.

Since the film's release, she'd been trying to figure out exactly how they were going to make the next film, and how she was going to make it better. She needed a large studio behind her. Video sales of *Banging Billy* weren't bad, but Steve at Cougar didn't care. She'd talked to him about letting her direct now that she'd made a feature-length porn film, but he just shook his head and said, "Sorry Sasha. My policy still stands. No fat drag queens in the director's chair. Wouldn't mind hiring that Billy, though." She'd heard almost the exact same responses from the other studios.

As she looked over at Billy now, she realized he looked a little bored. All week it seemed something was bothering him, but every time she asked, he said he was fine. She feared that if she didn't get a new film for him soon, he might go elsewhere. In his own way, he was as ambitious as she was. She thought of the world premiere party. The fact was that she hadn't invited anybody from the major studios partly because of the production quality, but even more importantly because she didn't want them snooping around Billy like a pack of thieves, calculating out just how easy he would be to steal. Billy was hers.

"Hey, Billy, and ah…" It was the bartender again, looking at Sasha and not knowing her name.

"Sasha, darling. Sasha Zahore."

"Sasha. That's cool. Listen, there's a VIP lounge upstairs, and I can get you in. Want me to take you up there?"

The young bartender, who introduced himself as Dick and said he wanted to do porn, left them on overstuffed burgundy chairs in a room draped with velvet. There were a few minor celebrities around, quite a few friends of staff, and plenty of coke. Sasha was happy to see Billy turn the coke down, but annoyed that he was approached very quickly by an attractive older man who said he was a record producer. Billy left with him, and Sasha had to make her way home alone. It was raining, so she took a cab. The peach-colored light from the streetlamps splashed in the gutters of West Pico Boulevard, and the cab driver's eyes kept glancing at her in the rear view mirror. The back seat felt empty without Billy.

The next morning Dale walked out of his bedroom at noon to find Mike lying on the sofa, complaining of a sore throat and a headache.

Dale reached down and put a hand on Mike's forehead. It didn't feel warm. "Maybe you just overdid it last night," he said.

They stayed at home all day and nursed their hangovers. Dale never asked about the record producer, although he wondered if the tall, grey-haired man had been a paying trick or a sport fuck. That afternoon they watched Dale's favorite movie, *Breakfast at Tiffany's*. Mike lay back on the sofa and Dale sat at one end, happy to have Mike's gorgeous legs across his lap. At one point, Mike turned around and put his head in Dale's lap, rubbing the fat on Dale's leg as though he were fluffing a pillow. He put his head down and said,

"You're comfortable, Dale." Very carefully, Dale put a hand on Mike's shoulder, and left it there.

On Sunday Mike was worse, complaining that his entire body ached. He had no appetite, and now his skin felt hot. Dale ran a washcloth under the cold tap, rang it out and placed it across Mike's forehead. Kneeling in front of the sofa, he realized then how much he had come to love that forehead. It was strong and unlined, in the mornings slightly covered at the edges by stray locks of Mike's beautiful, sandy brown hair.

At 10:00 a.m. Dale put on a pair of sweat pants and drove to the store to buy Mike some aspirin. He also bought, for the first time in his life, a thermometer. He'd never before had someone whose temperature he needed to take, and the thermometer felt like an incredible thing in his life. It was a tiny glass wand for a magical fairy, a silver bead at the end instead of a star. He picked up six cans of chicken soup and, once back at home, heated some in the microwave for Mike, serving it in a blue bowl on a wooden tray, with a plate of saltine crackers and a single red rose at the side.

He took Mike's temperature three times that day. Each time it was high. Mike moved from hot sweats to cold shivers, and the only time he got up off the sofa was to walk to the bathroom. That afternoon Dale made Mike watch his second favorite movie, *The Sound of Music*, and in an effort to make Mike laugh he stood up and sang 'Do Re Me' like one of the Von Trapp children. It was good to see Mike smile, in spite of his not feeling well.

Climbing into bed at the end of the day, Dale realized he and Mike had never had a weekend like that before, where they stayed in both Saturday and Sunday, hanging out at home together for two days straight. He couldn't help but feel happy.

When Sasha came out of the bathroom on Monday morning, ready for work, Mike had just woken up and he looked horrible. His color was off. He still had a fever, and he didn't even touch the coffee she brought him. Sasha immediately picked up the phone and made two calls, one to Steve, to tell him she was staying home sick, and one to her doctor's office.

She sat down on the edge of the sofa. "Baby, I'm taking you to the doctor today. We have an appointment in just two hours."

"You think I need to go?" Mike asked.

"You're very sick." She reached out and slowly stroked his hair. He looked up at her. He didn't push her hand away. The feeling that suddenly came over her then surprised her, but she accepted it, felt it.

She wished Mike were sick more often.

"I don't have the money for a doctor," he mumbled.

"Don't worry about the money. I'll pay. It's my doctor. She lets me pay in installments. It's like buying a dress on layaway."

Mike turned his head, pushing his cheek into her hand. "Thank you."

When the time came, she grabbed her favorite green vinyl handbag and picked up Mike's car keys. "Let's take your sexy old car," she said. "I'll drive."

She was disappointed when Mike made her stay in the waiting room. She wanted to be with him. She flipped through an old Woman's Day magazine, and the entire time a little girl nearby kept staring at her. When the mother turned away, Sasha shot the girl a quick, nasty look, all snarling mouth and bulging eyes. The girl leaned into her mother and whined annoyingly, but she stopped staring.

It seemed like a very long time before Mike came back out.

15
Doctor Wesley

THE DOCTOR'S NAMETAG said 'Dr. Wesley,' but she introduced herself as Barbara. She didn't wear a white coat. She looked at Mike plainly, without judgment. She had chocolate skin and large, kind eyes which calmed him.

He didn't know why she asked what he did for a living. Maybe it was because he came in with Sasha, or because of something else about him. He gave her the truth. "I'm a stripper, and I've started doing porn."

She didn't flinch. "Are you straight, gay, bi?"

"Men. I do it with men."

"How many sexual partners would you say you have in a month?"

"Depends," he said. "Sometimes only ten, sometimes closer to thirty. I need to be tested for HIV. Three months ago a guy came inside me." It was only the second time he'd ever told anyone exactly what happened. The first time was Toby, and Toby didn't seem to care. Mike had never even given specifics to Dale, and now it felt weird to say it out loud.

"How often do you have unsafe sex?"

"Never. Not normally. It wasn't my choice. He held me down."

The doctor paused. "Do you want to talk about that?"

He looked at a painting of the sea that hung on the wall. "I just need to be tested. Can you do it anonymously?" He knew how it was supposed to happen. You weren't supposed to give anybody your name. If you turned out positive, it would show up on your medical record. You'd be blacklisted.

"I'm afraid it's not anonymous if I do it. But I'll give you a list of clinics where it is. You can get tested there. When was the last time you were tested?"

"About a year ago," he said, thinking about Bob, one of his regular johns back in Cincinnati.

Bob wore tweed jackets with elbow patches. After getting fucked by Bob off and on for years, one night, drunk and upset, Bob had admitted to being positive. Mike felt sorry for him and continued to see him. Mike's rule was to treat every trick like they were positive anyway. Technically it didn't change anything. They'd always used condoms. Even so, the next time they had sex Mike couldn't get his mind off Bob's HIV. It felt like he had a gun up his ass that could go off at any moment, just a thin piece of latex to stop the bullet. He just couldn't handle knowing, and he wished Bob hadn't told him. After that they only did oral, and eventually Bob stopped calling. Mike felt bad. It was then that he had gotten tested and found out he was negative. That was the last time he knew for sure.

"Here you are," the doctor said. She handed him three brochures: one with a list of places around LA that provided free and anonymous testing, one with safe sex tips that he already knew, and a third with a phone number for a rape help line. Mike folded all three and slipped them into the back pocket of his jeans.

She had him strip to his underwear and sit on the padded table. She listened to his chest, had him breathe deeply in and out. She told him to lie down and she felt around his neck and groin. "I'm checking your lymph glands," she said.

Once, years ago, Toby had told him that when your lymph glands were swollen, it meant you were sick. It was one of the first signs of HIV.

Mike looked up at the doctor. "Are they swollen?"

"Yes, but that doesn't necessarily mean anything. It's possible you have nothing more than the flu. Although sometimes people do have cold symptoms when they seroconvert."

"You mean when they become positive?"

She nodded.

Mike wondered, if he found out he was positive, would he keep it a secret from Dale? Would he still try to become a porn star? He didn't know. Thinking about it felt like slipping into a large, terrifying hole.

"But that doesn't mean you have HIV. Of course, you have to be tested to know."

When Mike walked back into the waiting room, the doctor stepped in behind him to greet Sasha. "Hello, Dale." she said, all warmth and smiles as she shook Sasha's hand. "How are you?"

"Oh, I'm fine. Turned out I was just being paranoid the other day. Thank you so much for answering my questions."

"Any time."

After the doctor walked out of the waiting room, Mike said to Sasha, "What questions? What were you afraid of?"

"Oh, nothing."

"Were you sick?"

"No. I had a little food poisoning scare. You know me, just a silly drag queen. Are you okay?"

"When? Why didn't you tell me?"

"Last week. Didn't want to worry you. I'm fine. What about you?"

"Well, she tells me I just have the flu. She gave me this." He held up a prescription.

"Give me that, baby. We'll get it filled on the way home." Then she walked up to the woman at the front counter and slapped down a twenty dollar bill. "Tell Doctor Barbara I'll send more next month." She slid her hand into the crook of Mike's elbow, as if she were a dainty little lady, and they walked out to Mike's car together.

Over the next two days, Mike started feeling better. Sasha nursed him attentively, making sure he had everything he needed before she left for work in the morning – food and videos and magazines and books. They had a fight one evening when Mike mentioned he'd done a bit of a workout at home, just some push ups and sit ups. Sasha scolded him for exercising when he should have been recuperating. She wouldn't listen when Mike tried to explain that he wasn't that sick anymore.

By Thursday afternoon his energy had returned completely, and he decided he would go to the clinic the following morning to get tested. His stomach turned in knots.

When Sasha came home from work, he got up and started making dinner. She'd pulled two chicken breasts out of the freezer before leaving that morning, and he'd decided to cook them himself. He was feeling agitated and bored, a little tired of Sasha waiting on him.

"Get back on the sofa," she ordered immediately. "You should be resting."

"I feel all right." He took out a pot, put in some water from the tap, and set a metal vegetable steamer inside. "I've been laying on that couch all day." He put the pot on the stove.

"I want you to rest. You've been sick." Her voice was sharp. Mike turned around and was surprised to find himself standing face to face with her in the middle of the kitchen, their shoulders squared toward each other.

"It's okay," he said. "I feel okay. I'll make dinner." Two large potatoes and a bundle of asparagus were setting on the counter. The pink chicken breasts were thawed in the sink, still under plastic wrap on a black Styrofoam tray.

Sasha's voice became harsher. "You are still sick. You need to rest. You should not be up."

Mike became even more determined. He did not need to be waited on any more. He spoke firmly. "I feel fine Sasha. Fine."

"Go lay down!" Her voice had deepened and was so quick and loud that Mike actually jumped. She took a step toward him. Her right hand shot out, grabbing him by the red sweatshirt he was wearing. She began physically pulling him toward the couch.

"Stop it!" Mike yelled, astonished at what she was doing, and instantly furious.

She continued to heave and pull, using her weight to her advantage. Mike gripped her hand and began wrenching it away. She was bigger, but he was stronger. There was a grunt and a turn and a ripping sound. He pushed her hard in the chest, her foam breasts compressing under the force of his hands, and she stumbled back.

He looked down. There was a tear in his sweatshirt, along a diagonal seam from his neck toward his armpit. "Look what you did!" he shouted.

Sasha looked as though she'd just been slapped across the face, angry but surprised. "Oh baby, I'm sorry." Her hand was over her mouth.

"You fucking ripped my shirt!"

"I'm so sorry." She reached out to touch him, but he pushed her hand away. She opened the cupboard where she kept the scotch and poured herself a drink. "You want one?" Her voice was now soft and sweet.

"I'm making dinner." He turned toward the stove as though she were no longer there.

"I'll buy you a new shirt."

"That's not the point."

"I just want to take care of you, baby. That's all. I like taking care of you."

"I told you I'm fine," he said, still fuming. "You've been taking care of me for almost a week. But I can't stay on that couch forever. I feel better. I want to do something. I wanted to make you dinner." He began ripping the plastic wrap off the chicken.

"Are you sure you're all right?" Sasha asked.

"Don't ever grab me like that again."

"Never, baby."

He didn't know what to do, so he attended to the small things. He tossed the potatoes into the microwave – Sasha's trick to avoid boiling them. He threw the chicken breasts down into the hot pan. Then he looked back at his sweatshirt and walked into the living room, taking it off and throwing it onto the floor. Sasha's bedroom door clicked shut as he began riffling through the grey duffel bag in the corner where he kept his clothes. He found a T-shirt and put it on, then picked up the sweatshirt, looked at the rip, folded it and put it in the bag. When he started back into the kitchen, Sasha came out of her room carrying the black Styrofoam tray from the chicken.

He looked at her oddly, looked at the tray in her hand.

"I thought I could cut this in half and make shoulder pads for a dress," she said. "But it won't work." She followed him into the kitchen and threw the tray away. "I can sew it for you, baby, your shirt. If you want. But I have to say, it looked sort of sexy. You might want to leave it that way. Cut the sleeves off. It'll look fabulous."

He turned his back on her and flipped the chicken, which had already begun to turn golden brown.

16
Tiny Bottle

SASHA FELT TERRIBLE about the shirt, and was humiliated that she'd actually tried to force him back onto the sofa. She was ruled by her emotions; she knew she was. But he was sick. He needed to rest. Besides, she'd been upset. She'd had special plans for that chicken.

She saw her opportunity when he walked out of the kitchen. She went directly for the Styrofoam tray that he'd left sitting on the counter. It was rectangular and still full of the runny juice from the chicken. She picked it up, careful not to spill a drop, and moved quickly into her room as Mike had his back turned. She set the tray down on her vanity and shut the door.

Sasha's room was small and cramped, but the bed was big. The walls were an intense, hot fuchsia. Her room was always a mess, her shoes piled in a heap on the floor of her closet, pieces of fabric across the bed and in piles in the corners. Along one wall stood an enormous clothes rack stuffed with sequins, feathers, and lamé. A window in the corner looked down onto the street.

Her vanity was near the foot of her bed. It was cluttered with makeup brushes, small canisters, and lipstick tubes. She picked up a small glass bottle. The cap was a beautiful blue-green, and the glass was clear. Until yesterday, it had contained some old blemish concealer. Secretly, she had cut off the makeup brush that slid into the bottle from the cap, and then she washed out the bottle in the bathroom sink. The water had turned the color of her skin.

Now she unscrewed the cap, lifted the Styrofoam tray, and carefully, from a corner, poured the liquid into the bottle. She only spilled a little onto the vanity, which she promptly wiped up with a tissue. She screwed the cap on tightly, tipping the bottle this way and that to make sure it didn't leak. The liquid inside was cloudy and pink, like a sunrise.

She had thought this through very carefully. There was no guarantee that it would work, but it was worth a try. Doctor Barbara had answered her questions. Now, if all went well, Sasha would get what she wanted. She wiped the tray clean with another tissue and opened the door.

17
Tested

MIKE HEARD DALE up and making coffee the next morning, heard him go into the bathroom and then heard Sasha come out. They sounded different.

Lying on the couch with his eyes closed, pretending to be asleep, Mike took in the quiet slide of Dale in his green silk robe, followed by the louder rustling of Sasha, the jingling bracelets and smell of perfume. She put his morning cup of coffee down on the table beside the couch. He never once opened his eyes, and she didn't try to wake him. Dinner the night before had been silent and forced. Sasha had drunk too much scotch, apologizing several more times about the shirt.

Now, as soon as the door shut and the key outside turned in the lock, he opened his eyes. He waited a few moments to make sure Sasha didn't come rushing back, looking for her sunglasses or her car keys, then he sat up. He walked over to his bag and pulled out the calendar he'd bought back in Denver. He wanted to double-check, just to be sure. There, next to a picture of Mount Elbert, was today. It was April 21st.

He was too nervous to eat, so he drank the coffee, jumped in the shower, and left. One of the addresses on the brochure the doctor gave him was in West Hollywood, just over on San Vicente. He decided to walk. He wanted to be outside, wanted to move.

When he stepped out onto the sidewalk, the noisy morning wrapped around him. There was never much traffic on Orlando Avenue, but he could hear the cars over on

Melrose Avenue to the north. He turned back and looked at Dale's building – dusty beige and unimpressive, a two-story concrete thing with tiny windows. Someone began yelling down the street. A car honked on Melrose.

For a moment Mike found himself actually longing for the absolute stillness of Brewerton, the calm way the mornings unfolded, the crickets becoming still and the birdsong opening slowly. There was a way the light hung in the trees there. He'd yet to see that in LA, and he didn't think he ever would.

He walked down the alleyway that ran behind Dale's building, passing service entrances for shops on Melrose, and then he stepped out into the heat and noise of Melrose Avenue itself. He walked by a hair salon and a bookstore, looked in the windows of expensive furniture stores. He passed the discreet entrance to the Manhole Sauna, which he'd visited a couple of times, just for fun. It was open twenty-four hours, and an older man was going in now.

Near the Lighthouse Café he bumped into Kerry on the street, one of the other guys who stripped at Exposé. Kerry looked hung over and tired.

"Just getting home?" Kerry asked, his curly blond hair catching the sun. His body was lean and strong and tall. Even hung over and tired, he was very handsome.

Before Mike got sick they'd done some overtime together, each of them down on their knees in front of an English guy named Simon. Kerry had a green and blue tattoo on his left hip. "It's an Egyptian ankh," Kerry had explained, as they were undressing in Simon's hotel room, Simon watching nearby. "It means eternal life."

Here in the daylight of the street, Mike thought of Kerry's left hip.

"I just got up," Mike finally answered. "Thought I'd go for a walk."

"A walk? In LA?"

"Yeah. You know, just around."

Kerry shrugged. "That's cool. I just got away from a trick. He wanted me to stay all night, wanted me to sleep next to him."

"Just sleep?"

"No. First I fucked him."

Mike thought about the clinic. "Well, I gotta go."

"Right. Your walk."

"Are you working tonight?" Mike asked.

"Yeah."

"Cool. I'll look for you."

Kerry smiled. "Cool."

Mike moved on. He came to the enormous Pacific Design Center, which everyone called the Blue Whale, and he turned and headed up San Vicente Boulevard until he got to the other side of West Hollywood park and reached the clinic.

It wasn't as clean and new as Doctor Barbara's office had been. There were no potted plants in the corners, no art on the walls. The carpet in the lobby was grey and worn. A woman at the front desk said hello and gave him a code. He was Y7349A. In a small room he gave the code to another woman who talked to him about safe sex and took his blood. He watched the silver needle going in, watched his blood fill up a small test tube with red.

She said, "What would you do if you found out you were positive? Do you have a support system? Friends or family you can talk to?"

"I've got lots of friends," he said. "I'd deal with it. I'd be okay."

She told him to save his code and come back in a week for the results. He made an appointment with the woman at the front desk, and then he left.

18

El Mexicano

THIS WAS THE third shop Sasha had entered that afternoon, and she was in a hurry. She hoped desperately that they would have what she wanted. There were rows and rows of running shoes, tennis rackets, and golf clubs all around her. She felt like she was back in the boys' locker room of her high school gym, surrounded by the trappings of an athletic, masculine world she loved to look at, but where she would never belong.

The sweatshirts were hanging on black plastic hangers toward the back. There were grey ones, black ones, white ones. Finally she found a red one. It wasn't the same. Across the front, in large white letters, was the word 'Champion.' But she smiled to herself, thinking of Mike's favorite gay top, Luke Champion. This was perfect.

On her way to the register, a rack of tiny Speedos distracted her. Sasha loved Speedos. For a long time she'd dreamed of making a film about a randy swim team who couldn't keep their hands off each other. There would be sexy shots of men doing the butterfly naked – the swimming stroke she found the most powerful and erotic – and there would be sex in the pool, in the showers, everywhere. And of course there would be a hairy-chested coach with a whistle around his neck, demanding to be serviced by his star swimmers.

Standing in front of the rack, touching black nylon now, she thought of Mike. He deserved a tiny swimsuit for his perky little butt. She found a medium and walked up to the counter, her hands full of red and black.

As she smiled to the sales girl, her mind was in several places. How silent and awkward dinner was after the incident last night. How happy she hoped Mike would be when she gave him these little presents. But there were other things on her mind as well: confirming the reservation for tonight and, most importantly, getting to LAX by 5:30.

A week ago, when Steve first mentioned that a director and two models were coming in tonight from New York, she'd been irritated. Steve was always looking for directors for his successful series, *Muscle Party*. He was currently filming Volume 5. A different director filmed each scene. Sasha had been begging Steve to allow her to direct a scene for the series, but he said no. It was criminal that he was flying in a director when he had her, the wonderful Sasha Zahore, right under his nose.

She handed over her credit card to the sales girl and was pleasantly surprised to find she hadn't yet exceeded the limit. She took the bag and walked quickly out to her car. If traffic wasn't too bad, she still might make it to the airport on time.

The director Steve was flying in was Blane Handsome, and Sasha hated him not only for being successful, but for being five years younger than she was. He had no right. He and his two models – a top and a bottom – were arriving for a weekend of LA fun before they filmed their scene for *Muscle Party* 5 on Monday. In spite of her irritation, when she'd learned last week that Steve was flying people in, she volunteered to help out immediately. She was determined to make herself indispensable, by whatever means necessary. It wasn't until Steve asked her to arrange dinner that she realized she could turn it all to her advantage. She'd promptly booked dinner at El Mexicano.

* * *

At the age of eighteen and new to Los Angeles, waiting tables at El Mexicano had been Dale Smith's first job. Under a ceiling strung with brightly colored piñatas, he served enormous burrito platters and frosty margaritas. He didn't mind the work, but he couldn't bear putting on the dreary uniform every day – a boring white shirt and black pants.

The first time he showed up wearing a skirt, he was a nervous about how his boss would react, but he just couldn't help himself. It was such a fantastic skirt – bright yellow, full and ruffled, trimmed with burgundy ribbon. He wore a white blouse with it, and full makeup, a jet black wig in an attempt to look Mexican, open-toed sandals, and then he finished it all off with a beautiful orange sash.

His boss was the man who owned El Mexicano – a Cuban man named Jorge who worked long hours in the kitchen to support his wife and two small children. Dale liked Jorge because he pretended to be Mexican in front of the customers, in order to give his restaurant an air of authenticity.

On the day Dale showed up in drag, Jorge stood stock-still and took a long look at him. It seemed as though he was about to yell at Dale, but then he broke into a smile that was clearly flirtatious. "Beautiful," he said. "You are like a big piñata. My customers will love you."

From then on Dale came to work in drag every day, and he was so thankful for Jorge's acquiescence that two weeks later, when Jorge began hinting that he was in need of a blow job because his wife refused, Dale was more than happy to oblige. After he was done, Dale got up off his knees, wiped off his chin, and said, "From now on, call me Sasha."

Sasha made far better tips than Dale, and she had a lot more fun. "Buenos tardes," she would say as she approached her table. Sometimes she would curtsy. Sometimes she would turn her head to show off a miniature sombrero pinned to her wig, or earrings shaped like tiny guitars. As she took orders for enchiladas and quesadillas, she made jokes and got people laughing. She spoke conspiratorially with the women and called them "girlfriend." She flirted with the handsome straight men out on dates. "Ay caramba!" she would say, directly to the man's face. "Muy guapo!" Her hand would go to her chest, and she'd flutter her fake eyelashes feverishly. Then she'd turn to the girl he was with and add, "Mmmm, honey, when you're done with him, would you mind sending him my way?"

Soon customers were showing up to see Sasha as much as to eat Jorge's food, and the other waiters became jealous. All the customers wanted to sit in Sasha's section, so Jorge offered her a job as hostess. From then on she greeted every-one at the door with a spectacular smile, seated them, and wandered around asking people if they wanted another Corona, Dos Equis, or perhaps a pitcher of margaritas. She helped clear dishes when the waiters got busy, and she chatted briefly with each table, making sure everyone was in on the fun. With Sasha working the floor, eating dinner at El Mexicano was like being at a carnival, and Jorge's business took off.

The sole reason Sasha quit after three years was because the job made it too hard to do drag shows. The work was exhausting. The kitchen didn't close until eleven. By the time she got out it was usually close to midnight. Although she

106

tried, it was difficult to run to clubs after that and give an audience her best.

Jorge said he was very sad to see her go, and in the years since they'd managed to maintain a kind of ongoing friendship. Sasha frequently took people to El Mexicano to have a good Mexican meal and check out the new drag queen hostesses that Jorge hired in his never-ending attempt to fill her place. An astute businessman, Jorge had once explained, "This is now our point of difference." Years ago he'd moved the restaurant down the street to a bigger, more upscale space. Even at the new location Sasha always walked in as if she belonged there. She would sashay through the door with her head high, dismissing the new, substandard hostesses with a wave and heading straight into the kitchen to speak to Jorge, who would greet her warmly. After closing time, in the kitchen or in Jorge's car, she still indulged him in a friendly blow job now and again, which she enjoyed giving as much as he enjoyed getting.

* * *

Sitting in traffic on her way to the airport, Sasha felt a little conflicted. Her lasting fondness for Jorge made her feel bad about what she was going to do in his restaurant. Nevertheless, it was an obvious choice to book Steve's dinner party at El Mexicano. The food was still good – better, she thought, than when she'd worked there – the margaritas were fantastic and the girls at the door made it fun, even if they were a bit bland compared to her. Most importantly, at no other restaurant would she be able to do what she needed to do. Really, she had no choice.

It was 5:45 when she pulled into short-term parking at LAX. She walked inside and went immediately to a phone booth, where she called Jorge to confirm her reservation.

"Hola, Sasha!" Jorge said. "I'm looking forward to seeing you, my big piñata." After all these years, he still called her this from time to time, affectionately, and Sasha didn't mind. Sometimes she called him "my little Mexican sausage" in return. She confirmed her nine o'clock reservation, wished him well, and hung up the phone.

There would be six people at the table that night – Steve with a new young lover Sasha hadn't yet met, Blane Handsome, the two New York models, and of course herself. In an uncharacteristic act of generosity, Steve was paying. No doubt this was because Blane had directed the movie that won Best Gay Video at last year's Adult Entertainment Awards. It featured two incredibly muscular men making tender love on a New York rooftop, dressed as jewel thieves. These were not, unfortunately, the models that were accompanying Blane today.

Sasha suspected that Steve was paying for dinner in an attempt to woo the award-winning director to do even more work for Cougar. But as far as she was concerned, it wasn't Blane's directing that made that scene win the award. It was the two models, who were so obviously into each other, and who looked very good in black – but even better out of it.

She had agreed to meet Blane at the luggage carousel, and she saw him from a distance now, recognizing him from photographs of the Adult Entertainment Awards in *Rod & Shaft* magazine. He was a tallish, appropriately handsome man who had broad shoulders. She could tell just by looking at him that he was as dumb as a box of rocks.

With him were the two models. They were like pathetic puppy dogs at Blane's heels, carrying his luggage and yapping *yes-Blane-yes-Blane* every chance they could. It made her stomach turn. Nobody, not even second-rate talent, should behave with so little self-respect. If her models ever became that sycophantic she would slap them, one by one, over and over, until they stopped.

She took a deep breath and walked in their direction, waving with a tiny finger wiggle and a tilt of her head. The two models came over to her immediately and introduced themselves by their porn names, Max Pole and Phil Dass. With names like that, it wasn't hard for Sasha to figure out who was the top and who was the bottom. She liked Phil's name in particular; her only regret was that she hadn't thought of it herself.

Max was tall and well built, but had a permanent, goofy smile on his face, as though he was continually confused and too embarrassed to say so. Phil was a pale redhead, which Sasha liked because you didn't see many gingers in gay porn. But really there was nothing special about either of them. There was no sparkle, no electric fire. Nothing like her Billy.

"Thanks for picking us up, Miss Sasha," Phil said. "It's super nice of you."

There was such a look of wonder on Phil's face that for a moment Sasha actually suspected he might never have met a drag queen before.

"Not a problem, doll. And you can just call me Sasha." She winked.

While she asked the two about their flight, Blane Handsome hung back, some distance away, scowling arrogantly and refusing to walk over. Eventually Sasha was forced to approach him. She put her hand forward in her most lady-like way, palm down, and as Blane reached out to take it she quickly moved it upwards, so the back of her hand approached his mouth, almost obliging him to kiss it. He did, and Sasha smiled victoriously, pleased with herself that in her small way she'd already begun to subjugate him, like the Pope making a Cardinal kiss his ring.

"It's a pleasure to meet you, Blane," she said.

She waited as they gathered up the rest of their luggage, and then she led them to her car. She carried nothing. They were to stay at Steve's, and as she drove up the ramp onto the San Diego Freeway she asked questions about the films they'd made. She quickly learned that this was to be Phil's first sex scene.

"So you're a virgin?" she said into the rearview mirror, winking back at Phil.

"Not exactly," Blane interrupted. "Half of New York State has had that ass."

"Lovely," Sasha said, and continued asking questions to make conversation. More than anything, she knew, people liked to talk about themselves. It soon became clear that this was especially true of Blane.

"I've lost count of the films I made," he said, never once looking at Sasha as he spoke. "I've made so many. Must be over sixty now. Damn fine films, every one of them."

"Oh my," Sasha said, merging into the faster traffic. "That is impressive. And how many of those films have won awards, Blane?"

Secretly, she already knew the answer.

He pushed his jaw forward. "Best Gay Video last year for some great rooftop sex in my film *The Family Jewels*. Very hot."

"Of course. Silly me. How could I forget? So, of those sixty-odd films, is it just the one award?"

"Well, I've been nominated for quite a few."

"And how many have you won, doll?"

He paused. "Ah, just the one."

"Oh, I see," she said quickly, as though she sincerely regretted causing him any embarrassment.

After being trapped in the car with Blane talking non-stop for what seemed like an eternity, they finally approached Larchmont Village and she pulled out a piece of paper. Steve's assistant, Günter, had drawn a little map. As she turned on Windsor Boulevard and saw the house, a little spasm of resentment ran through her. It was a beautiful faux-Spanish villa, all white stucco and red tile roof, with three graceful archways framing the porch. Although it wasn't the largest house in the neighborhood, it still reeked of money. Off toward the end of the street, up in the distance through the hazy smog that hung over LA, the Hollywood sign was visible in the hills.

Steve, she knew, wouldn't be home. Much to her delight his new lover walked out to greet them wearing a pair of red Speedos. He looked like a carbon copy of Steve's last lover, only slightly younger: cute, blond, tanned and muscular, but not so big as to make Steve look puny.

Sasha climbed out of the car and greeted him with her arms in the air and a smile on her face, as though she'd known him forever. "Why hello you gorgeous thing you! You must be the new edition."

After introductions – the new lover's name was Marcus – Sasha explained that she had to run home to change and pick up a few things. "See you boys at the restaurant at nine!" she yelled, and drove off.

She was disappointed that Mike wasn't home when she got there, because she wanted to give him his presents right away. She changed into a dress that matched the Mexican flag, with ruffled folds of red, white and green, and then inspected herself in the mirror. Yes, perfect. She opened the drawer of her vanity and reached in, picking up the small glass bottle that contained the chicken juice from last night. She held it to the light.

There was, of course, no guarantee. She knew from talking to Doctor Barbara that results could range from absolutely nothing to extreme and dangerous illness. What she hoped for was something in the middle, but it was a risk she was willing to take. Her biggest concern was that illness didn't occur for two to five days after infection. If it didn't happen quickly, it would be too late. She dropped the bottle into a small woven handbag and headed out the door.

Sasha arrived at El Mexicano ten minutes early in order to make sure everything was ready. She slid past the scrawny hostess at the front door with not so much as a nod. In the kitchen, Jorge greeted her with open arms and a big "Hola!"

"Hola, doll. Now, listen here. You need some better signage out front. How about this?" She gestured upwards toward an imaginary billboard. "It would be in big letters, so everyone can see it from a distance. 'El Mexicano: Burritos as big as your head.'"

Jorge smiled and set his hand on his belly, which had grown considerably over the years. "Yes, Sasha. I like it. You're always good to me. May I use it?"

"Of course. Now let me get to work. I've got important people coming tonight. Big directors and producers, you know."

Jorge looked impressed.

She asked quickly about the specials for the evening, set her handbag down in the small hallway that led from the kitchen to the dining area, and got busy. She went around straightening and polishing the silverware, fluffing Jorge's new cloth napkins, and making sure the wooden tabletop was spotless. Everything had to be perfect. She ordered a pitcher of margaritas from the bar and placed it in the middle of the table.

When Steve and his entourage arrived, she stepped in front of the hostess and greeted everyone individually with dramatic kisses to the air. Before she kissed Marcus she said, "Oh, I almost didn't recognize you with your clothes on." She turned to Steve and added, "You've got a hot little number here, boss!" She smacked Marcus on the ass and Steve looked proud, as though someone were admiring his new thoroughbred horse.

Sasha herself led everyone to the table, although she let the emaciated hostess carry the menus. Then Sasha made a big show of telling them all where to sit. Steve was at the head of the table and Marcus at the other end. She sat Blane on Steve's left and then herself on his right. "So I can be close to the kitchen," she said. Max and Phil were on either side of Marcus. The effect was of a table that separated things according to their kind – the directors from the models, the watchers from the watched, the desirous from the desired.

The hostess began telling everyone about the specials when Sasha interrupted. "Don't you worry, honey. I'll tell them the specials. I already talked to Jorge." Then she dismissed the skeletal creature with a wave of her hand.

Max pointed to a picture on the wall. "Hey, Sasha. That's you."

Ever since Sasha left, Jorge had been covering the walls with glossy head shots of every drag queen who ever worked there, interspersed with large tourist posters of Mexico. A photograph showing a much younger Sasha was near the entrance, overlooking the hostess stand.

"Yeah. I got my start as a drag queen here," she told Max, who was smiling in his dim-witted way. "This whole Mexicano drag queen shtick is because of me."

Phil spoke up then, gazing at Sasha. "That's really great, Sasha. You're great."

Sasha suspected that if the boy wasn't already putting on dresses, he would be soon. "You're very sweet, doll. Thanks," she said, feeling a small stab of guilt for what she was about to do.

She began pouring the margaritas as she told everyone about the specials and embellished them with her own recommendations. She was pleased with herself that she managed to talk Blane and Phil into getting the beef enchiladas.

A new waitress named Emily took their orders in a rush. She was obviously very busy. Not long afterward, Sasha got up to check on things.

"The food won't be ready yet," Steve said.

"I'll just see how it's going." She walked into the kitchen and asked Jorge about their meals. She'd committed everybody's order to memory.

"It'll be another fifteen minutes until they're ready," Jorge said.

Waiters and waitresses were running in and out of the kitchen. The restaurant was full. It was good that it was so busy. Little things would go unnoticed.

She looked at her watch, helped herself to some corn chips, and wandered back out of the kitchen. On the way toward the table, she checked her handbag.

The hallway that led from the kitchen to the restaurant floor was painted a dark blue. On the left side, where Sasha had left her bag, there was a long countertop. This was where the wait staff added up their bills and ran credit cards through the machine for approval. On the right side there was a service window where staff ordered drinks from the bar and gave cash to the bartender. Sasha was relying on the fact that, except for moments when the waiters were dealing with bills, this space was usually empty. Staff passed through quickly, and few lingered.

She opened her handbag now and checked that both things were there: her compact and her small bottle of chicken juice. There was nothing else. She knew better than to leave a handbag full of money on a countertop in LA. She pulled out the compact now and checked her makeup. Spectacular.

Back at the table, she joined the conversation for exactly ten minutes. Blane was rambling on about some stupid movie he'd made in the desert outside Las Vegas.

When she got up to check on the food the second time, everything was nearly ready. Emily rushed by and Sasha grabbed her elbow, saying, "Honey, I'll serve our table, don't you worry. You seem a bit busy."

Emily was delighted. "That would be great, Sasha. You don't mind?"

"Not at all, honey."

Emily thanked her again and ran out to a table that was waiting to order.

Although it had been years, Sasha knew the routine. She grabbed one of the large oval serving trays and began arranging the warm dinner plates side by side. Six fit if you let some hang over the edge. She set a side of salsa between two plates and heaved the tray up on her right shoulder. Loaded with meals and full of food, the trays had always been heavy. But Sasha had done this many times in the past, and she was still capable.

She walked out of the kitchen and stopped in the hallway to set the tray down on the counter. She opened several cupboards, pretending to look for salt and pepper shakers. Then, when she was sure that nobody was around, she put her left hand into her handbag and pulled out the bottle. She moved quickly and discreetly, unscrewing the top with her right hand and then, in one sweeping motion, pouring the raw chicken juice across the top of the two beef enchiladas.

She knew that sometimes there were public health investigations at restaurants, and she didn't want it to look like Blane and Phil got sick here at El Mexicano. If they'd ordered chicken it would be too obvious. This was the least she could do to protect Jorge – and herself.

If she got caught, she'd lose her job at Cougar and never be welcome at El Mexicano again. Steve would be shocked and angry and, even worse than that, Jorge would be terribly hurt. She could almost see Jorge's sad, stunned eyes looking at her, his beautiful Cuban accent asking, "Why do you do this to me, Sasha?"

She quickly threw the empty bottle back in her handbag, picked up the side of salsa, and dumped some across the top of each enchilada, to help hide the juice.

"What are you doing?" A waiter was standing beside her, looking over her shoulder. Sasha didn't know how long he'd been there.

Fortunately, she had years of practice with quick thinking on stage, ad-libbing responses to hecklers, and dealing with awkward sound failures in humorous and entertaining ways. Out of mere survival her mind had become sharp and swift. Her face could hide the deepest insecurities and fears.

She held out her fingers now, as if she was counting things to do, continuing a private conversation she'd been having with herself. "Extra salsa, okay." She turned to the waiter. His eyes were jet black, as though they were all pupil, and it seemed as though he was looking right through her. She cleared her throat. "Now, tell me, doll. Where's the salt and pepper?"

He looked at her for a moment, and she thought she saw the most vague suspicion pass across his face. It bloomed up slowly, but then died back.

"Here you go." He reached up into a cupboard and pulled down two clear glass shakers, then he turned away and began adding up a bill.

Sasha took a deep breath. She was okay.

The noise from the kitchen and the restaurant floor mixed there in the hallway – sounds of people talking, plates clattering all around, everything loud and chaotic. She loved the energy at El Mexicano when it was busy. Even back at the old location, which was smaller, the liveliness of it all had always made her feel good. As she thanked this waiter now, it seemed for a moment that she was eighteen again. There was so much ahead of her.

When she went to lift the tray, she struggled and quickly set it down. "Oh!" she moaned out loud. "Please," she said to the waiter. "Be a doll and help me with this, would you? I told Emily I'd do it, to help her out, but these trays are just so much heavier than when I used to work here."

It wouldn't be good for Steve to see her serving the meals. She didn't want to look suspicious.

The waiter said, "Sorry. I got a table that needs their bill."

She put a hand on his arm and gave him the most charming pout she could muster. "Oh, help an old girl out, won't you?"

He paused. "Sure." He lifted her tray onto his shoulder and headed out to the table. Sasha walked out behind him and sat down. She directed everything from her seat. "The taco salad is over there, doll. The beef enchiladas go to those two sexy men..."

She sat down and watched as Blane and Phil brought forks full of salsa and beef to their mouths, chewing it, swallowing it down. She kept refilling their margarita glasses, as well as everyone else's.

"This is great," Blane said. "The beef's delicious."

"Mind if I try?" Steve asked.

"Sure." Blane pushed his plate toward Steve.

Sasha did not want Steve sick. She did not want it to be obvious which meals had been bad. Just as Steve was reaching forward with his fork, she lifted her hand quickly, so that her own nearly-full margarita glass toppled in Steve's direction, spilling across the table and running into his lap.

"Oh, I'm so sorry!" she yelled. "I'm such a klutz." She waved her hands in the air. "No more margaritas for Sasha!"

Steve had quickly moved his chair back and was already wiping his pants with his napkin. He did not look happy. Blane threw his napkin onto the margarita puddle in the middle of the table.

"Missy!" Sasha called the hostess over. "This big ol' girl made a big ol' mess. Would you be a dear and bring us some more napkins?"

By the time the mess was cleaned up and Steve had gone to the men's room to dry his lap with the hand dryer, the meal was almost over. Luckily Steve forgot about his desire to taste Blane's enchilada. Sasha watched as Blane and Phil ate their last bites. The deed was done. She folded her hands under the table and made a small prayer to the goddess. Please, she thought, let it work.

19
Stripping at Exposé

MIKE WAS STANDING by the bar, ready to do his first number for the evening. He was disappointed that Kerry hadn't shown up yet. He wanted to chat.

After his first number, he knew, the customers would monopolize his time, trying to talk to him and buy him drinks. Usually this was fine. It was what he was here for. Exposé only paid him ten bucks an hour, and it was the extras the customers paid for that that made stripping worthwhile. But tonight he wanted to talk to Kerry. He thought of Kerry's blond hair in the sun in front of the Lighthouse Café that afternoon, of his little smile, the ankh tattoo hidden on his hip.

There weren't many customers in the bar yet – just a few old lechers in the corners, a couple of teddy bears up by the stage. The lechers were always trying to fondle him. The teddy bears just wanted to talk. There was one guy in the audience who, whenever Mike did a private dance for him in back, always tried to touch more than he'd paid for.

The private dances were what made him the most money, without sex. Mike charged twenty bucks minimum for a private, the length of one song. Although most of the guys charged only ten, Mike had no shortage of customers. For the twenty bucks he let them touch his chest, back, arms and legs. For a thirty dollar dance they could also touch his ass. For forty, his crotch. In the private rooms they weren't supposed to have sex, not even a hand job, although some guys offered it. Mike didn't. There was a window in the door and the bouncers could check. Mike never did overtime – full-on sex after hours – for anything less than a hundred. If the guy was ugly, or if he looked rich, it was more.

The good thing was that Mike didn't have to do overtime if he didn't want. It wasn't expected. But he did it, because the money was good, and he was used to sex with strangers. He pushed away his fear. He was always careful. He didn't leave with anybody bigger than him, unless the guy was a regular, and even then only if the bouncers had said the guy was okay.

From behind the bar Pascal, the owner and bar manager, caught Mike's eye now and gestured to the stage. Mike stepped in back and went into the changing room, where he unlocked his locker and pulled out his tool belt and hardhat, and then put them on. He was wearing work boots, jeans, and a flannel shirt with the sleeves cut off. The costume was silly, but that was part of what made it entertaining. It was construction drag. He'd learned from Sasha. On the nights she showed up at Exposé to watch his routine, she invariably gave him helpful advice and feedback. And she spent a lot of time with him at home putting together his costumes. He always smiled to himself when he put them on – whether it was construction drag, police drag, or football drag. He wore his costumes in the same spirit as Sasha wore her dresses. "You're *supposed* to smile," she told him. "It's *supposed* to be fun." As the costume came off it was also – unlike Sasha's drag – going to be sexy.

He walked through a narrow passage now, to the doorway at the back of the stage. He parted a curtain and stepped out. 'Brass in Pocket' by the Pretenders started playing, which he'd told Sasha he wanted to dance to even though she didn't like the song. The room was almost empty. He'd rather dance to a crowd, but the shows were supposed to start at nine. He moved to the music, swaying and smiling.

He unbuttoned his shirt and let it hang open, leaned back to show off his abs. He let the shirt fall behind him and put his hands on the back of his head to show off his hairy armpits, his biceps. He winked and side-stepped. One by one he took off the hard hat, the tool belt, the work boots. The boots were untied, with the laces tucked in, to make it easy.

With his back toward the audience, he bent over in his tight jeans and wiggled his butt. One of the old lechers whistled. Mike turned back around and squinted through the lights to see if Kerry had come in, but he couldn't see him.

The first song ended and 'I Don't Want to Live Without You' by Foreigner started up. Sasha had picked the song, helped with all the choreography. "This song is how I feel about you," Sasha had said, and Mike didn't know what to say.

He almost always danced to a slower song for his second number. The first number was good for getting the customers horny and getting their energy up, but the second number was for enticing them into requesting extras.

Mike moved his body, gently rubbing his hands over his torso and thighs. He slipped off his jeans, then his socks, and danced in a white jockstrap. He liked how the elastic straps in back pushed up his butt cheeks and accentuated the curve of his ass. There was no full-frontal nudity on stage at Exposé. Everyone knew you had to pay more for that.

When the second song ended, one of the teddy bears held up a five-dollar bill. The five-dollar dances were easy. Mike stepped down off the stage in his jock strap and walked over as a the DJ started a new song. After the two songs that Mike had chosen, the DJ played anything he wanted.

The customer was someone Mike recognized. This guy had once paid Mike for five private dances in a row, and then talked about his holiday in North Carolina nearly the entire time. He was in his fifties, with grey hair and a wedding ring.

Mike stood directly in front of him now and held his arms over his head, his hips jutting out. The guy pushed the bill down into Mike's jock strap. That was as much contact as he would get for that money. Touching during a five-dollar dance wasn't allowed. Mike began moving, very close. One of the bouncers watched from the corner. If a customer started groping, Mike was supposed to step out of reach, but if the guy was sexy, Mike stepped away very slowly. If the guy continued trying to touch, a bouncer would come over. Pascal always said this was a high-class place, not a common whorehouse.

Mike was swaying back and forth in front of the customer when Kerry walked in. The strippers always came in the back. Kerry walked out through the door beside the stage and moved over to the bar. He caught Mike's eye, nodding and smiling, as though this five-dollar dance were for him. Mike kept his eye on Kerry as he danced. Eventually the customer looked over his shoulder to see who Mike was looking at, and he said, "Hey, I paid you," pointing at himself. After that Mike was careful to keep his eyes off Kerry.

When the song was over, he was happy that the guy didn't ask for a private dance. The bouncer was still watching. Mike wouldn't have been able to say no, and he wanted to go talk to Kerry. Although the strippers at Exposé weren't expected to do overtime, they were expected to do privates if a customer requested it. It was part of the deal.

He walked back up on stage, turned around again and wiggled his rear end, then went backstage.

In the changing room, he pulled the five-dollar bill out of his jockstrap. It was warm and damp. The changing room had lockers along one wall and a long bench in the middle of the room. Mike sat down and waited for Tony to come with his clothes. Tony was the new waiter, and this was part of his job: serve the drinks and pick up the clothes. The waiters didn't dance, but they had to be handsome. Tony was sexy in an Italian way, and he flirted with the customers even though he was straight.

"That was a good," Tony said, coming through the door in his waiter's uniform, tight black pants and a white shirt. He was carrying Mike's clothes and boots.

"Oh really?" Mike said. "You better stop watching. Your girlfriend's going to get jealous."

Tony laughed and ran back out into the bar. There were rumors that he had a daughter with an ex-girlfriend, that he saw her every other weekend.

Mike put the construction drag back on, except for the tool belt and hard hat. He stuffed the five-dollar bill it into the pocket of his jeans and went out to talk to Kerry.

"Hey," Kerry said. "Damn, you're the hottest guy here."

Mike was taken aback. He smiled. "Thanks, but I don't think so. The hottest guy here is this dancer named Kerry. Know him?"

"Vaguely. What are you drinking?"

"Miller light."

Kerry turned to the bartender and got Mike his beer. The strippers didn't pay for alcohol, although part of their job was to get customers to buy them drinks anyway. Mike liked that Kerry ordered his beer.

"You enjoy your walk today?" Kerry asked.

Suddenly worry shot through Mike's chest. He didn't want to think about being tested, didn't want to think about waiting an entire week for the results. "It was fine," he said, then added, "Have you recovered from that all-night trick?"

"Yeah. Wasn't so bad. He had a nice apartment. He smelled good. I got an extra hundred for staying."

"Cool." Mike looked at the empty stage. He took a sip of his beer. It was the hardest thing, just talking. Not when he was with a customer – that was easy, it was his job. It wasn't real. But it always felt difficult to maneuver when he was with guys he was attracted to, guys he liked. Ever since he and Kerry had done their trick together, Mike thought Kerry was nice. He'd been gentle when he fucked Mike in front of the English guy, almost kind, like he was handling something precious.

Mike never mentioned Kerry to Sasha. Customers didn't make her jealous, and neither did simple one night stands. But hearing about a guy he liked – a guy who was tender when he fucked him – this, Mike knew, would upset her.

"You live with that drag queen, right?" Kerry asked.

Mike was surprised. It felt like Kerry was reading his mind. "Yeah. Sasha. Her name is Sasha. Dale, really. He's Dale."

"I hear she's always after guys to do jack-off scenes for her. She's into video."

"Yeah. She's a director. I did a jack-off scene for her. And we shot a movie together."

"Hardcore?"

"Yeah."

"Why'd you do that?"

"I wanted to. It's fun"

125

"I'm not so into porn."

"It's safer than turning tricks. There's no risk of being beat up."

"I prefer real sex, without cameras."

"It is real sex."

"And some day I don't want to be doing this anymore." Kerry gestured around, to the stage and the men in the bar. "I don't want some video of me having sex hanging around afterward, reminding me."

"It's what I want to do. Porn. I want to be a big star."

"She's sort of gross. So damn fat."

"Sasha? She's not gross. She's just Sasha. Sort of beautiful, in a way."

"You think she's sexy?"

"No, I don't mean sexy. I mean she's really nice. She'd do anything for me. I trust her."

Kerry laughed. "She's fuckin' hideous, man."

Mike stopped. He looked at Kerry sternly, like a warning. "She's my friend," he said, his voice short and clipped. He was no longer so sure about this lean, blond stripper in front of him. Where was the tender man who fucked him?

Pascal walked up and tapped Kerry on the arm. "You're on."

Kerry nodded to Pascal, then turned back to Mike. Something in his face said that he didn't want to walk away right now.

"The stage," Pascal said, watching.

"Sorry, man," Kerry said to Mike. Then he downed the last of his drink and began walking to the stage.

The change in Kerry's gait told Mike that he was already performing. It was a loping swagger. His head was high, chest forward, shoulders rocking just a little with each step, first

126

the right then the left. The difference was subtle, but Mike knew it wasn't Kerry's usual walk. This was the walk Mike had also learned to do when he was on the streets, so men would recognize he was for hire. Around the bar, customers' heads were already turning toward Kerry, even before he made it to the stage.

The music started, and Kerry began dancing. He didn't do costumes. He stripped in street clothes, tight jeans and muscle tees. Mike felt it didn't convey the same sense of fun, sexy play that costumes did, but it was still good. Kerry had been doing this for a long time, much longer than Mike, and as Mike watched he took note of the expert expression on Kerry's face.

Stripping, Mike had decided, was as much about the face as it was the body. You had to look like you were enjoying it, or it wasn't sexy. Of course you had to have a good body. But even if you had the body of a god, if you looked bored or annoyed or self-conscious it wouldn't come off right, wouldn't really be sexy. At the same time, if you had just a decent body you could still go a long way with a flirtatious, sexy expression or a mischievous smile.

Mike thought that a large part of what made a guy appealing was not just his body or the features of his face, but how he carried himself, how he held a gaze or turned away just at the right time. There were men, just average guys he'd seen around, whose ability to be attractive was destroyed merely by holding their chin out too far, their neck stiff and tight, or slouching terribly – things that revealed a lack of ease with themselves, and consequently made them ugly. The sexiest men wore their bodies well, like a loose robe. They carried themselves in a manner that implied there was something relaxed and still just under the surface of their skin, some effortless way of being – a thing you could get at and touch, if you got close enough. This was an act Mike had always tried to mimic. Yet at the same time he knew, above all, that you had to come off as genuine. You couldn't seem affected or cheesy at all. Nothing was as big of a turn-off as an obvious fraud. You had to be completely comfortable with yourself. Then the act became true.

By the time Kerry was done with his two songs, he was standing in the middle of the stage in a tiny black G-string. Mike hated G-strings. They weren't sexy. Jock straps were sexy. He watched Kerry, watched his long, sinewy muscles stretch down his arms and legs. One of the lechers against the far wall held up a five-dollar bill. Kerry glanced in Mike's direction and then walked over to the old man. Mike stood at the bar drinking. When the song was over, Kerry and the lecher walked into the back together. Mike watched them go.

20
The Results

FOR DALE, THE weekend passed with an almost unbearable slowness. After climbing into bed Friday night, he slept for a few hours but then woke up at four am feeling horrible for what he'd done. He thought of the risk of serious illness and hospitalization. He wanted to call Steve's house immediately to make sure that Phil and Blane were okay, but he knew he couldn't. It was too late. He had to keep quiet now.

Around 4:30 a.m., he heard the door in the kitchen open and heard Mike come in. He saw the light from the living room flash on under his door. Although he wanted to get up and talk, it would be too hard to face Mike right then. He rolled over and tried to get back to sleep. The next day he made a point of not asking if Mike had gone home with a trick. More and more, Dale didn't like to know.

He brought out his presents on Saturday afternoon and watched as Mike opened them with an enormous, child-like smile. He felt incredibly happy as Mike took off the shirt he was wearing and slipped on the red sweatshirt immediately. It fit. It looked good. Then, standing in front of Dale, Mike took off his jeans, the sweatshirt, his underwear, and he put on the pair of black Speedos. His lean body was already beginning to fill out with a bit more muscle from his workouts. He turned around and showed Dale his ass.

"Does my butt look big in this?" he asked, laughing.

"*Huge!*" Dale said, staring at the beauty of Mike's rounded ass.

Dale wanted to watch movies on the sofa with Mike on all day Sunday, but Mike had plans, although he didn't say what they were. Dale feared that if he put too much pressure on Mike to stay home, or to spend time together, he might go away entirely. Mike left Dale sitting alone at noon and didn't come back until after seven that evening.

Dale waited for Mike so they could eat dinner together. Over potatoes warmed in the microwave and some quickly pan-fried steaks, he asked how Mike's day was, but Mike only mumbled a vague answer about how he'd just been "hanging out." Dale decided to let it go.

On Monday morning Sasha left for work in an understated yet comfortably glamorous pink velour tracksuit. There was a purple rose embroidered above her left bosom. She might have to work late, and she wanted to be practical.

In fact, she had absolutely no idea what she'd find when she walked in the door of Cougar Studios. She was dying to know the results of her hard work, but it was important not to do anything out of the ordinary. She walked to her desk in no hurry, put her enormous green handbag under her desk, and made a cup of tea before poking her head into Steve's office. She planned to thank him for the lovely meal at El Mexicano, but she was delighted to find him standing outside his office, shouting frantically at Günter.

"What do you mean, Austin's not available?" Steve was clearly stressed. "What about Montgomery, can he do it?"

Sasha knew Austin Wagner and Montgomery Boss were directors. She suppressed a smile.

Günter, wearing a dark grey mesh tank top, had a stunned expression on his face. "I called Monty already," he said. "He's at Fire Island on vacation." In the urgency, Günter's voice seemed to have lost any trace of German intonation.

"Then get me Peter's number," Steve said.

"Peter?"

"Peter Wolff. If he can't do it, we're in serious trouble. And get the talent book. Start making calls. We need a bottom too."

Sasha interrupted, sporting her best look of concern. "What's wrong, Steve?"

"Fuckin' pain in the ass, Sasha. Both Blane and Phil are sick. Really sick. In bed and moaning. The only time they get up is to run to the bathroom. Marcus is at the house taking care of them."

"Oh, Steve, that's awful. They'll be okay, won't they?"

"Yeah, we think it's food poisoning. They ate at some nasty diner on Saturday afternoon. They're in no condition to work, and we're supposed to film tonight at Built."

"Built?" Sasha knew it. Built was the big, gay West Hollywood gym.

"Yeah." Steve raised his hands to his face and briefly massaged his temples. "But I've only got the location for to-night. If I can't get this scene shot tonight it's going to throw off our entire production schedule. I'd direct it myself but I'm on a plane at five."

"That's terrible!" It was too perfect, Sasha thought. It was fantastic. The goddess had heard her. "Where are you going?"

"I'm judging a talent search at a leather bar in Atlanta tomorrow night, and I've got business there the next morning. Local producers."

Günter handed Steve a piece of paper and said, "Here's Peter's number." Steve turned toward his office.

"Steve," Sasha said. "I'm available."

"What for?"

"To direct."

Steve smiled. "You?"

"Yes, moi. You know I've directed before. What's more, I have the ability to make sure a certain bottom you're very interested is available."

"Billy Knight? The one from your amateur movie?"

"It wasn't entirely *amateur*, Steve. The problem was budget."

"How do you know he's available?"

"For me, he'll be available. I'm practically his mother."

"Look, you get him for me, and I'll owe you a favor. Now I'm calling Peter." Steve walked into his office.

"No, Steve." Sasha stepped through the door behind him. He was already reaching for the phone. "You don't get Billy Knight unless Sasha directs. We come together. So to speak."

His hand stopped and he looked at her. He seemed to be considering the idea, then said, "In that case I don't need Billy Knight." He picked up the phone.

Sasha stood watching as he called. She made another tiny prayer to the great drag queen in the sky.

"Hi, Peter!" Steve spoke into the phone. "Yeah, Steve Logan here. How are you? Look, I know we haven't used you in a while but I'm in a bind here. It's short notice, but I need a director for a shoot tonight. Yeah, that's right. I've got a crew and a location and most of my models but I need a director. What do you mean? But Peter, this is for *Muscle Party*, high profile stuff, good for your career. Can't you reschedule that? So what, they'll come another night. You mean there's just no way you're willing to do it? God damn it, Peter. Fuck you!"

Steve slammed down the phone, then looked up, surprised to find Sasha still there.

"What's wrong, Steve?" She was trying hard not to look happy.

"He's got an orgy at his place tonight."

"Oh, that's a shame." Her voice had turned saccharine. She walked over to him and whispered in his ear. "Sasha and Billy are all yours. You just say yes, and all your problems will be solved, like that." She snapped her fingers and stood up straight, then walked out the door.

21
Partners

WHEN MIKE WOKE on Monday morning, Sasha had already left for work. He lay with his hands behind his head and looked around the room, at the intense red walls, the ugly feathered masks, the pink sewing machine against the wall.

Sometimes, when Sasha worked on a new costume in the evenings, the sound of the sewing machine reminded him of his mother. But he'd been sleeping on this fake leather couch for three months now, and he was tired of it.

The sheets slipped away and his skin stuck to the vinyl when he rolled over. He wanted a bed, his own bed. He wanted to walk into his own room and close the door, to be able to bring people home, somebody like Kerry, without Sasha or Dale watching. But he didn't want to leave, had no desire to live alone. He didn't want Cincinnati all over again.

He sat up and went over the weekend in his head. On Friday night Kerry had left Exposé with the lecher he'd been doing private dances for all night. In a way, Mike was happy for Kerry. He must have made a lot of money. But Mike was even happier when Kerry had stopped by before leaving.

"Hey Mike," Kerry had said, reaching out and touching his arm. Mike was standing near the bar with a customer, a teddy bear who was offering to buy Mike a drink. Kerry's hand was warm and big. "I'm really sorry I insulted your friend," he said. "I didn't realize."

Mike paused. "Sure."

Kerry turned toward the teddy bear and said, "Just a sec. Do you mind?" He pulled on Mike's arm, walking a few steps away, so the music of the bar would give their conversation some privacy. Over by the door Kerry's lecher stood waiting. Mike's teddy bear watched from the bar.

"Let me take you out to lunch," Kerry said. "To apologize."

"I guess that'd be cool."

"You guess?"

Mike decided to speak the truth but soften it with a flirtatious smile. "Kerry, I'm not so sure how nice you are."

Kerry took his hand off Mike's arm and gave a surprised laugh, then nodded.

"Don't ever say anything mean about Sasha," Mike said.

"Okay. I won't"

"Promise?"

"Promise. What about lunch?"

"Yes."

Kerry looked pleased. "I'm working all day tomorrow, but can you meet me at the Lighthouse Café on Sunday? Say noon?"

"Cool." Mike reached out and, with the back of his hand, lightly hit Kerry's stomach. It was tight like a drum. Then he nodded and walked back to the teddy bear, still waiting at the bar.

Now Mike stretched out on the couch and rubbed his chest. There was a pleasant soreness in his muscles from the workout he did with Kerry yesterday. Lunch at the Lighthouse had been fantastic. The conversation was easy. They talked about customers, the ones they liked, the ones they didn't. They giggled like kids. They talked about where they grew up. Mike didn't talk about his dad, didn't tell Kerry what happened the night he left home. He didn't talk about that with anyone.

They both said they didn't want to work at Exposé forever. Kerry wanted to save his money so he could quit and travel around Europe. Mike, of course, wanted to become a major porn star. The only uncomfortable moment was when Kerry tried to talk him out of doing any more porn. He just looked at Kerry and said, "Back off." Kerry did.

They recovered with a conversation about working out, and after lunch Kerry invited Mike to join him at his gym. Kerry worked out at Built, not too far from the Lighthouse, and they stopped by Kerry's apartment so Mike could borrow some workout shorts. They almost didn't make it back outside, but Kerry insisted, saying that he really wanted to work out, that he hadn't been to the gym in four days, and that if Mike was a good workout partner he'd bring him back home afterward and fuck him.

Mike had never worked out in a gym before, and Kerry showed him the different equipment and how to use it. They took turns spotting each other during bench presses, counting out each other's repetitions and saying "Come on, one more."

It was different than Mike's workouts at home. It was harder. Kerry pushed him more, taught him things like the correct posture for squats and how to do reverse flys. Mike enjoyed moving his body in new ways. It felt like a kind of meditation to put all of himself into doing the same movement eight times with an especially heavy weight, then repeat for two more sets the way Kerry did.

After their last set Kerry leaned in close with a mischievous smile and said, "You were definitely a good partner. You deserve to be fucked."

Mike began laughing and getting hard all at the same time. Nobody had ever made him do both those things at once.

When they got back to Kerry's apartment, Kerry kept looking him in the eyes and telling him how beautiful he was. "You're lovely," he said, over and over, using Simon's word, the English guy they'd first had sex with. He did his best imitation of a British accent. "You are so *lovely*."

Mike pushed away his fears of being HIV positive, as he did every time he had sex now. He was always safe. He wasn't going to infect anyone. He got down on his knees and watched the intense green of Kerry's ankh move back and forth as he sucked his dick. Later, when Kerry finally fucked him, it was even more tender than the first time – so much so that if Mike let go entirely he would have begun crying, not out of pain or sadness, but out of a kind of weightless joy.

He couldn't believe it when he woke up, still in Kerry's arms, and it was already seven pm. He kissed him affectionately and showered and rushed out, feeling a little guilty that he'd left Dale home alone all day – especially after Dale had given him presents the day before, and taken such good care of him when he was sick. Yet in spite of this guilt, or perhaps because of it, he decided not to tell Dale where he'd been.

The phone rang, jolting him away from his weekend thoughts and back to Dale's living room. He let it ring at first, but on the third ring he got up off the couch to answer it.

"This is Billy Knight's agent calling for Billy and have I got a job for him!" It was Sasha. You could tell it wasn't Dale by the way she talked. Sasha spoke in a higher pitch, and she was always excited and loud. Dale was quieter, lower, softer. Right now Sasha sounded even more excited than usual.

"What's up?" Mike asked.

"You're not going to believe this. Steve here at Cougar is filming on location tonight and his director and one of his models are sick, the poor things. But get this. Steve has come to me, Sasha Zahore, and asked me to direct the scene. A scene for Cougar! Big budget! Studio backing!"

"Sasha, that's great!" Mike knew how much this meant to her, and he was genuinely happy, although a little surprised.

"But listen, Billy," she continued. Her voice was frantic and trilling, like wedding bells. "They were looking at other models. They need a bottom. I decided to take a risk, and I told Steve that I would *not* direct unless they hired *you*."

"Oh, Sasha." Mike sat down on the floor by the phone. "You didn't."

"I did. I laid down the law. We're partners! He was considering some other models, but I simply refused. And Billy, Steve Logan wants me to direct so badly that he agreed to use you."

"He wants you so badly?"

"Let's just say he's finally come around. The point is, I've got you a scene with Cougar!"

"Seriously?"

"Baby, would I lie to you?"

"No, you wouldn't. Wow. A Cougar film!" Mike stood up again. He turned to the left, then the right. He didn't know what to do.

"Well, one scene. But it's a start. Short notice, I know. Listen, you call that Pascal at Exposé and you tell him you can't come in tonight. Meet me at Built gym at eleven. We're filming after hours. Come rested because we'll be working all night. I've got so much to do before then, I'm working straight through."

"I'll be there. Sasha, thank you so much."

"My pleasure, baby. You and I are going places together."

As Mike hung up the phone, it seemed like doorways were opening up for him everywhere, and he was dizzy with possibility.

22
Cliff Hardman

ALTHOUGH THE MOMENT when Steve asked Sasha to direct a scene for Cougar had been brief, it felt enormous to Sasha. She had been gazing absentmindedly at a list of video shops she was supposed to call that day when out of the blue there was Steve, standing in front of her, looking feeble and defeated – like the king of a conquered country, she thought. She almost said so, but knowing the stakes were high she managed, albeit only barely, to hold her tongue.

"Sasha," he said, "So long as you can get Billy Knight, the scene is yours."

It was that simple. After all that time, just one sentence. She refused to show him her happiness. He'd made her work too hard for this moment. It was unfair, the lengths she'd had to go to, the years she'd put in, just to get him to give her this. So she maintained her composure, kept her face pleasant yet firm. Then slowly, with a kind of mock military seriousness, she said, "You will not be disappointed, Mr. Logan," as though she'd just been given a top-secret assignment to save the world. Immediately she began asking about the logistics, the schedule, the crew, equipment, and supplies.

Steve sat down with her at her desk. It was the first time he'd ever deigned to do so. He explained what he wanted, simply and clearly – enough footage for a final cut of between fifteen and twenty minutes, plus soft core stills for the box cover and any magazine spreads. The crew was to consist of Sasha, a cameraman, a sound technician, a production assistant, and a makeup artist. The two models, of course, would be Max Pole and Billy Knight. Steve would have a contract drawn up for Billy to sign that night.

"I'm relying on you to keep things in line and keep production tight," he said. "I've got a lot going on this. I'm paying for the entire crew, plus two models, not to mention the six hundred bucks for the location fee. This scene must be finished tonight, ready for editing."

Sasha lifted her right hand, her fingers decorated with fake red nails and a large, synthetic emerald ring. "Scouts honor," she said.

Steve shook his head. "I hope so."

"Doll, with Billy Knight in front of the camera and me behind it, you can't go wrong. Is there a script?"

"No need. Just give me hot sex in the weight room, on a weight bench, and we're good to go. That's what I want. Oh, and one more thing. You need a good name. For title credits we're listing you as Cliff Hardman."

Sasha could barely contain her anger. She glared at Steve. He got up and took a few steps away. It was unclear whether he was leaving or seeking the protection of distance. She stood up at her desk and spoke through a clenched jaw.

"My name is Sasha." Her voice was a low, seething growl. "Sasha Zahore. And so help me, goddess. *Nobody's* calling me Cliff Hardman."

"Then choose another name. Something strong and manly."

She realized then that she could acquiesce. She could decide to surrender this particular battle in order to win the larger war. What did her name matter, really? She could just let it go. She could shut her mouth and sit back down. But Sasha Zahore had never excelled at compromise. It was one thing to hold her tongue in order to avoid insulting him. It was quite another to agree to hiding her name, as though it were something to be ashamed of. She was *Sasha*, and years ago she had come to Los Angeles to live out loud. She would not go back into hiding. Steve was pushing too far.

She said nothing. She simply reached under her desk and pulled out her green vinyl handbag. From her desk drawer she grabbed her emergency lipstick and eyeliner, and her spare jar of foundation. She snatched up her address book and business card file. She threw open a filing cabinet and pulled out two pairs of high-heeled shoes. Then she hurled everything into her bag in a hot, steaming rage.

Steve stared, the way someone would watch a tornado approaching, a mixture of wonder and terror on his face.

When Sasha swung the bag onto her shoulder and walked toward him, he took a large step backwards. She paused, looked him directly in the eye. "Steve Logan, you can take your *Muscle Party* and shove it up your ass."

She stepped past him and walked out into the hallway, past Studio B and Studio C, and then out into the mid-morning April sun. The sky was bright blue. She held her car keys in her hand. The door to Cougar's offices swung shut behind her, and she did not look back.

She got to her car and unlocked it, threw everything into the back seat, climbed in front and sat behind the wheel. Then she waited. In the rearview mirror she could see the front door to Cougar Studios. Any minute now, Steve would come rushing out, realizing that he'd made a terrible mistake. Not only was she a great director, but she was his best salesperson. He needed her.

The door didn't open. She slid the key into the ignition. If he didn't come out at the count of ten, she'd start the car.

One. Two. Three. Surely he would chase her. *Four. Five. Six. Seven.* Just how dumb was he, anyway? *Eight. Nine.* Christ. *Ten.*

She did not start the car. She looked back at the door. What was he doing? Was he telling Günter to bring him another phone number? Was he calling everyone and cancelling the entire shoot? He was in there with an entire porn empire at his fingertips, and here she was sitting out here with nothing but her principles.

Would it really be so bad to be called Cliff? Yes, of course it would. But just once? Just one teeny, tiny time? After all, once Steve finally realized how amazing she was as a director, surely he would begin *begging* her to direct, under any name she wanted. She could call herself Dick Cheese and he'd agree. Wouldn't he?

Then, Sasha remembered a terrible thing. If she didn't get a movie for Billy soon, he might leave her. He might get a movie with somebody else.

Steve was yelling at Günter when she walked back into his office. He stopped yelling and looked at her, confused.

"Steve," she said. "You win. You can list me in the credits just this once as 'Cliff Hardman.' But I want you to know that in my heart of hearts I am still, and will always be, Sasha Zahore."

Steve smiled. It wasn't a friendly smile. It was overbearing and triumphant. "Cliff, buddy," he said. "Welcome to Cougar." He put out his hand.

PART THREE

WEIGHTS

23
Muscle Party

SASHA WAS DETERMINED to make the best *Muscle Party* porn scene ever, damn it. She hurried out of Steve's office and back to her desk. She had to call home immediately and secure Billy for the shoot that night. It was important to be positive, to be grateful. Even if she did have to give up her name, even if she did have to be called Cliff, at least she had a movie.

Or rather, she had just one small scene. But it was something.

When Billy answered the phone and she started talking, it seemed she was helpless to stop the truth from coming out upside-down. She just couldn't tell Billy that it was him Steve really wanted, not her. If Billy thought that *she* was riding on *his* coattails, rather than the other way around, he would surely leave. Had she done a bad thing, to lie in order to keep him?

After she hung up the phone, she sat looking at her hands. Now that forty was just around the corner, it seemed time was catching up with her, starting with the backs of her hands. The skin was becoming thinner and crisscrossed with tiny lines, like crumpled paper somebody had tried to make smooth.

She opened her handbag and pulled everything back out – makeup, address book, business card file, shoes, everything. She was staying at Cougar. She took out her compact and looked at her face, at the relatively new and subtly deepening lines under the outside edges of her eyes. There was so little time. No, she could not take the risk of Billy leaving her. She had done the right thing. With him she was stronger.

By the time Steve was finally ready to leave for the airport just a few hours later, Sasha had smoothed things over with him as best she could. He gave her the contract and she signed it. She didn't tell him that she'd already typed up a draft script. It wasn't much, just a quick set up and some blocking for the sex. There was only one scripted line of dialogue, but it was absolutely essential to the plot. She said goodbye to Steve, told him not to worry, and he walked out the door. She felt like she'd been handed the keys to the kingdom.

She went directly to the art department. Her production assistant was named Toshi. He was little and cute. She asked him to go through the studio supply room to pull together the condoms, lube, enemas, and paper towels they'd need for the shoot, plus a spray bottle filled with water to simulate sweat. She also asked him to run out for a supply of snacks – cola, fruit juice, muffins, bananas and, because she knew Billy liked them, plenty of apples. It was fantastic to have a budget for food. There was no telling how late they'd be filming, and a hungry crew was a distracted crew.

"And Toshi, doll," Sasha said. "Bring me some takeaway for dinner. Anything. Being a big shot director makes a girl hungry."

The total budget for Sasha's scene was almost four thousand dollars, which was a lot considering she'd made an entire film out of *Banging Billy* for half that. It felt like progress.

She went back to her desk and started making calls. An hour later she had ten people lined up to be extras, a mixture of men and women. She didn't want two guys just fucking randomly on a weight bench in an empty gym, as Steve had requested. Good sex was psychological. It needed to be framed by a concrete situation, one where the prospect of sex was a genuine possibility, however remote. Desire, she believed, was a kind of hope.

When Toshi brought her a burger and fries for dinner, she was in the midst of scribbling notes on the mood she wanted, and possible camera angles. She wanted to be clear with the cameraman. Too many extreme close-ups, she felt, ruined a film. Of course you had to have insertion shots for confirmation that penetration was happening, and dropping them in here and there could be hot, but she preferred seeing everything all at once – beautiful, long shots of the top behind the bottom, holding his hips, or the bottom straddling the top, bouncing up and down. She wanted to capture the human interaction, the facial expressions while they were fucking. You could put two machines together and show their parts intertwining, but outside the context of human feeling it was nothing, just mechanics.

When she finally set her pen down, she felt sleepy. She walked into Studio C, hoping to find it empty for a quick power nap, but it was being converted into a circus tent for Steve's big-budget circus flick. Late shift workers were building platforms and hanging red and yellow striped fabric off the back wall. It was noisy with hammers and saws. She walked out and went into studio B, which was empty and quiet, almost peaceful. It still had the barn set from *Country Cousins* so she lay down in the hay Steve had shipped in from Napa Valley. She looked up at the studio lights, thought about the men who had had sex right where she was laying now. She'd watched some of the filming, and it was hot. If

Sasha had the body, she would be a porn star. She would love to be that free, that unafraid of lying naked under bright lights, completely exposed. Her powder-blue eyelids grew heavy, and she slept.

When she woke up it was already late and her crew was looking for her. She straightened out her dress and pulled the hay out of her wig. Then she gathered everyone in the hall and gave an impromptu pep talk about how they were going to make the hottest scene ever. It was important to inspire, to give people a common goal and drive them toward excellence. They loaded the cameras and sound equipment into the Cougar van and headed toward Built.

Billy was there, out front already wearing gym gear when the van pulled up. She saw him from the back seat. He was so damn sexy. There were still occasions when just laying eyes on him could cause her heart to do yet another tiny flip. She opened up her compact and checked her makeup in the dark as best she could. After climbing awkwardly out of the van in her blue platform shoes, she stood tall and smiled, "Hello Billy!" She was so happy to see him there, leaning against a wall, ready to be in another one of her films.

Nearby there was her small group of extras. Billy stood separate from them. She imagined, for just a moment, that they were paparazzi, waiting for her as she walked into a fantastic film premiere. She smiled and waved. "Hello boys and girls!" The women in the group were wearing leotards, shiny spandex, legwarmers, and elastic headbands. The men were wearing biker shorts, tight muscle shirts, and tracksuits. Sasha nodded at the group in approval, then walked over to Billy and gave him a light kiss on the cheek.

"Are you ready?" she asked, proud to be the one who knew him, to be the only one here to have earned the right to walk up to him and give him a kiss.

"Ready and willing," Billy said. He didn't seem as nervous as he'd been before the *Banging Billy* shoots. "Where's my scene mate?"

Sasha looked around. "He's not here yet, but you'll like him. Lots of muscle, and tall." She reached out and touched Billy's arm. "When he gets here, give him your quiet charm. Make him want you. I know you can do it."

The crew was already taking the equipment inside, and Sasha and Billy followed them into the lobby. She handed Billy his contract and a pen, telling him not to bother with the contact details, just give a signature. Billy sat on a sofa nearby to sign.

"Toshi!" Sasha yelled. "Find a room for the extras to wait in." Then, partly talking to herself and partly asking anybody who would answer, she said, "Now, which way to the weight bench thingies?"

Nobody answered, and as she started turning toward a hallway to her right Billy got up off the sofa. She felt his hand on her arm.

"That's the aerobics room," he said. "The weights are over that way. Up those stairs."

She looked at him and paused. "How do you know?"

"Oh. A friend of mine brought me here, once."

"Really? When? I didn't know that."

He shrugged. "You don't know everywhere I go."

She felt a tiny stab, and she recoiled. It must have been obvious, because Billy's face turned immediately apologetic.

"It was just yesterday," he said.

"With who?"

"With my friend..." He paused, and then blurted out a word. "Joe."

"*Joe*? His name is *Joe*?"

Billy looked at her, paused again, shook his head. "No. I'm sorry. His name is Kerry."

"Kerry? Why did you say *Joe*?"

"It's Kerry. He's just a guy I work with. I'll show you the weights. I signed the contract. It's over there." He gestured toward the sofa.

She didn't like that he brought up the contract now. This had nothing to do with the contract. "So you were here *yesterday* with some *stripper*? That's where you were? Why didn't you tell me? You just said you were hanging out."

"Yeah. Hanging out. Working out. Whatever. It's no big deal, Dale."

She snapped. "That's *Sasha* when I'm in drag, boy."

"Sorry." He turned and walked up the stairs.

She grabbed his contract and threw it into her handbag, then followed him. She tried to tell herself that working out with a friend meant nothing. She simply wasn't used to the idea of Billy having friends. Yet by the time they'd reached the top step, she'd decided there was something more to it than that. There was something secretive that made it troubling.

At the top of the stairs she said, "Which one is he? Have I seen him dance?"

"Maybe. He's tall and blond. He has an ankh tattoo on his hip."

Sasha remembered the ankh, and nodded slowly.

Billy turned and led Sasha into the large weight room. She tried to focus, to concentrate on the work at hand. Hugh, her cameraman, approached her and wanted to discuss spots for shooting. Billy walked away. She began walking around with Hugh, looking at angles and mirrors. It was difficult knowing Billy had been in that very gym yesterday, sweating with some stupid stripper – someone who wasn't a paying customer, someone whose name Billy at first didn't want to share.

She found a good location with weight benches, no mirrors to catch the camera, and lots of step machines, treadmills, and rowing machines perfectly placed in the background.

"This will be good for the lead-up" she told Hugh. "But not the sex."

Hugh looked at her critically. He had a large belly and thinning hair. "Steve told me he wanted sex in the weight room, on a weight bench."

She glared. Hugh was like an old, smelly dog, stupidly loyal to its owner. "I'm the director here. Set up the lighting, please." She waved her hands dismissively toward the benches. Hugh shook his head but got to work.

Sasha called out for the sound guy to get moving. Then she found Toshi and told him to set up a table downstairs in the aerobics room with the food.

When Max showed up with his dim-witted smile, she walked over to greet him. "Doll, I'm so sorry that your friends aren't well."

"Yeah. It's a real downer," he said, his smile fading for a just moment. "They're really sick." Max was wearing a tight green T-shirt with a large white '69' on the chest. Sasha had to admit that the T-shirt showed of his gym-toned pecs very nicely. Suddenly he looked at her directly in the eyes, with an unmistakable aggression, and he said, "Blane should be directing this."

She paused. Did Max suspect something? "Well, daddy's not here," she said. "And I am. And the show must go on." She put a hand on his chest as though to soothe him, then saw Billy at the other end of the room playing with the weights.

Max saw him too. "Is that the bottom?"

"Yes, it is. You don't know how lucky you are today, Max. There are a lot of men who pay good money for that ass."

Max nodded slowly and Sasha yelled out, "Billy, come here. I want to introduce you."

As Billy walked over she pushed everything away, all her thoughts about Billy's possible secrets, all her own fears, and she began a kind of performance. She became playful and silly, smiling and speaking in a cheerfully naive voice, as though reading a children's bedtime story. "Billy," she said, gesturing to Max. "This is the big, bad top who's going to pounce on you and fuck your sweet little ass. Max, this is the eager bottom who's going to give it up to you like sugar on a Texas hotplate. Now, you two just get acquainted."

She immediately turned to walk away, wanting to leave them alone, and she saw Billy offer Max his most charming smile. This did not upset her. This was work. It was why they were here. Although the cameras hadn't yet started rolling, she knew this moment was crucial. If the models weren't into each other, if they weren't put entirely at ease, all the careful lighting and cutaways and insertion shots and post-production editing would add up to nothing. Some directors got so caught up in elaborate plotlines, fancy camera angles, and moody effects that they forgot the most important fact: the heart of any good porn film was not just good sex, but human connection. And you didn't get the good sex without the connection. She always gave the models time together before a shoot, always tried to make them comfortable with a joke and a smile.

She was looking around for a second location in the gym when she saw Günter standing on the other side of the room. He was wearing yet another mesh tank top. This one was red. He had no reason to be there. It looked like he was flirting with the sound guy. She stomped by various weight machines to get to them. "Günter, what are you doing?"

"Steve asked me to keep an eye on things," he answered. His melon-shaped biceps bulged. His voice sounded decidedly German today.

"So, you're like his little Nazi spy, is that right?"

He smiled, showed his bright white teeth. "I suppose so."

"Listen. Number one: stop distracting my crew. Number two: if you get in my way at all, or make one tiny peep while filming, you're out of here. I don't care what Steve says. And number three: people who watch, work. Go downstairs and help Toshi with the food." Sasha turned to the sound guy. "Doll, what's your name again?"

"John."

"John, darling. Stop drooling and get back to work."

Günter paraded off. John turned away only when Günter was out of sight. Sasha looked around for Terrence, her makeup artist. "Terrence! Let's start makeup. Billy, Max, over here." They'd been sitting on the floor in the corner, talking and laughing. They were leaning in close to each other. It was a good sign.

She led the three of them into the men's locker room. This was her first time to have a real makeup artist, and it felt fantastic. It had always been up to her to pull out some of her foundation and cover any blemishes on her models. She told

Billy and Max to undress. "Terrence, I want their balls shaved. And Billy's asshole too."

Billy began taking off his shirt, and Sasha watched. Even under the glaring fluorescent light of the locker room, his skin was flawless. "Billy, you are damn beautiful," she said, watching him as he took off his jeans. "Now grab one of those enemas and make sure your butt's clean while Terrence starts on Max."

"Yes, ma'am," Billy said, saluting and giving her a teasing smile.

As he walked naked toward the toilets he passed in front of her, and she reached out and slapped him playfully on the ass. He jumped and shouted, then poked her in the stomach with the enema box before running away. She smiled. Maybe, just maybe, it was going to be okay.

Max hadn't even started undressing. He was looking at his face in a nearby mirror.

"Max," she said. "On the double. Get your clothes off."

He gave her a look that seemed almost shy, somewhat hesitant, and then began moving slowly, slipping off his gym shoes, gradually pushing down his long basketball shorts.

When she saw the bare skin of his legs, she screamed. "Ah! What's that?!" There, on Max's tanned and muscled thigh, was an enormous dark purple bruise.

"Rough trick yesterday," he said.

"Be careful with those tricks, doll. And no rough stuff before filming, even if you like it, and even if they pay extra. Bruises and cameras don't mix." She sighed and moved closer to inspect the damage. "What were you doing working yesterday anyway? You should always take a day or two off sex before shooting."

"Huh? Why would I not have sex?"

"You're joking, right?" The look on his face showed that he was not. She rolled her eyes in exasperation and looked up at the ceiling, as though talking directly to the goddess. "Do I honestly have to work with this?" Turning back to Max, she explained. "Doll, taking time off gives you more cum. A better money shot. One to two days off is best. But you should never take more than two, because then you get too excited and chances are you'll pop too soon."

"Don't worry." Max smiled. "I eat lots of egg whites. And I took zinc before I got here. I'll come buckets."

"Oh, doll." She shook her head. Egg whites and zinc had nothing to do with it, even though so many silly models swore by them. "Listen, if you ever do another movie for me, no sex for two days before filming. Got it?"

"Blane doesn't make us do that."

"Do I look anything even remotely like your precious *Blane*?"

Max sneered. "No. You're just a stand in. You're not even supposed to be here."

"Jesus fucking Christ. Would somebody give me a sign that says, 'I'm the director?!' Is there not a single person here that believes a fat bitch can direct?!" She stared down at Max. He was naked. Her pink tracksuit covered her from head to toe. "Listen to me very carefully, Max Pole." She spoke in a low, hushed voice. "If you refuse to cooperate with me tonight, not only will I inform *Steve* of that fact, but I myself, *Sasha Zahore*, will personally smear shit across your name from here to New York City. Don't mess with me. Got it?"

He looked away.

"Got it?" she repeated.

He nodded. "Got it."

She looked him up and down. His body was much more attractive than his face, and his dick was huge, which made up for his dopey looks entirely. She pointed to his bruise. "Terrence, you know what to do. After you're done shaving those balls, hide that nasty thing. It ruins the view."

Terrence took out shaving foam and a razor and led Max toward the sinks while Sasha wandered around the locker room. She still needed one more location, a private place. There would be no sex in the weight room. It was going to be better, more real. She looked in the showers, but they were too open, too public. The toilet stalls were too cramped; it would be difficult to film in there.

She'd almost given up on the locker room altogether when she found a large metal door. It led to a kind of boiler room with a hot water tank and a furnace. Pipes and metal ducts ran across the ceiling. There was an old stationary bike missing its pedals in the corner, and a stack of thick, blue floor mats up against one wall. In the middle of the room there was an open space, big enough for two people and a cameraman. To one side there was a weight bench with a cut across its vinyl surface.

"Eureka!" Sasha yelled. She would give Steve sex on a weight bench, only better.

After some time, the lighting and sound were ready. Billy and Max were clipped and made up. Billy's ass was clean as a whistle, and everyone was prepared to start shooting. They began with the publicity stills, which Sasha knew had to come first, so the models weren't too sweaty and tired.

Hugh was doing both the video and the stills. She explained what she wanted from the stills and then supervised it all. First they shot Max, and then Billy, and then the two of them together. Max, fortunately, did as he was told. Together the boys posed in their gym gear, then semi-naked, then naked, standing by the weights and sitting on weight benches with stiffies.

Hugh called out directions. "Eyes here. Elbows in. Breathe out. Abs are tight. Flex your dick."

From time to time, Sasha interrupted. As Billy was sitting on the weight bench with his back to Hugh, she called out, "Billy, squeeze your shoulder blades together! Arch your back. Now point your asshole directly at the camera. Perfect!"

When they were finished with the stills, she had Billy and Max put their gym gear back on. She explained that Max's character was aggressive and assertive while Billy's was shy and inexperienced. Then she instructed Toshi to bring up the extras so she could place them around the gym, on step machines and treadmills. She told the extras that they should never ever look at the camera. They were to stay in the background, working out, so it would feel like a real gym, a real situation. Two of the extras stood off to the side, ready to walk past in the background when she pointed. It felt good being the center of it all, giving directions. People were starting to listen to her.

"Max," she said. "I want you to start out sitting here on this weight bench, doing some workout thing, something with your legs spread wide."

"I could do seated shoulder presses," he said. Then he showed her what they were, sitting on the end of the bench and lifting his arms over his head with two black dumbbells. He spread his legs.

"Fantastic, doll. Thank you." She was relieved to find that he was actually being helpful.

She walked through the blocking with the boys. Then Hugh picked up the video camera, and John held the boom.

Sasha sat in front of a monitor nearby and yelled, "Action!" The extras began rowing and stepping. Billy walked up to a seated curl machine, which was positioned directly facing Max. He glanced at Max. They shot Max throwing back an interested glance, and then filmed Billy doing curls as he stared at Max's open legs.

"When's the sex?" Hugh asked from behind the camera.

"You just be patient," Sasha said. "This is build-up."

Next she asked Billy to do something to show off his ass, and Max suggested stiff-legged deadlifts, which he showed Billy how to do. Billy stood straight while holding a barbell in front of him, then bent forward, keeping his back arched and tight. "Oh, Billy," Sasha said, and turned toward the room. "Everyone, just look at that bubble butt! The boy is truly blessed!" The people standing around nodded in unison.

Terrence began spraying Max and Billy with a water bottle so that they looked naturally sweaty. They filmed Max doing biceps curls as he watched Billy's deadlifts. Then Sasha pulled Max aside and gave him the one line of dialogue that she'd included in her script. She told him to relax and to avoid speaking stiffly. It had to seem casual. "Pretend you're really trying to pick him up," she said. "I'm sure you've had practice at that."

Max smiled.

After Sasha yelled "Action!" again, he walked over to Billy – the cameras rolling, John holding the boom – and he delivered his line.

"Hey buddy, could you give me a spot?"

It was horrible. His voice was awkward. He sounded like an idiot, insecure and scared.

"Cut!" Sasha marched over to him. "What was that?!"

Max looked at her apprehensively, but said nothing.

"I'll tell you what it was!" she screamed. "It was wooden and horrible. I want the wood in your dick, boy, not your voice." Suddenly she realized what she was dong. Max was drawing back. He wasn't at ease. She calmed her voice, placed her hands on his arms, and gave him a loose, quick massage. "Oh, you just relax, doll. I'm sorry. You've been helping out. You're great. Really, this is easy. He's a hot guy in the gym and you want him. That's all. Nothing new." She turned over her shoulder. "Billy, do you think Max is hot?"

Billy nodded. "Fuck yeah. Can't wait to get that big dick in my ass."

Sasha smiled warmly. She knew Billy would say just the right thing. He could be such a thoughtful boy.

"See, Max?" she said. "He wants you. Hell, I want you. Everybody here wants you. You're hot. You've got a beautiful body and a cock that deserves to be worshiped. Just think of how big your dick is when you say this line. Confidence, doll. Confidence. Now, let's try again." She gave him a tender pat on the cheek. "Okay?"

It took three more takes, but finally the line came out smoothly and believably. Sasha ran up to Max and pushed her cheek against his, holding his head with one hand. "That was wonderful," she said.

"Really? You think so? Honest?

"Listen, doll. You will always know where you stand with me. Absolutely. It was perfect."

He beamed. "Thanks, Sasha. Thanks a lot."

She had wooed him. He was once again a little puppy dog.

The last shots they did in the weight room were of Billy and Max spotting each other as they did bench presses. There was a lingering shot of Billy lying down on the bench, ready to do a set of bench presses, and Max standing behind the barbell, his crotch close to Billy's head. Sasha screamed, "Stare, Billy! Stare!" She couldn't help it. They'd have to edit her voice out in postproduction. Billy took a long look up at the bulge in Max's shorts. "Max, grab your beautiful crotch!" she yelled, and Max did. "Now look at Billy and gesture toward the locker room," and Max did. Finally he led Billy off camera, as directed.

Next they quickly filmed the scene where Max and Billy looked for a place to have sex in the locker room. Sasha had one of the extras changing as they walked by. Max and Billy found the large metal door that led to the boiler room, slipped inside, and shut the door tightly behind them.

"Cut!" Sasha yelled. "Excellent!" She went out and yelled to the extras. "Now, all you good people, you can go home. You're beautiful and I love you all! Thank you! Thank you! Billy and Max, take a break while we set up for the next scene. There's food in the aerobics room. Don't eat too much or your tummies will bloat. You two are fantastic on camera! Fantastic!" There was clearly an energy developing between them, a mounting desire, as well as a growing confidence in Max, which she needed for the scene to work. She was relieved. It was going well.

The boiler room was hot, dark, and far from spacious. It took the better part of an hour to figure out how to set up the lighting without having the lighting stands show up on film. Sasha's video monitor had to be set up just outside the boiler room, but that was okay because she was still within yelling distance. Terrence started doing touch-ups on Max and Billy, and especially on Max's bruise since the makeup had rubbed off under his shorts.

When Sasha saw Günter disappear into the toilets, she suspected he was in search of something stronger than caffeine and she followed him. Through a stall door, she heard the distinctive sounds of someone preparing lines on the toilet seat and snorting coke. "Get ouuuuut!" She began screaming, pounding on the stall like a mad woman. "Ouuuut!"

Günter opened the door with a shocked look on his face, wiping his nose and sniffing.

"Nobody does coke on my shoot!" she yelled. "Nobody! I don't care if the Queen of Sheba sent you! We're here to work, bitch, not play! You leave!"

"But..." Günter said.

She cut him off, shrieking and shaking her head. Her earrings rattled and her eyes bulged as she pointed toward the door. "Ouuuut!"

Günter stood frozen for a moment, dazed and clearly frightened by what was in front of him. It wasn't until Sasha took a step toward him and yelled "Now!" that he finally turned and walked toward the door. He didn't come back.

Sasha walked out into the locker room, where the crew was standing, and she clapped her hands twice to get their attention. They were already watching. "Listen up! If I catch anybody else doing anything stronger than coffee before we're done with this shoot, you can join that little tramp out in the gutter. Now back to work!"

By then it was nearly 1:00 a.m., and they hadn't even started filming the sex yet. Sasha led Max and Billy back into the boiler room and walked them through the blocking for the scene, telling Max how she wanted him to start by throwing some of the blue mats down onto the floor next to the old weight bench. Then she wanted Max to push Billy onto his knees to begin the oral. Finally she explained that she wanted the anal to start with Max sitting on the weight bench and Billy doing a reverse cowboy.

"What's a reverse cowboy?" Max asked.

She looked at the ceiling again and sighed, then looked back at Max. "You've been in a couple movies for Blane, right?"

"Well, yeah."

"Didn't he teach you anything? How else will you improve your craft? What kind of director is he, anyway? Billy, tell him what a reverse cowboy is."

Billy smiled flirtatiously at Max and said, "It's where I ride your dick with my back to you."

"Oh," Max said, smiling like an idiot. "Cool."

Sasha continued. "Your sex will focus on this weight bench and on the floor mats. Once we have the reverse cowboy shots, we'll talk about the next positions. And Billy, what's the golden rule of porn?"

Billy smiled again. "Always look like you're into it, like you're having fun."

"I don't think I'll be pretending," Max said, staring at Billy.

Sasha nodded. "Oh, you're such good boys. Now, everyone in your places! Action!"

As Max and Billy began having sex in the boiler room, Sasha sat outside watching her monitor, shouting directions and encouragement. When Billy was giving Max his blow job, she yelled, "Good length, Billy! Remember good length! Move up and down on that dick! Fantastic! Max, give me some noise. Moan! Tell him to suck that dick!" When Max began reciprocating with a blow job for Billy, it quickly became clear he wasn't very good at giving oral, so Sasha cut the take short and went straight to the anal. Toshi brought out the box of condoms. Max slipped one on and sat down on the weight bench, leaning back. Billy held Max's dick and slid his ass down onto it. He moaned. He started sliding up and down, slowly at first, then faster.

Although she couldn't say why, knowing that yesterday Mike had secretly come here to work out with that stripper Kerry bothered her more than watching Billy get fucked by Max in front of her now. In fact, she really liked watching Billy get fucked.

She shouted, "Beautiful! Now, Max, pull his hips down onto you! Fuck that ass! Gorgeous! Arch your back, Billy! Show off that beautiful rear end."

Sitting back didn't stop Max from thrusting hard, rocking his body into Billy. He clearly was better at fucking than sucking. Sasha was relieved. He was taking control of Billy's hips now without being told, and he was getting verbal, saying to Billy "Oh yeah, you like that dick?" Billy moaned, "Yeesss!" Sasha was careful not to yell over the top of them, so that their impromptu dialogue could be saved in the editing room. A good fuck was almost always verbal. Sasha had always believed that the ears were one of the most important sex organs, right after the eyes.

As she watched, Billy was transforming, becoming entirely lost in the sex. It was amazing the way he stayed hard while being fucked, without even touching his dick, which a lot of bottoms couldn't do. How she hated the sight of a floppy cock on a moaning bottom.

She shouted out directions to Hugh. "Move in and give me a quick insertion shot from that angle! Perfect! Now a full body shot from the other side!"

Everyone else had fallen silent and still, as though a kind of magic snowfall had begun to cover everything. Terrence and Toshi stood several feet behind her, peering over her shoulder at the monitor. John was diligently holding the boom through the doorway.

When the reverse cowboy shots were done, Sasha called the boys out of the boiler room and explained what she wanted next. The lights and the sex were making it hot in there and the sweat looked fabulous on Max and Billy, standing naked on either side of her. Max had pulled off his condom. They both listened to her directions carefully, pulling on their dicks absentmindedly while she talked, just to stay hard.

She was careful to be very specific about the next shots. Models performed better when they knew what to expect. First, she wanted Billy on his back on the weight bench, legs in the air butterfly style as Max fucked him. It was, she explained, her favorite position to see on film. She talked to Max about cheating his torso toward the camera during the side shots, so you could see the penetration. Then she wanted Max to push Billy down onto the mats, onto his stomach, and fuck him in the missionary position, but aggressively and hard. She explained that any good fuck film had anal in at least three positions. She liked four. For the last one, she wanted some intense doggie style, then the cum shots. After that, the only bits remaining would be the final close-ups, which would be edited back in at various spots – shots of their faces as they pretended to come, or of Billy acting like he was sliding down onto Max's dick for the first time in the reverse cowboy, or of Max pretending to be enjoying a blow job which was, in fact, long over. Sasha hoped to be finished and have everyone out of there by 5:00 a.m.

Terrence briefly touched up the makeup, Max slipped on a fresh condom, and they were ready to start filming again, but as soon as Billy lay back on the bench with his legs up in the air, Sasha screamed. "Aaack! Billy! The bottoms of your feet are filthy. Terrence! Get in there and clean him up!"

Billy lay there on the weight bench with his feet in the air as Terrence cleaned off the dirt with wet paper towels, then he wiped off Max's feet for good measure. The floor of the boiler room was dusty and grey, and from then on Terrence stayed on foot-cleaning duty.

When Sasha screamed "Action!" again, she watched in her monitor as Max moved up to Billy, held his ankles in the air, and pushed his dick into Billy's ass. "Beautiful!" she yelled. "Now pull back out, Max! Hugh, lay down on the ground under Billy's ass and get that insertion in extreme close-up."

What came across her monitor then was absolutely incredible. There was no doubt about it, watching Max's huge dick slide into Billy's ass was one of the most beautiful things she had ever seen. This dear little Billy was amazing, so beautiful, so charming, and he could take anything up his ass. He would go far.

Yet as the monitor cast a glow over her features, she still couldn't help herself. She kept thinking about him there yesterday, in that very gym, with that damn stripper – somebody he'd chosen to spend time with instead of being with her.

Then suddenly it hit her. An image came to her mind: Mike Dudley and Stripper Kerry doing an unthinkable thing. The image was not of them fucking. Sasha pictured them sitting together at a nearby café and actually having coffee. It was a horrible thought, horrible. They would be talking and laughing at a table for two, and Mike would be looking up over the rim of his coffee cup, smiling at this Kerry, ridiculously, like somebody smitten. Kerry would be smiling back, looking all handsome. Sasha remembered him clearly from Exposé. She hated to admit it, but Kerry had a fantastic body and a full head of hair. Who could compete with that?

A knot turned in the hollow of her stomach. She could lose him, her Mike, her Billy. She could lose them both. It was utterly terrifying.

In the monitor now, she saw that Hugh had backed up and was shooting Max and Billy from the side again. It was a gorgeous long shot, and it wrenched her heart.

She was afraid, and she was angry. "Now Max, push him onto the floor and fuck him hard!" she yelled. Then she watched closely as Max did just that.

24
Fear of the Body Failing

MIKE WAS THRILLED to make five hundred dollars off the scene, the same as Max. Sasha said she was pleased. When they were finished filming at the gym, Mike went with Sasha to Cougar to drop off equipment and the footage. By the time they got back home it was light.

They slept right through Tuesday morning and into the afternoon. Sasha went to work, saying that she was only going to sit and review the footage with the guy who would do the editing. Steve wouldn't be back until Thursday, so they had to wait to hear what he thought of the footage before the editing began. Still, she said, she wanted to be ready.

Mike sat home that afternoon, wanting to call Kerry and tell him all about the shoot, but he was worried about what Kerry would say. More than anything he wanted *Kerry* to pick up the phone and call *him*, to ask how it went. He decided to wait. He didn't want to seem desperate.

Standing in the kitchen and pouring himself a cup of coffee, it felt like something was wrong. He should be happy. He'd just done his first scene for a big studio. He'd had a fantastic time with Kerry the other day, something that actually felt like a date, with no money changing hands. It felt like romance. Only then did it dawn on him, lifting up one of Sasha's thick pink coffee mugs to his lips, that he'd never actually had a date before. He'd slept with more men than he could count, picked guys up off the street or in bars, had fuck buddies here and there, and lots of johns of course, but he had never had anything that could even remotely qualify as a genuine date, like normal people had. Yes, he should be very happy. At the age of twenty-three, he'd finally had his first date.

He went into the living room and opened the small side pocket on his duffel bag to find the thing that was bothering him. He pulled out a white piece of paper and read it again. "Your code: Y7349A," it said. "Your appointment: 2:00 p.m. Friday, April 28th, 1989." It was three days away.

Kerry never called that day, and when Mike called Kerry that evening, there was no answer. Maybe he was working. Mike left a message. "Hey there. It's Mike. It'd be great to catch up. Give me a call." He wanted to seem casual. He kept thinking about his appointment. Everything seemed connected to it.

Mike expected to see Kerry at Exposé the following night. When Kerry didn't show up for work, even though he was scheduled, Mike began seriously wondering if it meant something. Pascal complained about Kerry pulling a no-show, about strippers having no sense of responsibility, but Mike wasn't listening. He was wondering if Kerry knew something, if he'd intuitively figured out that Mike had AIDS and was going to die. It was a crazy idea, but he couldn't stop it. Waiting to go up on stage and take off his clothes, he feared his body was already failing him, and he thought of Freddy.

* * *

In Mike's entire life he'd only had one john he'd ever fallen a little bit in love with. Freddy Wilson was a middle-aged black man with small love handles and a successful Cincinnati business – a fish market called "Freddy's Fish." He was an unusual john because he never wanted to actually have sex, or if he did he never said so. Sometimes they'd jack off together watching porn, but Freddy was so afraid of infecting somebody that he wouldn't even let Mike suck his dick. Instead they kissed, on the lips, mouths usually closed, like modest lovers before marriage.

When Mike first met him at the Spares 'n' Strikes, Freddy didn't look sick at all. He was dressed neatly. There was a shiny gold chain around his neck and a small diamond stud in his left ear. He was friendly and gentle, smiled a lot, had a deep, sexy voice. Sometimes he would tease, pretending to be rough, like a street-smart thug. "Yo bitch, I'm gonna beat yo' white ass," he'd say, a lighthearted flicker in his eye. Mike always laughed. He knew from the very beginning that Freddy would never hurt him. They spent time together. Freddy paid well. He was the only regular Mike took back to his own place, that apartment on St. Clair above the bar. It was nice having Freddy there, hearing his low voice fill those tiny rooms, seeing him piss into the toilet naked with the door open like he lived there, like Mike wasn't really alone. That was the first time Mike was able to imagine how it might be, if there was no money.

Within a year Freddy started losing weight and visiting the hospital a lot. They stopped watching porn. Instead Mike would go to his apartment and they would eat sandwiches at the kitchen table and go for a short walk. Every once in a while, if Freddy was feeling good, they'd manage to go out to dinner. Freddy started giving him advice about business, how to deal with customers. "Keep 'em interested and they'll keep coming," he'd say. "People pay more for the good stuff." One day he took hold of Mike's hand and said, "You be careful when I'm gone. Don't let anybody hurt you."

Mike stopped taking Freddy's money, and he started showed up at Freddy's place just because he wanted to. It was like visiting an ailing uncle, someone you really liked a lot. Maybe even loved.

Once, when Mike hadn't talked to Freddy in a couple of weeks, he phoned to see how he was. Mike was afraid there'd be no answer, but then there was Freddy's voice, just as deep as ever, although tired now, and Mike felt an incredible sense of relief. Mike asked if he could stop by, and Freddy said yes.

Freddy lived in a high-rise apartment building downtown. At the front door to the building Mike rang the intercom and Freddy buzzed him in. Mike walked through the sterile white lobby, took the elevator up to the tenth floor, and knocked on Freddy's door. He heard Freddy yell, "Coming!" It took a long time for Freddy to get to the door. Standing in the hallway, Mike called out, "What are you doing Freddy? Hiding the go-go boys?" He couldn't hear if Freddy was laughing, only heard him say again, "Coming!" Mike teased some more, "Slow poke!"

When the door finally opened, the guy standing on the other side was just a shadow of Freddy – a frail, thin man in a robe, leaning on a cane. Usually Mike gave Freddy a kiss on the cheek when he saw him. He didn't now. Freddy looked so sick.

Walking behind Freddy into the apartment, looking at the suddenly slight waist and withered legs, Mike saw that Freddy could barely walk. He'd aged decades since the time they'd first met at the Spares 'n' Strikes. Pill bottles lined the coffee table. The apartment had an odd, sour smell.

Freddy laid down on the couch, put his leg up because he said it hurt, and they talked. It was only then that Freddy admitted he'd just gotten out of the hospital the day before.

He joked about a hot orderly. "A beautiful brother," he said. "Goatee and a shaved head. He was fine." Then out of nowhere, he said, "I can't get my earring in. It's been out for a long time. I think it grew shut. Will you help me?" Freddy's old diamond stud was sitting on the coffee table. He must have noticed Mike hesitate, because he said, "There's gloves over there, if you want," and he pointed to a box of latex gloves on the kitchen counter.

The thought had rushed through Mike's mind that there could be blood when he poked the earring back through the hole in Freddy's ear. He looked at the gloves, not knowing what to do. He didn't want Freddy to think that he was suddenly afraid of him. He sat for a moment, then got up, walked over to the box of gloves and put on a pair, feeling bad the entire time, as though he was admitting to some small failure. It was odd touching Freddy's ear with one hand, and holding the diamond stud with the other, but not actually coming into contact with anything, feeling only the powdery insides of the latex gloves against his skin. When he pushed the earring through, Freddy didn't even wince. There was no blood. Mike took off the gloves and finally touched Freddy's arm, skin to skin. He wanted to kiss him on the cheek, but he couldn't. Three weeks later Freddy was dead.

* * *

In the days before his appointment, Mike couldn't get his mind off Freddy. It was odd the way people could come back to you like that, as though you had never really left them behind, as though everybody you once knew was still inside you somewhere, just under the surface of your skin, even if they were dead. Full of his own fear as he was, Mike's thoughts of Freddy gave him no comfort.

On Thursday afternoon he was working out at home and trying not to think about Freddy – the latex gloves he wished he hadn't put on, the small kiss he wished he'd given him – when the phone rang. As he picked up the receiver he was hoping it was Kerry, but it was Sasha, calling from Cougar. She had good news. "Steve watched the footage, and he loves it!"

Mike tried to sound happy, but it felt like the movie didn't matter. Sasha explained how at first Steve had scolded her for kicking out Günter and then complained because what he'd wanted was sex in a gym, not a boiler room, but in the end he admitted that he really loved what she'd done, that the premise of two guys sneaking off to fuck in secret was hot, that she'd captured some really great sex.

"He's really happy with our work," she said, and went on without pausing for breath. "We have to go out tonight to celebrate, a fancy place. Something special. We'll go to the Ballroom in West LA. The food is beautiful and the waiters are *delicious*. My treat. I'll drive."

"Sure, Sasha," Mike said. "Sounds great." Mike was uncomfortable in nice restaurants; he wasn't used to them. Still, at least it would be better than staying home and worrying about his appointment tomorrow, about Freddy, about Kerry.

Sasha barely heard him and continued rambling on. "I'll come home early and change. The Ballroom is classy. You put on a nice shirt with a collar and those sexy black pants that show off your ass. I'll go in man-drag and wear a suit."

It was strange going out with Dale dressed like that. It seemed almost unnatural, like everybody should be staring, but nobody did. For once, going out together, they almost blended in. Dale's suit was dark grey. His only nod to drama was a purple paisley ascot and a shiny black cane, which he insisted on taking. Mike had tried to talk him out of the cane because it made him think of Freddy, although he didn't say so.

The restaurant had linen tablecloths and a fountain in the middle of the room. Even though it was called The Ballroom, there was no place to dance. They served Argentinian food, there was a white candle on every table, and tango music played quietly. Mike had a hard time pretending that he was happy, and he sensed that he was letting Dale down, like his own worry was quickly becoming a black haze over them both.

Dale was holding open the menu and saying, "You order anything you want," when he looked up at Mike, shut the menu, and said, "What's wrong? Don't you like it here? We'll go somewhere else. Where do you want to go?"

"No, Dale. It's fine." Mike looked around the room, at the carved stone fish on top of the formal fountain, at the handsome waiters with red bowties and cummerbunds, at all the rich people everywhere. "It's great," he said. It's fantastic. I'm okay."

Their waiter interrupted then, standing at the side of their intimate table for two, and Dale said something in Spanish. They ordered, and the waiter left. Then Dale looked back at Mike. "You're obviously not okay. What is it?" He leaned forward, put his hand on Mike's. A woman at the next table looked over. She had large diamond earrings, and she stared at Dale's hand on top of Mike's. Dale turned and glared at her until she looked away.

"It's that guy I mentioned," Mike said. "Kerry. He hasn't called me back, and he wasn't at work last night."

Dale's face fell. "Oh, is that it?" He began staring at the fountain. "Why did you say his name was Joe? At first, you told me his name was Joe. Why?"

Mike didn't have the words to say why he did it, to explain how his first instinct was to try to keep Kerry for himself, and at the same time protect Dale, protect Sasha. He shook his head. "I don't know."

Dale sighed. "So you haven't heard from him at all?"

"No."

"Well, easy come, easy go, right? The boy is obviously a flake. Don't you worry. I'm here. And I'm not going anywhere."

Mike forced a smile. "Thanks Dale."

The waiter came back with a bottle of Chardonnay Dale had ordered, and he made a big show of presenting the bottle to Dale, then opening it and setting the cork down, pouring Dale a little taste. Dale picked up the cork and inspected it, then tasted the wine, gave an assertive nod toward the waiter, and said, "Gracias." Only then did the waiter pour them each a glass. Watching Dale, Mike thought it was an amazing performance. It looked as if Dale ate in places like this every day, as if he had an entire closet full of dark suits at home – instead of brightly colored sequined dresses, feather boas, and pink track suits.

"Now," Dale said, " I want no more talk of that Cory boy."

"Kerry," Mike said.

"Whatever." Dale lifted his glass. "This is a celebration, and I propose a toast. To Sasha Zahore and Billy Knight, the dynamic and inseparable duo, bound for greatness. Long may they live." Dale shook his head as though flipping back hair he didn't have, and looked off into the distance with such melodrama that Mike laughed, happy to see Sasha still poking through the suit.

It wasn't until the end of the evening that Dale obviously became frustrated. By then he'd driven them back to Orlando Avenue and was dropping Mike off in front of their building before finding a parking space. Mike got out without saying anything, turned and started to shut the car door.

"Hellooo," Dale said. It was an annoyed voice, as though he were calling out to Mike across a great distance. Mike turned back, leaned down and looked into the car. Dale shook his head and said, "How about saying, 'Thanks for a great night, Dale?'"

"Oh, I'm sorry." He felt awful. He'd let Dale down again. "My head is somewhere else. Thank you."

"What the hell is it with you tonight? Are you *that* hung up on your stupid stripper? Is that all this is?"

"He's not stupid, and it's not just him." Mike looked down the street. A car pulled up behind Dale.

"What is it then?" Dale said.

"Nothing. I'm sorry. Thank you for tonight." He shut the door and walked up to the building.

Once inside he went straight to the sheets and blankets that he kept on the floor in the corner, and he began making up his bed on the couch. He brushed his teeth and was just starting to undress when Dale came in and sat down on the couch, on top of the sheets and blankets.

"Stop." Dale patted the couch. "Come here and sit down. Talk to me."

Mike had already taken off his shoes and one of his socks and was standing in the middle of the room, his shirt unbuttoned and untucked. Dale seemed so worried, sitting on the couch in his ridiculous purple ascot, so genuinely concerned.

"Sit down," Dale said again.

Mike didn't move. He felt the weight of all the fear and sadness he'd been carrying around with him ever since that guy came inside him in that hotel room in Cincinnati. Standing there, one foot bare and the other still covered in a black sock, he began to cry. He was amazed by the sudden force of his own tears, and tried to push them back, but they were unstoppable.

"Baby, baby," Dale said, and got up off the couch to give him a long, tight hug.

Mike put his head down on Dale's chest and let go. He sobbed. He felt Dale's hand stroking his hair, heard Dale's voice saying "What? What? It's okay. Sshhh." Dale's shoulders moved back and forth, rocking him gently. Mike clung to the sock in his hand as he cried.

Dale pulled Mike toward the couch and said, "Come here, baby. You sit down." Then Dale went to the bathroom, brought out a box of tissues, and set it on the coffee table. He reached into Mike's hand and took the sock. "You talk to me," Dale said. "You tell me what it is."

Before Mike knew what was happening, he was telling Dale everything – about the guy who beat him in Cincinnati, about how much it hurt, about how scared he was when the guy came inside him, how he'd been feeling so afraid for the past three months, about his HIV test, about the appointment to get the results tomorrow. But it didn't stop there. He began going on about Kerry, how Kerry didn't know, how nice it was when Kerry had held him in his bed, how great Kerry was, how Kerry's dream was to travel around Europe, and how much he didn't want to get sick because he secretly hoped to be able to go with him. In the wild blur of it all, he even mentioned Freddy, how scared he was now that he too was going to die. He'd never spoken a word of any of this to anyone, and it came tumbling out.

Dale put his arms around him again. "You're okay. You're going to be okay."

Mike found himself muttering words without thinking about Dale's feelings. "If I'm positive, Kerry won't want me."

"Shhh," Dale said, and Mike heaved.

When his tears and words finally ran dry, Dale leaned back and looked him in they eye. "My darling Michael, I can't believe you've been carrying this around inside you all this time. Why didn't you tell me earlier?"

Dale's hand touched his knee.

"Listen," Dale continued, "I'll go with you tomorrow. I'll call in sick. I'm in Steve's good graces now. I'll go with you to get your results. You don't have to do all this alone, you know."

Mike liked the idea. He sniffed and nodded. "Thank you."

Dale pulled several tissues out of the box and held them out. "Dry your eyes. No matter what happens tomorrow, I'm here."

Mike had for so long felt that he was alone in the universe that it was almost unreal to have Dale sitting in front of him, holding out tissues. He took one.

"There, there," Dale said. "Buck up, little fighter."

Mike smiled.

"You like that?" Dale said. "My mom used to say it all the time. *Buck up, little fighter.* It's a good expression. But you have to be careful not to get the B and the F turned around."

Tears still in his eyes, Mike thought about the letters and started to laugh.

"See what I mean? Terrible," Dale said. "You don't want to say that to someone when they're down."

"No, you don't." Mike looked at the sheets and blankets beneath them.

"You're scared tonight. You sleep in my bed."

Mike shook his head, said, "No."

"No funny business. Scouts honor."

"You were never a Boy Scout, were you?"

"Well, once I wanted to bake brownies with my sister's Girl Scouts troop, but my mom wouldn't let me. Does that count?"

"Afraid not."

"Okay then. Cross my heart and hope to, er, well... I promise. We'll sleep like sisters. No groping. I give you my word as a gentleman and a lady."

He looked at Dale carefully, and then nodded. He believed him.

"Can I just put my arm around you?" Dale said. "While we sleep?"

Mike paused. "Okay. Like sisters"

Although he normally slept in his underwear, he put on a T-shirt and sweat pants before he climbed into Dale's comfortable bed later that night.

Dale was wearing a pair of enormous pink pajamas. "Made them myself," he said.

Mike fell asleep quickly, lying on his side next to Dale, his back to Dale's warm stomach, Dale's arm wrapped around him. It surprised him how safe he felt.

All night long Dale kept his promise, and in the morning they both put on jeans and tennis shoes and walked over to the Lighthouse Café for brunch. Over bacon and eggs, Mike said, "If I'm positive, I won't be able to be in Steve's movies."

"*Steve's* movies?" Dale asked.

"Well, yeah."

Dale waved something away with his hand. "If I'm positive, if I'm positive," he said, mocking Mike tenderly. "We'll cross that bridge *if* and when we get there. I for one wouldn't tell anybody if you were positive. Anyway, you just might be negative."

Afterward, they wandered in and out of shops, killing time before the appointment. They began walking down Melrose, and Mike realized they were headed in the direction of Westbourne Drive, where Kerry lived. He decided not to mention it.

Dale stopped to look in a shop window at some dresses and sighed dramatically, "So many frocks, so little time!" Then he put his hand on his forehead and leaned back as though about to faint, turning to see if Mike was watching. Mike saw that Dale was trying to entertain him, to put on Sasha and make him smile. In front of another shop Dale said, "Let's go in," and inside he bought Mike a pair of sunglasses, making him try on different styles to see which looked the best.

"It'll be your birthday present," Dale said. "Only I get to choose." He selected a pair of mirrored aviator frames. As they walked out he stopped to look at Mike again and said, "You're the most beautiful man in the world."

"Thanks, Dale." Mike felt incredibly fortunate to have this fat, unattractive man at his side, caring for him, buying him things, and taking care of him.

"I'll teach you a game," Dale said as they continued along the sidewalk. "It's called Husband Hunter." He explained the rules.

"You take turns and you have three chances. When your turn starts, you look at the first man who passes us by. You have to decide instantly if you want to marry him. Think carefully because you'll be stuck with him for the rest of your life. Before he passes us by, say 'yes' or 'no.' If you say 'no' to the first *and* the second man we see, then you're stuck with the third – no matter how nasty he is. Even if he's ugly and has scabs on his nose. Then it's the other person's turn. The winner is the one with the hottest husband."

They played over and over, laughing as they walked. Once, on Mike's third chance, a tiny little man with an egg-shaped head and enormous, furry eyebrows walked by, talking to himself and spitting. It was all Dale and Mike could do to hold off laughing until after the man had passed. Dale said, "Ooo, just think of the honeymoon you two will have. You and his big eyebrows." When it was Dale's turn, a beautiful bodybuilder approached, and Dale was about to say "yes," but at the last minute the man turned and walked the other way. "Noo!" Dale yelled. "My dreamboat has gone!"

After that it was Mike's turn again. The first man was as fat as Dale and Mike said, "No way," without hesitation. Then he paused, hoping the sharp rejection hadn't hurt Dale. When he saw the second guy he couldn't believe his good luck. There, walking toward them down the street was Kerry. Mike turned to Dale and whispered an emphatic "yes."

Mike walked up to Kerry and said, "I always see you on the street." He felt simultaneously happy and nervous, and was overwhelmed with relief when Kerry smiled and gave him a quick kiss on the lips and a hug.

"You're going to start thinking I'm some common street whore," Kerry said. "And not a highly trained, professional dancer."

Mike reached out and touched his arm. "Where have you been?"

"I went to Vegas. It was sort of last minute, with a client. We drove back this morning so I just got your message today. I called you right away, just now, and left a message on your machine."

"Mine," Dale said. Mike and Kerry turned. "You must have left a message on *my* machine. It's *mine*."

Dale seemed to be glaring at Kerry, but Mike couldn't be sure. He took a step back to include Dale in the conversation. "Sorry. Kerry, this is my friend Dale. You know, I live at his place. Dale, Kerry."

"Yes," Dale said.

Kerry nodded coolly. "You're Sasha."

"Well, she's me."

"I think I've seen your show at the Lucky Pony."

"Many people have. They love me."

There was an awkward pause, a kind of tension. There were no polite smiles, no signs of friendliness at all.

Mike turned to Kerry and said, "Pascal was pretty bent that you weren't at work the other day."

"I figured he'd be upset, but I made four times the money with this guy in Vegas."

Dale stepped forward, put his hand down firmly on Mike's shoulder. "Baby, we're going to be late for that appointment."

"Yeah. Okay."

"So sorry, Kevin," Dale said. "We're off to the beauty parlor. I'm getting Mike here a pedicure. I'm getting one too, of course. Then facials. It'll be *hours*."

"It's Kerry," Kerry said, and he turned to Mike. "Beauty parlor?"

"Um, yeah," Mike said.

Kerry looked surprised. "Are you working tomorrow night?"

"Yeah, I'll be there."

"Me too. If I still have a job anyway. See you then?"

"What about tonight?"

"I have another job."

"Okay." Mike wanted to touch Kerry again, but Dale was standing close, his large hand still pushing down on his shoulder. "I'll see you tomorrow night then."

It was Kerry who leaned forward, gave him another hug, and in doing so pushed Dale's hand away. Mike felt the edge of Kerry's lips kiss him awkwardly on the ear as Dale watched.

Dale grabbed Mike's arm and began pushing forward. "Now, now. Off we go. Bye bye, Cory!"

When they were out of earshot, Mike said, "His name is Kerry."

"Whatever," Dale said.

"And beauty parlor?"

Dale shrugged. "Sorry. It was the best I could do on such short notice."

"Kerry knows I don't go to beauty parlors and get pedicures."

"Would you rather I told him where we're really going?"

Mike winced and fell quiet for a moment, then said, "He's going to feel my feet and wonder if you were lying."

"Pardon me?"

Mike said nothing.

"Well, then," Dale said. "It's simple. Keep him away from your feet. Oh, sorry. I guess that'll be tough when your ankles are behind his ears."

Mike hit Dale softly and smiled. "You're just jealous."

Suddenly Dale stopped in the middle of the sidewalk, staring Mike in the eyes. A woman behind him had to swerve to avoid walking into him. Dale was oblivious. He looked as though he were either angry or in pain. "Yes," he said. "I *am* jealous. You're a genius for figuring that one out."

Mike knew he'd made another mistake, but he had no idea what to say. He moved closer to Dale, put his hand in the crook of his elbow, nudged him forward down the street. "Dale," he said, as if more words would magically follow. He tried desperately to think of something that would make Dale feel better, make himself not feel guilty for liking Kerry, but there was only an empty quiet. He leaned in toward Dale as they walked, squeezed his arm gently, but he said nothing.

25
The Clinic

DALE DIDN'T LIKE the look of the clinic. It was dingy, tattered, and felt faintly desperate, although he didn't say so to Mike. The nurse was cold. She wouldn't let him go in with Mike to receive the results, and it didn't seem fair. Mike shouldn't be alone. Dale felt himself becoming loud and pushy. "Is it because we're faggots? If he were my little wife, would you let me go in then?"

"No," the nurse replied calmly. "I'm afraid not. No couples, straight or gay. I'm sorry."

So Dale sat in the lobby, waiting, watching the wooden door Mike had disappeared through. He was physically uncomfortable. His jeans were pinching his waist. Inside the heavy denim his thighs were sweating. Dresses were so much easier. On the other hand, wigs itched and high heels hurt. There was no winning.

The door opened and a young blond boy came out. His eyes were bloodshot. He'd clearly been crying. Dale tried to look away, but failed. Their eyes met for a moment, and then the boy walked quickly outside. The noise of the passing cars became briefly louder, then the boy was gone, and the lobby was still again.

Dale was very much aware of the possible paths that were in front of him. He'd been through this before. He began saying the list in his head. It was something he did from time to time, a kind of prayer, names like repeated rosary beads. You should never forget the names of the dead. Darryl, Rick,

Ellen, Rex... He included the ones he'd been close to as well as the ones he didn't know very well, and he remembered various, embittered voices which said only in passing that *so and so* was dead. It was scary, the way people disappeared.

He should be dead himself. Sometimes he wondered if he'd survived this long simply because – even back in the 70s, way before safe sex – he'd never much cared for the taste of cum, and he didn't like to be fucked. It was amazing, that your life could come down to that.

His mind went back to Rick now, the one he'd helped the most, a good friend he'd done drag with years before. Dale had done everything he could. He scrubbed Rick's toilet, did his grocery shopping, cleaned out that nasty parrot's cage when Rick was afraid the bacteria in the bird shit would finish him off. Then, when nobody wanted the bird after Rick died, it was Dale who sold it back to the pet shop, gave the money to an AIDS charity. He hated that damn bird.

He figured now, still watching the door, that if Mike walked out with a smile on his face, they would keep going forward as they had been. He would continue finding Mike jobs in films, and Mike would continue sleeping on his couch, and maybe sometimes, upset and sad like last night, Mike would sleep with him in his bed. Dale hoped so.

But so much could go wrong. If Mike were negative, Dale worried he'd eventually be left behind. It could happen in any combination of ways, and he couldn't help himself now: he began going through each frightening scenario as he waited.

He hadn't told Mike everything. While it was true that Steve was happy with Sasha's work on the *Muscle Party* project, it was obvious that Steve was even happier with Billy's. There was no doubt in Dale's mind. Steve still wanted Billy for Cougar movies more than he wanted Sasha. In fact,

Billy could end up overshadowing Sasha entirely. It was possible that he might actually become the more successful of the two, that he would step over her and continue on until she became just a hazy memory for him – just one of many who'd helped him on his path to becoming a huge star, just some old drag queen. Fat, failed and forgotten.

Of course there was that other scenario for losing Mike, the one that would hurt more. He could end up leaving for love. He could end up leaving for someone like that Kerry.

Dale looked down at the worn carpet and rubbed the short hair on top of his balding head. Kerry was stupid and shallow. That much was obvious just from looking at him today. It didn't matter what Mike said. Kerry had none of Mike's vulnerability, or warmth, or charm. In no way was he worthy of Mike's affections. Dale paused, staring at the floor. For a moment he imagined having to continually pull Mike away from men on the streets.

He looked up at the door again. It was a pale wood. The light switch on the white wall to the left was slightly grey from hands touching it so many times.

Gradually Dale came to a conclusion, one that was twofold. First, even if Mike walked out with a smile on his face, even if he was fine and healthy and good and negative and wanted to make more movies, Sasha was going to have to stop relying on him. She was going to have to prove her worth to Steve without Billy, on her own, to show that she could do it even without such an intensely burning performer as him. Secondly, unless Dale wanted to lose Mike to love, something would have to be done about that Kerry.

But there was, of course, yet another possibility altogether, and Dale turned to it now. If Mike's eyes were bloodshot, if he looked like that poor blond boy, as though he'd been crying, if he was positive, then everything would change. Mike would start counting T-cells, would in time begin struggling to fight off one thing and then another. He would need help. He would need Dale. And certain threats would disappear. *If I'm positive, Kerry won't want me. If I'm positive, I won't be able to be in Steve's movies.*

A new thought came to him then, strangely, like some exotic flower blooming in time lapse photography – as though something which normally took hours, days, weeks was now visible in one smooth and flowing, beautiful instant. He realized that if Mike became sick, it wouldn't be all bad. There would be long talks at Mike's bedside. There would be more nights with Mike sharing his bed – his small, feverish body next to him as he slept, his slow and steady breathing. There would be all the little things he could do for Mike, things that Mike would want and appreciate. He could get Mike's prescriptions filled, drive him to the doctor, bring him coffee, and buy him apples by the bushel. He would have Mike all to himself.

As soon as he thought it, Dale felt horrible. How could he want such a thing? Only when he followed the idea, this possible future that continued to blossom in front of him now, when he continued to stare it down and watch it happen, did he realize that he did not want it at all. It was a death sentence. After being sick, after needing him more, Mike would surely fade and die. All over Los Angeles, men were dropping like flies. What was he thinking? Dale didn't want to lose this one too – especially not that way, especially not that slow, wasting, skeletal way. Mike was the most precious one by far. Upon seeing this path's inevitable conclusion, Mike's death, Dale finally stopped the thought. He turned away from it, shocked and sad. He felt guilty and ashamed.

189

And then there was Mike, standing at the door. He looked at Dale blankly, and Dale didn't know what to do.

But then, suddenly, like a great beaming sun, Mike smiled.

Dale rushed over to him and hugged him, and Mike whispered in his ear, "I'm okay. I'm negative." Dale, in spite of himself, in spite of wanting Mike to be okay, felt ashamed and guilty all over again because there was, suddenly, rising up inside him – he felt it in his chest – a strong and undeniable pang of disappointment.

26
A Distinguished Friend

IT WAS ONLY with the results behind him that Mike began to realize how the entire thing had shaken his confidence so deeply. He'd always felt that his most reliable source of power was his body – the way he looked, whatever it was that people saw in him – but for the past three months his belief in that power had been shaken. He'd felt vulnerable, full of fear that his body was no longer fully his, that something foreign had lodged inside it and would soon start taking control.

So as he walked out of the clinic with Dale that Friday afternoon, slipping on his new sunglasses and looking down the street, it felt like he finally had command of his body back, and with it all of his power again.

"I want to meet Steve," he said, smiling and looking at Dale.

"Why?"

"What do you mean, *why*? I'm his next big superstar. I'm going to be the first big bottom in gay porn. Will you call him when we get home? Let's go to Cougar today." He grabbed Dale's arm and pulled him closer.

"No. I called in sick this morning." Dale pretended to cough. "I'm supposed to be in bed."

"What about tomorrow? Can I go to Cougar with you in the morning?"

"Tomorrow's Saturday. I'm not going to work. Besides, it's your birthday and I just decided I'm taking you out for brunch."

Mike smiled. "Okay. We'll go to Cougar together on Monday."

"You can't go in with me. Steve might not be there. But I'll talk to him about it. We'll see."

"Dale, thank you for coming with me today."

"I wouldn't have it any other way."

"I'm so fucking relieved I'm negative," Mike said.

Dale nodded. "Me too, baby. Me too."

The next day Dale took Mike out for brunch as promised, then they went and saw a movie together. That evening Mike went to work early, hoping to see Kerry before it got busy. When he finally saw Kerry come in, Mike went up to him and hugged him. There were two customers already there, two old lechers sitting at the bar. They stared. Mike didn't care. He kissed Kerry full on the lips. He looked over and saw the lechers watching. He liked it.

Kerry laughed and pulled away slightly, but kept his hands at Mike's waist. "Well, you seem happy. I guess a good day at the beauty parlor works wonders."

"Nah. I'm just glad to see you. When I didn't hear from you, I figured you were blowing me off."

"Vegas was a good chance to make some money."

"You could have called me. That would've been nice."

Kerry looked away. When he turned back he said, "When are you going to come back to my place?"

Mike felt the growing warmth of Kerry's hands, still lingering on his waist. "As soon as I get an invitation. It's my birthday today."

"Really? Well, how about tonight, after work? We can celebrate."

"I'd like that."

"Good. Me too."

"I made another movie."

Kerry's eyebrows rose. "Did you?"

"Well, it's just one scene. But it's my first studio shoot. I'm really excited about it. Dale told me the producer really liked what we did."

"You did it with Dale?"

"Yeah. He directed."

"That guy's an asshole."

"What?" Mike looked at Kerry closely.

"On the street yesterday. 'Mine. It's mine.' What the hell was that about?"

"That's just Dale. He's a little bit jealous. He protects me. He's helped me out a lot."

"He's a porn freak who likes a pretty boy and wants to use you."

"Stop it, Kerry." Mike pulled away. "He's given me a place to live and helped me find work. He's the closest thing I have to family here."

"Family? How long have you known him?"

"Long enough." Mike paused. It had really only been three months. "You know, Kerry, I couldn't wait to see you tonight. I wanted to tell you what I'd done. I missed you even. But you're ruining it."

"I already told you what I thought of porn."

"Yeah. Well, it's what I do. Take it or leave it." Mike turned and walked toward the bar. The two lechers smiled and quickly offered to buy him a drink. He said yes. One of them put his hand on his waist, where Kerry's had been.

Behind him he heard Pascal talking loudly. "Well, if it isn't King Kerry who thinks he can come and go whenever he pleases..." A new song started and it drowned out their conversation, but it was clear that Kerry was making excuses to

Pascal. The lechers continued smiling. They asked Mike if Kerry was his boyfriend. He said no. Then suddenly Sasha's voice was booming.

"Hello doll! How *are* you?"

When he turned around he was surprised to see Sasha actually giving Kerry air kisses, pretending like she'd found an old friend. She wore a bright orange, knee-length dress with long sleeves and blue feathers that circled each wrist. Her blond wig was topped with a blue headband, and she wore the blue platform shoes that she had on during the *Muscle Party* shoot. Behind her was a grey-haired guy in khaki pants and a navy blue blazer. He had a paunch and a fat, gold watch. He looked familiar, and Mike remembered he'd seem him before, at the premiere of *Banging Billy*.

Mike nodded toward the lechers on either side of him and excused himself, smiling and squeezing one of their knees just to keep them interested. He might need them later. It was always important to have options.

As he approached Sasha, she was reaching out and patting Kerry's shoulder and saying, "Aren't *you* the sexy one tonight?"

The moment she saw Mike she yelled "Baby!" and gave him a big hug. "I've come on a mission of peace, in honor of your birthday. I thought I could share a drink with you and Kerry here, to get to know him a bit better." She looked at Kerry, who stood alongside her watching everything carefully, and she squished up her nose at him, trying to look cute. "Oh, but I have such bad manners," she said, waving her arms in the air, the feathers on her wrists fluttering wildly. She turned to the man with the gold watch. "I brought my distinguished friend Burt here, just to keep me company. You know, I thought you two boys might be working hard, and I didn't want to sit at a table all by myself. Burt, you remember my darling Billy."

"Yes." Burt looked Mike up and down. "Happy birthday."

"Thanks," Mike said. "I remember you. You told me I look good in a cowboy hat."

"Did I?" Burt said, but he was already staring at Kerry.

"And this is Billy's new friend, Kerry," Sasha said. She leaned in toward Burt as though about to whisper a secret, but she spoke loudly. "I'm hoping he won't be a bad influence on my dear boy." She turned and offered Kerry a warm, friendly smile.

Although Burt hadn't shaken hands with Mike, he did now with Kerry. Mike noticed the gold wedding ring on Burt's left hand. Sasha marched over to a table with a good view of the stage and told everyone where to sit. She placed Kerry next to Burt. Mike looked across the table to catch Kerry's eye, trying to figure out what Kerry was thinking, to see if he was going to be nice to Sasha. Kerry was looking at her suspiciously.

Pascal's house rules were clear. Dancers couldn't sit and talk to friends unless the friends were buying them drinks, and even then they could only talk for a limited time. The dancers were here for the customers, not for their friends. But the lines weren't always clear. Friends sometimes became customers. Customers sometimes became friends. Sasha knew the rules, and she immediately offered to buy drinks for everyone.

Mike was happy to see her at Exposé again. It was nice knowing she'd be in the audience as he danced later on. She always clapped and cheered loudly for him.

When the waiter named Tony came over, Kerry announced to the table, "This is Tony. He's straight."

Tony ignored him and smiled, "What would you like to drink?"

"Oooo," Sasha squealed. "Now tell me, doll. What would a nice straight boy like *you* be doing in a *nasty* gay place like this?"

"Waiting tables, ma'am." He said 'ma'am' without a trace of irony, as though he really believed he was talking to a woman. "What would you like?"

She laughed. "That depends. Are you on the menu?"

"Afraid not." Tony smiled again, directly at Sasha. It was unquestionably flirtatious.

"Oh, doll. I bet you get some good tips," Sasha said.

Kerry nodded. "That's what keeps him coming back." He reached out and slapped Tony's ass.

Tony hit his hand away. "Not for sale. What can I get you to drink?"

"Not for sale," Kerry repeated. "You're the worst kind of tease. Frustrating the poor guys that come into this place. At least Mike and I make an honest living. At least we put out."

"Drinks?" Tony repeated. "Ladies first." He turned to Sasha.

She ordered a cranberry and vodka and said she wanted to file a complaint with the management that the waiters weren't on the menu. Burt asked for a gin and tonic. Mike and Kerry each ordered a beer. Sasha proposed a toast. "To the birthday boy, Billy Knight!"

Afterward she turned to Kerry. "Now, Kelvin – I mean, I'm sorry, Kerry. Really, you'll just *have* to forgive my geriatric memory. Next stop, Alzheimers! Anyway, how long have you worked at Exposé, Kerry dear? I've seen you here before, but we've never had the chance to become acquainted."

196

"A year."

"I hope you're looking out for my Billy, since he's really still a newbie and all."

"You mean Mike? He's smart. He can take care of himself."

"I understand you took him to the gym the other day."

Sitting alongside Sasha, Mike was watching closely, ready to intervene if things turned nasty.

"Yes, that's right," Kerry said.

"Billy, you should join that gym. There's only so much you can do at home. Maybe Kerry can become your workout buddy. Show you what exercises to do." She looked at Kerry. "It's all very complicated, I imagine. All those big machines."

"I don't really use the machines. Free weights are better," Kerry said.

"Really?" Sasha said. "And why is that?"

"They activate more muscles, because you have to stabilize the weight. Plus, they involve balance and coordination. You get a better workout."

"Well, you're smarter than you look. I mean – " She cut herself off. "It's not that you look stupid, Kyle, er, Kerry. I didn't mean that. It's just you're just so handsome that, honestly, one never knows."

There was an awkward pause. Kerry said, "I'm not sure if I've just been insulted or complimented."

"Complimented, doll. Complimented. Really, it sounds like you know a lot about working out. You should be teaching Billy and working out together on a regular basis."

"Good idea," Mike said. He didn't understand why Sasha was encouraging them to spend time together, but he liked it. It was a nice birthday present, better than the sunglasses Dale bought him earlier. She must have changed her mind about Kerry.

After Tony came back and served the drinks, Sasha proposed a toast. "To new friendships." Everyone clinked glasses. She turned briefly to Kerry and said, "Kerry, Burt's headed off to Europe next month." Then she turned to Mike.

Kerry and Burt began to talk.

Sasha began asking Mike what number he was going to do first, which costume, which music. He answered slowly, half listening to Kerry and Burt. It was clear from the bits Mike caught that Burt was an experienced traveler. Kerry was asking question after question. At one point a quiet song started and Mike could hear Kerry ask, "What's it like, seeing the Eiffel Tower for the first time?"

Mike turned away from Sasha to hear the answer.

"Magical," Burt said. He lifted up his gin and tonic. "Paris is like stepping inside a painting. The city was never bombed, you know. So it's still beautiful. I have an apartment in the seventh. I spend six weeks every summer there, and also a couple weeks throughout the year." He took a long, slow sip. It looked like a very expensive gold watch, and it was a thick, gold wedding ring.

"What's the seventh?" Kerry said. A few more customers walked by and sat down at tables near the stage.

"The seventh arrondissement. Paris is divided up that way. It's a nice area. The only problem with my apartment is that you can't see the Eiffel Tower very well. The problem is that it's too close."

"Too close?" Kerry was leaning in toward Burt now, laughing lightly. "Your complaint about the view is that the Eiffel Tower is too close?"

"Yes. But it's still very nice. As I'm sure you can imagine."

"Yes, I can imagine."

"Kerry," Mike said. "Aren't you up next?"

Pascal was standing by the bar, looking in their direction. When Kerry looked over, Pascal nodded.

"Well, a boy's gotta work," Kerry said, standing up.

"Yes, indeed he does," Sasha said.

Since Kerry didn't do costumes, he just walked up on stage as his music began to play, wearing the acid-washed jeans and yellow Ocean Pacific T-shirt he'd arrived in. Sasha cheered almost as loudly for him as she usually did for Mike, and Mike took it as a kind of endorsement. He looked over at Burt, who was watching closely as Kerry danced. Already he had a bad feeling about Burt. He didn't like him, wanted him to go away, wished Sasha hadn't brought him.

Sasha said to Mike, "He *is* really a beautiful man, your friend Kerry."

Mike nodded.

"Yes," Burt said softly. "He is." Then suddenly Burt let out a loud, piercing whistle, just as Kerry began unbuttoning his jeans.

"That's some whistle," Mike said, covering his ear. He pointed to Burt's wedding ring. "You're married."

"Am I?" Burt looked at his hand. "Thank you."

"Does your wife go with you to Paris?"

"Billy," Sasha said. "Don't pry."

"It's okay Sasha," Burt answered. "No, Billy. She stays home. We have an understanding."

Mike turned away. The two old lechers from the bar moved down to a table near the stage. When Kerry was down to his G-string, one of them held up a five-dollar bill. Kerry stepped off the stage, danced over, and let the lecher stuff the money into his G-string. Then he gave him a five-dollar dance, but he backed away a little early, when the lecher began stroking Kerry's tattoo. Burt whistled again. He was so close that it hurt Mike's ear.

When Kerry was done, Mike went backstage to find him.

"I'll take it," Kerry said when Mike walked up to him.

"What do you mean?" Mike asked.

"You said you do porn, take it our leave it. I'll take it. I mean I accept it. I'll try to accept it. Just because it's not for me doesn't mean it's not for you. I'm sorry I keep fucking up." Kerry stood there in his jeans now, shirtless, all long arms and flat stomach, remorseful smile. "Maybe I'm a little jealous too."

"Jealous?"

"Of course I am. Cute guy like you, and you're spending so much time with that fat old hag instead of me."

"Kerry." Mike was stern.

"Oops. I should say, 'with that distinguished older gentle... ah, gentleperson.'"

"She's not that old."

"She's fat though."

"Kerry."

"Sorry. See? I can't help myself." Kerry put out his arms. "Forgive me?"

To Mike, Kerry's arms felt like two wings opening, and he walked in. Kerry's skin, still warm from dancing, wrapped around him. Mike took a deep breath, filled himself with Kerry's faint, musky cologne, his fragrant sweat. "I don't like Burt," he said.

Kerry shrugged. "He seems like a nice enough guy."

"Did you see his wedding ring?"

"Yeah. And his watch. He's loaded. I'd love to see his apartment in Paris."

200

Mike poked Kerry in the side. "I bet you would."

Later that night, after Kerry and Mike had both danced several sets, Sasha and Burt got up to leave. Sasha gave Kerry and Mike big hugs.

Burt said, "Kerry, are you busy later? After you're done here?"

Kerry paused. It looked like he was about to accept Burt's invitation.

"Sorry, Burt," Mike interrupted. "Kerry and I have plans."

"Oh." Burt said, not even glancing at Mike. He was looking only at Kerry. "Maybe another time, then. How can I reach you?"

Kerry went to the bar and wrote his number down on a napkin, then came back and handed it to Burt.

"Excellent," Burt said. I'll call you."

Sasha pulled on Burt's arm. "Time for the old folks to get back to the rest home." She looked at Kerry and Mike. "Where are you two young'uns headed tonight? You'll be finishing off the birthday celebrations with gusto, I expect?"

"Don't know where we're going," Kerry answered. "Maybe just back to my place." He put his arm around Mike.

"Well, don't do anything I wouldn't do," Sasha said.

Mike smiled. "That doesn't rule out a whole lot."

"Smart ass. You probably won't be coming home tonight, then?"

To Mike, this felt like another endorsement, like Sasha was accepting the fact that he was going to be in Kerry's bed all night long. "Yeah. Don't wait up for me."

"Okay, but you two be careful. Kerry, please take good care of my boy for me."

"I will," Kerry said.

She looked back at Mike and shook her finger in the air. "Play safe. And no dilly-dallying all day tomorrow, Billy. I'm making Sunday dinner. Roast pork. I expect you home for dinner by five."

Mike looked at her warmly, rolled his eyes and smiled. "Yes, Mother. Whatever you say."

27
Country Cousins

DALE WAS GRATEFUL that Mike was home in time to set the table. He'd been nervous, thinking maybe Mike wouldn't show for dinner, but then suddenly there he was, yelling out, "I'm hungry! Let's eat!" as he walked in the door.

Everything started out fine. They sat down and ate, talked, laughed and sipped Chardonnay. Mike was in rare form, telling stories about johns he'd had years ago: a Cincinnati fishmonger, a man in a pink bunny costume.

Sitting there at that small kitchen table together and sharing that meal mattered to Dale, in a very important way, although he couldn't say exactly why – other than the obvious fact that he loved being with Mike. The evening was everything it should be. There was nothing fantastically raunchy about it, or extravagant, nothing terribly exciting at all. Just the pork he'd thrown in the oven with some potatoes, some vegetables, followed by an easy dessert, apple crumble because he knew Mike liked it. Comfort food. It was a simple Sunday dinner, but it was grounding and good.

Over dessert Dale said, "Mike, there's something I haven't exactly told you about our *Muscle Party* scene. Nothing bad. I mean, not for you at least."

Mike looked at him, concerned. "What?"

"Well, I'm not getting credited as Sasha Zahore. The only way Steve would let me do it was if he could credit me as Cliff Hardman."

"But you directed it as Sasha. I saw you."

"Tell that to Steve. Anyway, if I didn't agree to being listed as Cliff then Steve wasn't going to let me direct, and then I couldn't have gotten you a part. So really, I did it for you."

"Oh, Dale." Mike stood up, walked around the table, and hugged Dale from behind. "Thank you."

After dinner they moved into the living room and sat on the couch. It was then that Dale opened a second bottle of wine. Perhaps that was his first mistake. He'd left his advance copy of *Country Cousins* sitting on the coffee table. Perhaps that was his second. He'd planned to watch the movie at some point later that evening, in preparation for selling it at work the following day. The box cover showed two shirtless young men in cut-off denim shorts, red bandanas around their necks, sitting on hay bales.

Dale and Mike sat on the couch talking a little while longer, and then Dale finally said, "Do you mind watching this together?" He picked up Country Cousins. "Cougar's newest film. It's business."

Mike paused, then said, "Sure." He smiled. "We'll watch it like sisters."

Initially they enjoyed talking about the movie, noting which models had strong oral technique and which guys they'd personally like to jump in bed with. Dale pointed out a couple of flaws. There were too many long, drawn out insertion shots, too many strange cutaways to farm equipment.

"It's not perfect," Dale announced, "but I think Sasha can sell it."

Mike nodded. "Of course she can. Check out the dick on that guy."

The sex got hotter and they kept watching and then finally both fell silent, focusing on those young LA boys pretending to be farm hands having sex.

Everything was fine until Dale pulled out his dick. After all, he thought, what was a little jack-off together, between sisters?

Mike immediately got up, went into the kitchen, and started doing the dishes.

Dale finished himself off alone, feeling the emptiness of a sad orgasm. Then he wiped himself up and fast-forwarded through the rest of the movie. Mike never came back out. Eventually Dale went into his bedroom and shut the door, without even saying good night.

The following morning Sasha sat at her desk, dreading the thought of getting on the phone to sell *Country Cousins*. She had such a bad feeling associated with that movie now, the lonely orgasm it had given her. But the movie was going to be released soon, and the calls had to be made. The merchant list sat on her desk next to the box cover, and she knew she would be on the phone most of the day.

There was also a 1:00 lunch appointment with Edward Derwood, who owned the Backstreet Theatre and Video Shop in Chicago, and who was in LA on business. Steve expected her to sell Edward at least 20 copies of *Country Cousins*, and also wanted her to get Edward interested in screening Cougar's big circus flick when it was ready at the end of the year. The studio didn't make a lot of money from theatre screenings, but it was good publicity and drove up video sales later on – which was where Cougar turned its profit.

She tried to escape her thoughts of last night by calculating how many copies of *Country Cousins* she could sell altogether. The standard porn movie only sold about 2,000 tapes. But at $50 each, that came to $100,000 in sales. Movies by solid directors usually sold about 5,000 tapes. If you had a big star like Luke Champion, you could sell as many as 20,000 tapes, but that was rare. She hoped to sell 4,000 copies of *Country Cousins* in total. Of course it wouldn't all happen today, but that was her goal. Sasha always had goals.

The sales of *Banging Billy* were disappointing. Stunning Productions hadn't done much in the way of marketing, and so far the film had sold only 1,000 tapes. Lately she'd begun taking matters into her own hands, giving pitches for *Banging Billy* while she was selling her Cougar films. Steve would be furious if he found out, but she didn't care. It was something she had to do.

She glanced over at the merchant list, all the places that sold Cougar films across the country. It was an unbearably familiar list. She'd been calling these same damn numbers for almost four years now, building relationships, cultivating vendors. Although the owners changed every now and then, and the occasional video shop or adult bookstore would close or re-open here or there, for the most part the list stayed the same and the routine never changed. She made the call. She said she hoped business was going well. She asked about something personal – maybe she checked her notes to re-member the name of the person's partner, or maybe she just asked about the weather where they were. Finally she made the pitch and recorded the sale. In spite of her initial enthu-siasm, it no longer seemed to matter if she was selling hot gay porn or no-nonsense kitchen knives. She wasn't cut out for a desk job. She was bored.

When she thought about what she wanted, what she really needed to be happy, it was simple. There were only three things. She wanted more time to do drag shows. She wanted to direct one full-length studio film after another, in her own name, or at least the name she'd chosen for herself. And finally, she wanted Billy.

Sasha wanted this young man in a way that she'd never wanted anybody her entire life, not simply as a friend, or a fuck buddy, or even just some common lover, but as a profound companion in all things – from sex and love to play and food, absolutely everything. Inside her there was an ache in the shape of him, a feeling like a void where her lungs should be, or her heart, some kind of vacuum that became stronger the longer she didn't have him the way she wanted. This feeling of excruciating lack was so profound that she imagined if she couldn't stop it or fill it she'd actually begin to collapse, to crumple back onto herself, like an empty milk container with the air sucked out.

If, of her three desires, she could only have one, she would choose Billy. She would choose the young man she'd made dinner for last night, who slept on her living room sofa week after week, who so often lay exposed in the mornings with the sheets kicked back, wearing that adorable white underwear, fast asleep inside all that beautiful skin. There was no question it would be him.

Yet she didn't want to be forced to make the choice. She had three wishes damn it, and she wanted them *all* to come true.

Ever since she was a little boy, she'd been steadfast in the conviction that her life was her own kind of fairytale, a story she could create with her own two hands, any way she wanted. The possibilities had always seemed limitless. But in recent days – it was terrible to admit, but true – she was beginning to doubt herself. Things weren't going according to plan. She hated the fact that she'd be listed in the *Muscle Party 5* credits as 'Cliff Hardman.' The very thought of it made her skin crawl. There was only one thing more disappointing than that name. The exclusive directing contract Steve should have obviously handed her after seeing her *Muscle Party* work had never materialized.

Slowly now, she began to realize something as she sat at her desk, something she'd never allowed herself to consider before, and it was like leaning over and looking down into a great chasm. She felt a kind of vertigo. But there it was, one horrible, undeniable fact: it was entirely possible that she could spend years working toward her goals and never achieve them.

She began flipping the pages of her desk calendar until she came to the small red 'x' she'd drawn in the corner of the 18th of May 1989, marking her secret. Not even Billy knew, and it was less than four weeks away now. A tiny twinge of self-doubt and fear ran through her. The 'x' marked the day she would turn forty. Could it be that her peak was, in fact, behind her?

Steve's voice came barreling in from the hallway, and she looked up just as he turned the corner. She turned the calendar pages back quickly, away from that small red stain.

"Why are you keeping Billy Knight from me?" Steve said. He stood in front of her desk with his shoulders squared off, a stern look on his face. "Why haven't I met him yet?"

"Well, good morning, Mr. Logan. And how are we today?"

"There are no contact details on his *Muscle Party* contract. Günter says he lives with you. Is he home now? I'll call him." He stepped over to her phone and picked up the receiver. "What's the number?"

Leaning over her, she could smell him, an adamantly masculine combination of deodorant and cologne. "Just a minute," she said. "Billy's not there. He's a very busy young man. Have a seat. Let's talk."

He remained standing, holding the phone in his hand. "I don't want to talk to you. I want to talk to Billy Knight."

She looked away and fell silent. Was this the start of it? Was this the place where Billy's path diverted from hers, and he began to become a success without her? Was this the point where he began to leave her?

"I have to meet him," Steve said.

She forced a smile. "Well, you certainly do have a bug in your britches."

"I want to offer him an exclusive."

"Oh, really?" She raised her eyebrows. An exclusive contract meant that Billy would be paid well, and wouldn't have to struggle for work. Cougar Studios would take care of him, would nurture and promote his career. It was a rare opportunity any model would jump at. "And what are you going to offer me?" she said. "I want to talk about my future as a director with Cougar."

Steve finally set down the phone. "I never made any promises. Your scene for *Muscle Party* was a one-off. I want Billy. If you don't put me in touch with him, I'll find him another way. Günter told me where he works. I'll track him down myself if I have to. But it won't make me very happy. It'd be a real CLM on your part."

"Excuse me? CLM?"

"A Career Limiting Move, babycakes." Steve stroked his mustache.

Sasha rolled her eyes. Jesus, this man annoyed her. "And how can you limit my career any more than by not letting me direct?"

"At least today you have a job."

"Look, you know I'm your best salesperson. And you know I want to direct. I scratch your back, you scratch mine. I thought you liked what I did with my *Muscle Party* scene. You said it was good sex."

"Billy Knight is good sex. A monkey could direct him and you'd have a top notch scene."

"A monkey? Is that how you see me?"

"Of course not. But you know you're not right for us. In sales, yes. In the director's chair, no. Your whole image is wrong. Even changing your name, I still can't get rid of… of this." He gestured to her body, from her large wig to the rolls of her stomach. "My customers don't want fat drag queens directing their porn."

"Excuse me? Do you hear that?" She looked around the room, then back at Steve. "It's a broken record. How can you still be going on about that? Listen doll, as long as our customers get off, they don't care if *Captain Kangaroo* directs their porn. Damn it, I'm good. I can direct."

Steve stood stock-still and said nothing. Sasha, keenly aware of the futility of repeating the same arguments, began down a different path.

"I can make you a lot of money," she said. "I discovered Billy, picked him out of a crowd in a smoky bar. I can sniff out talent like a bloodhound. You let me direct, and I can bring you more and more like him."

For a moment it looked as if Steve was actually considering this. But then he turned away and sighed, and she could almost feel her entire future being brushed away. He didn't even argue. He just walked out of the room and stopped at the door, looking back at her. "Will you bring him in, or won't you?"

Sasha leaned forward and held her head in her hands. She wanted to hide her face. It felt like she might actually cry, right there in front of Steve. The edge of sadness was too close.

"Well?" Steve said at the doorway.

There was a long moment when nothing was said, while Steve stood watching her and she continued looking down. The pens in the coffee mug in front of her pointed at odd angles. Fluorescent light bounced off the cold, white walls. Down the hall, a phone rang. Finally she shook her head, braced herself, and looked back up. She would not cry in front of this horrible, annoying man. She would not give him that. Her face became a thick veneer.

"Steve," she said. She spoke softly. "If you really want him, and you don't want me, there's nothing I can do about it. I love that boy. *Love him*, I tell you. And if you're willing to offer him a Cougar exclusive, that would be fantastic for him. I'll bring him to you. You can have him."

"When? Today?"

"Umm, he's in New York right now. Yes. He left over the weekend. I'm afraid he'll be there until the end of May sometime. He's playing boy toy to some rich client. Travel companion. Whatever. I'll bring him in when he gets back. How's that? Deal?"

Steve eyes narrowed. "If another studio gets him before I do, your job's on the line."

"Of course it is, doll. I understand."

"But you know, I'm not a bad guy. If you bring him in and we manage to sign him, I'll give you a finder's fee." He smiled, obviously proud of himself for having thought of the idea, and then quickly walked out.

Sasha mumbled to herself after he was gone. "Well, lah-dee-fucking-dah." She looked down at the skin on the back of her hands. From the top of her desk, the young men in the *Country Cousins* box cover photograph remained blissfully happy in their perfect, fake world. Alongside them, the merchants' list looked like a death certificate. She thought of all the calls she had to make that day, and the next. She felt chained to that horrible office chair. This was death from monotony, death from having her three wishes remain so far away. She'd always thought this job was a means toward an end – a kind of stopover on the way to her true destination – but maybe it wasn't. Maybe this was actually the end.

Maybe this was as much as she was ever going to have.

28
The Happy Couple

IT WASN'T THE sex Mike liked the best. It was the few minutes just after he woke up in Kerry's bed, hearing that steady, comfortable breathing on the pillow next to him. He would lie there completely still for as long as he could, trying not to break the moment, looking at the way the midday light came in around the edges of the thick blind, at the square shape where Kerry's white ceiling met his chalky green walls, at the peaks and troughs of the sheets all around them. Eventually, when Kerry stirred, Mike would roll over and cuddle up against him, lay his cheek down on his chest, and breathe.

He began waking up at Kerry's at least twice a week, often three. They would meet at Kerry's late at night after doing overtime with clients. Then, like an old married couple, they would watch a movie on TV, or order Chinese from a late-night takeaway nearby. They would curl up on the couch together and talk about the clients they'd just seen, saving their own tender fuck for the morning.

Sometimes they would go out, meeting at Tricky Dick's or The Powder Room, dance clubs around Los Angeles where the music was intense and thumping and they could hold each other, where they could stand in the middle of the room and kiss if they wanted. They would drink beer and dance and laugh and sweat.

Mike liked getting drunk with Kerry. There were so few times when he didn't feel the need to stay in control. Only with Kerry was he free to allow himself to let go, without fear, without wondering if Kerry would cross some kind of line or do something to hurt him.

When Dale told him that Steve Logan was in New York for a month, that he'd have to wait until the end of May to meet Steve and talk about a contract, Mike was disappointed. He decided that he could pass the time by allowing himself to be completely distracted by Kerry. There was nothing else worth thinking about. He went with Kerry to join Built, and he began paying monthly gym fees. It seemed like a kind of stability. Mike hadn't paid anything monthly since his rent back in Cincinnati. They worked out together regularly, and it felt as though in Kerry he'd found not only a first-time boyfriend – someone who had never once paid him for sex – but a personal trainer as well. Kerry showed him how to do reverse flys and military presses and Bulgarian split squats. Once he tried to pull Kerry into Built's boiler room, but the door was locked. When he explained that was where they'd filmed the *Muscle Party* scene, an angry look flashed across Kerry's face, but it faded quickly and was replaced with a sigh.

At work they flirted shamelessly, putting their arms around each other in front of all the teddy bears and lechers, grabbing quick kisses before they went up onto the stage. Mike thought they'd get in trouble for it, but Pascal never told them to stop. It turned out the customers liked it. Everyone talked about them, called them 'the happy couple.' They developed a routine where they stripped together – Mike getting down on his knees in his jock strap and pushing his face into the crotch of Kerry's G-string, then Kerry holding him from behind, pretending to fuck him while all the lechers cheered and the teddy bears smiled.

Sasha had said it was important to make sure your act never got old, and he enjoyed having a new routine, especially because it was with Kerry. Most nights he would catch Kerry's eye as they stood side by side, thrusting their hips at the crowd, and Kerry would give him a little wink, as if even up on stage they were still sharing some great private joke together, as if nobody else mattered.

Pascal warned them never to actually have sex on stage because he was afraid of being closed down. By then Mike had heard that even dances in private rooms were supposedly prohibited in LA. Mike figured so much illegal activity was already going on at Exposé that it would hardly matter if they had sex in front of everyone. But they did what Pascal said just the same. Kerry never wanted to actually have sex on stage, and Mike didn't want to lose his job for fucking in the wrong place, although it was tempting when the crowd cheered for more. Instead they arranged to do their overtime together as much as possible. It was great to be paid to have sex with your boyfriend, even if somebody else had to join in.

He was aware that Kerry had begun turning frequent tricks with Burt. Knowing about Kerry's clients didn't normally bother him, but it felt different with Burt. Kerry talked more about Burt than any other client he'd ever had – about how rich Burt was, about how well he knew Paris. It made Mike uncomfortable, gave him a hollow feeling in his gut.

To help Mike get over his unease, Kerry asked him to do a three-way with Burt. "You should get to know him. He's really nice," Kerry said, and Mike eventually agreed to do it.

It didn't go well. Mike felt jealous. Burt paid more attention to Kerry. Even when Burt was simultaneously fucking Mike and kissing Kerry, it was obvious. Mike's ass was just a place for Burt's dick but Burt's real attention, all his energy and focus, was directed at Kerry. Mike felt unwatched and nonessential, completely powerless. He wanted to push Burt away, to shove him off the hotel bed and yell, "Back off, he's mine!" but he knew he couldn't. Burt was Kerry's regular. Burt was Sasha's friend. So Mike lay there and tried to imagine that he was somewhere else. He disappeared, the way he'd first discovered he could years before, so that he wasn't really there anymore, wasn't in the bed with Burt kissing Kerry. It was a relief when it was finally over.

Afterward, he asked Kerry not to see Burt again. Kerry got angry and actually started shouting, something he'd never done before.

"Why would you not want me to have such a great regular?! How can you be so fucking selfish?"

Mike had begun to suspect that it was true, that he was selfish. He let the topic drop. After that, they stopped talking about Burt.

29
Home Alone

DALE NEVER FELT Mike's absence as intensely as when he knew Mike was away with Kerry. It was all the time now. Very quickly, weekends became tedious and empty. The evenings, in spite of the slowly lengthening days of spring, seemed to grow darker. Mike was never home.

After coming home from work Dale would step out of the bathroom, having removed the dress and the makeup, and he would be in his pajamas by 7:00. He would shuffle into the kitchen and stare into the refrigerator. It was all he could do to move a frozen dinner from the freezer to the microwave. He ate alone, in front of the TV, sitting on the sofa where Mike might or might not be sleeping that night.

Mike's bag of clothes sat in the corner, and sometimes Dale would open it, just to touch Mike's T-shirts and underwear, just to make himself feel not quite so abandoned. Other times he would lose himself in sewing costumes for Sasha, the TV on to keep him company. Wednesdays at the Lucky Pony had become the only evenings he wasn't at home alone, but even those fabulous performances had begun to feel just a little bit empty, because Mike was never in the audience anymore.

Still, Dale did what he could to keep Sasha fresh – new costumes, new dances. It was important to never let the people who watched her get bored. Dale pushed white satin under the presser foot and thought of songs Sasha could do in this fabric or that, what music went well with purple taffeta or teal crêpe. He would spend hours working on the movements Sasha would do in this new skirt or that blouse.

Eventually, as each lonely evening at home came to an end, Dale would brush his teeth in front of the bathroom mirror, staring at the flesh under his chin that lately had begun sagging even more. Then he would walk back out into the TV room, throw the plastic tray from his frozen dinner into the trash, and slip into his bedroom. Sometimes he would pull the chair from his vanity over to the window in order to do a little mending where he had a view of the street. If Mike came home then, Dale had an early warning, and he would quickly run back out into the TV room, sit on the sofa with a book in his hand, so that he could be there when Mike walked in, as though he'd been there all along. More often than not he just climbed into bed, rolled over and turned off the light.

He would wake at odd hours of the night and wonder if Mike was out there, on the other side of the bedroom door. Often Dale would slip out of bed, open the door quietly, and walk up to the sofa. The only light in the room was from the street lamps outside and the pale green glow of the display from the video player. He would find himself leaning over in the darkness to see if Mike was there and, if he was, feeling a sudden tiny bright spot of joy, but if not, feeling only the cold void of the empty room, his own solitude. Either way he would turn around and slink back into his bedroom, close the door behind him, and struggle to return to sleep. In the darkness, lying alone, he would think about his plans to get rid of Kerry. He hoped it would happen soon.

30
Piercing Whistle

MIKE DIDN'T KNOW why Kerry wasn't meeting his eye. They were stripping together, the audience cheering, but Kerry was always looking past him, or down, as Mike bounced and danced.

Kerry reached out and grabbed him, twirled him in. Somebody in the audience whistled loudly and everything in the room spun. With his back to the audience and facing Kerry, Mike wiggled his ass. Kerry looked off to the left.

Mike was glad this was the last set. Although he still enjoyed the power he felt when the audience was watching him, dancing almost every night was becoming tiresome. It would have been so much more honest, so much more sincere to suck Kerry's dick right there on stage. After all, wasn't sex what people really wanted when they pretended to want to see you strip?

Mike trailed a hand across Kerry's chest now, but every time he tried to catch Kerry's eye, Kerry was again staring out to the left. Somebody whistled again, from over where Kerry was looking, a loud and piercing shrill.

It was only later, when the five-dollar dances started, that Mike saw Burt holding up a bill and waving it at Kerry, doing that horrible whistle. It looked like a fifty. When they were done, Kerry and Mike ran back up on stage and bowed together, then slipped through the burgundy curtain and into the changing room. Tony came in behind them with their clothes, saying "Nice one, guys." He left right away.

Mike pulled a five-dollar bill out of his jockstrap and said, "Was that a fifty Burt gave you?"

"Yeah." Kerry was already pulling on a pair of khaki dress pants over his purple G-string. "I have to talk to you about him."

Mike paused. He threw his five-dollar bill into his gym bag with a bunch of others and pulled out a bottle of water, taking a long drink. "What about him?"

"Well, I don't know. Tonight I'm staying at his place."

"You and I have plans. After overtime. We're getting Chinese."

"His wife's away. He wants me to spend the night with him."

"So tell him no." Mike looked at Kerry head on. "Tell him you're busy."

"I can't. He's leaving for Paris in a couple days."

"Thank God. Get the creep out of here."

"He's asked me to go with him."

Mike froze. All around him the air felt cool where it touched his skin, still damp from dancing. He said nothing. He watched as Kerry put on his shirt. It was new, blue with long sleeves. It had a Polo logo on the chest. It was expensive.

"I already told him yes," Kerry said, and he sat down to put on his socks, as if what he'd just said was no big deal. "Burt's only going to be there for a month, but he told me I can stay longer. I can stay in his apartment in the seventh. I can travel. I just have to be there for him when he comes back to Paris."

Mike leaned down slowly and set his water bottle on the long bench in the middle of the room. The music was thumping out in the bar. This was what he'd been afraid of, and now here it was. He cleared his throat and spoke carefully.

"I'll save some money and come join you in Paris, when Burt's gone. Okay?"

"I'm sorry, Mike. I'll be busy." Kerry was already slipping on a pair of brown, tasseled loafers. These new shoes had shown up in the past week, along with the expensive shirts. He'd suddenly begun dressing like a preppy boy. "I'll be working," Kerry said. "Or traveling."

Mike felt like he was going to cry. "It's okay. I'll travel with you. I'll work with you."

Kerry stopped fiddling with his shoes and looked up at Mike. "It's not going to happen that way. I'm sorry."

"What do you mean?"

"I'm going to be in Europe alone."

"What have we been doing together, Kerry? What have we had here? Nothing? Have I been alone in this?"

"No. Look, we've had a lot of fun. You're a great guy. But now I'm going." Kerry stood up on the other side of the bench. The blond curls in his hair spun circles. He seemed very far away.

"Is it because I do porn? Is that the problem?" Mike could hear that his voice was starting to crack.

"Not at all. It's just, well, I have Burt now."

"What do you mean, you have Burt? He's just another john, no better than the lechers out there. He's just got more money."

"Don't make this ugly." Kerry pulled out a gold watch from the pocket of his dress pants and put it on.

"Don't make this ugly? Me? You're suddenly dumping me like this? In the fucking *changing room* at work? You're going with some married closet case to be his kept bitch, and you think *I'm* the one making it ugly? Fuck you, Kerry. I might do porn but at least I stand on my own two feet. Nobody owns

221

me."

"Sasha owns you."

"What? She does not."

"Do you pay rent?"

"What the fuck do you know? You can go to hell!"

Mike looked at the floor. It was true. He didn't pay rent. He hadn't given Sasha any money since they were saving money to make *Banging Billy*. She bought the groceries every week, never said anything about money.

"I'll leave now," Kerry said.

"That's it?"

"Pascal already knows it's my last night."

Mike stood facing Kerry, his water bottle on the bench between them, his clothes still on the floor where Tony had left them. "You mean you told the fucking *owner of the bar* before you told me? I had no idea you were such a god-damned coward. Or such a fucking asshole."

"Take care of yourself, Mike." Kerry stepped closer, reached out across the bench and put his hand on the side of Mike's neck, rubbing it gently. Mike smacked it away. Kerry turned, fully dressed, bag in hand, and walked out into the bar.

"Fuck you, Kerry! Fuck you!" Mike was shouting wildly at a disappearing blue shirt, but at the same time he was feeling an overwhelming desire to run forward and wrap his arms around that patch of expensive blue cotton, to stop what was inside it from getting away. He imagined bolting through the door beside the stage and into the bar in his jock strap, running up to Kerry as he was probably kissing Burt hello. But what would he say when he got there? And why would he want to chase a man who was leaving him this way?

When he turned and saw that Kerry's locker was empty,

the lock gone, he shut down, went blank. He didn't cry. Instead, he slipped into a kind of autopilot, where everything was tucked away. He was at work. He held it together. He moved deliberately, so the air would not shatter. He walked over to his clothes and picked them up off the floor – a pair of short denim cut-offs, his flannel shirt with no sleeves – and threw them in his locker. He put the water bottle in his gym bag, pulled out a pair of jeans and a T-shirt, put them on slowly, in silence, feeling mechanical, empty. He wanted to get to Sasha. She would comfort him, hold him. She would make him feel safe.

He put on his tennis shoes and walked to the door at the side of the stage so he could peek into the bar. Already there was no trace of Kerry. The teddy bears and lechers were talking and drinking, ogling the other strippers who were leaning against the back wall. Tony was serving two young guys some drinks. Pascal stood by the bar, laughing about something with the bartender. Nobody seemed to notice the emptiness in the room. It was as though Kerry had never been there, had never existed at all. Somewhere out on the streets of Los Angeles, Burt was probably even now driving Kerry back to a big house or a nice hotel somewhere, telling him what to pack.

Mike stepped backwards and let the stage door swing shut. It felt like he was watching himself from a spot in the ceiling. There he was, stepping back into the changing room, picking up his gym bag, grabbing his car keys, moving out the back door and into the parking lot. Then he was stepping into his old blue Nova, pulling out onto Sunset Boulevard, and pointing his headlights in the direction of the Lucky Pony. Everything quivered as he drove. The streetlights passed him one by one.

31
Old Fashioned

AS THE FLUTE intro started and the lights came up, Sasha stood in the middle of the stage. She was wearing an enormous white satin hoop skirt, covered with lace and pink ribbons. Her blouse had puffed sleeves, white satin to match the skirt, and pink ribbon at the shoulders. Her brunette wig was done in ringlets and dainty bows. This was her new number, and she began mouthing the words as Ella Fitzgerald sang, "I'm Old Fashioned."

She batted her eyes, trying to look quaint. She held her hands together behind her back and swiveled her body to the right and to the left as demurely as her large waist would allow. After the first lines, the rhythm picked up, the melody started, and she pulled out a frilly pink folding fan.

She knew that behind her the two shirtless dancing boys were already jumping out through the silver streamers and approaching her on either side. She had sewn their black satin shorts herself, and had found their black bow ties at a second hand shop in Burbank. It was a well-known fact that satin shorts and bow ties were all the costume a dancing boy ever needed. When their muscular bodies appeared in front of her, she pretended to be shocked at the sight, putting her hand to her chest and leaning back melodramatically. Mock palpitations ran through her, and she fluttered the fan as though she were about to faint. The boys caught her just as she was collapsing, and they propped her back up again, smoothing her dress. Then suddenly all three of them were happily doing synchronized dance steps. Step, shuffle, step, spin.

The trumpets blared and one of the boys pulled the pink fan from her hand, replacing it with a long black riding crop. She looked at it as if she didn't know what it was but, when the boy leaned over in front of her, she gave him a light smack on the behind and then gave the audience a wicked smile. Both boys abruptly spun behind her and pulled at her blouse. The Velcro she'd sewn down the back made it come off easily.

Underneath was a shiny black leather bustier with a bodice that was tight around her protruding stomach. Below her waist, the lace and ribbon of the hoop skirt clashed wonderfully with the bustier. She had hoped to appear in this moment as a fantastic hybrid – Little Bo Peep the Leather Dominatrix – and now, as the audience cheered in front of her, it seemed it was a complete success. She smacked the crop into the palm of her hand, just as she'd done a few moments before with her little pink fan. The crowd cheered.

The music crescendoed and the boys came up behind her, pulling at the last line of Velcro so that the hoop skirt fell down around her legs in a spectacular cascade of white satin. The transformation was complete. She stood in black leather hot pants, fishnet stockings, and amazing, six-inch high, black patent leather stilettos. If she fell she was sure to break an ankle, but the effect was dazzling, and entirely worth the risk.

She slapped her thigh with the riding crop and pushed both boys to the ground. One went down on his hands and knees in front of her, while the other wrapped his arms around her right leg. The song slowed to the closing lines and she batted her eyes again, bringing the act full circle, acting quaint and trying to look as innocent as possible.

After the last notes of the flute faded, she could barely hear herself yelling "thank you" over the applause and whistles. She bowed four times before finally slipping behind the silver streamers at the back of the stage and heaving a sigh of relief. It had worked. They loved her. She may be sad and lonely, but at least she still had this. She told the dancing boys to stay put, and she went back out for one final bow on her own.

She was thrilled to see Billy in her dressing room when she got there. She was still high from the performance as she whirled in and gave him a big, sloppy kiss on the cheek.

"Well, hello baby!" she said. "What a nice surprise. Better than a dozen roses waiting for me. Now, quick, untie me. I can barely breathe."

The back of her bodice was laced tightly and tied at the bottom. She could reach it herself, but she wanted to be close to her Billy. She turned around and felt his hand near the base of her back, untying the string. The bodice loosened.

"Ugh! How I suffer for beauty. I'm like a stuffed sausage in this thing. Now unzip the shorts, baby." She felt his hand slide down her backside. "Oh, you're an angel."

Unzipped and untied, she felt the blood rushing back. She took off the shoes, then the bodice and the hot pants. It didn't matter if Billy saw her there in her large underpants and padded bra. This was who she was. She left the wig on. The bows and ringlets made her look cute.

"The crowd loved my new number!" she said. "How they cheered! It was fantastic. Did you see it?" she asked.

"I caught the end," Billy said. "You were great."

"Oh, go on, flatter me." She turned around again, gestured to the clasp on her bra, and said, "Be a doll, won't you?"

He struggled to unclasp it.

"Jesus Billy, you're hopeless with a bra. No experience, I suppose."

She reached behind her back and undid it herself, turning to expose her waxed chest, the saggy flesh of her man-boobs, her belly protruding over the flesh-colored underpants. She quickly slipped on her fuzzy pink bathrobe, then sat down and began taking off her rings. All of a sudden it was clear that Billy was troubled.

"What's wrong? Why do you look so sad?" She set down her rings, leaned forward and put her hand on his knee.

"Kerry's going to Paris with Burt," he said.

"Oh, baby."

"It doesn't sound like he's coming back, at least no time soon. He doesn't want me to come visit."

"I'm so sorry." She stood up out of her chair and moved toward him, bending over so that she could hug him as he sat. He put his arms around her, pushed his face into her shoulder with such force that it surprised her. She held him that way for a while, awkwardly, standing as he sat, before Billy slowly pulled away. "When are they leaving?" she said. She sat back down and pulled her chair closer to Billy's.

"I don't know. A couple days. He already quit his job at Exposé. He broke up with me at work."

"Fucking bastard. I knew there was something I didn't like about that boy. I was trying so hard to be nice on your account, Billy."

"I can't believe I was so close to him and I had no idea he was such a mother fucking prick. It's like I was totally blinded because I cared so much about him."

227

"Don't blame yourself." She reached out and touched his arm. "I'm just sorry I brought Burt in with me that night, on your birthday even. Oh, if I'd known this was going to happen, I never would have done it."

"It's not your fault."

"But I feel terrible."

"Don't."

Sasha looked down. When she first told Burt that she knew of a working boy who might be interested in traveling to Paris with him, she had made it clear that if it all worked out she needed Burt to do two things for her in return. First, he was *never* to tell Kerry the true reason she'd introduced them. Secondly, he was to feign a certain disdain for Billy, and ask Kerry not to see him again. She had never before asked Burt for a favor, and he was happy to comply. If it worked he was going to get a beautiful boy.

What made her feel justified now, even slightly smug, was that the entire thing had been a test of Kerry's character. If he truly cared for Billy, he would not go. But if he could be bought, if Kerry valued Burt's fat wallet more than Billy's warm heart, he would be on the next plane to Paris. The answer was in the fact of his leaving.

"That boy is obviously cold-blooded, Billy. Strictly mercenary. Boys like that don't know how to love. He's not like you and me. Good thing we have each other."

"But Sasha," Billy said. He was leaning back in the old tattered chair next to her vanity, his legs spread wide. "I really liked him." All of a sudden, her Billy was crying, small fits at first, then more.

Her smugness fell away. She felt horrible. Billy was heartbroken. In the four months that she had come to know him, somehow an invisible line had grown from Billy's heart directly into hers, a kind of reverse umbilical cord that fed her all his emotion. During the good times, his happiness filled her with joy. During the bad times, his sadness destroyed her. His tears now made her feel responsible and guilty, but these feelings were tempered by her resolute knowledge that this was in fact good for him, that she had saved him from an even greater heartache if the entire charade with that Kerry had gone on longer. She had rescued her Billy from a cruel and unfeeling monster. He must never know.

She reached toward the counter and pulled a few tissues from a box, handing them to Billy.

He took them and held them to his face. "I really thought it was something. He was so gentle."

"Oh, baby, baby. This hurts so much right now, I know. I know. Come here."

She pulled him forward and he came out of the chair easily, moving onto his knees in front of her and resting his head on her lap. He sobbed. She put one hand on his back and with the other she stroked his hair. She said nothing. His tears wet her bathrobe. She sat there, petting him like a small kitten, until he finally became quiet and still.

"Billy, I have good news for you. But first I have to tell you something I've done that's very bad."

He looked up at her.

"I'm sorry to tell you now," she said. "But it's the good news that will make you happy."

Small strands of pink fuzz stuck to the stubble on his jaw. She brushed her hand across his face, careful not to scratch him with her long, plastic fingernails.

He looked confused.

"I've been keeping a secret from you," she said. "I don't know why. I'm so sorry. I was so afraid of losing you."

He sniffed and shook his head. "You're not going to lose me."

"Oh, but when you find out what I've done. What I've been hiding from you."

"What?"

"Steve hasn't been in New York. I told him *you* were."

He leaned back slowly until he came to rest on the chair behind him. He was staring at her.

"Billy, he doesn't want me at all. He only wants you. I was afraid he'd take you away from me. That you'd leave me behind and forget about me."

"You lied to me? And you told him I was in New York? Seriously? Why?"

"You're a very talented boy. Steve wants to offer you an exclusive contract. He wants to make you a star."

Billy's face lit up. "Really?"

She nodded and smiled.

"No way! Me? He wants to give me an exclusive contract? Are you sure?"

"He gave me the contract. It's sitting on my desk, waiting for you to sign. He wants you to come in and talk to him. Discuss your career with Cougar."

Billy stood up. "Sasha this is great! I can't believe it!" He stopped and looked at her. "How long have you known this?"

"A couple weeks. Almost a month."

"He told you this a month ago?"

"I'm afraid so. I'm sorry."

"How could you keep that a secret? You know how much this means to me."

She looked down and braced herself for his anger. "I know, baby. Like I said, I was so afraid of losing you. He doesn't have a contract for me. He wants me stuck behind that horrible desk doing sales calls for the rest of my life."

"When were you planning on telling me?"

"I don't know. I wasn't thinking. I've just been so scared." She pulled at the tissues, dabbed her nose. "Billy, being with you makes me so happy. I'm afraid that if you become successful without me, you'll forget who I am. After all, I'm just some fat, old slob in a dress, who can't even direct. And you're so incredible, so beautiful, so young. I think how much you must hate me."

"I don't hate you."

"It's not going to work Billy. I'm not going to be able to do it. They don't want me. None of the studios want me. I tried talking to the others again, and they all say the same. I'm not right for them. I'm just a piece of smelly shit nobody wants. I'm so scared of ending up all alone. And now you hate me too."

"I said I don't hate you. You're like my family."

"Really?" Her heart lifted.

"Yes. And you can so direct. You're great. Just look at *Banging Billy*, look at our *Muscle Party* scene. It's all great. Everything you do is great."

"Steve says it's you. He says you're such good sex that even a monkey could direct you. He called me a monkey."

"A monkey?"

She nodded, blew her nose into the tissues. "I'll take you in and introduce you to him next week. He's wanted to meet you for a while. He doesn't care about me."

"How can he call you a monkey? God damn him."

"Look at me, Billy. How can anybody take me seriously?" She turned toward the mirror. Billy stood behind her. Her mascara was starting to run. Her robe was falling open. Her lipstick was smeared. She began laughing. "Ugh! Would you look at that ugly bitch! She's a mess. Get her out of here!" Then she sighed and looked up at Billy in the mirror. "I'm going to have to butch it up if I want to succeed in this business. Maybe Steve did me a favor calling me Cliff Hardman."

"Sasha, no. The problem is with Steve, not you. The problem is with the studios and all those old fags that run them. They're fucking dinosaurs from the 1970's. They think we should all look like the Village People."

"Baby, don't forget that I was at my peak in 1970. I *sucked off* one of the Village People, okay? Well, come to think of it, *several* of them."

"But you're no dinosaur. You're fantastic, Sasha. You're amazing."

"You're very sweet. I turned forty yesterday."

"What? Why didn't you tell me? I would have done something. Had a party."

"No, Billy. So help me goddess, you tell *anybody* I turned forty and I'll shoot you dead."

"Well, happy birthday."

"The clock is ticking. I'm going to have to become Cliff Hardman."

"You are not. You're Sasha. It's who you are."

"Well, I suppose there's one thing I could do." She had always felt so much pride. What she was about to say was incredibly difficult. She had always made her way on her own. "You could help me," she said sheepishly.

"And you could have told me about that contract right away. You didn't."

"I know. But I've told you now, and it's not too late. I was just so afraid of losing you. I am so incredibly sorry. It was wrong." She paused. "Please help me?"

Billy said nothing.

She shook her head and then began pulling off her fake eyelashes as she spoke, staring into the mirror. "You're right. I can't ask anything of you. I'll figure it out myself. What am I thinking? It would be far too much to expect some old-fashioned *gratitude*. After all, I haven't done anything for you, really. Just a staring role in your own movie, your first scene with a major studio, now an exclusive contract ready for you to sign. Oh, and a place to sleep and a fully stocked refrigerator. You don't owe me anything. I'm just so selfish, out for my own glory all the time, never doing anything for you. How can you even stand me?"

Billy sighed. "What is it? What do you want me to do?"

She turned and looked at him. "Don't sign that contract."

"What do you mean, don't sign?"

"Tell Steve that you won't sign unless he gives me a contract too. A contract to direct. For Sasha."

"Oh." Billy walked over to the dressing room door. He stood there, staring at the bright blue sequined dress that she had left hanging on the back of the door. He reached out and touched the material. "I don't know. I mean, of course you should have a contract too, but…"

"I'm sorry." She turned her back to him again. "I shouldn't have asked. You don't owe me anything."

Her turned and looked at her. "Why would I do that for you after you've been lying to me?"

"I haven't exactly been *lying*, Billy. I was, well, *hesitating*. Out of fear. And I regret it. It was stupid of me. You just mean so much to me. I get all confused."

233

He came over to her, stood beside her and looked at her in the mirror. He reached down and picked up one of her makeup brushes. "What if Steve said no to me? What if he said, 'Fine, I don't want you if you come with Sasha.'"

"You're right. Absolutely right. I don't want to drag you down with me. That wouldn't be fair. I'm a fat monkey on your back, some horrible weight you're carrying. You go on without me. I'll be fine." She yanked off her wig and looked in the mirror. "I'm Cliff Hardman."

Mike put down the brush. "Stop it."

"The eighties will be over soon. Sasha is history. The nineties will be all about Cliff Hardman. That's me! Cliff! Cliff!"

"Stop."

"Call me CLIFF!"

Suddenly Mike exploded with anger, his voice bouncing off the walls of the tiny room. "Shut the fuck up, Dale!"

Dale, stunned, set the wig on the counter, leaned forward and opened the jar of cold cream, then began rubbing it into his cheeks.

Mike sat back down in the chair near him, but Dale ignored him. They sat in silence for several minutes.

Finally, staring at the floor, Mike whispered the word. "Okay."

Dale's face was covered in a white mask of cold cream. He turned and looked at Mike. "What?"

"I'll do it. After all, we're partners."

Dale couldn't believe it. He felt like his heart might burst. "Really?" he said. "You won't sign unless Sasha signs too?"

"Sure."

"There are no promises," Dale said. "Steve might sign us both, but he could just as easily become furious and dump us both. You'll take that chance? Don't play with me, now. Do you *seriously* mean that you'll do this?"

Mike nodded, and he looked almost surprised. "Yes," he said. "I do."

PART FOUR

SILVER DICKS

32
And the Winner Is

MIKE WAS STANDING at the bar in a crowded theatre lobby as he dug a finger into the collar of his tuxedo shirt and pulled at his bow tie.

"Here you go." The bartender pushed a gin and tonic toward him. "That's three fifty."

The smallest bill Mike had in his wallet was a hundred. "It's all I have," he said, handing it over.

The bartender raised an eyebrow. "I can't break that." He looked around. "Look, it's on the house." He winked and turned to take care of someone else.

Mike took a sip and looked at the old theatre around him. It had seen better days. Somebody had tried to spruce the lobby up a bit for the occasion, but the silver garland strung across the doorframes only made the room seem even shabbier. A large banner read, "1993 Silver Dick Awards."

There were scuffmarks on the walls and the carpet was worn thin in places. Even so, the people filling up the room looked amazing. There were well-built, handsome men everywhere, and almost every one of them was wearing a black tie. The women in the room wore evening gowns, as did some of the men. Everybody had cleaned up well.

Luke Champion was on the other side of the lobby, holding a drink and talking with two other models. His tuxedo was skintight black leather from head to toe, and his muscular body filled it out nicely. The two models he was with were less famous than Luke, but then again most everyone here was. Mike knew who they were. One was Jeff Shaw, whose career had almost been ruined last year when an ex-boyfriend released a video of him letting a dog lick gravy off his balls, and the other was Kevin Bender, whose legendary dick turned sharply to the left. Many bottoms were afraid of Bender. Mike wondered what it would be like.

Bender said something now, and in response Luke tipped back his five-o'clock shadow and threw laughter at the ceiling. Mike had met Luke on several occasions, but each time the superstar top had been distant and aloof, not talking and laughing like this, not smiling. Each time Mike's heart fell.

"He's gorgeous," the bartender said.

"Huh?"

"Luke Champion. He's gorgeous."

"Oh, yeah. He's okay."

"Okay? He's a fucking god. You've met him, haven't you? What's he like?"

"He doesn't seem to remember me."

"Doesn't remember *you*? I doubt that." The bartender smiled again, this time more flirtatiously. There was something genuine in his smile, almost boyish. His dark black hair contrasted nicely with his rosy, flushed cheeks.

Mike shrugged. "He's Luke Champion. I'm just some bottom."

The bartender rolled his eyes. "Yeah, right. Just some bottom, my ass."

"No. *My* ass," Mike said, smiling.

"I'm Greg," the bartender said, and he smiled back. "Are you here alone tonight?"

"No, I'm with someone." Mike looked around the room.

"Well, listen, I'm sure this happens to you all the time, but, well, here's my number." Greg was already writing on a bar napkin. "If you ever want to meet for a drink, or whatever."

As Mike said thanks and took the napkin, somebody came up and grabbed his elbow.

"You're Billy Knight," a voice said.

When he turned, he saw an old man standing right behind him. His eyes were red and watery. His face was blotchy, and his stomach was huge.

"Yes, I am." Mike smiled. It was important always to smile, to be pleasant to the people who recognized you.

"I've seen all your movies. I'm your biggest fan. Will you sign me?" Suddenly the old man was pulling up his shirt. There, across his distended belly, were the signatures of at least twenty other models who were there that night. The man held out a black pen. His stomach was blotchier than his face.

"Sure," Mike said, his smile frozen into politeness. In the muddle of names he saw Luke Champion's signature, larger than the rest. He signed above it, slightly larger, just under the man's right nipple. His hand rubbed against the man's skin. "That's quite a collection you have there," he said as he gave back the pen.

"Yes! Touched by all these porn stars! How lucky am I?" There was a fanatical eagerness in the man's smile. "I won't bathe for weeks!"

Mike leaned forward and put a hand on the man's shoulder. He knew how to make people feel special, and he knew that the sole reason he was now able to bring in $1,000 per scene was because people like this bought his videos. He had to remember to be grateful. The old man would probably tell his friends about this moment for years to come, about how one night Billy Knight put a hand on his shoulder and smiled. It was an easy thing to give.

"Which of my movies is your favorite?" Mike asked. It was a selfish question. He always wanted to know.

"Oh, it has to be *Big Top Bottoms*. You with that sexy ringmaster, and then the strongman. Amazing."

Mike nodded. "That was my first full-length video with Cougar." It seemed like a lifetime ago, but it was only four years.

"I know. I've got your entire videography memorized. Even your very first movie, *Banging Billy*, although not quite as professional as your Cougar films, is absolutely fantastic."

Banging Billy had developed a bit of a cult following among Mike's highly dedicated fans. It was re-released by Cougar two years ago, when they bought the rights from Stunning Productions.

"Thanks. I was so damn nervous when we made that."

"You? Billy Knight? Nervous? Impossible."

"No, really. I was. I mean I loved it, don't get me wrong. But I was nervous at first." Mike paused. "How about my more recent movies? How do you like those?"

"Oh, those are good too."

He wondered if it was just his imagination, or if the man's voice sounded less enthusiastic. Out of the corner of his eye he saw Bender laughing with Luke on the other side of the room. "You know," he said, "for your autographs, you should get Kevin Bender too. See? Over there." He pointed through the crowd. "I hear even his signature is crooked."

As the man laughed and craned his neck, Mike said, "Now, if you'll please excuse me," and then he slipped away, offering a nod to the bartender as he went. He heard the old man yell out, "Nice meeting you, Billy!" and Mike waved back a little goodbye. He couldn't help wondering how the guy had gotten in. Tonight was invitation only.

Mike headed toward the back wall, pretending he was walking toward somebody in particular. Other people said, "Hi Billy," as he passed, and he smiled and nodded. He knew pretty much everybody of any consequence in the room – the other established models, the directors, the producers and cameramen. It was true that he didn't know all the little production assistants, the editors, or some of the new models, but it was safe to say they knew him, or rather they knew Billy Knight.

"Billy, good luck tonight!" somebody said. Mike didn't know the guy, but he smiled back and held up two crossed fingers in the air as he walked on.

Years before, he'd figured out that nobody liked an arrogant porn star, not really. People might pretend to, but behind their backs they said terrible things. It happened time and time again. He'd watched the models with long careers and realized that the way to make a career last was to be liked, be easy to work with. Too many guys showed up for shoots strung out, late, or – it was hard to believe – didn't show up at all. Mike had carefully built a reputation for being hardworking and professional. The average model's career lasted only three years. Mike was now in his fourth. He was concentrating on longevity.

He saw the back of Steve Logan's head, the old army-style brush cut, and he tried veering off to the right, but it was too late. Steve had turned and was already walking over.

"Billy! How are you?" Steve gave Mike a handshake that was a little too strong. "It's been a while."

"Yeah, it has. I'm good, thanks. You?"

"Oh, great. Never better. Keep churnin' out the fuck flicks." Steve thrust his hips lewdly.

"I saw Cougar's latest movie," Mike said. "That new bottom's hot."

"Harry Hole? He's something, ain't he? Quite an ass on that boy."

"Definitely." Throughout the 80s most of the popular models were hairless, with waxed chests and shaved assholes. This new Harry Hole was going against all that. He looked more like a 70s model, with a hairy chest and a manpussy to match. Mike himself was naturally not very hairy, so he'd never had to wax his chest, but he still always shaved his hole. Hairy assholes always looked dirty to him. Even so, he wondered now if a shaved hole would eventually date him. He'd have to watch the trends.

"Harry's talented," Steve said, stroking his mustache, "but he's no Billy Knight. Nobody has your enthusiasm on screen. When are you going to work for me again?"

"Don't know." Mike gave a friendly, challenging smile. "When are you going to make it worth my while?" There was a difference between arrogance and standing up for yourself. There was a place where one ended and the other began.

The exclusive contract Mike had with Cougar ended the year before, and he'd chosen not to sign on with Steve again. He wanted to pick and choose his own films, deciding which directors and studios he wanted to work with, jumping from one to the next with every project. He absolutely refused to make a movie unless he could choose his scene partners. It had become common knowledge in the industry that you didn't fuck Billy Knight unless Billy Knight wanted you to. So far, the only one who had refused to do a scene with him was Luke Champion.

Since leaving Cougar, Mike had been managing his career more or less himself. At this point it was important not to be overexposed. In his first three years he'd made over 30 hardcore videos. He'd done 92 scenes in total. Mike knew that his initial rush of films had to be carefully followed up with not-too-frequent, top quality releases. A new Billy Knight movie had to be an occasion. People would have to wait for it.

He felt that his career was at a crossroads. He could cement his superstar status, getting himself firmly planted at the top of the heap with the major superstars, or he could slip downhill, becoming just another fading model who had stayed too long at the fair. The $1,000 Mike pulled in for a scene was nothing compared to someone like Luke Champion, who could pull as much as $8,000 per scene. Not only did Mike still dream of doing a scene with Luke, but he wanted to make the same money as Luke. He wanted to be that famous, that highly sought after.

"I got you started in this business," Steve said now. "When are you going to pay me back?"

"Steve, my friend." Mike put his hand on Steve's back. He knew he could say almost anything, be as confrontational as he wanted, as long as he said it with a smile on his face, or maybe a flirtatious nudge. This was how he dealt with men like Steve. "First of all, Sasha got me started. You took over from there. And while I'm really grateful you gave me that exclusive contract, let's talk about who owes who. For my one-off fee, you've got footage of me that you can sell and sell and sell. When you put that footage in multiple movies, there's no additional payment for me. You're still making a shitload of money off me, but right now I'm not making anything off you. So when are *you* going to pay *me* back?"

"What are you talking about? Model royalties on video sales? You know that's rare."

"Might be rare, but it's fair." He smiled and playfully punched Steve's arm.

"Wasn't in your contract," Steve said.

"That's right. My problem's not with you, it's with your contracts. And that's why I'm not working for you."

"Well, until you come to your senses, I guess we'll just keep recycling what we've got. You know you'll be in a new Cougar movie soon. *The Best of Billy Knight: the Cougar Years.* I haven't officially announced it yet. It's a bit under wraps, but it should be out soon."

"Steve, I wish you wouldn't. I don't want to be overexposed."

"Overexposed? It's a little late for that, don't you think? Beside, you got no say in it, do you Billy?"

"So what are you going to pay me for it?"

Steve laughed. "Like I said. Wasn't in your contract. All that footage is mine."

"Yeah. See you around Steve." Mike turned and walked away, leaving Steve standing there alone.

He passed a few more people who said hello, and he thought about what Steve had said. Suddenly it hit him. His dislike for Steve Logan was blinding him. This new movie wasn't a bad thing after all. Only the biggest stars had 'Best of' compilations, and they were always tops. This would be the first time a total bottom had a 'Best of.' It could make Billy Knight more marketable. He hadn't shot a new video since *Between a Cock and a Hard Place*, which was almost four months ago even though it was just now being released. The studios knew Mike was demanding bigger money now, and nobody wanted him. This could change that. In the meantime, there were other ways to pay the rent.

Mike had progressed from stripping into the upper echelon. He was a private escort, turning all his tricks through an agency – but they weren't tricks anymore, and they weren't johns. They were clients. Rutherford Models took all his calls and contacted him on his pager with times and locations. They even sent over a driver to take him to the client. He could turn down a job if he wanted, but the more you did that the less you got work. Going through an agency provided a certain amount of safety. Somebody always knew where you were and who you were with. Rutherford Models was known for screening all their new clients carefully. Of course they took a third of the fee, and you had to tip the driver, but it was worth it.

He'd tried working independently for a while, but it was too difficult and too dangerous. Independent escorts had to run their own ads in the papers, and consequently they had to deal with all sorts of stupid things, like crank callers who just wanted phone sex, and guys who made appointments but no-showed. There were so many difficult clients out there: the ones who got a strange thrill out of having escorts come to the door just to reject them, the ones who refused to pay afterward or who paid less than agreed or who tried to use bad checks and stolen credit cards, and of course there were the ones who turned into stalkers or became violent.

Now if Mike ever had a problem with a client he just told the agency and they put the client on their blacklist, which they shared with other agencies. Mike would never have to deal with the guy again, and it would protect other escorts too. But bad clients didn't happen too often with Rutherford Models. The agency was top of the line, and Billy Knight charged out at $300 an hour. The agency took a third of that, and Mike walked with the rest after he'd tipped the driver. Clients didn't usually agree to pay that kind of money and then act up.

Although once upon a time Mike had imagined getting into porn would be a way out of prostitution, the money had become so much better that he couldn't stop. And the truth was, even with his status he wasn't really making enough out of porn to completely earn his living. Besides, there were a lot of guys who paid top dollar to have sex with a porn star. Likewise, there were cheap hustlers all over the world who longed to do even just one widely distributed porn film, so they could charge higher rates. The LA escorts who didn't do porn were charged out at only $150 an hour. In other cities it was just $100. Mike was happy he'd already made it this far, that he could pocket almost $200 for an hour's work, plus sometimes a tip. Whenever he got sick of it – if he had to have sex with someone who was ugly or disrespectful – he reminded himself that there were worse ways to be making money. He thought of washing dishes back in Luigi's Tavern. There was no way he could ever work in a restaurant or shop again. Still, he knew there were risks. He remained diligent about safe sex. He got an HIV test every three months, like clockwork, and every three months breathed a sigh of relief.

Mike felt someone slap him lightly on the ass now, and he turned around.

"Hey there." It was Rafael.

"Where'd you go?" Mike asked.

"I was in the bathroom. Sorry." Rafael was big and dark, with a broad chest. He was wearing a black tuxedo and a shiny red bowtie. He sniffed and brushed his nose.

Mike shook his head. "Let's go sit down." He started walking toward the theatre doors without waiting for an answer. Rafael followed. The crowd narrowed at the doors, and Rafael stood close behind him, his hand on Mike's ass again.

People began jostling to get through the doors and grab a good seat. Mike paused to let Gloria Glimmer step in front of him. Her dress sparkled and her low voice came back at him booming. "Thank you, Billy." She sounded like a football player. "At least there's one gentleman in the crowd tonight. All these old fags forget their manners when there's an award on hand."

Mike and Rafael ended up sitting next to some production coordinators they'd never met. They told Mike that they loved his work, and he thanked them. Then he turned away and settled in.

When the curtain came up, a beautiful drag queen began lip-synching to Ethel Merman doing "There's no business like show business." The queen's name was Amanda Manning, and she had on a long green dress with a high slit that revealed surprisingly feminine legs. Mike had met Amanda twice. She was far too thin and gorgeous to be doing Ethel Merman. Sasha should be the one up on that stage.

Rafael leaned over and said, "She almost looks real." His eyes were wide.

Mike kept staring at the stage and just said, "Yeah."

Out came ten buff dancing boys. They were bare-chested and wearing purple spandex briefs with matching feathered hats and boas. Amanda was surrounded in a sea of feathers and muscle. She fell back and two of them caught her, lifted her up above their heads and carried her to the front of the stage. Mike wondered how many buff boys it would take to

249

carry Sasha. They all danced and twirled, and it became clear that each dancing boy had a shiny silver letter on his ass. At the end of the number they lined up and began turning around to push their muscle butts out at the crowd. Their tiny briefs spelled out the words "SILVER DICK" in metallic letters. Amanda took a bow in the space between the two words, and the curtain came down.

Rafael clapped frantically. "She was great!" He was yelling to Mike above the din of the applause.

Mike nodded slowly and continued staring at the stage. Out of the corner of his eye, he could see Rafael's fawning smile. There was a time when he wondered if he loved Rafael, but that time had passed.

Rafael's company was fine, good enough, at least when he wasn't snorting coke, which Rafael did too frequently for Mike's taste. But often, like tonight, Mike couldn't help feeling annoyed with him. With only two films under his belt, Rafael still spent too much time staring starry-eyed Mike's way. Yet they always had great sex, and there was nobody else for Mike that he could see, at least not now. He absentmindedly lifted his hand to the jacket pocket that held the bartender's phone number.

When Mike thought about it, which he tried not to do too often, he was sometimes able to admit to himself that what he really wanted was somebody who could make him feel the way Kerry once had, back in the early days. But now whenever he remembered Kerry he cringed.

A few years ago he'd bumped into Burt at the Manhole Sauna and had asked about Kerry. He couldn't help himself. The words just came out into the mist of the steam room as he and Burt sat next to each other wrapped in their white towels. Mike learned that Kerry was still in Paris, in Burt's apartment by the Eiffel Tower. It became clear that Burt was firmly established as Kerry's sole keeper, that Kerry had managed to become one of the elite escorts whose sponsor paid for everything. Mike knew it would be costing Burt somewhere between $10,000 and $20,000 a month just to keep Kerry.

Mike himself held his clients at arm's length – even his regulars. They could only contact him through the agency. He had no desire to give himself over to just one sponsor the way Kerry had, or even to a few sponsors who would share him, as some guys did. Sponsored escorts always said they still maintained their freedom, but he didn't believe it.

What Burt had said next hurt most. "Kerry is such a tender fuck." Mike's stomach heaved at the words. "I shouldn't even put it like that," Burt added, and then spoke more slowly, wistfully. "He doesn't fuck. He makes love."

That was the moment Mike finally decided that he'd never really had anything special with Kerry at all, not even briefly, that the gentle way Kerry had fucked him had nothing to do with the way Kerry felt. It was simply a question of technique. Mike left the Manhole that night without even jacking off. He didn't feel like it anymore. He just went home.

Now, as the applause for the skinny Ethel Merman finally died down, Mike saw that a small podium had been set up on the stage. Out walked the Master and Mistress of Ceremonies, a sexy man and woman dressed as Tarzan and Jane. It was Miles O'Beef and Lady Lesbos Lavender. Having them as MCs for the night had been somewhat controversial. The Silver Dick awards were just for gay films, hot man on man sex or solo scenes only. Miles and Lady Lesbos only did bi and straight films.

Miles' career had been established on the fact that he looked a bit like Miles O'Keeffe, who'd played the lead in the 1981 Tarzan film. But Miles O'Beef was well known for not caring what he fucked. He just needed a place for his sizable dick. His first and most famous film was the ape-man spoof he did with Lady Lesbos called *He Swings Both Ways*. Although Miles had never made an exclusively gay film, there was no denying that he was beautiful, so he was popular with the Silver Dick audience.

As far as Lady Lesbos went, rumor had it that her name was a lie, that in her private life she had no lesbian proclivities at all. She just had sex with women on video to get the straight men hot. Even so, the fact that she could deep throat a guy as big as Miles and take a dick up her ass better than most of the gay men in the room gave her a great deal of esteem with this crowd.

Miles and Lady Lesbos were making jokes and saying what an honor it was to be hosting the Silver Dick awards. They spoke surprisingly well and almost seemed like real actors, which Mike figured must be why they were asked to MC. When they introduced Larry Jones, who founded Stud Studios back in the early 70s, they called him the granddaddy of gay porn. Jones came up to present the first award and said, "To be honest, I'd much rather be somebody's daddy than their granddaddy, but at my age I'll take what I can get."

They started giving away all little awards first: Best Set Design, Best Lighting, even Best Food on Set, which Mike thought was pretty stupid. He pulled out a pen and a piece of paper and handed them to Rafael, saying, "Would you mind doing it? I told Dale I'd write down the winners."

"No problem," Rafael said, and began dutifully taking notes.

Looking along the row in front of them, Mike started counting how many people there he'd had sex with. Only three. Up on stage, set designers and lighting guys walked off with their shiny Silver Dicks in their hands. Every once in a while there would be a break between awards where they'd have another act. A comedian came out and did stand-up about the industry. A bunch of dancers did some kind of modern dance which made no sense to Mike, but the guys wore almost nothing and they looked hot, so that was cool. Miles and Lady Lesbos changed costumes a few times. A priest and a nun. A prisoner and a lady cop. Eventually they got to the more interesting awards, like Best Wrestling Video, Best Leather Scene. After that came Best Flip-flop, where the bottom and topped switched places midway, and then came Best Orgy.

When they announced the winner of the Best Solo Scene, Mike perked up to hear the presenter call out, "Antonio Savage!" People started clapping and up walked Tony, the old waiter from Exposé. He accepted the award with the director and cameraman, and said, "Mostly, I'd like to thank my girlfriend for all her support."

Finally they came to the nominees for Best Three-way. Mike was up for this award. He'd spent two days skewered like a rotisserie chicken in an expensive house in the Hollywood hills, and he was glad all the hard work had led to a nomination. The film, *Confessions of a Hollywood Pool Boy*, had sold well, and he'd been the star, but that was almost a year ago now.

He sat on his hands as the presenter read out the other nominations for Best Three-way.

"Mark Adonis, Max Pole, and Randy Scott in *Dick Him When He's Down*, directed by Montgomery Boss, videography by Derrick Lamont. Enrique Verga, Ramón Fuerte, and Alfonso Gómez in *Spanish Harlem Hunks...*"

The competition Mike was most worried about was from *Spanish Harlem Hunks*. It was a hot scene with three gorgeous men in an alley. He eyed Enrique Verga sitting up toward the front of the theatre, eager to collect his Silver Dick.

"Good luck, Mike," Rafael said, and squeezed his hand.

The presenter said, "And the winner is..." then made a big show of opening the silver envelope in his hand. "*Spanish Harlem Hunks!*"

Mike began clapping enthusiastically. It was the only way he could think of to hide his disappointment. He felt Rafael's hand squeeze his leg.

One of the production assistants to his left immediately leaned over and said, "You should have won, Billy." Mike gave a pained grin and thanked him.

Rafael leaned in from the other side. "I'm so sorry. At least you've already got a couple Silver Dicks under your belt."

Mike nodded slowly and continued staring straight ahead. He'd won two awards before – Best Newcomer in 1989 for *Big Top Bottoms*, and Best Leather Scene in 1990, when he was strapped into a sling and worked over by a guy wearing nothing but a black leather vest and a biker cap. Still, he would like to have won Best Three-way as well. He took solace now in the fact that the two awards that mattered the most to him tonight were still to come: Best Sexual Performer, and Best Director.

Best Sexual Performer was Mike's last chance for an award this evening. He didn't think his chances of winning were very good. In the short history of the Silver Dicks, the Best

Sexual Performer award had never once gone to a bottom. The industry still lionized all the big, macho tops.

Mike wanted the award, in part, because of Luke Champion. Luke won Best Sexual Performer in 1991, and Mike thought that if he himself could win it this year, he'd finally be able to get Luke to agree to do a scene with him. It would be like being the Homecoming King and Queen together, only better. It would secure his place as a superstar.

Rafael started whispering into his ear. "You are so great. You're the best."

Finally he turned to look at Rafael. He knew this was why he kept Rafael at his side – this constant adoration. Deep down, Mike needed it.

Before they'd met, Rafael hadn't made a single movie, and sometimes Mike wondered if the real reason Rafael picked him up at the Tricky Dick's a year ago was professional interest, a way to start a career. Within five minutes of being introduced, Rafael had said that he wanted to do porn. As they rolled around in bed later that first evening, Mike suspected that the sex was some kind of audition. It hadn't bothered Mike. If Rafael was trying to prove what a good sexual performer he was, Mike certainly benefited from the demonstration. He'd been benefiting ever since.

Up on stage now they gave away the awards for Best Music, Best Editing, and Best Videography. Rafael jotted down the names and titles. Finally it came time to announce the winner of the Best Sexual Performer. Mike felt his palms beginning to sweat. Rafael reached out and put a hand on his arm.

Miles and Lady Lesbos stood on stage dressed as a doctor and a nurse and announced the presenter. It was Luke Cham-

255

pion himself. He swaggered out in his tight leather tux, smirking at the cheering crowd.

"Each year at the Silver Dicks," he said, "some lucky guy wins the Best Sexual Performer award, like I did two years ago." His voice was low and steady. He flashed a cocky smile at the audience, and somebody whistled. "The award is given for work that sets a standard in the industry for high quality sexual performance. This year's nominees are…"

Mike knew this list by heart. Rick Hunt, a top. Derek Rockland, a top. Brett Titan, a top. And finally, last but not least, him. He was nominated for his work in *Midnight Barracks*, where he'd serviced a roomful of army guys in the final scene.

He tried to tell himself he should just be happy with being nominated. It was good to be in such company. The other nominees were all highly regarded in the industry. He told himself it was okay to lose, but he didn't really believe it. He wanted that award.

Luke Champion finished reading the list of nominees. He cleared his throat as he slowly opened the small silver envelope. "Ladies and gentlemen, I'm very pleased to announce to you that the winner of the 1993 Best Sexual Performer award goes to none other than the incredibly talented…" Here he paused. He cleared his throat again. Then he leaned forward and spoke directly into the microphone, lowering his voice further and speaking louder so that the words reverberated around the theatre. "Billy Knight, for his work in *Midnight Barracks!*"

Mike felt like he'd been jolted in the chest. Everyone was clapping. Some were whistling. He was only vaguely aware of Rafael hugging him as he stood up and then began stepping over people to get to the end of the row. Several different hands slapped his ass as he went by. When he finally got to the aisle, it felt like the stage was a mile away, and he concentrated on not tripping, on moving down the faded red carpet smoothly and negotiating the steps up onto the stage with as much confidence and sex appeal as he could muster, given the swirling in his head and the tightness in his chest.

Luke held out the Silver Dick – its smooth and chrome-like surface reflecting all the lights, the long shaft and the perfectly round silver balls. Mike swore there was something new in the way Luke stared at him as he approached the podium. His dream fuck was actually smiling at him, almost leering, and as Mike took the award in his hands, those thick arms reached around him and gave him an enormous hug right there on stage, brushing dark stubble against his cheek. It was all so abrupt and unexpected that Mike held the award awkwardly with one hand as he put the other around Luke's wide back. For a moment he became lost in a wall of muscle, and what nobody in the audience heard that night were the two words Luke whispered into his ear. *Congratulations, kid.*

Mike hadn't prepared a speech, but he knew who he wanted to thank most of all. "I'd like to thank Steve Logan of Cougar Studios for his part in launching my career, and all the others I've worked with as well, including Gavin Kennedy of Magnum Man and Joe Butch over at Hard Bodies. But most importantly I'd like to thank Sasha Zahore, who has helped me and supported me more than anyone I've ever known in my entire life." He wanted desperately to be able to express how much she meant to him, but he wasn't sure how to put it. There was something big inside him where his thoughts of her lived, right next to his thoughts of Dale, something so large it felt beyond measure. "I carry her around inside me," he blurted out. It was an odd thing to tell this audience, in this moment, but he paused and nodded to himself. That was it. That was what he felt for her. He gathered himself and moved forward. "Also, a huge thanks to my fans. I'd like to take this opportunity to make an announcement, something my fans will like. I've got a new movie coming out soon, *The Best of Billy Knight: the Cougar Years*. It's gonna be hot. Check it out." He gave his most charming smile and lifted his Silver Dick in the air. "Thank you so much."

The audience applauded wildly as he walked backstage. There was a photographer waiting for him, and he posed for a quick publicity shot with the Silver Dick in his hands, which was just a stand-in award. After the shot he had to give the award back to the photographer. Mike would have to pick up his own Silver Dick, with his name engraved, from a warehouse in Burbank the following week.

Miles and Lady Lesbos were already announcing the next presenter as Mike slipped quietly back into the audience. People whispered congratulations to him as he slid down the aisle toward Rafael, who gave him a soft kiss on the cheek and said, "You are my star."

Mike waited impatiently as they gave away the award for Best Assistant Director, then Best Videographer. Finally there were only three more awards to go: Best Director, Best Sex Scene, and Best Video of the Year.

The Best Director award was making him anxious. He'd been worried about it all night, almost more than he'd been worried about his own nominations.

Larry Jones came out again, this time to present the Best Director award, but he began by talking about what it was like to direct porn in the 70s, how it was completely illegal and how they had to keep their locations a secret so the cops wouldn't raid the sets. Larry seemed excited, like an old man rambling on about his youth, about the good old days. Finally he read the nominations. "And the nominees for Best Director are: Weston Pierce for *When Cops Go Bad*, Blane Handsome for *Man Quest*, Taylor Cooper for *Lumberjack Jack-off*, and Sasha Zahore for *My Swim Coach Loves Me.*"

Mike's heart was thumping in his chest. He leaned back in his chair as though he were about to fall. He wanted it for Sasha so badly. Rafael leaned in and touched his arm again.

This was the third time that the name 'Sasha Zahore' had been read out in a list of nominees for Best Director. She'd never won. Earlier that night Mike had tried to convince Sasha to come with him to the ceremony, but she absolutely refused, barking, "Why should I go? So they can snub me again? The motherfuckers." She stayed home. Mike called up Rafael at the last minute and asked him to take Sasha's place.

In 1991 Sasha had been nominated for Best Director for her work on *Beach Boy Bingo* and again in 1992 for *When the Cock Crows*, but Mike knew that *My Swim Coach Loves Me* was particularly important to her, that she'd dreamed of doing this film about a university swim team for years. It was a Cougar film, and although Steve hadn't allowed her to film the synchronized swimming scene she'd wanted – naked guys with erections rising up out of the water – she'd been able to do most everything else: the swim coach with the whistle, the spunky young men playing in the pool, the shots of athletic swimmers doing the butterfly naked. Mike was in three scenes himself, as he played the star swimmer and the coach's favorite. They had been long, difficult shoots, but the results were spectacular.

On stage Larry rustled the envelope. "And the winner is..." Larry looked twice at the name, and actually looked offstage as though there had been some mistake. He stared back at the audience and said, "Ladies and Gentlemen, this wouldn't happen in my day. Drag queens didn't direct porn back then, but here it is. The winner of the Best Director award is Sasha Zahore, for *My Swim Coach Loves Me.*"

In that moment, Mike found that he felt even more pleased than when he himself had won. Sasha had wanted this for so long. He wished that she was sitting at his side right now, wished he'd been able to talk her into being there.

Over the audience applause, Larry announced, "Sasha Zahore couldn't be with us tonight. Accepting the award on her behalf is Billy Knight."

Mike stood up and began his second trip to the stage that evening. People cheered. Everyone in the industry knew that Sasha and Billy went together, like bookends. There were rumors. Some people said they were lovers. Others assumed that it was a professional arrangement, that Billy was being kept. Once Mike had caught wind of gossip that Sasha was actually Billy's real-life uncle. It made him smile. He didn't care. People were always making up theories to explain things they didn't understand.

On stage he pulled out the small piece of paper Sasha had given him just in case, and he read the one sentence she'd written. "Miss Zahore wanted me to tell everyone that she's terribly sorry she couldn't be with us tonight, because she's home ill." The rest he made up on his own. "Three years ago, when Sasha had the vision to start these Silver Dick awards, she did it because we weren't getting enough recognition at the straight Erotic Entertainment Awards. Everyone knows that she discovered me, but not everyone knows that every single person in this room owes her. We wouldn't even be sitting here tonight if it weren't for her. We wouldn't have the

Silver Dick awards. She's been fantastic at raising the profile of gay porn and bringing in some much-needed fun."

"People who have worked with her on shoots know how tough she can be, and we all know she's got a reputation for being a major bitch." Mike heard a ripple of laughter from the audience. "That's why we love her. She's tough because she wants the best. She's worked really hard throughout the years to bring us some of the hottest, best quality porn around, and she deserves this Silver Dick." The audience gave an enormous round of applause, and the only thing wrong was that Sasha wasn't there to hear it.

The moment he got backstage, Mike handed over the stand-in award and began looking along the narrow back hallway for a red 'Exit' sign. The door he found was heavy and green, with a large metal handle that went down with a thunk as he pushed. Outside it was dark, and the air was warm with the leftover daytime heat of mid-July. He was standing in an alley, and the broken glass on the pavement looked like stars. As he walked out toward the sidewalk, he didn't even care about what was happening inside the theatre, didn't mind missing the awards for Best Sex Scene and Best Video. His movies weren't nominated. Neither were Sasha's. It didn't matter who won. He'd find out later. Right now he just wanted to talk to her, to tell her. Rafael would figure out where he was.

He felt buoyant and happy as he walked down the street, and he realized it was happiness mixed with gratitude. In the past four years Mike had begun caring for Sasha almost more than he cared for himself. She'd made him less selfish.

There was no phone booth on the sidewalk, so he kept walking, trying to think back to when it all started, to when his feelings for Sasha began to take on their current shape. It could have been the day he sat alone with Steve at Cougar that very first time, looking at all the pictures of porn stars with exclusive Cougar contracts.

That was the day he told Steve he wouldn't sign the contract unless Sasha got one too. It had been terrifying, having what he wanted on a platter in front of him, and pushing it away. But it made sense. Sasha had wanted it for even longer than he had. She was the one who dreamed up *Banging Billy* and got him the part in the *Muscle Party* shoot. If he hadn't said no to Steve he would have felt like he was taking something from her. He even lied, saying that he'd been in New York with a client to corroborate Sasha's story. Until that day, turning down that contract in that office, he had never placed anybody else before himself, never made that kind of sacrifice. It felt like working out a specific muscle for the first time: it wasn't easy, you had to concentrate, you had to connect to that spot in your body that you'd never consciously made work before, and afterward it ached, but in a good way, a way that let you know you'd got it right.

Mike remembered the conversation as he walked down the street now, and he remembered what else he did for her.

* * *

"Look," Steve said, "I don't need Sasha. I need you. I need you in my movies."

"Sorry, Steve. It's both of us or neither of us." Mike hoped he wouldn't have to get up and walk out just to prove his point, because he wasn't entirely sure he had the strength to do so.

Then Steve changed. He smiled and said, "Jesus Christ, you two are as thick as thieves. You'd really put your neck on the line for that fat queen?"

"Yeah, I would. I am." Mike was a little amazed that he was actually saying it.

Steve paused. "Look, I can give her a little contract, but it's only for one movie. That's it."

It didn't seem like much. "Three," Mike said. "Make it three and we have a deal."

"I'm not giving her three goddamned movies."

"I can go talk to somebody else," Mike said. "Magnum Man or Stallion. They'll hire me." He leaned forward, but he couldn't make himself stand up, couldn't make himself leave the room. Still, he was leaning forward as though about to go. He'd managed that.

Steve shook his head in disbelief. "If you weren't so fucking hot on screen there's no way I'd let you take me by the balls like this." Then Steve pulled out a calendar and flipped through some pages. "Okay, three it is. Now sign your contract, would you?" He pushed forward a contract across his desk, held out a pen.

"No. When you have Sasha's contract, we'll sign them together." Mike was taken aback when Steve actually started laughing.

"You're like fuckin' Bonnie and Clyde." He paused and nodded. "Come back tomorrow. I'll have both contracts ready for you then."

"And she gets billed as Sasha Zahore."

Suddenly Steve changed again. His laughter stopped. His eyes suddenly narrowed. "So I offer a contract and you think you can tell me how to run my business? No way. That's a deal breaker."

"She just wants you to call her by her name."

"Did she put you up to this?"

"No."

"Cougar does not have directors with drag queen names. End of story. She knows that. Non-fucking-negotiable."

"Come on, Steve. Please?" Mike leaned forward as far as he could and smiled. He gave Steve all his attention, concentrated everything on him.

Steve stared back, and his eyes wandered down toward Mike's chest, his arms. "What are you gonna ask for next? A fucking limo?"

Mike smiled as flirtatiously as he possibly could. He mustered up all sex he had. "Only if you're driving."

Steve paused and leaned back in his chair. He put his hand near his crotch. "Oh yeah?"

It took only five minutes to suck him off. It wasn't so bad. Although Mike hadn't planned to do it, Sasha meant a lot to him. Just before he put his lips on Steve's short, stubby dick, Mike said, "She gets billed as Sasha?" and Steve moaned, "Yesss."

Even while it was happening, Mike felt a kind of surprise – not so much at the fact that he was giving head to a porn producer, but more at the fact that he was doing it for somebody else. He always assumed that if he had to suck somebody off in the industry, it would be to advance his own career. Yet it was clear to Mike that he was sucking Steve's cock for Sasha, and Sasha alone. He'd never believed himself capable of anything so magnanimous.

That was the moment he realized – while on his knees in that office, with the door shut and Steve's dick in his mouth – that he was starting to feel something like love for Sasha, and for Dale. For both of them, in different ways.

Mike finally found the phone booth he was looking for. He stepped inside, dropped some coins in the slot, and dialed home. Dale answered on the first ring, and Mike blurted out the news without even saying hello.

"Sasha Zahore is fabulous," he announced. "She won. She is the Best Director."

There was a stunned silence on the other end, and he thought he heard Dale crying.

33
Glamorous Life

SASHA HURRIED PAST Billy's bedroom door as she headed toward the bathroom, carrying her eyelashes in her hand. On her right, the wall of the long central hallway was hung with three framed, black-and-white photographs of Billy, semi-nude, which she'd taken herself. It was good to pass by them every day, to always have his beauty in front of her, even when he wasn't home.

In front of the bathroom mirror, she applied fresh eyelash glue and stuck the eyelashes back on. Earlier she'd put them on too hastily, and they hadn't been sticking very well. She held them now and tried to concentrate. She'd already had three glasses of scotch. Finally she let go, stepped back, shook her head, and batted her eyes vigorously. They stayed.

She jumped and hopped, testing them out. Then she started singing "The Glamorous Life" and drumming just like Sheila E. always did. Sasha watched herself in the mirror as her sizable stomach jiggled back and forth. She spun and twirled. They didn't make music like they made back in the 80s.

Since Billy called from the Silver Dicks just an hour ago, Sasha had been happy. This was the thing she'd always wanted, and now that she'd won she couldn't possibly miss the after party.

The last two annual Silver Dick ceremonies had been horrible – all those people coming up to her afterward, offering awkward consolations as though they'd just learned she was dying. The very first year of the awards, back in 1990, had been especially hard. She hadn't even been nominated. That was the thanks she got after spending so much of her own time putting together that first ceremony – from finding a Hollywood workshop that could make the awards, to organizing the presenters, the entertainment, the MCs. And even before that, getting all the studios behind the idea, convincing them to fund a gay-only awards ceremony. Nobody had ever thanked her, and at the time many of the studio dimwits simply hadn't understood what she was trying to do, didn't see that she was attempting to raise the bar, and do things right, to give the people in this industry something to feel proud of. Of course now every producer in town was trying to take the credit.

She paused, pointed at the mirror and spoke out loud to herself. "Stop ruminating, girl. Nobody likes a bitter old queen." She had to remain positive, to concentrate on gratitude. She jiggled her shoulders as if shaking off dust. The Best Director award was finally hers. Nobody could ever take it back. No matter what happened, she had this. Storms, hurricanes, earthquakes, loneliness, financial ruin – come what may. She would always be the Best Director of Gay Porn in America in the year 1993. Thanks be to the goddess.

A key clicked in the front door, followed by Billy's sexy voice. "Hello?!" he shouted. "Special delivery for the Best Director! Is she here?"

Sasha stood up tall at the bathroom mirror, held her shoulders back, and hiked up her dress. She moved over to the bathroom doorway and stuck one leg out into the hall for Billy to see. She was in her stocking feet, and wiggled her toes under her nylons. When Billy's laughter came back down the hallway, she spun around and leaned up against the doorframe, displaying herself fully: the black charmeuse dress with its slutty satin finish and long slits up either side, the immaculate cocktail hour makeup that she'd done in record time. Billy was walking toward her with something in his hands as she tilted her head back and batted her now well-glued eyelashes toward the ceiling. Speaking in a raspy voice, she said, "I'm ready for my close-up, Mr. Knight."

She smelled the flowers before she realized he was holding them.

"For you," he said. "For the Best Director ever."

It was a bouquet of small, perfectly formed yellow roses, incredibly fragrant. They hung in the air in front of her, such a soft, soothing yellow that they almost seemed illuminated from within. He had never given her flowers before.

"Oh, they're lovely. What a sweetheart you are." She reached out for them and put one hand behind his head, pulling him forward in the hopes of placing one gentle kiss on his lips. At the last possible moment, he turned and the kiss landed on his cheek. She was incredibly happy for the flowers, but suddenly very sad for this kiss, for that subtle turning of his head. You would think this young man was the most timid wallflower. If she hadn't spent years learning how to hide her true feelings from him, she could have easily ruined her makeup with tears. "Thank you, Billy. These flowers mean even more to me than that silly Silver Dick."

He stood in front of her smiling, looking fabulous in his tux, but then in one fast and painful moment she saw that his smile was entirely wrong. This was the smile of a boy who'd just given his mother a hand-picked bunch of yellow dandelions, when what she wanted was the smile of a man who'd just given his lover a dozen long-stemmed, red roses. This smile carried more juvenile affection than adult romance.

There was no longing in it, no desire. For years she'd been hoping for his feelings to change.

"I'll put these in water right away," she said, and she quickly walked past him down the hallway, toward the kitchen, so that he wouldn't see the disappointment she felt flashing across her face.

"Sasha! Who cares about water?! You won! Congratulations!"

She looked back at him in time to see that he was running toward her, laughing. He thumped into her and gave her an enormous hug. She returned it happily, holding the flowers out in the air so as to not crush them. Then all of a sudden he began shaking her back and forth and growling like a puppy.

Her laughter bounced off the walls as she yelled, "Billy! Stop! You'll ruin my dress! The flowers!" But she didn't mind, not really. She loved it. When he pulled away, the sadness had already begun to fade. He hadn't been in the apartment even five minutes and already she'd been pushed down and picked back up. This was the hidden emotional roller coaster she rode with him every day. She sighed and said, "You won too, Billy. Congratulations to you, too."

"That doesn't matter. It's you that's been waiting. It's you that's been overlooked for years."

"But you won Best Sexual Performer. That's huge!"

He smiled and his eyes became wide. "I know. It's great. Aren't we both fantastic?"

They looked at each other and began laughing hard, at nothing in particular, just out of the joy of having both won.

She knew that in previous years Billy had held back when expressing his enthusiasm upon winning at the Silver Dicks, no doubt because he was concerned about her own feelings. He was always careful not to make her loss more painful by rubbing her nose in his own happiness. But now here they were, both winners.

"Billy," she said. "This wouldn't have happened for me if it weren't for you."

"Yes, it would have."

"No. I don't think so. Thank you for what you did."

"Well, thank you for everything you've done for me."

After Billy had used his considerable talents to secure Sasha's first three full-length films with Cougar, she'd taken the chance and run with it. She'd worked unbelievably hard on those films, and then promoted each one with such gusto – and in such a novel way – that all three became successful sellers, proving to Steve Logan once and for all that Cougar's clientele didn't care if a drag queen directed their porn. In fact, they liked it.

She put her hand on his shoulder now. She wanted to say something to him, something more than just thank you, something that would make him understand how much he meant to her, but she paused too long. There was a knock on the door.

Billy said, "That's probably Rafael."

She opened the door to see Billy was right. "Oh, hi," she mumbled.

"Hey! Congratulations!" Rafael shouted, and he gave her a hug. She leaned forward only slightly, holding out the flowers again, but keeping her other hand on the door to block Rafael's way. She couldn't help thinking that Rafael's congratulations were more for himself than for her, because he now knew the Best Director personally.

"Thank you, Ronaldo," she said.

"Maybe I can be in one of your movies?"

"Mmm. We'll see."

Rafael looked over her shoulder toward Billy and said, "I'm double parked. I'll wait in the car. Will you two be long? I really want to get there soon."

Sasha rolled her eyes. He was so stupid. "Don't you know how important it is to make an entrance?" As the words came out she heard the sharpness in her voice, and she reminded herself to soften her tone. She must try to be nice to this one, for Billy's sake. No matter what an idiot Rafael was, he was no threat. He was really nothing more than a sex toy for Billy, some kind of dildo that could talk. "We'll be down in just a minute, doll," she said, as gently as possible, and Rafael turned and walked away.

She closed the door behind him and headed into the kitchen, where she filled a pale green vase with water and began carefully arranging the luminous roses. She took her time. Rafael would have to wait in the car a bit longer. These flowers had to be savored, even if Billy's smile *had* been all wrong, even if the kiss *had* just fallen on his cheek.

Billy walked into the kitchen and set a piece of paper down on the counter. "Here's the other winners. Rafael wrote them down for you."

"Oh, can he write?" She picked up the paper and scanned it quickly. "Antonio Savage won Best Solo?!" she said.

"Not bad for a straight boy, huh?"

"I heard he's going to do his first real gay sex scene soon," she said, setting down the paper and turning back to her flowers. She would study the winners later, commit them all to memory. Right now she had these pale yellow lights in front of her. She tilted her head to the left, turned the vase to the right slightly, then pulled one rose up just a little bit higher. "But it's a non-reciprocal scene," she said. "He's just

271

going to get sucked off. Hope his girlfriend doesn't mind." She looked up at Billy and smiled.

"He thanked her tonight," Billy said. "In his acceptance speech."

"What did you say in your speech for me?"

"I read your sentence."

"Good."

"Then I just said how great you were. I reminded everyone that there wouldn't *be* a Silver Dick award if it weren't for you."

"You're a dear." She shook her head. "I still can't believe I was up for Best Director against the likes of that Bland Handsome. *Man Quest* was the worst piece of porno crap I've seen in a long time. What were the judges *thinking*?"

"You won. That's all that matters."

"You're right. That's all that matters." She picked up the vase of flowers and walked through the doorway to the dining room, where she set it down on the table. It was a large, wooden table that sat six, and the roses looked spectacular holding center stage in the room. She loved this old Hollywood apartment, with its high ceilings and art deco flair. Two years ago Billy had found it listed in the paper himself, and they'd moved in right away, splitting the rent fifty-fifty. Billy had insisted.

Behind her now she heard him moving down the hallway to his bedroom, and she reached out toward the dining room wall and flicked off the lights. For a moment she stood in the semi-darkness. The roses caught the light that came in from the front room to her left and from the doorway to the kitchen behind her. The dining room walls were painted a soft cream. They captured shadows well. Billy had rejected the audacious colors of her Orlando Avenue place. Only her bedroom had bold color here – the same deep fuchsia of her old Orlando Avenue boudoir.

From where she stood she could see into the front room, the coffee table strewn with magazines, the faux leather sofa Billy used to sleep on, now covered with throw pillows, the burgundy upholstered armchair Billy brought home from a second hand shop shortly after they moved here. She walked out into the room and looked around, at Billy's two previous Silver Dicks on the bookshelf, at the beautiful painting they had bought together while on Fire Island last year – two hunky men in shorts and T-shirts, walking on a beach holding hands. The TV looked out from the corner next to stacks and stacks of videos – gay porn mostly but also the old movies Sasha loved, Audrey Hepburn and Katherine Hepburn in particular. She felt a sense of security in knowing this apartment was theirs, that in a drawer somewhere there was a lease with their names signed side-by-side, tying them together.

She headed down the hallway toward her bedroom. Billy was making noise in his own bedroom and she poked her head in as she passed. His room was always much neater than hers, although he rarely made his bed. The posters on the walls alternated between hunky shirtless men and 1970s muscle cars. He never brought clients home, just friends and fuck buddies – Rafael and the occasional extra one here and there, guys whose names she never bothered to learn.

Billy was standing at his open closet now, looking through his clothes. He had amassed a large wardrobe in the past four years, helped by her careful advice – fine Italian suits for some occasions, leather chaps for others. A man in his profession always had to have the right outfit.

"Should I change out of my tux?" he asked.

"Oh God no, Billy. You look a dream."

"Thanks." He shut the closet door.

She went back into her bedroom, grabbed her handbag off her bed, and checked her eyelashes once more in the vanity mirror. They were fine. She slipped on her shoes – black patent leather with dramatic high heels – and she called out, "Let's go, baby."

Down at the car, she opened the back door and said, "Ricardo, you don't mind if Billy and I sit in back together, do you? We're both just so happy tonight."

Rafael looked over his shoulder and said, "Uh, sure. I guess not." Sasha grabbed Billy's hand and pulled him in behind her.

Driving along, Rafael rambled on from the front seat about how great the opening act was at the Silver Dicks, how the drag queen did such a good job on the Ethel Merman number. He talked as though Sasha had never heard of Amanda Manning. Sasha responded as politely as she could. Of course she knew every drag queen in town, and she didn't really care to hear how fabulous Amanda was. It should have been Sasha Zahore opening the Silver Dicks. It should be a tradition. She should be asked to do it every year.

When they finally approached the bar where the after party was, Rafael started looking for a place to park, and Sasha saw that a small group of fans had gathered in front. It happened every year. Gay boys heard where the Silver Dicks after party was held, and they stood outside to catch a glance of a porn star or two.

Sasha leaned forward and touched Rafael's shoulder in the front seat. "Be a doll and drop us off, won't you? I've got these horrible high heels on and it'll ruin my feet for the night if I have to walk. We'll have a drink ready for you."

When Rafael hesitated, she added, "Oh Rafael, do be a dear and help an old girl out. You're such a gentleman. *Pleeease*?"

He acquiesced.

"Pull up so my side is on the sidewalk," Sasha said.

As Rafael crossed traffic and pulled up in front of the bar, some of the fans pointed. From the back seat Sasha leaned forward and touched Rafael's shoulder. "Oh, doll, I've just won Best Director, and I have to make an entrance. Be a sweetie and open my door for me, won't you?"

Billy was already climbing out on the far side as Rafael got out and opened Sasha's door. She'd practiced getting out of a car gracefully in a dress; it wasn't an easy thing to do. You had to keep your legs together and pivot around smoothly, so that your feet touched the ground almost simultaneously. Then you had to lean forward and rise up in one single motion. But after Rafael opened the door, he didn't know enough to put his hand out to help her, and she had to hold her hand up in the air for a moment before he understood to take it. Then she rose up onto the sidewalk perfectly, her back slightly arched, as Billy came to her left side. She hooked her left hand in the crook of Billy's arm and dismissed Rafael with a nod.

Someone yelled, "It's Sasha Zahore!" and somebody else said, "Billy Knight!" It was fabulous to be recognized.

They both signed several autographs as Rafael drove away, then the bouncer opened the door and they moved inside. Having Billy beside her made her feel like a queen, a real queen, like royalty.

Steve Logan immediately walked over.

"Sasha, I thought you were sick?" he said.

"Let's just say I had a *miraculous* recovery."

He congratulated her and Billy on their awards and invited them to join him at the booth he'd secured near the dance floor. She accepted Steve's invitation before she realized he was sitting with Harry Hole and Blane Handsome. As she sat down she gritted her teeth at the tediousness of the company.

Steve was scolding Billy for announcing the *Best of Billy* movie before he was ready, when Blane stuck out his hand and said, "Sasha, Sasha, good to see you. How is it you and I both work in the industry and we never get a chance to catch up?"

"Honestly, Blane, I have no idea."

"Congratulations about tonight. I've won my fair share of awards. It's about time to give somebody else a chance."

"How generous of you." She knew he'd only won two awards in total over the years. She kept track of these things.

Harry spoke up then. "Yeah, congratulations Sasha." He had a thuggish face and had unbuttoned his tuxedo shirt to show off his hairy chest. "I'd love to work with you some day."

"I'll keep you in mind, doll."

Billy went up to the bar without asking Sasha what she wanted, but he returned with the right thing, a beautiful pink Cosmopolitan. He knew what she drank these days. He also had a gin and tonic for himself and, tucked under his right arm, a Miller Light for Rafael.

By the time Rafael found them, two other people had joined the table and there was no room left in the semicircle booth.

Sasha looked up at Rafael and said, "Oh, they let you in?"

When Billy got up to find Rafael a chair, Sasha said, "Let Raul get it himself," but Billy went and got one anyway. She had already finished with her Cosmopolitan by then. She was there to celebrate, so she excused herself and wandered up to the bar to get herself another one.

Several people came up and congratulated her, and she was glad because that was really the only reason she'd come. She wanted to be respected, *venerated*. She wanted people to lay their good wishes down at her feet.

Back at the table, Gavin Kennedy came over to congratulate both her and Billy on their awards. He said to Sasha, "Are you ready to direct again for Magnum Man?"

"She's directing for Cougar next," Steve said.

"Now, now boys." Sasha held out her hands. "Lord knows there's enough of Sasha to go around. Gavin, I'd *love* to direct for Magnum Man again."

"And what about you, Billy?" Gavin said. "Best Director and Best Sexual Performer together in a new film? We want something big."

Billy smiled. "I might be available."

"Good."

"Watch out," Steve interrupted. "Mr. Knight here wants a lot of money. And royalties, for Christ's sake. Thinks he's a superstar."

Gavin looked at Billy. "Well, we'll see what we can do."

"Great," Billy said.

Sasha took a long sip of her drink. "Gavin doll, next weekend we start promoting our new Cougar release, *Between a Cock and a Hard Place*. It's a prison movie where poor, unsuspecting Billy gets thrown into a jail cell with muscle studs Erik Summers and Dom Cruz. Hot stuff. We finished filming four months ago, and it's finally on the shelves. We're doing an eight city tour." She glanced at Billy and squeezed his knee, then looked back at Gavin. "When I'm back in town let's have lunch and talk about a new Magnum Man film," Sasha said. "Something fabulous."

"We'll want one of your tours, too." Gavin said.

"Of course, doll. Everybody does."

"Call me when you're back in town then." Gavin smiled and walked away.

Billy went up to the bar and came back with another Cosmopolitan for her. She didn't know where her last one had gone. As he sat back down, Blane began going on about his latest film, how it was sure to win an award next year. Unfortunately he explained the plot in detail. "It's science fiction porn set in the future, in a world where people get psychic powers from dildos. The bigger the dildo, the bigger the power. Isn't that awesome? It's my idea totally. Imagine *Blade Runner* meets *Carrie*, only with hot sex and dildos everywhere. Isn't just the most amazing porn plot ever?"

"My dear Blane," Sasha said. "Never before has the world seen such genius as yours. It truly is astounding."

Blane smiled broadly. "It's going to be one helluva fuck film," he said. "I ought to be put in some Hall of Fame somewhere for this one, really!"

"Nobel Prize, possibly," Sasha said.

"Really? You think so? That would be awesome."

Sasha sighed. She couldn't endure another minute listening to this moron. She hastily tipped back her entire drink and asked Billy if he wanted to dance. He said yes, and she was happy, but her heart fell when he asked Rafael to join them.

The DJ was playing a re-vamped disco tune that she remembered from the first time around. Billy moved back and forth so quickly on the dance floor that she could barely keep track of him. Rafael kept grabbing him and kissing him and she was pleased each time she saw Billy pull away. She found herself thinking that Billy should keep Rafael chained in a little cage in his room and just let him out when he wanted sex. Rafael could be such a nuisance otherwise.

But then abruptly Billy gave in to Rafael's advances and they stood in the middle of the dance floor making out, right in front of her, as though they'd forgotten about her. She danced by herself for a little while, watching. They almost looked happy. Her heart fell even further. All she had was a small bouquet of flowers, the smile of a boy who held them out to his mother, while Rafael had all this: making out with Billy on the dance floor, his hand on Billy's ass now, Billy's tongue in his mouth. How could someone as dumb as Rafael get so much? She slipped away unnoticed, went to the bar, and ordered a shot of tequila. A bartender she'd never met told her she was wonderful and the shot was on the house. She ended up having two, and chatting with the bartender, who was incredibly cute and well built, so she asked him if he'd ever considered a career in porn. He smiled and shrugged and she pulled out one of her business cards, which she kept in her bra. It had a color picture of her and said, "Sasha Zahore. Transvestite Homosexual Pornographer." Although the card was a bit damp with sweat he seemed happy to take it. "Call me," she said, and then there he was again with the tequila bottle in his hand, so maybe it was three shots after all.

The music was better after that and she worked her way back to the dance floor. She couldn't find Billy anywhere, so she danced alone, the black charmeuse of her dress flowing beautifully across her thighs. Somebody began talking to her, but she didn't know who it was, and he kept saying how much he'd enjoyed working with her and how she treated her models so much better than some directors who treated them like dirt, it was really terrible. She kept nodding and saying oh, thank you, yes terrible, okay, see you dear and then he was gone and she was by herself again.

She hadn't eaten dinner that night, because she was so nervous. Maybe that explained why the floor kept shifting now. It was getting harder to dance and she looked for Billy again but she still couldn't find him, couldn't even find the table they had been at, couldn't find any of them – Steve or Blane or Harry or the other two and not even Rafael the talking dildo. Not that she wanted to find *Rafael* but at least then she would find Billy, as Billy was no doubt still attached to Rafael's face, or perhaps by now he was attached to some other part. Her stomach felt a little odd and she looked for the bathrooms and then she was in the stall and hurling into the toilet just like that. Billy's voice was calling her and she said I'm in here and he couldn't open the stall door because it was locked and she reached up and concentrated and undid the latch. Billy's arms were around her now and she looked at him and she said, "Take me drunk I'm home." He was wiping off her face and straightening her wig.

The lights were brighter on the dance floor and they hurt her eyes leaning into Billy as he moved forward. Then there was Rafael, who looked upset as he handed Billy some keys, and all of a sudden she was standing alone with that stupid talking dildo who should be locked in a cage. Where Billy was, she didn't know. She hated Rafael for touching her but when she pulled away the floor tilted dramatically to the left so she let him touch her again. They were standing by the bouncers at the front door and Billy came in and she leaned into him again, much happier to be touching her Billy instead. She sat down in the front seat of Rafael's car and

Billy was driving and Rafael wasn't with them. The floor next to her feet was dark and she kicked around and there was nothing and she said "My handbag" and Billy said "Don't worry I got it." The hazard lights were blinking orange when he helped her get out of the car, not at all graceful this time, and she laughed at herself because she could direct a porn film, she was the Best Director, but she could barely get out of a car on her own. It looked like the car was in the middle of the road but she knew it must not be because Billy was smarter than that and not drunk like her. Billy was saying things to her, apologizing about buying her another Cosmopolitan. She didn't tell him about the tequila, or the other drinks, let him think it was his fault. There was no elevator in their building so the stairs kept coming and kept turning and they were going up. Then there was the front door and the front room with the pillows on the sofa and the magazines on the table where she had left them. Without warning the wall tipped at an odd angle and it pushed up against her. Billy's arm was around her waist, holding her, leading her down the hallway. Her bedroom was there and her big beautiful bed, so soft, she was sitting on the edge of it with Billy next to her and he was saying what am I going to do with you. She turned and looked at him and focused on his face and in her heaven all the angels would look like this. She leaned forward because it was only just a little kiss she wanted, that was all, but it had to be on the lips – mouth open, tongue – it wasn't a lot, surely he had done much more with much worse than her. His hand on her cheek slowly pushed her face away. No Sasha you're drunk. Inside she wanted to scream and throw money at him, how much for just a little kiss, but she kept her mouth shut because it would be awful to say that and she had never said it and she never would. Billy stood up. She heard the next words as though somebody else was saying them but they were inside her own voice. *Billy why don't you love me the way I want you to?* It was horrible how the words came out sobbing and choking back at the same time. And then he was hushing her, shooshing her like a baby, stroking her wig with his hand. She had been his mother and she had been his father and now she was his child but never his lover, never although of course of course she understood even then that he loved her, but not like that, not with every part of him, not with his lips and his mouth and his dick and his ass and especially not with that very small part of his heart where he kept things hidden. But her bed was moving up next to her and the pillow was now under her head and Billy's hand was on her forehead saying sleep tight and then he was gone, just gone, and the bed rocked back and forth in the dark and the only thing that saved her from being swallowed by loneliness in that terrible moment was the deep and welcoming solace of sleep.

34
Sisterly Love

MIKE WALKED DOWN the hall to Dale's bedroom door at 3:00 in the afternoon, carrying a cup of tea. He knocked, but there was no answer, so he opened the door and went in. The room was dark, the curtains drawn and windows shut tight. The air was stale with the smell of fermented sweat. There were clothes all over the floor.

"Morning," Mike said softly, an almost inaudible whisper. He set the tea down on the nightstand and opened the curtains halfway, then cracked open the window. Traffic noise came in, horns honking out on Fountain Avenue.

Dale was lying on top of the covers in the black satin dress from the night before. There was a rip in one of the slits on the side, and his leg stuck out. Sasha's wig was on the floor beside the bed. A muffled moan came up from the bed and Dale rolled over. His white pillowcase was covered with makeup. His face was a slur of color.

Mike had planned to undress Sasha when he put her to bed last night – he knew she wouldn't want to sleep in that dress – but after what happened he'd decided that undressing her would have been a mistake. In the four years they'd known each other, she had never tried to kiss him like that. It was horrible, that moment, her drunk on the bed, wig crooked and makeup already a mess, holding him and struggling to shove her tongue down his throat. He'd pushed hard to get away. It felt even worse than that time she'd wanted to jack off together, just before Kerry left. Not only was last night more aggressive, but it was more personal.

The scales of sexual intimacy for Mike were very clear, and he didn't want any of it with Sasha, or with Dale. In Mike's mind, the least personal thing you could do with somebody was to jack off together. The next thing you could do was to let a guy fuck you, which was only slightly more personal than jacking off. Some people thought getting fucked was pretty intimate, but it wasn't, not really. At least it didn't have to be. You didn't have to look at the guy. It didn't have to be face to face. You could pretend you weren't there. Mike would much rather get fucked by a guy he wasn't into than to suck him off, because when you sucked off a guy he was literally in your face. You couldn't get away from what you were doing. But there was no doubt that the most personal thing you could ever do was to kiss. Not only were you facing the guy, but he was facing you and, even if you kept your eyes shut, there he was in front of you, all of that energy going back and forth between you. It was impossible to close down and imagine you were somewhere else.

Mike only kissed co-stars and clients because he had to. He'd met 'gay for pay' straight guys doing porn and escort work who would fuck a guy but wouldn't kiss at all, ever, as though they thought kissing alone made you gay. Once, Mike slipped up and kissed a straight top on the lips while bouncing up and down on the guy's dick. The guy jerked back and snapped, "I'm not a fag. No kissing." He understood. It was like they'd unexpectedly touched on a kind of universal truth, as though everyone, somehow subconsciously, knew that of all the physical acts you could do with somebody, kissing on the lips was, in its own strange way, by far the most intimate.

"Wake up, Dale," he whispered now, leaning down and touching Dale's nylon-covered leg.

Dale opened his eyes slightly and squinted at the light coming in the window. "Oh, Jesus." He shut them again.

Mike sat on the edge of the bed. "It's three o'clock in the afternoon. We've got rehearsal at four."

It was the first official rehearsal for the *Hard Place* tour, although Dale had been working on the costumes and choreography for weeks.

"Shit." Dale's eyes shot open again and he stared at the ceiling, suddenly alert.

"Do you want me to call and cancel?" Mike asked. "Maybe we can do it some other time."

"No, we can't cancel. We said we'd be there. We launch in less than a week. I don't want a sloppy show. Oh, fuck." Dale went to sit up, but quickly put a hand on his head. "Oh, Mike. Oh, fuck. My head."

"I'll bring you some aspirin."

"I don't know if I can keep it down."

"You can try." Mike brought in two small white tablets and a glass of water and sat back down on the edge of the bed.

Dale took the aspirin. "I'm sorry I got so drunk last night. Thank you for taking care of me."

"That's fine."

"Did I make a fool of myself at the after party?"

"No, I got you out of there before you had a chance to do that. Nobody but me and Rafael knew you were throwing up."

"God bless you, my child." Dale cracked a weak smile.

Mike patted his leg.

285

"What about here?" Dale asked. "Did I make a fool of myself here? With you?"

Mike paused. "Don't worry." He smiled. "We're like sisters."

Dale looked away. He looked incredibly sad.

"Now," Mike said. "If we're going, we should leave in half an hour."

"I stink like booze and other people's cigarette smoke. My face must look a mess. I have to take a shower. It's not fair. Sasha goes overboard, and I'm the one stuck with the hangover."

Mike whispered in a sugary voice. "Oh, poor, sweet, innocent Dale."

Dale laughed faintly and grabbed his head again. "Don't. It hurts." He sighed. "Can you start the shower for me?"

"You bet." Mike stood up and left the room.

Dale was still in the shower ten minutes later when the phone rang. Mike picked up and was surprised to hear his sister say hello. It felt surreal, sitting on the couch in the front room, the muffled sound of the shower coming from the bathroom down the hall as Lisa's happy voice said, "I got out of the hospital yesterday, Mikey. I had my baby. A little girl. Her name is Abigail."

"Abigail?"

"After Mom. Abigail Marie."

Years ago, when Mike first moved into this old building with Dale, he'd called Lisa to tell her he was living in Los Angeles. He'd wanted to sound like a success and he told her he was getting started as an actor. She'd asked for his new phone number and when he hesitated she sounded almost wounded, so he finally gave it to her. Ever since then she had been calling a couple of times a year, and always on his birthday. He returned the kindness by making a point to call on her birthday as well, and sometimes at Christmas, if she didn't call him first.

"Are you okay?" he asked her now.

"Yes, I'm fine."

"And the baby? How is it?"

"Fine. She's fine."

Although he genuinely cared for his sister, sometimes talking to her on the phone felt strange, like visiting a place where the past was kept behind glass, where the air in the rooms had become stale. He'd moved far away from their childhood, but she still talked about certain stories: the time they got lost together in the woods at Black Creek, the time they dared each other to eat Molly's dog food. Now here she was on her end of the phone, a married secretary with a new-born baby in the suburbs of Cleveland, and here he was on his, a gay escort and a porn star, and she didn't even know.

Two years ago he'd made up an excuse to avoid showing up at her wedding, and it was clear that it still bothered her. He felt bad about it. She had sent him money when he needed it most, all those years ago, but he hadn't been there when she needed him. From time to time she would still say, "It would have been nice to see you at my wedding."

Other times, randomly, she would throw comments about their dad into the middle of the conversation. "Dad asks about how you are. Why don't you talk to him anymore?" He never gave an answer.

He concentrated now on the sound of Dale in the shower down the hall. "Does it have all its fingers and toes?"

Lisa laughed. "Yes. Ten each. Perfect sets.

"Good."

"But she's not an 'it'. She's a little girl. Abby."

"Don't you think that's kind of weird?" he said. "I mean, that's Mom's name." The silence on the other end of the phone told him that he'd wounded her again. Down the hall the shower turned off.

"No. I don't think it's weird. It's honoring Mom."

He felt bad. He was always hurting her. "Sorry, sis. I didn't mean it. Not like that."

"We're calling her Abby. I want her to know her Uncle Mikey."

He felt refracted and split. Was it possible to use his mother's name when talking about his sister's daughter, his niece? And was it possible that he himself could exist simultaneously as two such wildly different people: both Billy Knight and now this Uncle Mikey?

"I figured it out the other day," Lisa said. "I haven't seen you in over twelve years. That's more than a decade. That's too long for a brother and sister to not see each other. I still can't believe you missed my wedding. Will you come visit? Please?"

He heard the bathroom door opening, Dale padding away down the hallway to his fuchsia bedroom, the door shutting behind him.

"Mikey?" Lisa said.

"Yeah?"

"Will you come?"

He didn't want to hurt her again. "Of course," he said. "Of course I'll come."

35
Drag Queen and Strippers on Tour

DALE LOVED THE tours, loved the travel, the new cities, the audiences, all the lights. As Mike drove them to the first official rehearsal for the *Hard Place* tour, Dale sat in silence, one hand on his head, remembering back to their very first tour.

It had been to promote Sasha's feature-length directorial debut with Cougar: *Back Door Delivery*, staring none other than Billy Knight as a very obliging courier. At the time, Steve hadn't believed the tour idea would work. So Dale, determined to make sure Sasha's first movie with Cougar sold well, had organized it all without any help whatsoever. Dale booked the venues. He sewed the costumes. Then he piled Mike and two other *Back Door* models into his car, said they'd have to buy their own food but he'd pay for gas, and he drove them all over Southern California, staying with friends and friends of friends. They performed in Laguna Beach, Palm Springs, San Diego, and of course back in LA.

The venue was always a gay bar, and the show always started with Sasha announcing the film and doing a drag number on her own. It was only with the second number that the models were revealed, coming out on stage to be her dancing boys. They were dressed in tight little courier uniforms. After that, she left the stage for a while and the boys danced and stripped down to G-strings. At some point during the evening Sasha would conduct a lottery and somebody in the audience would win a free copy of the video and a kiss from Billy Knight. She'd deliver a campy monologue about all the hot scenes in the movie, and then she'd announce that you could buy your very own copy in the back of the bar at a discounted rate. There would be a couple more numbers and, depending on the city and if they thought they could get away with it, the models would strip down to nothing and grope each other on stage. Sasha always kept her clothes on because she said, "The goal's to sell movies, not scare everybody away."

Audiences loved the *Back Door Delivery* show, and the stack of videos they brought each night often sold out. Afterward there was usually an article or two about the performance in the local gay rags, and a review of the film, often with a picture of Sasha and her sexy models. It was great publicity.

It was only after the *Back Door Delivery* tour was over that Steve realized it had been a wonderful idea. He saw the interest it stirred up, all the sales it created. From then on he was fully on board.

Now, for the *Hard Place* tour, Steve was finally paying for everything – the accommodation, airfares, and even the food. It was fabulous. Steve's financial investment was a big part of the reason Dale had refused to cancel their first official rehearsal in spite of the hangover. He couldn't just not show up.

When they arrived at the Lucky Pony to rehearse that afternoon, Dale pushed through the headache and the sour nausea and diligently taught all the choreography he'd prepared, pretending he wasn't hung over at all. He absolutely refused to look unprofessional, refused to let Steve down or be a bad example for the models.

The *Hard Place* tour opened at the Lucky Pony a week

later. It was the official launch of the movie, and that night their stack of videos sold out so early that Steve had to run back to the studio for more. From LA they flew to San Francisco, then Dallas, Atlanta, Washington D.C., New York, Boston, and Chicago. Steve stayed in L.A, so there were only four of them on the road together, the director and the three biggest stars – Billy and Erik and Dom. The tour went incredibly well, and the four of them were like a little family. They worked hard and took their performances seriously.

Dale was proud of the *Hard Place* show and pleased with the dances and the outfits – especially that moment when the boys came out in orange prison coveralls and slipped them off to reveal hot pink sequined G-strings underneath.

It was nice travelling around with three handsome young men as well, even though there was nothing sexual. Sex never seemed to happen, at least not when Dale was with them (although he wondered what they got up to when he wasn't in the room). Instead, when they were all together they laughed and gossiped and made jokes. To Dale it felt like he and the boys had become equal somehow. He fit in with the beautiful ones, in his own way. He was no longer the odd man out like he had been back in high school, secretly adoring Doug Kohler and the other football players from afar, even as they bullied him. Now, in this new world, the world Dale had created for himself, all the attractive young men liked him.

He knew Mike had clients scheduled throughout the tour. By that point there were guys all over the country who wanted a piece of Billy Knight. Mike's agency in LA had contacts with other agencies across the country, so it was easy for Mike to find work anywhere. Sometimes his clients would turn up at the *Hard Place* shows and stand in the back of the room, staring. Mike would point them out in the crowd if Dale asked, although lately just seeing them there made Dale feel jealous. He tried to tell himself that he had more intimacy with Mike than those bug-eyed johns ever would. Sometimes he believed it.

No matter what city they were in, Dale always made sure he shared a motel room with Mike, even if Mike didn't usually come home until the wee hours of the morning. They slept on separate double beds, but it was still nice – like a boyhood sleepover. Sometimes when they woke in the afternoons Mike would climb over to Dale's bed and sit on top of the covers to talk quietly before their day started. Invariably then Mike would work out in nothing but his underwear, right there in the room, push ups and sit ups, triceps dips off of chairs. It was beautiful. Mike was getting so good with exercise. He knew so much, talked about things like sets and repetitions, knew the difference between his trapezius and his latissimus dorsi. Dale just liked being able to sit in bed and watch Mike sweat.

At the same time however, and some days more than others, Dale found those near-naked motel room workouts terribly frustrating. They were alone, away from home. There was no cameraman. He wished Mike would just give him a mercy fuck. It would be easy, like a favor to a friend. Why not? Nobody needed to know. Did Mike really find him that disgusting and ugly? Was he any worse than those horrible johns who stood in the back of the bar and drooled? Dale knew what happened the night Sasha got drunk, remembered it very clearly, and it confused him. Here Mike was giving up his ass to total strangers left and right, but still denying even a simple open-mouthed kiss to someone he cared for. Dale could not, even in his most lucid moments, figure out why.

36
Can't Go Back

MIKE WENT HIS own way in Chicago. The tour was over. He set down his old grey duffel bag at O'Hare airport and gave Dale a hug. The bag was full of toys.

"Good luck in Ohio, Mr. Michael Dudley," Dale said.

Mike smiled. "Thanks." Hearing his name like that, it suddenly sounded false, like it was the name of somebody he was now going to try and pretend to be. He turned to Erik and Dom, gave each a quick hug and a slap on the back, saying, "See ya" and "Take it easy." Then he left them at their gate and walked toward his own. They were headed back to Los Angeles. He was flying on to Cleveland.

He'd enjoyed the tour. Dancing wasn't so bad when it was only once in a while. It was nice to have people in different cities tell you how much they adored you, how great you were.

Looking back over his shoulder as he walked away, Mike saw Dale sitting down in between Erik and Dom outside their gate, already laughing. He remembered Sasha running out on stage back in Atlanta, when the tape jammed during Mike's number. She'd saved the show, saved him from looking like an idiot, standing there awkwardly with no music. He always felt safe when Sasha had his back, when Dale was close at hand.

Mike had pocketed a good amount of money from dancing tips and from his work on the side seeing clients. In Chicago he'd spent that money on his new niece. He'd taken a cab to FAO Schwarz on Michigan Avenue, smiling at the cute guy dressed as a toy soldier by the front doors as he walked in. Mike wandered around for over an hour there, picking out all the toys he could for a baby.

Alongside the toys in Mike's duffle bag now, there were several tiny purple baby shirts that Dale had helped pick out, a silver necklace for Lisa, and a Chicago Cubs baseball cap for Paul, the brother-in-law he was about to meet. He continued walking to his gate. He'd already checked his main suitcase. Although the duffel bag was technically too big for carry-on, he'd hidden it from the woman at the departures desk. When he arrived at his gate and it came time to board, he had to smile and flirt with the woman taking tickets in order to be allowed to take the bag on.

"Please?" he said, smiling. "It's full of presents for my niece. I didn't want to check it. It's too important." He gave her all his attention, and eventually she waved him through.

As the plane took off there was a strange, sinking feeling in his stomach, and it stayed with him throughout the flight. He hadn't set foot in Ohio since that day four years ago when he left Cincinnati and drove all the way to California in his old Chevy Nova. And of course, as Lisa often reminded him, it had been over twelve years since he last saw her. The plane was a time machine, taking him into the past.

Lisa was waiting for him at the airport in Cleveland. She stood there alone looking so much older that for a split second he almost thought it was his mom. Then she yelled, "Mikey!" and he knew it was her.

She hugged him deeply, and when she finally pulled away he saw that her eyes were watery. "You look good," she said. "Why did you go away for so long?"

He wanted to remind her that she'd gone away first, that she'd fled Brewerton the year before he did, that she'd left him alone there with their father.

"You look good too," he said.

She was a well-dressed, suburban mom – nice wedding ring, a diamond pendant on a gold necklace, khaki pants with loafers, a pink polo shirt. Her hair was still long and brown, the way it was when they were kids, but different. It fell down across her shoulders like a daytime TV star.

"Let's get your bags," she said. "I have to hurry up and get home to Abby."

Mike had to remind himself that Lisa wasn't talking about their mother.

"She's a month old tomorrow. This is the first time I've left her. It feels so weird, like I forgot my arm. Paul said he'd pick you up, but you two have never met and I wanted to be here. Let's hurry back. I left Paul some milk but he's hopeless." She started walking toward the baggage claim.

Mike followed. "I can't wait to meet her."

"And Paul. He really wants to meet you. I've told him so much about you."

She was walking fast. Mike suddenly had an image of his sister organizing bank presidents, telling them when they had to be where, rushing them off to this meeting and that.

"And I have a surprise for you," she said.

"What is it?"

"It's a surprise."

As they stood in front of the baggage carousel waiting for his suitcase come around, Mike tried to think of something to say, but he couldn't come up with anything.

She turned to look at him. "Why was your flight coming in from Chicago? Why not LA?"

"I was visiting a friend," he said.

"Who?"

He thought quickly. "My friend Dom. He works at a prison. We met in LA."

"A prison? Really? Huh. Sometimes I still can't believe you live in California. But seeing you now, you look like you live there." She looked down at his arms. "My little brother has muscles! Do you have a girlfriend yet?"

"No." She asked this all the time. He always said the same thing.

"I can't understand why a good looking guy like you doesn't have a girlfriend." She smiled. "You'd better get one soon or people will start to say you're funny."

"Maybe I am funny."

For a moment she looked somewhat panicked, then she laughed. "Oh, God," she said, slapping his arm lightly. "You're such a kidder. You've always been such a kidder. Where are your bags? I have to get back."

He'd never been described as a 'kidder' by anyone. He let it go.

"Is Abby talking yet?" he asked.

She laughed again. "No, silly. She's only a month old. They don't start talking until they're almost a year."

Mike's brown Luis Vuitton suitcase came around the baggage carousel, and he picked it up.

Lisa was looking at it closely. "What a nice suitcase."

"Thanks." He didn't say that a client had bought it for him on a travel job, a week in Key West.

Her car was a four-door family thing. As she drove down the expressway, weaving in and out of traffic, he was struck by the feeling that he had no idea who this woman was. It was as though there had been some terrible mistake. This was not his sister at all. This was not the girl who ate Molly's dog food. He was in a random car with a stranger. She talked nonstop as she drove, mostly about Abby, how she woke five or six times a night, how they still needed to buy a stroller because the one they'd borrowed from Paul's sister wasn't very nice.

"I quit my job," she added suddenly. "We can live off Paul's executive salary, and I just want to stay home and raise kids. I'll organize large, complicated birthday parties instead of CEO luncheons."

Mike felt his own silence solidifying around himself until it became a wall. What could he possibly tell her in return? That he'd just finished a three-week tour, dancing around in a pink sequined G-string and simulating gay sex on stage? That two weeks ago he was paid by a highly respected U.S. Senator to wear cowboy pajamas and yell, "Fuck me daddy!"? There was nothing he could offer to match the small tidbits of baby and home that she was offering him. Why had he come here?

When she pulled into her brand new subdivision, Mike was struck by how large and perfect all the homes were, how small the trees were, one planted carefully in front of each house. Her house was beige, covered with the same brick as almost all the others on the street. The windows had fake cream-colored shutters that didn't close, and the flowerbeds in front were planted with brightly colored snapdragons. The neighbors were close on either side, given the size of the house.

Turning into her driveway, he saw the pick-up truck with the words *Dudley Produce* on the side in green letters. It took him a moment before he understood. His dad was standing on the front porch, holding a can of beer. Mike's chest

297

tightened. He looked at Lisa. "Is that your surprise?" He knew he sounded angry. He was.

"Yeah. Aren't you happy?"

"You should've told me."

"Why? Is something wrong?"

Mike said nothing. He just stared out the car window at his dad on the porch.

Lisa leaned over toward him. "You never did tell me what happened the night you left home."

"No," Mike said. "I didn't."

He stepped out of the car and looked across the lawn at his father.

* * *

The night Mike left Brewerton was his dad's poker night. On the first Saturday of every month, the old man would close the shop and drive over to Barry Ferguson's place to play cards, then he'd come stumbling up the stairs at one or two in the morning, always stinking drunk. Mike always had to open the shop by himself the following morning. He'd been doing that alone, once a month, since he was fifteen.

In Mike's dad's bedroom, there was a TV and a VCR, which Mike wasn't allowed to use. His dad always said, "That VCR is expensive and new. Keep your sticky fingers off it."

It was next to the TV on top of a locked wooden cabinet. Shortly after Lisa left home, Mike had begun using his dad's poker night as an opportunity to snoop, and one night he found the key to that cabinet in the bottom drawer of his dad's nightstand. Inside the cabinet was a large collection of porn videocassettes. *Nurses Nasty and Nice. Warrior Women. Sarah's Sticky Summer. Just Between Girls. Hildebranda of*

Bavaria: Volumes 1, 2 & 3. Given that the collection belonged to a man who'd never left the state of Ohio, it was surprisingly international – some American, some Italian, some German, some with subtitles, some without. Mike especially liked the German ones because, for whatever reason, they didn't seem afraid to show the guys' bodies before and after they fucked the women, and the men were usually in good shape, unlike many of the flabby, plain men in a lot of the other porn. He never watched the lesbian porn. It was boring, and he didn't understand it.

Over time, he began looking forward to his dad's poker night more and more. It was a real treat to be able to jerk off to porn.

He told his friend Charlie about this secret treasure trove. Charlie was the one he fooled around with in the Thompson's hay shed from time to time, and soon Charlie was begging to come over and see the collection.

So one night when his dad was playing poker, Mike told Charlie to show up around seven thirty. When Charlie appeared at the back door, Mike could tell that he was already horny. The summer night air behind him was sweet. There was the smell of freshly cut grass that would always, for the rest of his life, remind Mike of Brewerton. He stepped aside and let Charlie in.

"Upstairs," Mike said, and they moved silently together toward the stairs.

Mike and Charlie never kissed, never flirted. They behaved as though what passed between them was simply a substitute for the real thing, as though they both would have preferred sex with a real live girl but, since none were available, they had to make do with what was at hand. Mike never told Charlie that he didn't care about having sex with a girl, that in fact he really enjoyed being naked with Charlie. He knew enough not to say that.

Up in his dad's bedroom, Mike opened the bottom drawer, reached in back, and pulled out the small silver key. The room hadn't changed since his mom died. The lamp at the bedside had a ruffled shade. The bedspread had small, faded blue flowers that matched the blue walls. Normally Mike sat on the floor to jerk off – it didn't seem right to do it in his dad's bed – but Charlie insisted they pull back the covers and get comfortable. Mike agreed. He let Charlie get the bed ready while he opened the cabinet and turned on the VCR.

Charlie wanted to watch one of the lesbian films first, but half way through he asked Mike to turn it off, and Mike did. Mike was always careful to take note of what scene the film was on when he put the tape in, and then to rewind it to the same place before he took it out.

It was during *Sarah's Sticky Summer* that Mike went down on Charlie for the first time that night. By then they were both naked on the bed, jacking off side-by-side, so it was easy enough to slide down and put his mouth on Charlie's dick. Charlie never asked for it, but he never said no. He never went down on Mike.

Charlie was about to come when he pushed Mike's head away and said, "Let's watch one more."

"We don't have to watch them all tonight," Mike said. "You can come back next month."

"Come on," Charlie pleaded.

Mike looked at the alarm clock on his dad's nightstand. His dad wouldn't be home for a while. He put in *Hildebranda of Bavaria: Volume 2*, which was his all-time favorite because of the burly innkeeper who took Hildebranda in when she

300

got caught in the rain in the final scene. She was soaked, her long, blond braids dripping with rain, so the innkeeper warmed her by the fire. Mike would like to be warmed by the fire by a man like that.

He was sucking Charlie's dick again, jerking off as he did, and they were both incredibly close when the door opened and Mike – his lips still touching the head of Charlie's dick – looked up and saw his dad.

There was a look on his dad's face Mike had never seen before. His dad yelled something and turned around and ran down the stairs. Mike and Charlie, intense erections feeling suddenly vulnerable, scrambled to get dressed. Charlie had his jeans back on and was fumbling with his shirt when Mike's dad came through the door again and pointed the shotgun at Charlie's chest.

"Motherfucking faggot!" his dad screamed.

Mike fell down to the floor on the other side of the bed, clinging to the floral-print of the bedspread. He looked over the edge of the bed. It was the 12-gauge his dad used for deer hunting, which had been kept behind the cash register ever since they'd been robbed that night so many years ago. The gun was long and black and Mike had always been afraid of it. He'd always refused to go deer hunting with his dad.

Charlie was screaming now, wildly, not making any words, just noise. Mike's dad was standing broad-shouldered and blocking the door.

"Get the fuck out of my house!" his dad yelled. Charlie, still shirtless, bent down and picked up his shoes, his socks, held them with his shirt in his hands, and when Mike's dad stepped aside, Charlie ran out of the room and down the stairs. The thump of his bare feed on the wooden steps rang out. The back door slammed.

By then Mike's dad was already pointing the gun at Mike, not saying anything, just heaving as he held it, short shallow breaths. Mike stayed crouched down on the floor in his underwear, trying not to cry, knowing that would anger his dad even more.

"Stand up you little faggot!" His dad walked around the double bed and moved toward him.

Mike stood with his back against the wall. The ruffled lampshade was to his right, the closet to his left. Looking up he saw how close the gun was to his head, the dark black metal. He heard himself screaming.

"Shut up, shut up!" his dad yelled. "No son of mine's gonna be a faggot. No son of mine."

Mike braced himself for the impact. He felt it was inevitable, that there was no turning back. He truly believed that his father was going to shoot him. And in some way, merely by the fact of pointing a gun at him, his father had already killed something.

"Tell me you're not a faggot," his dad said. There was no bullet. No blast or bang. "Tell me you're not," he said again. He shot the words out.

"No, Dad. I'm not. I'm not a faggot, Dad. I swear."

His dad moved quickly then, and Mike didn't know what was happening until he felt a sharp pain. The back of his head slammed into the wall behind him as he fell. Only when he was down on the floor did he realize that the butt of the gun had hit him on the forehead. One hard, sharp thrust. Then there was a solid kick to his ribs, and his dad stepped back, yelling. "Get the fuck out of my room! I ever catch you doing that again and I *will* shoot you!"

Mike hadn't seen his dad since.

Looking up toward Lisa's porch, Mike saw the man now. There were his bulky hands holding his beer. There was his steady gaze, as harsh and mean as ever. But this man, the one in front of him now, looked thin and unhealthy. There were spots of grey beginning to form around the temples. The once-broad shoulders were stooped.

Suddenly Mike saw a pattern, like he was viewing his own life from a distance, and he recognized the shape of something that he hadn't been able to grasp up close. He'd changed cities twice in his life. The first time, it was his father attacking him – nearly killing him – that had made him leave Brewerton. The second time, when he finally left Cincinnati, it was another man who had attacked him, who could have killed him in a different way. Mike was forever fleeing, trying to find a place that was safe.

Lisa was already pulling his duffle bag out of the trunk and walking up to the house. She shouted playfully, "Are you coming in or are you going to just stand there by the car?" She had no idea what she'd done.

Mike had never told her what happened that night because doing so would have required him to admit to too many things – the least of which was jerking off to his father's porn. It was almost as though he and his dad were complicit. They'd agreed to allow Lisa to walk through her life inside a cloud of make-believe. She was not tainted by their secrets.

Up on the porch, his father didn't move. Mike stepped to the back of the car and picked up his suitcase. Then he began walking toward the house. He felt he had no choice.

Lisa yelled, "Dad, look who's here!" She waved Mike on and stood back.

"You didn't tell me he was coming," their dad said.

Lisa answered in a sing-songy voice. "It's a surprise. Dad, I asked you to please not drink on the front porch. The neighbors will see."

Two concrete steps led up to the porch, and Mike stopped in front of them. His father, standing at the top and looking down, seemed to be intentionally in the way. There were wrinkles around his mouth and neck. Up close he looked even more feeble.

Lisa said, "Give dad a hug, Mikey."

"Step back, old man," Mike said. "You're blocking my way." His dad moved to the right, and Mike walked up the steps to the porch, ignoring his dad as he passed by.

Up out of the shadows of the house came a tall, thin man with dark hair. He shouted "Hello!" through the screen door and stepped out onto the porch. "I'm Paul," he said, shaking Mike's hand vigorously. "Glad to see you made it. All the way from sunny California! Bring any movie stars with you?" His voice was loud and nervous.

Mike shook his head. "Nope. No movie stars. Just me."

"Well, that's all we need. Come on in."

There was a large, pale beige living room with matching off-white couch and armchairs, soft cream carpet, milky walls. Somehow the colors all seemed slightly blurred, in a kind of soft focus. On the table was a rose petal potpourri, and everything was orderly and pristine. Mike recognized the china cabinet in the corner. It held his mother's glass figurines.

From somewhere a baby started crying, and Lisa began directing everyone. "Paul, take Mike's bags up to his room, would you? Mike, you sit down and talk to Dad. I'll go get

Abbey. Dad, come inside and sit down. What are you standing out there for?" Then she and Paul ran up the stairs.

Mike's dad walked in the front door and set his empty beer can down on the coffee table. Mike sat with his back to the wall so he could see where his dad was at all times. He did the math and realized for the very first time that his dad was only four years older than Dale. It seemed impossible that this old man with the wrinkles around his mouth and the hunched shoulders could be almost the same age as Dale. Although Dale was fatter, and balder, he didn't seem half as old.

His dad sat down and looked at the floor, and neither of them said anything. It was like sitting in a room with a rattlesnake and no doors.

He saw now that his dad was a lot like the johns he used to meet in bars – not that his dad was gay. It was something else. All his life Mike had lived with his dad's drunken unpredictability. The man seemed to move back and forth at random between sadness and anger. It was never clear which one was next until you were alone with him.

It was Paul coming down the stairs that saved Mike now.

"Mike, how about a beer?" Paul said.

Mike's dad interrupted. "Sure, I'll take a one."

Paul hesitated, then nodded, picked up the empty beer can on the coffee table, and turned back to Mike. "How about you?"

"Nothing for me, thanks."

"Not even a Coca-Cola?"

"Okay." Mike wanted to keep his head clear. There was still a rattlesnake in the room.

Lisa came down carrying a little baby that was wearing only a diaper and a white T-shirt. Mike was amazed at how small it was. "Sit on the couch," Lisa said. "You can hold her."

"I've never held one before."

"I'll show you. It's okay. Sit down. You'll have to learn sometime. You'll be holding your own son or daughter some day. Abbey will need cousins, Michael Dudley. And you better provide." She smiled, clearly trying to soften her words.

As Lisa set his niece down into his arms, Paul was already leaning over behind her, saying "Make sure you support her head, Mike. It's all about the head." Lisa nudged him away.

Looking down at Abby, Mike was surprised by the surge of fear he felt. Here was this tiny little thing, still somewhat sleeping, so incredibly helpless, relying on the people around her for her very life. She was perfect. It was like holding a rare and fragile piece of china, one of his mother's figurines in the cabinet behind him – the lady with the billowing dress, or one of the porcelain doves. As a child he'd never been allowed to touch them. The most valuable things were always so easy to break. He touched Abby's miniature pink hand with his finger. She made little sounds, peeps and squawks. He laughed. "She makes noises like a chicken."

Lisa laughed too. "That's my girl."

"Hey, little chicken," Mike said. This baby had never seemed real before now, not even as he was buying it presents – *her* presents. Before she was just an idea, something mentioned over the phone. But now here she was. And she was delicate. And he was certain that he was going to break it.

"Take her, please," Mike said. He felt like an alien in this place.

Lisa frowned and reached out her arms. "Let's go out back."

There was no fence at all around the backyard. Everyone's patch of lawn was open to the others. Nobody here had

306

anything to hide. Lisa walked Mike around, showing him everything she'd planted, carrying Abby. "I did it all myself. This is the wisteria I planted last year." She pointed to a trellis at the back of the house. "It's coming in nicely, don't you think?"

Behind them, their dad and Paul had come outside. They were sitting down to drink their beers on the deck.

"Yes, very nice," Mike said. He was amazed by the fastidiousness of everything, the careful edging around every flowerbed.

"I was going to plant roses, but I hate those gosh-darned thorns. I planted marigolds instead. See? Aren't they pretty?"

Orange and gold flowers stood in perfect little rows, and Mike realized that he would never be able to tell Lisa about himself, about what he did for a living. There was no room for the prickly tangle of his life here in this garden, this perfect place that Lisa had made.

She turned to him and spoke quietly. "You didn't seem so happy to see Dad."

"That's clearly mutual."

"I wish you two got along better. I don't understand."

Suddenly Abby opened up her mouth like she was revving up for something. She had tiny pink gums. She began to cry.

"She's hungry," Lisa said. "All she does is eat and sleep and poopy-doop. I'll go feed her. You go talk with Dad and Paul. Be nice."

There were four white deck chairs. His dad and Paul were sitting in two, and the others were empty. Mike sat down and picked up his Coke.

"Great back yard," he said to Paul, trying to be nice.

"Thanks," Paul said.

Mike's dad spoke up then. "You're drinking soda pop like some sissy boy. Why don't you be a man, have a beer with us?"

Mike turned to look at him. This was the first thing the man had said directly to him since he'd arrived, and that made it the first thing he'd said to him in twelve years. It almost felt like the continuation of their last conversation. Mike shook his head. "No thanks, Dad. I'm okay."

"Los Angeles is makin' you soft, boy." His dad said the name of the city as though it rhymed with *cheese*. Los Angeleese.

"I work out every day, old man," Mike said with a smile. "Nothin's gonna make *me* soft." He slapped his hard stomach as he looked down at his dad's frail frame.

They fell into silence.

"It's a hot one today," Paul said. "Not a lot of rain lately."

"Mmm," Mike's dad said.

They were sitting in silence when Lisa came out, still carrying Abby, who had on a tiny yellow hat with a duck on the front.

"You're all so quiet out here," Lisa said. "Sounds like it's a funeral, not a family reunion. Paul, tell them about that new subdivision that's going up over the road." She turned to Mike. "It's full of mini-mansions." She sat down, holding the baby in one arm and a Diet Coke in the other. Her brown hair was catching the sun.

Mike took a long breath, looked out across the perfectly manicured lawn, and decided to leave. Tomorrow morning he would make up some excuse, tell some kind of lie that would allow him to return to LA early. He already knew that he would never come back here again.

37
Porn Star Roast Dinners

SASHA TOOK THE large chicken out of its plastic bag and set it in her brand new roasting pan on the kitchen counter. Its juices ran down her fingers. With her kitchen scissors she cut shapes out of tin foil: two circles, one triangle, and a few long straight lines. She set the silver shapes aside. It was then that she remembered to rinse. She picked up the bird and ran it under the faucet, inside and out, and patted it dry. Next she stuffed the chicken with apple slices, dribbled a mixture of apple juice and olive oil over the outside, and seasoned it with freshly ground cloves.

It wasn't easy to tie the wings up behind where the chicken's head should be, but she managed. This would be a new arrangement for the chicken, and she couldn't wait to see how it would turn out. She pushed the legs apart so that they weren't pressed up against the body and she placed the tin foil shapes across the cold skin, pushing them down firmly. Finally she put the chicken into the oven, along with another roasting pan full of cut potatoes, and she wiped her hands on her red and white gingham apron.

Billy had called yesterday to say he was coming home from Ohio early. He would be home today. "It's just too hard here," he'd said. She offered to pick him up at the airport, but he told her that Rafael doing that.

"I'll be home by 5:00 at the latest."

"It'll be Sunday. I'll make a roast dinner," she said.

"Yes, I'd like that."

Because of the *Hard Place* tour, they hadn't had a roast dinner together in over a month. That was far too long.

She smoothed out her apron now. Underneath she had on a conservative seafoam green dress that flared just below the knees. The look she was going for today was of a 1950s housewife. The dress was complemented by a pearl necklace with matching earrings, a very sensible bobbed, blond wig, and heels that were just high enough to give her some style but not so high as to make it difficult to go about merrily dusting and vacuuming, at least in theory. For a roast dinner, the fashion was as important as the food.

She never understood why Billy kept the charade going with his sister, saying that he earned his living as an actor, refusing to come out to her. Sasha refused to hide the truth for anyone, not even her family. Of course there had been a time, back in the days of the dinosaurs, when as an awkward teen she'd tried on dresses only in secret, but happily that time was long gone. Now Sasha marched into Women's Plus shops all over LA and made a point of looking surprised and insulted whenever the sales ladies told her there were no changing rooms for men. Invariably she would charm the staff and they would let her use the ladies' changing rooms, or sometimes the staff bathroom.

Unfortunately, her own family had never been as understanding as the Women's Plus sales staff, nor as easily charmed. Since moving to LA, Sasha had been entirely honest with her parents about her life, and they'd responded years ago by cutting off all contact. Some people just couldn't handle having a transvestite homosexual pornographer for a son. To make it worse, when her parents ended contact she also lost her two brothers. They were just memories now. If she called they slammed down the phone in a conspiracy of silence. It felt to her as though they were all dead, as though her entire family had been snuffed out by an awful, cataclysmic event.

There were times when she missed them. She had fond memories of her Nebraskan childhood, her mother's own roast dinners every Sunday, her incredible pancakes, the family trips to Lake McConaughy in the summer. Nevertheless, she was convinced that it was better this way, better to lose your entire family than to lose yourself.

The orange of the carrots and the green of the zucchini looked handsome in the silver pan on the counter. These roast meals, which had started intermittently in the Sasha-Billy household years ago, were now a firmly established and regular Sunday tradition. It was something to rely on, a kind of soothing constant in an otherwise erratic and occasionally perilous universe. Sometimes she invited others. Sometimes it was just she and Billy. She called them her Porn Star Roast Dinners.

In spite of the obvious potential for debauchery, the dinners were meant to be purely wholesome affairs. Most times they were. In fact, they had descended into orgies only twice – when she'd served far too much wine and invited far too many people (at least ten both times if she remembered correctly) – but nevertheless those two dinners were the ones everybody still talked about. People told stories about them in bars and on shoots. She didn't mind. A little infamy was good for the soul. Not being one to let an opportunity pass by, she'd naturally joined the orgy on both occasions, even though whenever she laid a hand on Billy, he quietly and rather predictably moved away. Each time she'd made do with the other young men in the room, who all seemed very happy to accommodate a director with such a sizeable talent as hers.

She put two bottles of chardonnay in the fridge and began setting the table. Tonight it was dinner for five. If this particular meal were a film she would perhaps call it *Roast Chicken Rumpus*, and the credits would say that it starred Billy Knight, Phil Dass, Günter Besenkammer, and that annoying Rafael Herrera. Sasha, of course, would direct.

She couldn't wait for Billy to get home. She had a surprise for him, and she was looking forward to telling him.

Günter was invited only because he was dating Phil now, and Sasha liked Phil. Up until recently, she'd only seen Günter as Steve's spying, coke snorting assistant, but rumor had it Günter had given up the cocaine altogether and mellowed as a result. If nothing else, at least the boy was consistently good eye candy. He did, after all, have the most beautiful biceps in Southern California.

By the time everything was ready, it was just past 5:00. Billy was a little late. She poured herself a glass of chardonnay, and then sat down in Billy's armchair in the front room. The burgundy upholstery enveloped her.

Looking over toward the gorgeous dining room table, she suddenly found herself wondering if her life could stay this way forever. She loved living with Billy. Would he ever tire of her and move in with some hunky lummox like Renaldo instead? She didn't think so. She hoped not. She had resolved, long ago, to never let that happen. Fortunately, although Billy slept with a lot of men, he hadn't become emotionally attached to any of them since Kerry. She would do it again if she had to – get rid of whoever threatened to take him from her, do whatever was necessary to keep him at her side. She had no qualms about it. Even if their relationship wasn't perfect, Billy was hers. She would never let him go.

She looked at the clock and realized he was a full fifteen minutes late. She got up and basted the chicken and then peeked underneath the foil shapes. Her new arrangement was working. It was going to look absolutely marvelous.

Phil and Günter were the first to arrive, even before Billy, and they each carried a bottle of wine. Günter was wearing jeans and a hot pink mesh tank top, but Phil – bless his queer little heart – was in full drag.

Long ago Sasha had realized that Phil was more ashamed of wanting to wear dresses than of actually getting fucked on camera for money. But now here he was, finally dressed like he should be.

From the moment they arrived, Sasha saw that Günter was treating Phil like a real lady – gesturing for Phil to enter the apartment before he did, allowing Phil to sit down first. Günter was clearly unlike the mass of gay men, who found drag entertaining but wouldn't be caught dead dating a man in a dress. It seemed Günter actually liked Phil in drag. Thank the goddess! Phil needed this. He needed to feel okay in women's clothing. What was wrong with it anyway? Why did it distress some people so much – even the ones who *wanted* to do it? Phil's dress was a low-cut, black sequined thing, far too flashy for a Sunday roast. He obviously needed some pointers on makeup, but the Audrey Hepburn-like French twist in his brunette wig and the elegant, majestic way he carried himself revealed that he was off to a very good start.

"Call me Phillipa," Phil said.

"Oooo!" Sasha squealed. "Girl knows how to work it." She poured two more glasses of chardonnay and proposed a toast. "To Philippa."

"Yes. To Philippa," Günter said, and although it sounded like he'd once again lost his notoriously unreliable German accent, he was looking over at Philippa with such a distracted, warm smile that this time Sasha found the loss almost endearing. They clinked glasses and drank, and then Günter reached over and kissed Philippa lightly on the cheek. Already Sasha liked Günter more than ever.

"And to you too, Sasha." Philippa raised her glass. "A toast to Sasha Zahore. For being such an inspiration to us all."

"Oh, stop it," Sasha said. "I'm just another run-of-the-mill cock in a frock."

Günter cut her off. "No, Sasha. It's true." He raised his glass. "To you, for being so, so... *you.*"

They clinked glasses a second time. Sasha mumbled "Enough already," and waved her hand dismissively in the air, although she loved it.

"I'm glad we're here first," Philippa said. "Sasha, Günter has something he wants to tell you."

Günter stared at the floor. He and Philippa were sitting like a happy couple side-by-side on the sofa, the sporty jock and the little queen. Sasha glanced toward the door, wondering where Billy was.

"Go on, tell her," Philippa said. "We made a deal. I came in drag, now you tell her the truth."

Günter paused, then looked up at Sasha. "I'm not German."

Sasha couldn't help rolling her eyes. "No shit, Sherlock. That accent goes in and out more often than my dildo."

Günter visibly winced.

"I'm sorry, doll," Sasha said. She had to remember to be kind to Günter. Philippa liked him. "So you're not from Frankfurt? Where are you from then? Lithuania? Albania? Bulgavadavia?"

"No," Günter said. "I am from Frankfurt, kind of. Except I'm from Frankfort, Tennessee. That's Frankfort with an O."

Sasha snorted but quickly regained her composure. "Really? Frankfort-with-an-O, Tennessee? I had no idea there was such a place."

"It's not really a town. More like a road with some houses on it. It's two hours east of Nashville, in Morgan County. Near Catoosa. Lots of game hunters there. Deer, wild boar, and wild turkey. We also hunt fox squirrels, gray squirrels, ruffed grouse, racoons, quail, and rabbits. Good fishing too."

"Well, well. Aren't you *both* full of surprises tonight?"

"Tell her the rest," Philippa said. "Go on."

"My name's not Günter."

Sasha leaned forward. "The wonders never cease. What's your name, doll?"

"It's Earl."

"Earl?" Sasha blinked, swooping her eyelashes like tiny birds. "That's fantastic. What a *fabulous* name."

"When I came to LA, I didn't think Steve would hire me at Cougar if I was some hick from Tennessee, so I said I was German. He still doesn't know."

Sasha could already hear the southern accent starting to creep back into this young man's voice. It was delightful. "Well, Günter – I mean Earl. Don't you worry about Steve. I'll take care of him. He'll be fine."

"And tell her the other bit," Philippa said, nodding toward Sasha as though to push forward the words.

Earl stared at the floor again. "It's too embarrassing."

"You're talking to men in dresses, bitch." Sasha snapped her fingers. "Spit it out."

"I play the banjo."

Sasha jolted back, put her hand on her chest, and gasped. "The banjo?!"

"It's horrible, I know."

Philippa reached out a thin, well-toned arm and patted Earl's knee. Her sequins shimmered. "He's very good, Sasha. You should hear him. He's really talented."

"Do you really, *seriously* play the banjo?" Sasha asked.

"To some extent a guy from Tennessee has no choice."

"Go on, tell her how good you are," Philippa said.

"Before I left Tennessee I was three-time Junior Banjo Champion for Tennessee State."

"Oh my God," Sasha said, standing up. "That's so fucking hot."

"Hot?" Earl looked up at her.

"Totally hot. How many gay muscle boys in LA can play the banjo?! You're like a rare and precious diamond! Why on earth would you hide *that*?"

He smiled.

Sasha began pacing. "Have you ever thought of getting in front of the camera, doll? Of doing porn?"

"Well, sure. Sometimes."

"That's it. You've got to. I want to film you shirtless, in little cut-off denim shorts, on a porch in the back woods, playing the banjo. Then some friend of yours comes up out of the shrubbery. You set down the banjo and immediately start fucking him like a hound dog in heat, right there on the porch where just *moments* before you were displaying your prodigious banjo talent! Earl, don't you know that talent is sexy?"

Sasha thought of the time she'd cast a real live street performer. He'd juggled knives and swallowed swords expertly before taking home several onlookers and swallowing dick in the same fashion. It was fantastic. This could be even better.

Earl was beaming from his spot on the sofa. "Wow. Banjo porn," he said. "I like it."

"Trust me, doll. You'll have more appeal as a genuine country boy from Tennessee than as a German phony. People know when you're being true. They can smell it. For me, Sasha is the most authentic, genuine thing I can be. I expect the same is true of Philippa here. We're not pretending. This is us. So, will you do it? The banjo porn?"

"Sure. Why the hell not?"

"Marvelous. Of course you'll have to do a screen test. I can arrange one tomorrow." She knew that Earl understood what she meant. He would have to jack off on camera, to prove that he could come on demand. She didn't always have a camera for a screen test. There were times when she just told guys to drop their pants and come. If they could do it they got a movie deal. "Assuming your screen test goes well, we can do a whole banjo-themed movie. I already know what we'll call it." She looked up in the air and gestured broadly. "*Appalachian Ass*, starring..." Here she paused for dramatic effect. "Earl!" She quickly turned back to him. "You don't mind going by your real name, do you? You won't even *need* a last name, with a distinctive moniker like that. I'll make you a star."

"Sure," Earl said. He put his hand on Philippa's knee. "But can Phil Dass play my boyfriend, the one who comes out of the, uh, shrubbery?"

"Of course!" Sasha yelled. "The fag rags will love that. I can see it now. 'Newcomer Earl tops real-life boyfriend Phil Dass.'" All at once she stopped pacing and looked at Earl. "But listen, no coke on my set, ever. Nothing stronger than coffee. You know that's my rule."

"Don't worry, Sasha. I don't want to be kicked off your set ever again. You're too scary."

"Good." She raised her glass, and they sealed the deal with another toast.

By the time they'd finished their second glass of chardonnay, Sasha had started to seriously worry about Billy. Where was he?

Earl said, "Billy is probably stuck in traffic, Sasha. Or maybe his flight was late. That's all."

At six o'clock the roast was done and still there was no Billy. She put the oven on low to keep things warm, and basted the chicken again. She didn't want it to dry out, but she didn't want to start eating without Billy. It would be all wrong. She would rather cancel the entire meal and send Earl and Philippa home with empty bellies than to start without her Billy.

She tried to make small talk, tried not to worry. She thought about calling Billy's pager, but he'd have to get to a pay phone to call her back, which wouldn't help at all if they really were stuck in traffic. Rafael couldn't drive his way out a paper bag. Maybe they'd been in some kind of accident. She'd kill that dildo if he hurt her Billy. She excused herself and called Billy's pager anyway, entered their home number, and then sat back down in the front room.

At six thirty she got up again and went to the kitchen. She started ringing a tea towel in her hands.

Philippa walked in and looked at Sasha with concern. "Are you okay? You look so scared."

"Billy is an hour and a half late. I left him a message on his pager but he hasn't called back. What if he isn't coming home? What if he's never coming home again?"

"Oh, Sasha. Of course he's coming home. Seriously, it's just LA traffic. I'm sure he's fine."

"You don't *know* that though, do you? He could be dead on the side of the road, and here we are drinking chardonnay. It's awful."

"Oh Sasha," Philippa said. "You love him, don't you?"

Sasha was surprised to hear the question. "Of course I do."

"Come back in the other room and let's chat some more. He'll be here soon." Philippa took Sasha's hand and led her back into the front room.

By the time the door opened at 7:00, Sasha was almost on the verge of panic. But suddenly there was Billy, sauntering in with his easy gait, flashing his charming smile.

"Hey there," Billy said.

Sasha stood up immediately, and she started screaming. "Where the hell have you been!?" Her voice was at full volume. She was waving her arms. "What the fuck have you been doing? I was expecting you over two god-dammed hours ago! You selfish asshole! I thought you were dead!" She pushed him in the chest.

Billy stepped backwards toward the door and put up his hand as though to stop Sasha from advancing. His eyes were wide. Rafael was standing behind him. Everyone was staring.

"Sasha, relax," Billy said. "We were stuck in traffic. It's okay. Relax."

"Oh my god, oh my god," she said, no longer yelling. She walked over him with her arms open. "I was so worried." She hugged him, and she could tell that the hug she received in return was tentative and distant.

"It's okay," he said. His voice was flat. "I'm sorry we're late."

Sasha couldn't help it. She started sobbing. She didn't want to be a fool in front of Rafael and Philippa and Earl, but she just couldn't stop the tears.

"Sasha, what's wrong?" Billy said. "I'm here. It's okay."

"Oh, Billy. I am just so afraid of losing you. For all I knew you were dead. You could have been dead."

"It was just LA," he said, pulling away before she wanted him to. "There was a terrible accident on the 405. Total gridlock. I got your call on my pager, but I couldn't get to a phone to call you back. We just came straight here. I'm fine. It's all right."

Her guests were staring at her now, and she suddenly felt vulnerable and exposed in the middle of the room. Of course Billy had been stuck in traffic. It was silly to have been so nervous. She threw her shoulders back and shook her head, trying to make her face go smooth again. "Oh, you know a mother worries. It's our lot in life." She hated the words as soon as they came out. The feelings she had for Billy were not the least bit motherly.

Billy put a hand on her arm now "You really were worried, weren't you?" His hand was warm and strong.

"Of course I was."

For a moment he looked her straight in the eye, deeply, and then said, "Thank you." He took his hand away. "Now, something smells good."

"That'll be your dried out, shriveled up roast chicken. I stuffed it with apples, the way you like it, but it'll probably taste more like beef jerky by now."

"Why didn't you start without us? I figured you would."

She was shocked. Did he really think she would start without him? Did he not understand anything at all? She looked at him and sighed. "Oh, Billy. You're the reason I made this damn roast bird. Because you were coming home. I would never start without you."

"You didn't have to do that, but I appreciate it." He turned to the others. "Sorry you had to wait, guys. You must be starving."

Sasha hastily introduced Billy and Rafael to the new Philippa and Earl, and after a couple quick questions everyone sat down at the table, but she wished they'd all go home. She wanted to be with her Billy alone, wanted him to hold her again, better this time. She needed him to tell her that everything between them was okay, that it would always be okay, that he would never leave her, that he would never stop coming home.

38
Bi Bi Billy

MIKE LAUGHED ALONG with everyone when Sasha brought out the chicken. She'd somehow roasted it so that it looked like it had a perfect tan line from a tiny bikini. The wings were stretched out like arms behind its missing head and the legs were sprawled apart. This was a sultry poultry at an imaginary poolside, naked. Mike didn't think the meat was dry at all. It tasted deliciously of apples.

Sasha served everybody seconds. She told them it was Sunday, and Sundays were meant for eating and everybody should eat more. There was an enormous amount of food – the chicken but also roasted vegetables, potatoes and an enormous green salad and applesauce too.

Mike was happy to have come home to this meal, to Sasha, to know that there was somebody in the world who made a special dinner with him in mind, somebody who worried so much if he was late, although it was a little odd that she'd been so upset. He tried to concentrate on how much he cared for her, on how nice the meal was. He hadn't felt this much at home since his mother died.

Still, he couldn't help feeling that – as was often the case with Sasha – it was too much. Her anger when he came in the door was disturbing. Sometimes her love made him feel claustrophobic and scared. It was like a weight on him, pushing him down. He long could he take it before it became too much?

Over dinner Sasha kept the conversation going with comments about new talent, about who was sleeping with whom, about which models had supposedly found sugar daddies. At one point Philippa said she'd heard a rumor that Max Pole had recently become HIV positive, and she didn't want to work with him anymore.

"Philippa, dear" Sasha said. "That's why we always use condoms on set. You have to act as if *everybody's* HIV positive."

"I don't care. I don't want him fucking me."

Sasha picked up her wine glass. "So on the strength of a rumor you refuse to work with the man ever again? Even *with* condoms?"

"Well, yeah."

Sasha shook her head. "That's the problem with our industry. Rumor gets out that you're HIV positive, and nobody wants to work with you anymore."

"Is that a problem?" Rafael asked. "Sounds like common sense to me."

"What do you know, Ralph?" Sasha sneered. "Billy, tell us about Ohio. How is the heartland?" She turned to the others. "Billy just came back from a visit to his family, you see. Came home three days early, just to be here for my Sunday dinner. So, Billy, how was it?"

Mike looked up and saw the entire table turned toward him. Sasha had seated him at the head of the table, as always, with her at the other end. Everybody was waiting for an answer, but how could he possibly tell them about his family? What could he say? He shrugged. "Ohio was fine. I met my new niece. I brought her presents. She's cute."

"How did your sister like the purple baby shirts I helped you pick out?" Sasha asked.

"She liked them a lot."

Earl cleared his throat. "Why'd you come home early?"

"For my Sunday dinner," Sasha said.

Mike shrugged. "Oh, family. You know. You can only take so much. My dad was there. He and I don't get along so well."

"Your dad was there?" Sasha said. "How was that?"

"He looks older, but he's the same."

"We all look older." Sasha sighed and flicked her short, blond bob. "Every single day I feel my beauty fade."

Philippa turned to Mike and asked, "Does your family know you're gay?"

"Hell no. They don't know I'm gay, don't know I do porn. I don't care what my dad thinks, but it would upset my sister too much. My mom's dead."

"Oh, I'm sorry."

"It's okay. Happened when I was a kid."

There was an awkward pause before Philippa said, "My mom still thinks I'm a hairdresser."

"Billy, dear," Sasha said across the table. "I was thinking we should spice up your career, do something to get you some attention. How about a bi film? I've got yet another great title in mind. *Bi Bi Billy*. You could do a three-way with a hot bi top and one of the major leading ladies from straight porn. You wouldn't have to fuck her, if you didn't want. Just suck a little nipple and maybe eat some pussy. Do you think you could do that?"

Mike smiled. "That's a good idea." He liked that Sasha was looking out for him. A bi film would get him some press, get people talking about him again, and it might even increase his audience.

"Of course, this would have to be after your upcoming film with Magnum Man," Sasha said.

Mike was confused. "What?"

"Oh, didn't I tell you?" She looked around at everyone. "Ah yes, of course. It's my surprise for Billy. Let me tell all of you at the same time. Ladies and Mental Men, an announcement!" She picked up her spoon and chimed it against her wine glass several times. "I've arranged something for my darling Billy. Call it a welcome home present. I met with Gavin Kennedy of Magnum Man while Billy was off in Ohio." She snapped her fingers in the air. "Got it, just like that."

"Got what?" Mike asked.

"Billy Knight in the next major Magnum Man production, of course. Working with somebody you really like, Billy. Somebody who will fuck you better than Ricardo here, I'm sure."

Rafael leaned forward quickly. "Who?"

"Oh, just some superstar top." Sasha looked down at her green fingernails.

"Who?" Mike asked.

Sasha looked up. "Six foot two. Massive amounts of muscle. Permanent dark stubble. Gorgeous hairy chest. Ten magnificent inches and the Best Sexual Performer of 1991."

"You got me a scene with Luke Champion?" Mike said.

"Two scenes, in fact. Plus a box cover photo with him. And don't worry, they'll be paying you at superstar rates. Really, what do you even *need* an agent for when you've got me?"

"No way!" Mike was thrilled. This would help his career enormously. All at once he no longer felt at risk of fading. "Thank you so much, Sasha."

"My pleasure, baby. Well, no. I take that back. The pleasure will be all *yours*. Ten thick inches worth." She smiled at Rafael.

Mike got up from the head of the table and walked around to the opposite end. He leaned down and gave Sasha a hug, then a quick kiss on the cheek. "You're the best."

"Best Director? Yes. I know."

"Best Friend," he said. Then he caught Rafael's eye and realized Rafael did not look happy.

"Let's celebrate with dessert," Sasha said, and she started clearing plates. Mike helped. Everyone congratulated him, except for Rafael.

In the kitchen with Sasha, Mike saw that the coffee pot was already on. He started pulling out the coffee cups, milk, and sugar. Sasha was putting leftover food into plastic containers.

"How much, Sasha?" Mike asked her quietly. "How much will they pay me?"

Sasha whispered. "$2,000 a scene. And you've got two scenes. One oral and one anal."

"Seriously?"

"Yes. They're banking on you, what with your recent award and your 'Best of' about to be released by Cougar. They expect sales. If we manage your career well, we can get you up to what Luke makes. It's simple math. If we can increase your popularity, you'll sell even more videos and the studios will be happy to pay you more. We need to get you out on the dancing circuit more, make it a big deal when Billy Knight comes to town. Just you watch. We'll get you earning as much as a superstar top in no time."

Suddenly Sasha turned and, as if by magic, she pulled out of the refrigerator five perfect bowls of chocolate mousse topped with strawberries. She began arranging sprigs of mint on top of each bowl.

He looked at her closely, at the 1950's TV mom outfit, at her belly, her thick legs under her flesh-colored nylons. She amazed him. He felt so deeply grateful to her, for the deal with Magnum, the scenes with Luke, this dinner, everything. He wished he could repay her. He knew that if he said, 'Let's go have sex now,' she'd say yes. There were times that he almost thought that he would, that he should. She'd be happy if he did, even if he said it right now, here in front of everyone. She'd follow him into his bedroom and tell the guests to help themselves to dessert. But the simple fact was that he loved her too much for sex.

She began carrying the mousse bowls out and placing them in front of people at the table. Everyone was saying how beautiful they looked.

An incredible peace came over Mike, and he stood in the kitchen faintly nodding to himself as he watched the scene out in the dining room. There was no way around it. Sasha was the closest thing he had to a parent. His own family was lost to him. Only by coming home early did he manage to avoid a scene. Of course he would keep in touch with his sister, but he understood now that Sasha Zahore was only the real family he had.

Along with this realization came another one, like the opposite side of the same coin: he would have to leave her some day. It would break her heart, he knew, but at some point it would have to happen. You couldn't live with your parents forever. You had to grow up. He dreaded leaving, not because he would miss her, but because he knew that Sasha would do everything in her power to stop him.

Mike still wanted to find a real lover, something more than Rafael but not at all like Sasha or Dale. He wanted someone constant at his side. Not a fuck buddy. Not a parent. He wanted something like the feeling he once had with Kerry. How strange, he thought, as Sasha set down the last of the desserts, that after all these years he still thought of Kerry, still missed him.

"Do you have the coffee, baby?" Sasha said. She was standing in front of him.

He looked at her and smiled. "Yeah."

He poured the coffee into the five cups and carried them out on a tray. Sasha, walking just behind him, carried the milk and sugar.

PART FIVE

ACTS OF LOVE

39
Two Hooligans

IT HAPPENED IN Texas, on a mild evening in late May 1997. Dale was pumping gas into the car he'd rented for the day when he noticed two young men inside the gas station. They were staring at him. He wasn't in drag so there was no reason to stare. They weren't cruising him. He knew what cruising looked like. This was something else.

The gas station was on an isolated stretch of road, and there were no other customers. Bright florescent lights lit the area around the pumps. Beyond that was an empty, falling darkness. The station attendant was inside behind the counter, but from where Dale stood, a rack of cigarettes blocked his view of the man. The two young hooligans continued to look out the large front window, wearing hooded sweatshirts and jeans, sunglasses on one despite the fading light.

Dale had flown into Houston for work two days prior – a talent hunt night at the Male Room on Pacific Avenue, Sasha's first in a year and a half. The Male Room, unfortunately, was not on the A List talent hunt circuit. It was run down and not very popular, but lately Sasha took what she could get. The owners had asked her to judge a wet underwear competition. The winner was supposed to get a part in a movie, assuming he passed the screen test Sasha conducted in a back room afterward. The winner turned out to be gorgeous but horribly nervous, and he suffered from total equipment failure. Sasha had no choice but to dismiss him, albeit gently, and call in the runner-up. That one came beautifully and got the job, or at least the promise of one.

Now Dale fumbled with the gas nozzle in his hand. He'd rented the car in order to check out a location almost a half day's drive outside the city. A friend of a friend owned an old ranch and was going to let Sasha film there. It was a fantastic opportunity, because locations didn't come so easily anymore. Still, Dale wanted to be certain it would work. He wanted to see the ranch himself.

Inside the gas station, the two hooligans had begun lurking near the magazines, pretending to read but looking out toward him, turning to each other and saying things, laughing. Dale tried to butch it up, tried to look like just an average forty-nine year old man perfectly comfortable pumping gas, someone who would draw no attention and inspire no rage.

Glancing down through the car window he saw the last two promotional copies of Sasha's most recent video, *Mama's Boys*, in the back seat. It showed Sasha in a large red dress with black lace, surrounded by shirtless porn stars. Dale thought he should cover those videos with something. It wouldn't be good to be seen with gay porn in the back seat. Not here.

He stared at the videos as he continued pumping his gas, hating that box cover. It was a reminder of a mistake.

The fact was that in the past two years not a single one of Sasha's movies had done well. There were so many troubles on set – strung-out models, unreliable crew – and Sasha simply hadn't been able to capture the sexual energy her early professional films were known for. To break the bad run she'd done a few 'chicks with dicks' movies, but they were niche market. Despite her hopes of making them appeal to a wider audience, they sold barely enough for the studio to recoup their money. After that, she went back to pure gay porn with beefy boys, and she cast herself in a non-sexual role, as the owner of a gay brothel in *Mama's Boys*. She tried to get Billy Knight to sign on as her star, but he was busy. Lately Billy was always busy.

The fag rags gave *Mama's Boys* horrible reviews. One reviewer actually said, "Sasha Zahore is the most dick-deflating presence you could ever find in gay porn. She should stay behind the camera, and definitely off the box cover." What she'd hoped would be hot sex interspersed with episodes of camp fun had turned out to be a dud. Some people around LA were actually saying that she'd lost her knack, that after just a short time at the height of gay porn director stardom, she'd fallen out of touch. Sasha hadn't directed a truly successful film since the string of money makers she did with Billy Knight back in 1994: *Romeo and Julius* co-staring Luke Champion, the straight crossover hit *Bi Bi Billy*, the much-lauded *Banging Billy 2* (sequel to the cult classic), and of course the two-time Silver Dick winner *Tender is the Knight*. But that was three years ago, and in gay porn time, one year was as good as a decade.

Dale had always assumed that once Sasha made it to the top she would stay there. She would be Queen of the Whole Wide World, forever. But a porn director's reputation was only as good as the sales of her last film, and it seemed Sasha's age and experience and willingness to try new things were all being played against her. Her first real failure was *Appalachian Ass*. But that was all Earl's fault. Anyway, the past was past. Her new Texas western full of outdoor sex and macho cowboys would make for a fabulous comeback. It would sell like hotcakes. It had to.

Earlier that afternoon, the owner of the ranch had greeted Dale with a frail handshake. The man was a lonely, retired farmer in his late 60's, and his only reason for wanting Sasha to film on his ranch, besides the location fee, was that he wanted to watch. He gave Dale a tour of the property. It was perfect – several large fields that were private enough to fuck in, a rustic stable and a corral, even a hayloft. The possibilities were endless. After showing Dale around, the old farmer made coffee and they sat on the porch and chatted. He'd seen some of Sasha's movies, said he loved the idea of a bunch of gay porn stars having sex on his land. Eventually Dale thanked him, gave him a copy of *Mama's Boys*, promised to be in touch, and got back on the road. He'd been driving for an hour when he stopped here for gas.

Now he looked toward the station again, smelling the acrid scent of gasoline fumes in the air. The hooligans were still there. The one with sunglasses was talking. The other was nodding.

The pump stopped. The tank was full. Dale returned the nozzle, screwed the gas cap on, and began walking up to the station to pay. He made a point of not making any eye contact, but he felt the two hooligans watching him the entire way. They mumbled something as he walked by, then snickered.

The gas station attendant looked even rougher than they did. His eyes were bloodshot and there was a tattoo of a spider on the back of his hand. If something happened, if the hooligans decided a little fag bashing would be fun, this man behind the counter would be no help.

Dale handed over his cash, thinking forward to his return flight to Los Angeles. It was scheduled for tomorrow, after one more night in Houston.

The spider came back toward him; the attendant handed him his change. Dale thanked the man and turned around. He had to walk past the hooligans just once more. Then he would be free. He looked down, ignoring them completely, mindful not to do anything to set them off, and moved toward the door.

They were no longer trying to hide the fact that they were staring. Their gaze seared his face as he approached. They stood in his way, didn't move aside. He stepped around them and kept moving and finally made it outside.

The night air was cool, and he moved quickly toward his car. He was almost there when one of them called out, "Hey there." He pretended not to hear and continued walking.

"Hey, wait a minute!"

He opened the car door and began to climb inside, planning to hit the lock right away, but his plan failed. As he was pulling the door shut behind him, it stopped. One of them was standing there, holding the door with a firm grip.

"Hang on," a voice said.

"Leave me alone." Dale was trying to pull the door shut, not looking up. He hadn't covered the videos in the back seat.

The young man leaned down and looked into the car at Dale. It was the one with sunglasses. "Hey. Why the hurry?"

"I'm just going now," Dale said.

"What's wrong?"

"Let go." Dale pulled at the door again, then snapped at him. "Get your hands off my fucking door!"

"Whoa. Easy. Are you somebody? What's your name?"

Dale paused. He didn't know why he answered. It seemed like a bargain. His name for his freedom. "Dale," he said. "Now let me go."

"But are you anybody else?"

The young man reached forward and turned his sunglasses up, resting them on top of his head, as though to get a better look.

It was only then that Dale was able see his face clearly. What he saw in those suddenly unshielded eyes was not antagonism or hatred, but curiosity.

"Some people call me Sasha," Dale said.

The guy turned and shouted to his friend. "I knew it! I told you!" He turned back to Dale. "I thought it was you. He said no, but I knew it. We loved your movies. You were a great director. Can I have your autograph?"

All at once Dale was hit with a wall of conflicting emotion. Relief that he was not about to be bashed. Delight to be recognized in such an unlikely spot. Joy at the compliment. But there was also something else – a sharp stab coming up from underneath. The young man had spoken as if Sasha's career was something already over. *You were a great director.* How could it all become history so quickly?

Three years ago, it wasn't unusual for fans in gay bars to come up to Sasha and tell her that they loved her films. But Dale, without the dress, had always been invisible. Certainly recognition had never happened like this – never out of drag, in a gas station in the middle of nowhere. Never in a place so hopelessly and desperately *straight*. In some ways this moment, here, next to the gas pumps, was even more meaningful than winning a Silver Dick. It was a revelation. There were young, man-loving hooligans in Texas who actually knew who he was. It could have been perfect, but for the past tense.

Still, Dale was so thankful he wasn't about to be bashed that he reached into the back seat and grabbed the two copies of *Mama's Boys*. He got out of the car and gave one to each young hooligan, who both looked suddenly more sexy than dangerous. Dale was happy to let those last extra copies go, to put that movie truly behind him. "It's not my best work, I'm afraid," he added.

"Cool," the one without sunglasses said. "I didn't know you were still making movies."

There was that stab again.

"Yes," Dale answered. "Yes, I am."

They laughed strangely. "Billy Knight's not in this movie?" They were both studying the box cover.

"No, he's not."

"Aw, man," one said.

"That's a bummer," said the other.

For a moment Dale actually feared they were going to give the movies back. "I do more than Billy Knight movies, of course," he said.

"But that guy's so hot."

Dale nodded. "Yes. He certainly is."

"Well, thanks anyway, man."

"Yeah, thanks."

The two young men said goodbye and walked off side by side, punching each other in the arm as they headed over toward a rusty pickup truck and drove away.

Later that night, finally back in Houston in the safety of his hotel near the gay bars, Dale called Mike's cell phone. He wanted to tell Mike about the day, about the ranch, about being recognized at the gas station, but there was no answer. He left a brief message. "Hi, baby. I'll be home tomorrow evening. I can't wait to see you."

As he hung up the phone he tried not to think about how distant Mike had been the day before leaving for Texas. It seemed like something was terribly wrong, but Mike had refused to talk. Dale told himself now that it was just a bad mood, that it was fine. He climbed into bed and began taking notes on the ranch, possible scenes and a loose storyline. Somewhere in this Western there would have to be at least one sexy hooligan, perhaps a horse thief, someone who would have to be punished by the ranch hands – forced to do unspeakable, lovely things. Images flashed through Dale's mind. He set aside his notes and touched his dick. As usual, the one in the middle of his fantasy was Mike.

40
Unprotected

MIKE PULLED OUT his good clothes first – his three suits, his one tuxedo, and all his dress shirts. He took them from the closet and laid them carefully in his suitcase one at a time. It was a small suitcase. Usually he liked to travel light.

Clients had taken him to Acapulco, Belize and Madrid. Last year one of his regulars took him to Paris for a week. Mike had been amazed by the silver swan-shaped faucets in their bathroom at the Ritz, by the restaurant roof that had opened as they ate, leaving them suddenly sitting under stars. Mike had spent enough time in fine restaurants that he'd actually begun to feel comfortable in them. All during that week in Paris he thought of Kerry, and he wondered if his old lover was still living there as a kept man in an apartment somewhere. He half expected to see Kerry come walking down some historic street toward him, but he never did.

Now Mike folded another dress shirt. This time he wasn't packing for a client. This was for himself. When the suitcase was full he zipped it shut, but there was still more to pack. He got up and went into the kitchen, passing the black and white pictures of himself along the hallway wall. He would leave those. Those were Dale's.

He grabbed a handful of garbage bags from the kitchen cupboard, took them back to his bedroom, and started filling them up with the rest of his clothes – all his jeans and T-shirts, his leather chaps, his harness, the tiny cut-off shorts he'd worn in *Tender is the Knight*, his work out gear, underwear, his collection of baseball caps, all of his shoes (combat boots, Italian loafers, running shoes), his sweaters and jackets, even the old red sweatshirt with the tear in the neck from when Sasha had pushed him when he was sick, which he'd never worn again but had never thrown away.

By the time his drawers and closet were empty, there was a pile of distended garbage bags next to him that looked like shiny black clouds. He began taking the posters down. It wasn't until he saw the emptiness he was leaving behind – the thumbtack holes in the walls, the bare expanse of white – that he fully realized how horrible it would be for Dale. He couldn't do it. Not like this. Although he'd planned this day now for some time, he suddenly saw how much pain it would cause. He wanted to protect Dale from that hurt, if he could. After all of their time together Dale deserved to be told face to face, not just come home and find him gone.

Mike reached into his back pocket for his wallet and pulled out the receipt for the U-Haul truck that was already parked outside on the street. The truck was large and orange and white and seemed sturdy enough to carry his life. He walked out to the front room, dialed the phone, and booked the truck for one more day. Then he called Nick and told him not to bother coming over. The move would have to wait until tomorrow. Dale was getting back from Texas later that evening, and Mike wanted to tell him to his face. Nick seemed to understand, and he said he could help out tomorrow instead.

"But you're not having second thoughts, are you?" Nick asked. "I mean, you're definitely still moving in, right?"

Mike said, "Yeah. I'm still moving in."

Back in his bedroom, he put the posters back up on the wall again – the Australian surf team in their Speedos, the muscleman standing next to a 1970 Mustang, the hand-signed poster of Luke Champion. ("To my favorite bottom," Luke had written.) Next Mike opened up a garbage bag and took out a change of clothes, enough to stay one more day. Then he shoved all the bags into his closet, along with the suitcase, and shut the doors tightly. He looked around. There was no sign that he'd been packing up all his things.

Two weeks earlier Mike had gone with Nick to Utopia. They were sweating shirtless on the dance floor together when out of nowhere Nick asked Mike if he wanted to move in.

Nick Demachio was known in the industry for his puppy dog eyes, his pouty Italian lips, and his slightly asymmetrical yet entirely masculine smile. He and Mike met on a shoot about a year ago. Mike liked Nick a lot. He was easy to be with. They talked about the industry and directors and difficult johns. They fucked from time to time.

Mike had always thought it would be nice if he could spend more time with Nick, not just because Nick was a great fuck, but because he really liked being with him. The problem was that Nick never stopped chasing new meat long enough to express an interest in anything serious, so Mike had always held back. He never dared to say that he would have really liked something more. So he was surprised and thrilled when Nick asked him to move in.

"Really?" Mike said, smiling. "Move in with you?"

Nick looked back and offered one of his lop-sided grins. "Sure. It would be good."

It seemed so simple that Mike didn't know what to say. He loved the idea, and in a flash he saw himself living with Nick happily – waking up side by side in the mornings, watching TV on the couch with their arms around each other, peeing with the bathroom door open and not caring at all if the other one saw.

"My roommate moved out," Nick explained. "I need help with the rent. You'd be as good a roommate as anybody."

Mike winced. "So uh, so you mean... move in just as roommates?"

"Well, yeah. Of course. You didn't think I meant—" Nick's eyes grew wide and he pointed a finger back and forth between them, indicating some kind of stronger, unthinkable, connection.

"No. Of course not." Mike shook his head vehemently and took a long drink of his beer. To want anything more, to even say it, was clearly a breach of some kind of unspoken agreement between them. What they had was friendship peppered with occasional and unconditional sex. They were fuck buddies. It was easy and it was free and that was all it would ever be.

Now Mike leaned his back against the closet doors, as though afraid the clothing-stuffed bags inside would come to life and push their way back out. He turned and sat down on the edge of his bed, looking back at the closet, at the indented brass doorknobs that reflected him back in miniature and upside down.

He hadn't really 'dated' anybody since he'd dumped Rafael three years ago. It was just a night here, a fuck there. For Mike, desire had begun to feel like a complicated ache, a discomfort, and while sex made the discomfort go away, it always came back. Yet even worse than that discomfort was the thing underneath it, a stronger pain that felt like something resonating, a deep desire that went beyond sex. Mike was lonely.

In the past few years, finding anyone even remotely resembling a boyfriend had become more difficult than ever. Billy Knight had become one of the highest paid and most well known porn stars in the business, easily making as much as the hot, famous tops. He'd had interviews and cover shots with every gay porn periodical out there – not only *Rod & Shaft*, but also *Gladiator*, *Hunkfest*, and even *Man Love Magazine*.

Mike had always thought success would protect him from sadness, but with his firmly established superstar status, an entirely new cause of heartache had arisen, a new problem. The guys who were turned on by Mike's larger-than-life porn reputation didn't want anything more than a star fuck, a video fantasy in the flesh, while the guys who were out there looking for relationships were put off by the fact that he got paid to get fucked on film and by wealthy clients in private. Porn celebrity made people weird – even weirder, it seemed, than with 'normal' celebrity – and Mike was sick of the way guys either fawned all over him or avoided him like the plague. There was nothing in between.

Years ago he'd learned to recognize the weird light in people's eyes that crept in when they were being affected by fame. It caused faces to change, and a feverish, awed blindness to occur. He didn't like it. He was grateful that at least there were a lot of people who didn't watch gay porn and who, consequently, had no idea who he was.

For a while Mike thought he'd found what he was looking for with a guy named Jay. Jay was small, smooth, and lithe – not normally his type – but Jay had a way of making Mike feel like he wasn't a porn star, and Mike loved that. They fucked off and on for over a month and things seemed to be going well, when suddenly Jay started asking Mike to fuck him without a condom. "Do me bareback," he'd say.

Mike didn't actually mind being a top off camera every once in a while, although his on-screen porn persona was still entirely defined by being a bottom. Occasionally he topped for clients, when they wanted it. Now and then he topped Nick. But he'd always been safe. He still got tested every three months, never did bareback.

He told Jay no, but Jay kept asking.

"It'll be fun," Jay said, trying any angle he could to make Mike say yes. "It'll make us feel closer."

Mike knew that some people weren't as afraid anymore. Guys were no longer dying like they used to.

"It isn't such a big deal if you get it now," Jay told him. "You just take the new drugs and you're fine."

The positive guys Mike knew didn't make it seem fine. Sure, you might not die, but it was still horrible, always fighting off some new infection, having to pop pills for the rest of your life just to keep yourself alive, all the nasty side effects they caused.

Regardless, it was clear to Mike that something was beginning to change. Even his clients were asking for bareback sex more often – although it was always him they wanted to take it up the ass unprotected, never themselves. Around West Hollywood there were gay video shops that had pulled all their old 1970s porn videos out of dusty storage rooms to display them in special sections called 'Pre-Condom Classics.' And there was one small, renegade gay porn studio that had actually gone back to making new bareback films – low-budget productions that showed guys eating cum and taking loads up the ass.

All the established gay studios still used condoms religiously, and they even blacklisted directors and models that didn't. If you decided to make a bareback film, you could pretty much give up on ever working for Cougar, Magnum Man, or Hard Bodies again.

In straight porn, however, sex without condoms was still the norm. Nobody was shocked by it or called it bareback. It was just sex.

Mike knew there were guys out there who were so tired of the constant, seemingly hopeless struggle to avoid HIV that they'd begun giving in and seeking it out, intentionally trying to get infected just to get it over with. Sure, it was rare, but it happened.

For almost three weeks, Mike had told Jay over and over that he wouldn't fuck him bareback. For some reason Jay still kept asking. Finally Mike began wondering if Jay might actually be a bug chaser. Maybe it wasn't just the supposed thrill and intimacy and freedom of unprotected sex Jay was after – maybe it was the virus itself. He quit seeing Jay after that.

Lying down on his bed now, Mike hugged his pillow and looked up at the posters he'd just put back on the wall. He'd come to the conclusion some time ago that it was easier to concentrate on a career than on a boyfriend.

Mike was proud of what he'd accomplished in porn. Billy Knight was widely credited with being the first bottom to make it to the top. The new young bottoms looked up to him like some respected elder.

He'd certainly come a long way from the days back in Cincinnati when he would jack off to Luke Champion videos, to actually doing his first scene with Luke in *Romeo and Julius*. He'd loved every minute of that shoot. Sure, Luke had a bit of an ego, but he also had an incredibly thoughtful, supportive side. They'd hit it off well. Mike realized that Luke's aloof exterior was a way of protecting himself from all the people who fawned over him. Mike understood. Since that first shoot together Luke had actually become something of a friend and mentor, like an older brother. Luke's advice had helped Mike to do well over the past four years.

With all his income from movies, dancing gigs, and clients, Mike was pulling in six figures. He'd started actually saving money. At Luke's recommendation, Mike only did three or four films a year, and in each one he tried to do something new, even if it was just licking a guys balls in a different way, or twisting his body unexpectedly while getting fucked, so that his viewers didn't get bored. He had to work hard to maintain his longevity – hitting the gym five days a week, watching his diet, studying sexual technique in porn and in person, continually. Billy Knight had become a brand, a business. He remembered Freddy's old advice. *People pay more for the good stuff. Keep 'em interested and they'll keep coming.* What would Freddy say now? Would he be proud?

Still, even with all Mike's success, he was getting tired. He'd been doing porn now for nearly eight years. He'd been hustling for thirteen years. He was thirty-two years old. Hadn't he left Cincinnati with the idea of quitting hustling? Somehow back then he believed that porn would bring an end to the hustling, but it hadn't. Now the idea of quitting seemed unfathomable. It was what he did.

One of Mike's enduring frustrations was that he hadn't been able to get any income from products, which could set you up in retirement. All the superstar tops made big money with dildos. Some company would sign a deal with them to make a rubber replica of their cock, sometimes slightly exaggerated in size, and market it with the star's name and photo on the box.

Luke had recently told Mike that the popular Champion Dildo was still earning him almost $50,000 annually, even though Luke had finally retired for good two years ago. Mike had tried pitching a 'Billy Bottom' – a fuckable replica of his ass – to several adult toy makers last year, but nobody took him up on it. They said things like that never sold as well as dildos. It was cocks people paid big money for.

Mike got up off the bed and walked out into the kitchen, opened the refrigerator and pulled out a can of orange pop. He leaned against the counter drinking it. The can was cold in his hand. He thought about Nick.

"You'd have your own room," Nick had said that night at Utopia. "I'm a trouble-free roommate."

Mike said yes right away, even though it wasn't really what he wanted with Nick. He was almost certain he could handle Nick as a roommate, and maybe every once in a while they could still slip into each other's bed for a convenience fuck. It could be handy, having Nick just down the hall. Later that night Mike pretended he didn't care when Nick left the bar with some guy he'd just met.

Carrying his orange pop, Mike walked out into the front room and looked around the apartment he shared with Dale. Here was the fake leather couch he'd first slept on eight years ago. There was the bookcase with all their Silver Dicks – his seven next to Dale's two.

Maybe Billy Knight was part of the reason Nick couldn't imagine being anything more than fuck buddies. Maybe somehow that colossal persona had got in the way even for Nick.

Mike looked over at the burgundy chair he'd brought home years ago, then up at that sappy painting Dale had insisted on buying on Fire Island – those two muscle men holding hands, frozen forever on some beach, mid-step, never getting anywhere.

It was so hard to know what to do with Dale. Although Mike cared deeply for him, sometimes living with him felt suffocating, the way all of Dale's attention was on him all the time, the way there was no place to relax, to feel unobserved, unless he was home alone or went into his bedroom and shut the door tightly behind him, turning the lock. He almost always slept with his bedroom door locked now. Sometimes he felt like Dale watched him in his sleep. Moving out was the best thing he could possibly do, although he knew it would break Dale's heart.

Lately he always had to check in and explain himself to Dale. *I'm going here, I'm doing this, I've been there.* Nick, on the other hand, was so indifferent to everything that he wouldn't keep tabs at all. Nick would give him space. Although Mike could afford to live on his own, Nick would provide company without the claustrophobia he felt with Dale.

Mike believed Dale had become stuck in his feelings for him, snagged on something that was actually stopping both of them from moving forward. But sometimes he wondered how much responsibility he had for Dale's feelings. In the beginning, after all, hadn't he tried to make Dale fall for him, to *want* him, just a little? Wasn't that part of the way he'd gained some kind of control?

But now he had to step out from underneath Dale's shadow. Mike was not the same young man as when they first met. He'd grown and changed. It was time. And it had to be abrupt. He knew if he gave Dale much warning, if he announced he was leaving in a month, Dale would spend that month moaning and complaining and generally trying to talk him out of it. He might even succeed.

Mike rubbed his hand across his stomach, took another sip of orange pop. It was unclear what he should do with his day now that his plans had changed. He'd always thought of himself as decisive and strong-minded, and he was surprised now to feel so hesitant and unsure, changing his mind back and forth this way. But he was leaving Dale. And leaving Dale perplexed him. As much as he wanted to do it, it was hard.

He could still take some things over to Nick's today. He could take his clothes, some boxes, a few tiny things that wouldn't be missed. He could drive them over in his car. It would be easy. Tomorrow he and Nick would use the U-Haul to take over his bed and dresser, night stand, the small TV from his bedroom and the bookcase where he kept his porn – all the things that would be too obvious if he moved them today.

He downed the rest of his orange pop and went back into his bedroom, picked up the keys to his car, and opened the closet doors again.

41
Save a Horse, Ride a Cowboy

DALE BOARDED THE plane in Houston carrying his old green shoulder bag in one hand. In the other hand he held a shopping bag labeled 'Western World.' He couldn't wait to give Mike his present.

The plane lifted him into the air, and he thought about how lucky he was to have Mike. As long as that beautiful man was at his side, he never felt like a complete failure. Mike Dudley was the only enduring and reliable stronghold of happiness in the muddle of Dale Smith's life. As the land fell away, Dale tried to figure out how he would ask Mike, how he would propose his latest idea.

He didn't think that Mike would say no, not this time. This film would be a hit, guaranteed. Mike's schedule hadn't allowed him to be in Sasha's last five films – or was it six? If Billy Knight's name and photo had appeared next to Sasha on the cover of *Mama's Boys*, sales no doubt would have been better. So Dale was planning to schedule filming for this new Western entirely around Mike's availability. He'd get Mike's buy-in even before approaching any of the studios. It was the same old dilemma. If Sasha could tell the studios that she'd already secured Billy Knight, she'd have a better chance of making it. She was going to make this movie, it was going to star Billy Knight, and it was going to be fabulous.

Later, as the plane began its descent, there was a twinge of anticipation in Dale's chest. Being away from Mike, even for short trips, had become increasingly difficult. Whenever

Mike went off on dancing gigs or travel jobs, Dale felt an emptiness that was unsettling. Things were just easier when Mike was nearby.

In LA Dale gathered his purple, floral-print suitcase at the baggage carousel and went to long-term parking to get his car. Soon he was driving along with the heavy congestion of the freeway, listening to Etta James on CD singing "I'll take care of you." Her voice boomed out about how much she longed to take care of the one she loved, and Dale sang along. He thought that Sasha should do a number to this. He looked towards the hazy slopes of the Santa Monica Mountains at the edge of the city and felt happy to be home. The sun was shining through the smog. The world was full of possibility.

He exited at Santa Monica Boulevard and headed into West Hollywood. When he got to Fountain Avenue, he double parked near a U-Haul truck, turned on the hazards, and ran up to the apartment.

There was Mike, sitting on the couch and watching TV Dale ran over and gave him a hug and saying, "Hello, hello, hello!"

Mike hugged him back, but he looked sad.

"Are you okay?" Dale asked.

"Fine. Fine."

"I'm double parked. Can you help me bring my suitcase up?"

Mike followed him back down to the street and took the heavy suitcase out of the trunk.

"Don't look in this," Dale said, handing Mike the Western World bag, then he drove off to find someplace to put the car.

Later, Mike sat on Dale's bed as Dale unpacked and told stories about his trip, about the wet underwear contest and how terrible it was that the winner couldn't come on demand, about how nicely the runner-up performed, about the two hooligans who had recognized him.

The entire time it was clear that Mike was only half listening.

"What's wrong?" Dale asked.

"There's something we need to talk about."

Dale didn't like the sound of that. "Wait. I have a present for you," he said, sitting down on the bed next to Mike and handing him the Western World bag.

"I don't need a present," Mike said.

"Well, I'm not taking it back to Texas to return it, so you're stuck with it."

Mike opened the box. He pulled out the beautiful dark brown boots, embroidered with just the right amount of detail – not so much to look frilly, but not so little as to look plain. "No way," he said. "Boots. Why?"

"I wanted to. They're size nine. I hope they're okay. Try them on."

Mike put them on and stood to look in the full-length mirror. Then he turned to Dale and said, "They're perfect."

But somehow Mike still looked sad.

Dale sighed. "Those make a hot guy even hotter. Look at you. What a hottie. Studly Dudley."

With that, finally Mike smiled. "Thank you."

"So you like them?"

"Yes. They're great."

Dale patted the bed until Mike sat down next to him again. "You'll look great in those boots in Sasha's new movie. It's going to be a sexy Western. The ranch I checked out in Texas is wonderful. You'll be the star, of course. Box cover. Top billing. Top dollar. Everything a superstar needs."

"What are you talking about?"

"Sasha's next movie. You'll be the star. I'm going to call it, *Save a Horse, Ride a Cowboy.*"

Mike didn't even crack a smile. His eyes seemed strange. "Dale, I'm really busy," he said.

Dale leaned in and lowered his voice into a whisper, tilted his chin down and began to trace a circle with his finger on the back of Mike's hand. "Oh, baby. You know as well as I do that Sasha needs to make a comeback before it's too late. Before everybody forgets her. Please? She needs your help. Will you star in this movie for her? For me?"

Mike pulled his hand away but then looked back. "When are you filming?"

"That totally depends on you. Since the problem lately has been your busy schedule, this time it's all going to be planned around you, Mr. Knight. When are you free?"

"What studio is it with?"

"Not sure yet, but one of the biggies. I wanted to make sure you said yes before going to the studios with the idea. You'll be the ace up my sleeve. I'm so happy you'll do it."

"I didn't say that." Mike turned so that he was no longer facing Dale. He stared at the floor for a moment. "I'm really sorry. I've booked my four films for the year and you know I don't do any more than that."

"What?"

"You'll find somebody else. Some cute, up-and-coming guy." He looked over his shoulder at Dale.

"But it'll be a fantastic movie. You'll see. You won't regret doing it. It'll be like before. Sasha and Billy. Billy and Sasha. Everyone will be talking about us."

"I really don't want to."

"But I said I'd plan it around your schedule."

"I'm sorry." Mike shook his head.

Something was happening that Dale didn't understand. "You mean you won't help me?"

Mike turned toward Dale a little more. When he spoke, his voice was soft. "Dale, how much have I helped you? I got you your first big contract. I was in your first four big films. I've done so much for you." He reached out and touched Dale's shoulder and said, very gently, "I can't carry you anymore."

The room seemed to shift. It was a horrible thing to say. Dale was shocked. "What do you mean, *you can't carry me*? You're where you are because I put you there."

"Look, I don't want to fight," Mike said. "There's something I need to talk to you about. Something else." He turned away again, so that Dale saw him in profile.

Dale didn't want to hear whatever it was that Mike had to say. It felt like something was unraveling.

"I don't really know how to say this, so I'm just going to say it." Mike was speaking slowly. "We've been living together for eight years now. We've had a lot of fun."

It was a knit dress, and it was unraveling starting at the bottom, working its way up. Someone was pulling a string. Dale felt like his clothes were disappearing.

"What are you saying?" he asked.

Mike continued to stare at the wall. "Dale, you know sooner or later I just need to go out on my own."

The string went out into the hallway, through the front room, out the apartment door and down the stairs, through the foyer and into the outside air of LA.

"I'm moving out," Mike said.

In one strong pull, the rest of the dress was gone. Dale felt naked.

"What do you mean?" he asked.

"I mean it's time for me to go, to live in another place."

"Not with me?"

Mike stood up and turned around to look at him. "I really care for you a lot Dale, but I need to do this. It'll be good for both of us."

"Oh. So you have to leave LA."

"No. I'll still be in West Hollywood."

"It's this apartment? You're sick of this apartment. So we'll move. We'll get a new place together."

"No, Dale. The apartment's fine. It's just... I need a little space."

"We'll get a bigger place. Maybe you need a bigger bedroom. We could buy a house together. That's it. A house would be nice, don't you think? We could even move to the suburbs if you want. I'd do that for you. Let's move to Lakewood. The streets are tree lined and it feels like a small town. Would you like that?"

"No. I don't want to buy a house. I'm moving in with Nick."

"Nick?" Dale said. "You mean that dopey-faced little street whore?"

"He's not a street whore."

"Bullshit. I saw him on Sunset Boulevard just the other night in a pair of little hot pants."

"I used to be a street whore."

Dale said nothing.

"He works for Premier Escorts," Mike said. "I doubt that was him you saw on the street, but even if it was, so what. Listen, you don't have to make up reasons to hate him. We're just going to be roommates. His old roommate left and I'm moving in. He needs help paying the rent. No need to be jealous."

"Jealous? What do you mean? Why would I be jealous of *him*?"

"So I'm moving my stuff over there tomorrow. Nick's coming over in the morning to help me."

"Tomorrow? Tomorrow? You're leaving just like that?" Dale paused. "Wait a minute. Is that U-Haul on the street yours?"

Mike mumbled, "Yes."

Dale was suddenly both hurt and angry. "You little fucker. You already have a truck."

"I'll pay you rent for the next month, so that you have time to find another roommate if you need to. But I'm taking my stuff, moving out tomorrow."

"Which stuff?"

"My stuff. My dresser and bed, my clothes, the little TV in my room."

"Your bedroom will be empty."

"It's my stuff. I'm taking it with me."

"You can't."

"I bought it. It's not yours."

Dale felt an enormous pressure behind his eyes, and the room seemed very far away. He did not want to cry. The Western World box lay open and empty on the bed, the tissue paper folded back. The boots were still on Mike's feet. Dale sat perfectly still and said, "So you're giving me twenty-four hours' notice?"

"I'm sorry. It's just better like this. I'm not leaving you in a lurch. It's really like a month's notice, because I'm still going to pay you rent for June."

"Oh, great. A month."

"If you haven't found another roommate by the end of June, then maybe I can pay you a second month's rent. We'll see. I don't want to cause you any trouble."

Dale looked at the empty box. "You're such a fucking boy," he said. "This is totally juvenile. At thirty-two, you're still a god-damned child." When he looked up, he saw Mike's brown eyes staring back. "It's not about the money, Mike. I thought you understood that."

"You'll still see me. I'll come around." Mike's voice had grown soft, trying to soothe. "I'll be here for porn star roast dinners. You can still have them."

The pressure behind Dale's eyes grew stronger. Mike was just standing there. "I can't believe that you're leaving me like this," Dale said.

"Relax. It's okay. I'm not leaving you. I'm just moving out. I'm sleeping here tonight."

"Oh, lucky me. One more night, then that street whore gets you." Dale stood up and turned his back toward Mike. "You're leaving me because my career's hit a rough patch."

"No, I'm not."

"I wish I could believe that. What else are you planning to take, besides your bedroom furniture?"

"Do you mind if I take the burgundy chair?"

"What?" Dale looked back at him. "Why would you do that? Why would you want to take our chair?"

"Sorry. Forget it. You can keep the chair." Mike forced a smile and reached forward and lightly punched Dale in the arm. "Hey. Buck up little fighter."

Dale had never wanted to hit Mike before, but now it was all he could do to stop himself from slapping him. He jerked away.

"Dale, it's not the end of the world. You'll find somebody else to be your roommate, maybe some new model who'll need a place to stay. He'll be younger than me, and hot. Maybe he can even be in your horse movie. He'll boost your career."

"I don't want just some *roommate*, or just a model for my movies. Do you really think that's all you are to me? I want *you*. I want you here with me. In this apartment. Together." Dale realized that he was crying, speaking loudly, making a mess of everything.

Mike looked away and said nothing.

"You really don't get it, do you Mike? You never got it. Damn it, you have no idea how much I care for you. You are the single most important person in the world to me, Michael Dudley. But you're so fucking selfish, so wrapped up in yourself that you can't see past the end of your own nose. You ride roughshod over everyone around you, totally insensitive to what you're doing to people, what you're doing to *me*. Goddamn you." Dale felt his hands shaking. "Get the fuck out of my room."

"Dale –"

"Get out!" Dale heard the intensity and fury in his own voice. It was as though the sound itself pushed Mike back, made him move toward the door, then out into the hallway. Dale walked over and swung the door shut. It slammed loudly.

As he turned back toward his room, his eyes came to rest on the picture of Mike that he kept in a small frame on his nightstand. In it, Mike was seated nearly naked on the floor with his jeans down around his ankles, turning his head to the side and looking at the camera. His left leg was raised, hiding his crotch, and his fleshy bubble butt was pushed against the floor. Dale had taken the picture before a shoot one day, and he'd always loved the way it had caught the sultry, relaxed look in Mike's eyes, the smooth beauty of his body.

He yanked the photo off the nightstand, threw it at the door, and let out a long, loud scream.

42
Moving Out

STANDING IN THE hallway, Mike heard something crash and fall. He heard Dale yell. He lifted his hand up to knock, but stopped. There was no point. He'd done enough damage tonight. He couldn't mend this right now, not in the state Dale was in.

He walked down the hallway into his bedroom and closed the door. The boots made loud clunks on the floor as he went. He took them off, set them aside, and once again began taking his posters down off the walls. He felt the sting of what Dale had said. It was probably true. He was acting like a boy. At heart, he feared he was still selfish.

Although he would never say so to Dale, Mike agreed with the poor reviews of Sasha's last few films. The fact was that the only successful films she'd ever made were the ones he'd starred in. It was confusing. Sometimes he wasn't quite sure how much he owed Dale, and how much Dale owed him.

Even so, he hoped that what Dale had said wasn't true. He hoped he wasn't leaving Dale because Dale's career had hit a rough patch. But he wasn't sure.

He finished rolling up all of his posters and had begun clearing things out from under his bed when a door slammed shut. He poked his head out into the hallway and called Dale's name, but there was no answer. He knocked on Dale's bedroom door, but there was only silence, so he opened the door. The room was empty. He went into the front room and opened the door to the hallway and called down the stairs, but there was no answer at all. Dale was gone.

That night he went to bed half listening for a key in the front lock, but the sound never came, and the next morning there was still no sign of Dale. It was then that Mike started seriously worrying. Even on the rare occasions when Dale found casual sex, he never stayed out all night. He always finished up and came directly home. Mike tried to tell himself that it was fine, that Dale simply didn't want to be there when Nick showed up, that everything would be okay. He'd see Dale soon.

When Nick arrived the next day, he was carrying two iced skim lattes and he handed one to Mike. There was something strange about Nick's manner. His lop-sided grin seemed hesitant. They drank their coffees before they got started moving furniture. As Nick sat on the couch and Mike sat in the burgundy armchair, it finally became clear what the problem was.

Nick said, "Mike, you pay your rent, right?"

"Of course I do."

"I heard something last night. Remember that guy who used to be German?"

"Earl?"

"Yeah. That's the one. Used to call himself Günter."

"What about him?"

"I was out on a job last night and Earl paged me," Nick said. "I don't know how he got my number. He said he wanted to meet me, had something urgent to tell me. So after I got done fucking this banker in Bel Air I drove over to meet Earl at Pinky's. He told me how Dale's kicking you out because you haven't paid your rent in over six months, how all your money goes up your nose."

Mike was surprised, but then he laughed. "That's not true."

"Really?" The look on Nick's face showed he wasn't sure.

"Hey, you know me. Earl's a total liar. He's the one with the drug problem." Everyone in West Hollywood knew the story of what had happened to Earl.

* * *

Four years ago, when Sasha first told Steve Logan that Günter-the-German-Assistant was really Earl-the-Tennessee-Backwater-Boy-Willing-to-Fuck-for-Money, Steve hadn't been upset at all. He knew an opportunity when he saw it, and when Sasha told him her *Appalachian Ass* idea, he immediately loved it. She promptly began planning the movie, securing the location, hiring models and crew. She was so caught up in her plans that she remained completely oblivious to Earl's sudden downward spiral.

What started for Earl as a secret return to his old coke habit very quickly grew into a strong and fanatical devotion to crystal meth. On the day he was scheduled to do his first big scene for *Appalachian Ass*, he simply never showed.

Sasha was forced to find a last-minute replacement to fuck Earl's then-boyfriend Phil Dass. The entire movie had been planned around Earl, and the replacement not only lacked Earl's perfect, melon-like biceps and rock-hard abs, but he didn't have the natural Tennessee charm or friendly, lilting accent. Sasha made him fake the accent, which sounded so obviously phony that it made the entire production come across as amateurish and a bit silly. To make matters worse, the replacement had never touched a banjo in his life when

Sasha – stubbornly wed to her original idea – made him play one naked on film. *Appalachian Ass* was a terrible failure.

As for Earl, by the time the movie had found its way to the discount bins at gay video stores across the nation, his love of crystal meth had grown so out of control that he'd already lost his job as Steve's assistant at Cougar, and then he eventually lost Phil too. Last Mike heard, Phil was back in New York doing drag as Philippa Phanny. Everyone knew Earl was currently making his living as a third-rate street and bar hustler, that he was now HIV positive, and that he was still hopelessly addicted to crystal.

* * *

"Who told Earl my money goes up my nose?" Mike asked Nick now.

Nick shook his head. "He wouldn't say."

Mike wondered what Dale was doing last night. "Nick, you know I'm a total light-weight. Nothing goes up my nose. And I always pay my rent. You can ask Dale."

"Where is Dale, anyway?" Nick looked around.

"He didn't come home last night." Mike paused. The rumor must have come from Dale, from Sasha. There was no other way. Mike could almost see Sasha sitting there at the Lucky Pony last night, telling Earl what to say, then slipping off quietly before Nick showed up. Mike was touched. Sasha wanted him to stay with her so badly that she was willing to tell pathetic little lies to stop him from going. It was an act of total desperation, but it grew out of love, and he was moved by it.

"Don't worry, Mike," Nick said. "I didn't believe Earl."

"Thanks."

Nick smiled. "But I'll tell you what, if you don't pay your rent, I'll fucking throw your shit to the curb and change the locks while you're out. Got it?"

Mike laughed. "Got it. Let's load the truck."

They carried everything Mike owned down the stairs and into the truck – except for the burgundy armchair. Nick didn't say anything else about Earl. After the truck was loaded, Nick waited outside while Mike went back into the apartment one last time to make sure he hadn't forgotten anything.

Opening the front door, it already felt like the space wasn't his. In the front room he looked at Dale's two Silver Dicks standing alone on the long bookshelf – one for *My Swim Coach Loves Me* and the other for *Tender is the Knight*. They looked lonely without Mike's own awards beside them. Mike couldn't help thinking that somehow the household looked less exceptional now, less talented. Then he felt bad for thinking it.

He wandered around, looking at all the rooms. His own bedroom was empty and clean. The kitchen looked like it was ready for someone to make breakfast, all the plates and cups just waiting. He stood by the kitchen counter and opened his wallet, left a month's rent in cash under a pink flamingo glass on the counter, along with a note with his new phone number. *Dale – Call me. Take care of yourself. M.*

He walked back down the hallway to Dale's bedroom door, opened it, stepped in, and stood there for a moment. Everything was chaotic in that room, makeup spreading across the vanity and even nearby on the floor, costumes and dresses thrown left and right across the bed and on the back of the chair. Video equipment and old cameras were stacked in one corner. Piles of fabric had nearly buried the pink sewing machine. Mike's photograph was on the floor in the corner. He picked it up, found the glass cracked in a long diagonal, and put it back on Dale's nightstand as it was. He wished he knew what to do with Dale, how to handle him, how to love him in a way that didn't hurt him.

Standing in front of the open closet, he took in all the glitter and feathers there. Dale's shoes were in a heap on the floor: men's loafers, women's platform boots, red stilettos, pink fuzzy things. Matching shoes were nowhere near each other. He leaned down and picked up a black woman's shoe with a chunky heel and realized it was a tap shoe. He laughed to himself. Dale didn't know how to tap dance. No doubt he planned to learn. Then Mike noticed the corner of a grey box, behind the shoes. He pushed aside some of the dresses and saw that it was a tiny safe. As far as he knew, Dale didn't have any jewelry precious enough to lock up. He'd always assumed all of Sasha's baubles were fake. What did Dale need a safe for? Suddenly he felt guilty for snooping. He returned the tap shoe, slid the dresses back, and quickly left the room.

Out in the front room he paused for one last look. The burgundy chair was waiting for Dale. The air felt stale. Then he left. He locked the apartment door behind him, and he ran all the way down the stairs.

43
Empty

DALE STEPPED INTO the apartment wearing a black flamenco dress and carrying Sasha's wig, which was still pinned with a tiny black veil. Upon seeing the Silver Dick shelf, his heart fell. Until that moment he'd held out a faint hope that Mike would still be there.

Some of the books were missing off the bookshelves. The burgundy chair was still in the corner. Dale dropped the wig onto the coffee table, stepped over to the Silver Dick shelf, and let his hand come down to rest on the spot where Mike's awards used to be. The lace of his dress sleeve dragged across the shelf.

He backed away slowly, then turned and began to move down the hall. Looking into Mike's bedroom hurt the most. It was entirely empty. He paused, took a deep breath to regain his balance, then stepped forward into Mike's room until he was standing in the very middle, looking at all of the things that weren't there. Bed. Dresser. Nightstand. Mike.

Indentations in the carpet marked the missing furniture. The walls were dotted with the blemishes of thumbtack holes from those adorable, silly posters. The room seemed drained, as though a plug had been pulled out of a spot in the middle of the floor and Mike and everything had swirled down and disappeared. Dale remembered Mike appearing like an angel under the disco ball at the Lucky Pony that very first night, all the stars turning around him. But now Mike was gone. Dale knelt, and then laid down on his side in a heap of black ruffles and lace. He wished for the floor to open up and swallow him too, to take him to wherever Mike was.

The realization came to him then, as he felt the texture of the carpet pushing against his cheek. His worst fear had come true. He was nothing. He was just a middle-aged man in a dress, lying on the floor in an empty room. Without Mike, there was nothing spectacular or fabulous about Dale Smith at all. He was entirely and hopelessly mediocre. If he'd had any real talent he never would have fallen, never would have failed, never would have lost Mike like this now.

There was a very straightforward choice in front of him. He could accept that Mike was gone, or he could fight it. It was that simple.

Long ago Dale had come to understand that what he lacked in talent, he made up for in tenacity. He would not give up yet. Although perhaps it was true that he couldn't make Mike love him, maybe, just maybe, he could somehow make Mike *need* him. If someone needed you, did it really matter whether or not they loved you? If they needed you they'd come back. They'd stay.

If they needed you, it might feel just a little bit like love.

44
A Shocking Proposal

MIKE'S NEW BEDROOM at Nick's place wasn't as nice as his old one. It was smaller and the one narrow window didn't let in much light. He'd been to Nick's place a dozen or so times before, when they'd gotten drunk and fucked, and it felt strange in the first few weeks to not be there for sex, to not be taking off his clothes in Nick's bedroom.

Very quickly they established new patterns, as roommates. They came and went at their own times, occasionally chatted over morning coffee, swapping bleary-eyed stories about their clients from the night before. Every once in a while they went to the gym together. They rarely hung out at home with each other, and they never had sex anymore. It was very clear that they were not boyfriends. Nick brought home a lot of guys. Mike would sometimes wake in the middle of the night to the sound of Nick's headboard banging against the wall between their rooms.

Mike didn't bring guys home. He hadn't done that since he'd broken up with Rafael. Now, if he picked a guy up in a bar they went over to the other guy's place, or went to the baths. He didn't feel like bringing anybody home unless it was an actual boyfriend. He laughed at himself. He was becoming conservative. He was practically a prude.

For over two weeks Dale didn't return Mike's calls, in spite of the multiple messages Mike left on Dale's machine. The first few days were especially unnerving, not knowing for sure if Dale ever made it home after he'd disappeared. Mike was tempted to stop by and check, but then he asked around and someone said they'd seen Sasha at Cougar. Just knowing that made Mike feel better.

Then finally, walking in the door after the gym on a Wednesday afternoon, he found a message on his machine. "Helloooo Billy! Sasha here. It's Hump Night tonight at the Lucky Pony. I'm doing something special. It'd be great to see you there. Kiss, kiss!"

Sasha had been appearing at the Lucky Pony every Wednesday night now for over fifteen years. On the rare occasions when she couldn't perform, the younger drag queens tried to fill her shoes, but only Sasha was synonymous with Wednesday at the Lucky Pony – so much so that a couple years ago she'd managed to convince the bar owners to market the evening as 'Hump Night with Sasha Zahore.' Now posters tacked up around LA and quarter-page ads in the gay rags promoted the night with a big picture of Sasha front and center, go-go boys around her like angels in the air.

Even if her directing career was on the rocks, Sasha's position as the main attraction at Hump Night was secure. In fact, her fleeting notoriety as a director had actually helped to boost her reputation with the Lucky Pony regulars. She was multi-talented – a modern Renaissance woman.

Mike set down his gym bag now and checked his calendar. He had a job that evening with Trent Conner, a big Holly-wood action star who was deep in the closet, but there would be plenty of time to get to the Lucky Pony afterward. Trent was always so excited that he came too soon.

Mike called Sasha back at Cougar right away, but she didn't answer. He left a message. "Hey Sasha. Great to hear from you. I'll see you there."

That evening, he managed to make Trent shoot his load in record time – ten minutes, all over the action-hero-sized bed in his private Malibu Beach House. It wasn't even 10:30 by the time Mike had driven out from under the 'June Gloom' fog that covered the coast in late spring and early summer. He headed directly toward West Hollywood, to the Lucky Pony.

Sasha was still up on stage, smiling and lip-synching with three go-go boys behind her. The people in the audience were laughing a lot, every time Sasha tripped and acted like a clumsy clown or batted her eyes at an especially hunky guy in the crowd. Mike watched carefully. Her shtick hadn't changed in years, but it worked. Everyone here loved her. At least she had this.

Just before her last song, she made an announcement. "Ladies and gentlemen, Sasha's going to do something a little different tonight. Hold onto your hats, 'cause this fat bitch is gonna *sing*." Suddenly all the multi-colored stage lights went black, and a single spotlight illuminated her face, causing her silver sequined gown to sparkle. "This is a song called 'I walk a little faster' by Blossom Dearie," she said. "She's of my faves. I'd like to dedicate this song to Billy." The music started. It was slow. Mike was surprised there were no pre-recorded vocals coming out of the speakers, just the melancholy notes of a piano. When Sasha opened her mouth in front of the hand-held microphone and her very own voice came out – mellow and surprisingly nice, if just a bit rough around the edges.

But instead of filling the stage with her usual camp energy, as she sang she seemed incredibly sad. It was a slow song. She sang about wanting to see the man she loved, about always hoping that he was just around the next corner. She added humor only once, when she began stumbling on her high heels as she sang about banging into things, about falling. But even the stumble was subtle, almost half-hearted compared to how she normally flailed about, and rather than evoking outright laughter from the crowd, it just made people smile with a kind of heartbroken sympathy.

The song ended on a sad refrain about her futile hopes of seeing her lover. It was somehow – in spite of the campy drag, in spite of the shabby bar – deeply moving. She performed with such emotion that when the song finished it left behind a stunned, powerful silence. A glass clinked at the bar. Then all of a sudden the audience broke into cheers and applause. Sasha took an uncharacteristically tiny bow, said absolutely nothing, and disappeared behind the tattered silver streamers at the back of the stage.

Mike waited. The lights came up and dance music started. Ten minutes later he saw Sasha walk out the door at the side of the stage and begin moving toward the bar. She'd changed costumes and was now wearing a white dress with a long purple cape and a blond bouffant wig topped with a tiny gold crown. She towered above everyone, and the crowd parted in front of her as she walked.

Every once in a while someone put a hand out to touch her and say something – a compliment no doubt, some kind of adulation – and she would give a coy look, say something that made everyone around her laugh, then she'd move on. Mike smiled as he watched her from the other side of the room. She was so much better at being famous, in her own small way, than he was.

At the bar her Cosmopolitan was already waiting for her, and the bartender pointed over toward Mike. When she saw him she beamed, raised one hand in the air and waved dramatically, then began hurrying over. Everywhere she went people stepped aside.

"Darling, so good of you to come!" She kissed him on the cheek and gestured wildly into the air. "Uh! There are so many people in here tonight, a girl practically has to grease her thighs just to make it across the room." Gone was the melancholy of the song. She was back to being herself.

"Thanks for inviting me," Mike said.

She sighed. "You know you're always on my guest list."

Mike didn't know how to talk about the song she'd dedicated to him. "You haven't been returning my calls," he said. "How are you?"

"Oh, you know. We get by." She looked around the room.

"Have you advertised for a roommate yet?"

"You don't waste any time, do you? Go right for the jugular. Well, Roommate schmoomate." She tilted her head back, opened her eyes wide, and spoke in a thick accent, "I vant to be alooone."

"You know I can't pay rent at two places forever, right?"

"Jesus, Billy." She shook her head and looked irritated. "I know that."

They stood in an awkward silence for a moment.

"You sounded nice," Mike said. "I was surprised you really sang."

"Well, the old girl still has a few tricks up her sleeve."

Mike laughed. "I'm sure you do. How's Earl?"

"Earl? Haven't seen him."

"No, of course you haven't." Mike smiled knowingly. He didn't want to humiliate her. He just wanted to her to understand that he knew, that he forgave her. "For some strange reason Earl thinks I don't pay my rent. He told Nick all my money goes up my nose."

"Well, imagine that." She looked up at the disco ball hanging above the dance floor.

"Where do you think he could have heard such a thing?"

"I wouldn't have a clue." Her face shifted then, and she looked at him closely. "The world is a mysterious place, Billy. Things happen all the time and we don't know why. Things we can't change. Try as we might." She looked away quickly.

Mike dropped the subject. He decided to let her have her pride.

Directly in front of them, two guys climbed onto the stage and began dancing shirtless. They had to be in their early twenties, laughing and beautiful, both wearing body glitter across their chest and back. They were dancing to some new song Mike didn't know.

Sasha smiled sadly. "Have you ever worn body glitter?"

"No. I can't say I have."

"Everybody should wear body glitter at least once in their life."

"They look so young," Mike said. "What are they, twelve?"

"How many years have you been in porn now?"

Mike shrugged. "Eight."

"Good God. You know in porn star years you're, like, fifty-six or something. You're *ancient*." She laughed playfully. Then she smoothed her dress across her hips as though she was preparing a speech. "Billy dear, I appreciate that you're concerned about people becoming bored with you."

"Well – "

Sasha put up her hand. "Shush. I need to talk to you about something. I need to talk to you about a movie."

"Oh, Sasha. I said no."

"Wait. I'm not done. This is something different." She cleared her throat. "Billy dear, you're always looking for that new thing to do, trying to keep the interest of your bug-eyed little fans, right? Well, let me tell you, I have the perfect thing." She paused for dramatic effect. "How would you like to do a bareback film?"

"What?" Mike leaned back a little.

She began speaking quickly. "We'll change the name of my Western, call it *Riding Bareback*. We'll still use the Texas ranch. The opening shots will be of you and some hot top horseback riding – without saddles, of course – and heading off into the fields someplace, where you both hop off your horses and Mr. Top immediately pushes you down and fucks you bareback in the open air."

"You're joking, right?"

"Well, no. Mark my words, bareback is the wave of the future. We'll be in the vanguard. Sure, it's only low-budget renegade stuff today, but mark my words. Before you know it, bareback will be huge. Huuuge, I tell you. It's the next big thing."

"I'm not having unprotected sex."

"But of course we'll have all the models tested."

"That's no guarantee, and you know it. It takes a while for the virus to show up. What's wrong with you? You've always demanded safe sex. Are you high?"

"Oh, Billy, don't be silly. The times they are a-changing. Adapt and evolve, or become a dinosaur. There's a market for this now."

"Sasha, I'm not about to risk getting sick for a fuck flick. Besides, you know as well as I do that it's career suicide. The big studios are all against it. Suggesting I do your movie bareback makes me want to do it less, not more."

"Baby." She put her hand on his shoulder. "You're not as young as you used to be. You really do need something new.

We could do an entire *series* of bareback films. We could even do *Banging Billy 3: Billy goes Bareback*! It could totally revitalize your career. You'd have everyone's attention."

"I don't need to revitalize my career. My career's fine. I have everyone's attention. You're the one without their attention."

"No need to be nasty, doll. Listen, your career might be fine now, but how much longer until those young glitter boys over there take your place?"

Mike looked over at the young guys dancing. He shook his head and set down his beer. "I don't need to hear this. I didn't come here to have you tell me I'm washed up and need to start getting fucked bareback."

As he walked across the bar and toward the door, he heard her yelling to him from behind, but he just kept moving.

45
Another Little Job

AFTER HER LAST set, Sasha went directly to Pinky's Boy Bar and settled herself comfortably onto a barstool. She'd left her crown and purple cape back at the Lucky Pony. Her white dress looked crisp and bright against the wood of the bar, and the fabric picked up the pastel tones from the Christmas lights over the pool table.

She hated the way Billy had stormed out. She was an idiot for even asking.

Dave, the bartender, walked over. The man was in his early sixties now, close to retirement she supposed. He was almost completely bald, and still had his signature open collar with two silver chains. It would be a sad day when Dave left Pinky's. "The usual?" he said.

"Yes, Dave. Thanks."

As Dave turned to mix her drink, she looked around the room. The place had definitely gone downhill. Nothing had been done with it since she first brought Billy in eight years ago. Still, the place was full of the same familiar mixture of sellers and buyers. Two brawny men in very tight jeans were playing pool. A couple of skinny twinks lurked nearby. Sasha didn't care about any of them. She was looking for one person in particular. She wanted Earl.

"Here you are, Sasha," Dave said, setting her Cosmopolitan in front of her. She smiled to herself. Having a Cosmopolitan at Pinky's was a bit like eating caviar at McDonald's.

"Dave, have you seen him?" she asked.

"Yeah, he's here." Dave looked around the small bar. "Must be in the john."

"Did you get a chance to watch him after I left him here that night?"

"Of course. You know I'm good for my word."

"And did he end up talking to that Nick Demachio?"

"Yes, he did. They were sitting here at the bar, talking about your boy Billy. Nick looked a little upset at whatever it was Earl had to say."

"Good. Thanks, doll."

"Anytime Sasha, for you."

Dave turned away to reach for a bottle. Sasha continued scanning the room.

When she'd hired Earl to do that teensy-weensy job, she'd felt somewhat hesitant. After all, years ago he'd proven himself so unreliable. She was still a little bitter about *Appalachian Ass*, which could have been so good, but in her more magnanimous moments she recognized that the loss was equally Earl's. The big-biceped banjo boy could have been a superstar, could have shot straight to the top. In spite of her initial concern over hiring him again for anything, clearly he'd come through just fine this time. It didn't take much. Only 50 bucks and a few drinks.

While Sasha was sorry to be reduced to spreading lies about the man she loved most, she now realized that getting Billy back would require much more just a little fib or two. This was why she needed Earl again. Just one more time. It had to be Earl. She didn't know anybody else who was desperate enough to do what she wanted done.

Finally, there he was standing at the back of the room, talking with another working boy. One of the tragedies of Earl was that he was still wearing mesh tank tops now after all these years. Tonight's version was purple. Sadly, his biceps were no longer the most beautiful in Southern California. They'd gone a bit soft. His face had also become slightly gaunt. The poor boy was living a hard life now. Even so, every once in a while you could see hints of his former glory.

She winked and waved him over to the bar. He said something to his friend and then began walking over to her alone. She suppressed her urge to offer fashion advice and instead gave the barstool next to her a lively slap, indicating exactly where she wanted him to put his ass.

"Earl, doll," she said, and she gave him a big kiss on the cheek. "I have another little job for you."

46
The Color is Blue

IT WAS NOON when the phone rang. Mike had just woken up, and he fumbled with the receiver. As soon as he said hello, Dale's voice launched into an apology.

"I'm so sorry, Mike. I'm just so stupid. I don't know what I was thinking last night. I'll never ask you to do a bareback film again. I was silly to even think it."

Dale sounded so sincere that Mike didn't know how to respond. Dale continued talking.

"I'll start looking for a roommate right away. And of course your career doesn't need to be revitalized. I know that. You're not washed up. I really am so sorry."

Mike hesitated, then he said, "Thank you." He was stunned by Dale's total turnaround, and he wondered what had caused it.

Dale cleared his throat. "Listen, I'm going to a party this weekend, and wondered if you'd like to join me. Let's try this again."

"I don't know, Dale."

"What do you mean you don't know? You don't know if you want to see me?"

"No, that's not it."

"Good. I promise I won't even *mention* making a movie. The party's at Rob Lessing's mansion up in the hills. Big Hollywood director from way back. Queer as a three-dollar bill. Wants drag queens and porn stars to give his little soirée some color. Half of gay LA will be there. You'll come with me? Please, baby? So I don't have to go alone?"

Later, as Mike hung up the phone, he couldn't figure out why he'd said yes. He still felt angry with Dale for suggesting that he do bareback, yet at the same time, even after all that, he felt tied to Dale, connected in a way he could not name. It would be terrible to lose him altogether.

It was Sasha who picked him up that Saturday night. She waited in the car and honked the horn. "Look," she said as he climbed into the passenger seat, gesturing to her outfit. Her dress was a deep, iridescent blue that shimmered in the overhead light. She had on a large fake sapphire ring. "The color for tonight is blue. We'll only drink things that match my dress."

"Blue drinks?" Mike said.

"Yes. And just in case the good Mr. Lessing's bar doesn't have tonight's special color, I've brought my own." She reached behind the seat and pulled out a bottle of Blue Curacao. "Blue tropical drinks all night. I even have pineapple juice. You'll join me with blue drinks, won't you? As my companion this evening, it would be dreadful if your drinks didn't match my dress."

Mike laughed. "Well then, blue drinks it is."

She paused and looked at what he was wearing – black jeans and a black dress shirt, loose at the collar. "You don't have anything blue to wear, do you?"

"I'm wearing this."

"What about that vivid blue dress shirt that client of yours gave you last year? You know, the one with the silver buttons? That would look fabulous. We'd be a Blue Dream Team."

He smiled. She was a fun-loving man in a dress trying to make everything between them feel light and easy with the color blue. He'd considered talking to her tonight about how terrible her bareback request had made him feel, but he decided let that go now. They didn't need to go over it again. They understood each other, and it was good not to have things feel heavy between them. "You really want me to run back in and change?" he said. "So I can match a bottle of blue booze." He shook his head and laughed.

"Oh, would you? Billy, you're such a dear. We'll make a fantastic entrance. Besides, that way we can spill our drinks all over ourselves and nobody will know." She winked.

He looked at her. This was part of why he loved her – this sense of play, these innocent, ridiculous demands. He opened the car door and went back inside.

The cars were already parked down the street when they pulled up to Lessing's front gate a half an hour later, both of them in blue. They parked further on and walked back, Sasha carrying the bottle of Blue Curacao in her hand, Mike carrying the pineapple juice.

The house was modern and had a flat roof. Mike thought it looked like an office building, all grey and white. Inside there were white tile floors everywhere and high, empty ceilings with windows that ran up to the night sky and looked out over a large pool out back, with the nighttime lights of Los Angeles spreading into the distance. The guests were an odd mix of sophisticated older men and women with grey hair and nice clothes, surrounded by groups of younger gay muscle boys, a few drag queens, and the occasional cluster of pretty straight girls in little dresses. Mike wondered if Lessing had actually called a talent agency to hire young people for the night, so the evening would feel less like a retirement convention and more like a party.

Lessing himself greeted Sasha and Mike as they came in. "Just look at you two, visions in blue!" He had a lisp and his upper lip was sweaty.

"Don't we look fabulous?" Sasha said.

Lessing gave her a big hug, and then leered at Mike, saying, "This one needs no introduction. Pleased to meet you, Mr. Knight."

Mike shook Lessing's hand, which was frail and clammy.

They quickly left Lessing behind and moved through the house, then out the back doors. Sasha ran off to arrange their blue drinks and left Mike standing at the edge of the pool. It was lit underwater so that a soft greenish-blue light shone up onto the people and palm trees nearby. Mike walked to the edge of the garden and looked out at the city lights below. In the dark, from a distance, was the only way this city was beautiful.

When Sasha came back, she was carrying two blue drinks – each with a tiny umbrella propped at the rim. "Blue Hawaiians," she said, holding one out for Mike. "Drink up."

Mike took the drink. It was sweet, tasted of rum and pineapple and banana, and went down easy, like candy. They stood for a moment at the edge of the garden, separate from the party, looking down at the city.

Sasha said, "With the right person this would almost seem romantic."

Mike looked at her. "Let's join the party." He turned to walk back toward the other people, but Sasha stopped him with a hand on his arm.

"Mike, I don't ever want to lose you." Her voice had dropped and Mike felt suddenly like he was talking to Dale.

"You're not going to lose me," he said, and then he gave her a small kiss on the cheek and walked back toward the party. She followed.

They were standing near the pool again when Mike saw a man in tight black dress pants and a black mesh tank top looking their way. It took him a moment before he realized the man was Earl. He felt instantly awkward.

Earl looked at him and walked over. "Mike, hi. How are you? Sasha, hello."

"Earl," Mike said. "Funny seeing *you* here."

There was an awkward pause. Mike saw Sasha give Earl an expectant look and then tip her head in Mike's direction.

"Hey, Mike," Earl said. "Um, I'm just really sorry."

"Sorry?"

"Yeah. I, uh, I heard something about you, and I thought it was true, and I told Nick, but it's not true, and I'm sorry."

Mike looked at Sasha, then back toward Earl. "It's okay. I understand." Then he looked at Sasha again. "Let's just forget about it."

"Cool," Earl said. "Thanks."

"Well, happy, happy!" Sasha said. From her spot between Mike and Earl, she reached out and put an arm around each of them. "Let's do this. Let's have a celebratory drink to make amends and move on. Earl, the bartender has a secret bottle of Blue Curacao under the bar. If you go tell him that Sasha sent you for a Blue Hawaiian, he'll set you up. You can drink blue drinks with us."

Earl smiled. "Sure, Sasha. Thanks." He quickly turned and walked away, glancing back at Mike as he went.

Mike turned to Sasha. "Sasha, okay, fine. He apologized. That's nice. I appreciate it." He looked at her closely. "Really, I do. But why do we have to have a drink with him? That guy totally screwed you over with *Appalachian Ass.* Totally ruined your movie. You don't have to act like he's your best friend."

"Billy, dear. When you get to be my age, you realize that holding on to a grudge does you no good at all. Earl struggles. We all struggle. It's not easy, none of this." She gestured around into the air. "Cut the poor man some slack. He apologized to you. And as for my movie, Jesus, that was four years ago. And besides, it's a proven medical fact that grudges are the number one cause of premature aging. Nothing is worth another wrinkle."

Earl came back holding a blue drink with an umbrella that matched theirs. He held it up in front of Mike and said, "Cheers."

Mike reluctantly raised his drink. They all clinked glasses.

"Onwards and upwards," Sasha said, taking a small sip. "After all, if the fucking homos can't stick together, then nobody can. You might as well blow up the planet and call it a day."

As the evening progressed, somehow Earl was always nearby. He was laughing and talking with Sasha, or asking Mike questions about his latest movie, about his dancing gigs. Every once in a while, Earl reached out and touched Mike and said how good he looked. Mike didn't like Earl, but the more he drank the less he cared.

When he woke up the next morning, he recognized immediately that he was in Dale's bed. There was no other room he knew of that had such intense fuchsia walls, or a pink sewing machine in the corner. The bedroom door was open. His head hurt. He reached down and found he was wearing nothing but his underwear. Dale was in the kitchen, singing.

It was a struggle to get out of the bed. His body was moving slower than he wanted it to. He felt horribly hung over as he walked down the hallway toward the bathroom and then peed. When he came out he saw that his old bedroom door was closed. He opened it slowly and stepped in. It was still empty. He walked out and went into the kitchen. Dale was mixing pancake batter.

"Mikey!" Dale said. "Welcome back to the land of the living. How are you feeling? Coffee?"

"Yes. Terrible. What happened last night?"

"Oh, I've never seen you so drunk. Those Blue Hawaiians pack a wallop, and they go down so easy! Here, drink this." Dale handed him a mug of hot, black coffee.

"But did anything happen? I mean…"

"You mean, between you and me? God no. As always, we slept like sisters. You passed out in a deck chair by the pool and I brought you home."

Mike tried to remember a deck chair, but couldn't. He had vague recollection of sitting in the back seat of Sasha's car, with Earl and Sasha in front.

"Was Earl with us? When you brought me home? I remember Earl."

"Oh, yes. Well, I gave him a ride home. Pancakes?"

"I seriously don't remember last night. I don't feel so good."

Dale was already pouring the batter into his old cast iron skillet. "That's why you should eat. If you end up puking, you'll get rid of the toxins. If you don't, it'll give you strength!"

As the batter hit the hot skillet, it sizzled. Dale hummed.

47

A Lonely Summer

DURING THE MONTHS that followed the Lessing party, Dale felt that time had begun to move unbearably slowly.

He didn't see Mike nearly enough all summer long. He was lucky if he saw him once a week, for a ten-minute chat at Hump Night. In spite of the promises upon moving out, Mike was never available for Porn Star Roast Dinners on Sundays, and Dale refused to host them without Mike. Sometimes Mike would meet Dale at a restaurant for dinner midweek, or occasionally for lunch, but it always felt like a rushed catch-up with a friend instead of a pleasant visit at home with a loved one, as it should feel.

Mike was clearly very busy and preoccupied with his own life – arranging another dancing tour to promote his latest film, meeting new clients. Although nobody supported Sasha the first time she wanted to promote a film with a tour, now a promotional tour was practically an industry standard. One afternoon Mike told Dale over lunch that he was taking a course to become a certified gym instructor, and that he was already three weeks into it. Dale was surprised – not by the course or the fact that Mike was taking it, but by the fact that Mike had been doing something for over three weeks entirely unbeknownst to him. There was a time when he knew every single movement Mike made, or intended to make, even things as small as going shopping for a new pair of shoes. Clearly that time had passed. Mike was his own man now.

Dale had a lot of spare time on his hands, which he'd never had when Mike was living with him. So he began to revisit old haunts. Frustrated that Sasha's Texas Western still had no backing and was going nowhere, he put on a wig and dress and began visiting Venice Beach again, small video camera in hand. It was almost like the old days.

All that summer Sasha could be found walking along the Venice Boardwalk most Saturday afternoons. Venice was at its glory on the weekends, when it was most crowded. Even after all those years it was still one of the most fantastic spots in Los Angeles. Sasha loved the cheap jewelry and T-shirt shops, all the people selling sunglasses, the postcards and tourists everywhere. It was like a tacky carnival every day.

Each weekend she watched a parade of humanity – shirtless muscle men, penniless musicians, and chainsaw-juggling entertainers. There were activists shouting "Meat is murder!" alongside bikini-clad women with fabulously artificial breasts. Cyclists and roller skaters streamed by, wearing almost nothing.

Occasionally she would retreat from the bedlam of the boardwalk and collect herself over a cup of tea at the Rose Café, where she could look out at the 30-foot transvestite ballerina clown above the entrance to the Venice Renaissance Building across the way. Sasha loved LA.

Once, as she sat in the Rose Café having tea, she saw two plain-looking men walk in, both with salt-and-pepper hair and plaid shirts. There was nothing remarkable about either of them, but somehow they fascinated her. One wore a baseball cap. The other had a thick beard. They each had a small paunch at their stomachs. Baseball Cap kept absentmindedly touching Beard's arm. There was an obvious ease between them that suggested they'd been lovers for years.

The waitress led them to a table nearby, and Sasha watched closely. When Beard actually pulled out the chair for Baseball Cap, Sasha couldn't help but smile. She wondered for a moment what it would be like to be with somebody for such a long time, as lovers, somebody your own age, who declined and deteriorated as you did. She was, after all, almost fifty years old and not getting younger. No doubt Beard and Baseball Cap knew each other's bodies well – knew not only every wrinkle, mole, and little flap of sagging skin, but all the special places too, those spots that still, after so many years, liked very much to be touched. She felt herself envying them deeply, in spite of the fact that they were relatively unattractive and decidedly unglamorous. The feeling became so strong that eventually she had to turn away. It was like staring at an eclipse, something that hurt your eyes. She shifted in her seat and looked down into her teacup, concentrating in what she saw there, as though she were reading her own tea leaves, looking for her future. She left shortly after that.

When her Billy finally left LA for a dancing tour he'd been talking about for months, Sasha began going to Venice even more. Sometimes, to console herself, she bought little trinkets from the beach-side shops – plastic rings and cheap baubles. Other times she would visit the galleries and vintage-clothing stores on Abbot Kinney Boulevard. On one occasion, trying to stop herself from missing Billy so much, she had her aura adjusted by a woman on the boardwalk with purple hair. It didn't help.

Every time she visited Venice, she eventually found herself standing at the edge of the outdoor gym near the beach. She would whistle and jeer and the men would laugh, sweating in the afternoon sun. It felt like the old days. Every now and then one of them would walk over to her, and if they were sexy enough she would give them her card, explain that she did video. When one finally agreed to show up at her house to be filmed the next day, she felt a kind of relief. She hadn't coaxed a bodybuilder home since before Billy. She still had it. She could still catch men.

But when the musclehead got there on Sunday afternoon, everything went wrong. They got started right away, but it took him forever to come. After he finally shot his load, he said he wanted a hundred bucks – not the fifty they'd agreed on the day before. He got aggressive, so she paid him the money just to get rid of him. Afterward she sat alone on her couch, looking at the walls, and she spotted some cum which had dripped onto the faux leather besides her. The sight of those drops filled her with a terrible sadness. Even after quickly wiping them up, the bad feeling stayed. She began wandering around her apartment trying to find some kind of respite, but everywhere she went, there was that same feeling – a kind of emptiness. She opened up Billy's bedroom door and looked in but didn't dare walk inside, afraid the emotion there would overwhelm her. She couldn't wait for her Billy to move back in.

48
Handsome Buildings and Men

MIKE WAS IN Miami, and he was exhausted. He stood in an empty changing room in a South Beach bar and slipped on his red jock strap. He'd been on tour since the end of August, and he wanted to go home, wherever that was now. He told himself that as soon as he got on stage everything would be okay. The crowd would energize him. One more city after this, and the tour was over.

It had been good to be out of LA for the last four weeks. That smog-choked city felt too crowded all summer long – too busy and ugly and full of tourists. On top of that, Dale's neediness since he'd moved in with Nick had worn him out. He liked it here in Miami, especially South Beach. Just that afternoon he'd wandered around the Art Deco District, checking out the buildings and the men.

Now he picked up his black knee-high socks. There was no place to sit in this changing room, and he leaned against the wall to put them on. Next he stepped into the pants – tightly fitting yellow brocade, the legs ending snuggly around his calves.

He didn't quite know what to do about Dale, about the incessant phone calls that had continued all summer long. It was like having your mother living in the same city as you, wanting to see you all the time. It was horrible. Just because he still cared for Dale didn't mean he wanted to hear from him every day, or catch up over yet another lunch. And Mike *did* still care for Dale, although he was very happy to not live with him anymore. In spite of everything there was an enduring bond between them, and Mike couldn't imagine the world without Dale. He just wanted a little bit of space.

If Dale could find a boyfriend, or at least a new roommate, that would be perfect. The double rent Mike paid through June had extended into July. It was easily covered with extra clients, but when August came he finally told Dale he wasn't paying him rent anymore. Now it was already the end of September. He was worried that Dale was struggling to pay the rent for that place on his own, although of course Dale would never say.

Reaching down to his enormous gym bag on the floor, Mike pulled out a white shirt with ruffles down the front. He slipped it on, followed by a brocade jacket that matched the pants. There were epaulets on the shoulders, and a high-cut waist. The entire outfit was Dale's handiwork. Mike leaned against the wall again and put on the small black dance shoes Dale had insisted on. Finally, a black matador's hat finished off the look.

He stood in front of the full-length mirror that was the only attempt at furnishing this room, and he looked at the costume. Dale could sew. Every seam was perfect. The pale yellow material caught the light and almost seemed to shimmer. This outfit had been from Mike's most recent Cougar movie, *Bullfight*. He'd played a matador who was pursued and eventually conquered by a large, bullish man. Sewing costumes was the only part Dale played in the making of the film. A new young guy named Larry Gear had directed. Dale never complained. He took what work he could. Lately, it seemed he had resigned himself to the fact that his career as a professional director was over.

"Billy, you're on." One of the guys that worked in the bar was standing at the changing room door. "Follow me."

Mike grabbed his red cape, and the guy led him down the hall to a tiny doorway at the side of the stage. Mike had reached the point in his career where he could tour on his own. Billy Knight's name alone was enough to draw a crowd now, and he appeared at gay bars and sex venues across the country about once a year.

Although he made good money from dancing fees and the tips guys shoved into his jock strap, the real money on tour came from the dates his agency in LA arranged for him in every city. Clients now paid $600 an hour for Billy Knight. After his agency and the local agency both took their share, Mike still walked with two thirds of that. His daily rate was $1,500 and his weekly rate was $5,000. But in spite of all the money coming in, Mike just wanted this tour to be finished. He was tired of dancing, tired of turning tricks. Still, the money was like golden handcuffs.

Out on stage, the bar manager yelled out to the crowd. "Let's give a big round of applause for Billy Knight!"

Everyone was cheering and clapping as Mike walked out, then the music started. It was a disco flamenco song that a DJ friend had mixed especially for the tour. Mike waved the red cape around and people whistled. He followed the music, tried to look like he was having fun. He knew this act like the back of his hand.

He'd already taken off the jacket and was unbuttoning the shirt when he first noticed the tall blond standing in the back by himself, leaning up against the bar and drinking a beer. The guy was hot, and in fact looked a bit like his old boyfriend Kerry. As Mike danced he kept looking back at the guy. The crowd continued to shout and cheer. Of course that couldn't really be Kerry, since the last he had heard Kerry was still living as a kept man in Paris. In fact, he was so certain it couldn't be Kerry that he'd already slipped off the ruffled shirt, the black dance shoes, and the long black socks before he realized it actually was.

That tall blond, the one standing in the back of this bar in South Beach watching him dance, was Kerry – the man of the soft, slow fucks and the greenish-blue ankh on his hip. Mike was surprised at how happy he suddenly felt. He was at the part in his routine where he started waving the cape around again, draping it over his body, but the entire time he was doing it he kept staring off toward the back. He couldn't stop himself no matter how hard he tried. Some of the guys in the audience actually turned around to see who he was looking at. Kerry just kept looking back up at him, smiling.

The music ended and the bar manager came out again carrying the microphone. Mike walked over, bare-footed and shirtless but still wearing the yellow brocade pants. He made sure the audience got a good view of his ass. Somebody whistled. Standing next to the manager, he tried not to think about Kerry, tried to concentrate.

This was the brief interview part of the show, which Mike never really liked. He put up with it because he had to. Everybody wanted to hear the porn star speak, like some tea-drinking chimp on television. They always asked the same questions. *What sort of sex do you enjoy most off camera? What kind of guys are you attracted to in real life?* He knew enough not to answer truthfully. The point was to convince all of the guys in the audience that they could have you, that they could be the kind of guy you'd go for. You had to fulfill all of their fantasies at once. It had become a kind of game with Mike: how much could he make the audience want him, how many guys could he get desperately aching for him at once? It was the only thing that relieved the monotony of these tours.

He answered broadly, said that he was into all kinds of men, that he really just loved cock and as long as a guy had one of those he was good enough for Billy Knight. If he answered right, he could make the audience laugh. He'd learned that much from Sasha. People liked to laugh. But the key was to smile and flirt with as many guys in the audience as you could, to make them feel like they themselves were desirable, like they had something special that even you, superstar Billy Knight up on stage, really liked.

After the manager was done with the interrogation and after a couple more questions from some guys in the crowd, the music started up again, and Mike did his second number. This time he finally slipped off the tight yellow pants and danced in just the red jock strap. He waved the cape around again and the audience cheered, but the only thing that mattered was that every time he looked toward the back of the bar, Kerry was still there.

When the music ended, Mike ran back stage and threw on his biker gear for the next number as the manager made some announcements. Then he ran back out again. It went on like that for almost an hour, changing costumes four times. The shows always involved a lot of running around, dancing, working up a sweat. Tonight, after every costume change, he checked again to make sure Kerry was still there. It felt good to see him each time, although he wasn't sure why. Kerry had been such an asshole. It didn't make sense to be happy to see him.

For his last number he came out dressed as a sailor, but when he looked toward the back, Kerry was gone. There was just empty space where he'd been, and an empty bottle of beer on the bar. As the music started, Mike scanned the crowd, checking to see if maybe Kerry had come up to the front or moved to the side, but he was nowhere. The music thumped, but Mike no longer wanted to dance. He wanted to run off stage, out into the streets in that stupid white sailor outfit, looking for Kerry. As much as he'd been surprised at how happy he'd been to see Kerry, he was absolutely astonished at how terrible he felt now that Kerry was gone. Still, after all these years, after Kerry had abandoned him so abruptly, why should he even care?

He pushed the thoughts away and began to dance, eventually stripping down to his sailor underwear. He had to. Everyone was watching. When it was over the bar manager came out and asked a few more questions. *When's your next movie coming out? What city are you appearing in next?* Then finally the manager said, "Let's give another big hand to Mr. Billy Knight!" and everyone clapped and cheered and Mike was free, waving and smiling and walking off the stage as quickly as he could.

Kerry was waiting in the changing room. He looked incredibly self-assured, as though he had a right to be there. Mike walked in carrying the sailor suit bundled up in a ball in front of him and wearing just the white sailor briefs, a red anchor embroidered across the back. All over the floor the other costumes were sprawled out. Immediately Mike felt torn between wanting to hug Kerry and wanting to tell him to get the fuck out, but the conflicting feelings were so equally strong that they cancelled each other out. He was left just staring, holding the sailor suit in his arms.

"Hey there," Kerry said.

Mike didn't answer, didn't say hello. What could he possibly say?

"You look great," Kerry added. "I heard you were in town, so I came to see you."

"You live here?" Mike's voice was cool.

"Yeah. Been in South Beach a couple years now."

"A couple years." Mike repeated, watching closely.

"Yes. And it's been eight years since I saw you last. I've counted."

"Is that really how long it's been since you dumped me in Exposé that night? When you just walked out?" Mike didn't know where the words were coming from. A moment ago he had been happy to see Kerry.

Kerry stared at the wall, then the floor. "That was a mistake."

"A mistake." Mike set the sailor suit down on the floor. "If you'll excuse me, I have to change."

"Go ahead." Kerry gave a small, tentative smile. "It's nothing I haven't already seen. By the way, that anchor on your ass looks great."

"Get out."

"Listen, Mike. I want to talk."

Mike felt everything tipping toward anger. "I wanted to talk eight years ago, Kerry. Eight fucking years ago. But you had to go. No warning. Nothing. You just left."

"Mike – "

"Don't make me call security. I get stalkers like you all the time."

Kerry looked hurt. "I'm not just some fucking stalker."

"What are you then?"

"I'm your friend."

396

"Bullshit, Kerry. You lost the right to call yourself that a long time ago."

"I was afraid you'd talk me out of it," Kerry said. "That's why I left so badly, why it was so abrupt."

"Really?" Mike thought about how quickly he'd moved out of his place with Dale, about the reasons why.

"Yes, really. When Burt asked me to go with him to France. I was afraid you'd talk me out of it if I told you. You know I'd always wanted to go. And then out of the blue there was somebody saying he'd take me there, pay for everything, and give me a place to live. How could I say no?"

Mike had the feeling that absolutely no time at all had passed. It could have been only a matter of minutes since that night at Exposé, and now their conversation was picking up from the point they'd last left off, here in another changing room, in another city. He pulled his jeans out of his gym bag and started putting them on. Nothing had changed. He still cared a lot about Kerry, and he was still very angry.

"It was a mistake," Kerry said.

"You already said that." Mike zipped up the jeans. Kerry's body was so close. "When did you figure it out, that it was a mistake?"

"A while ago. But it hit me again just now when I saw you on stage and my heart sank."

Mike paused, looked back at Kerry, slipped on a T-shirt. "Where's Burt?"

"He traded me in for a younger model and finally kicked me out. That's when I came to South Beach."

"Serves you right." Mike pulled his gym shoes and his socks out of the bag, leaned against the wall, and started putting them on.

"I suppose I always knew that he'd get rid of me some day."

When Mike reached for a shoe, Kerry picked it up and handed it to him. Mike looked up at Kerry, took the shoe, and put it on.

"Are you busy now?" Kerry said.

"Yeah, I've got a date." Mike started shoving all his costumes into the enormous gym bag.

"A client?"

"Yeah."

"Cancel."

"The guy booked two months ago. He's paying six hundred bucks an hour. The agency expects me to show up. I'm not about to cancel for *you*."

"Please?"

Mike looked up at Kerry. "You show up out of nowhere, corner me here in the changing room and expect me to drop everything like that? You've got some fucking balls."

Kerry smirked. "I always thought you liked my balls."

Mike finished shoving things into the bag.

"It's just that I want to see you," Kerry said.

Mike zipped the bag shut, ignoring him.

"How much longer are you in Miami?"

"This was my last show here. I'm here tomorrow, working. Then I fly out the next day."

"Where to?"

"One night in Fort Lauderdale, then back to LA."

"You have any free time tomorrow?"

Mike stood up. He almost felt like he was going to cry. "Kerry, I was really upset when you left. You fucking broke my heart."

"I'm so sorry, Mike. It was a mistake."

"Stop saying that."

"You hate me."

Mike said absolutely nothing. He tried to push away his feelings.

"I just want to meet for coffee," Kerry said. "That's all I want. Maybe a drink."

"I've got clients to see."

"You can't be scheduled twenty-four seven. Come on. Coffee. That's all."

Mike took a long breath. He could tell Kerry to leave and he'd never see him again. Or they could meet, somewhere, and just talk. He rubbed the back of his neck and looked up. "I'm staying at the Adonis Guest House on 14th Street. Call me there tomorrow at three. We'll see."

"Okay. I will. Thank you."

"Now I have to go find the manager and get my money, and then meet my client."

"You know. You're still wearing that sailor underwear with the anchor on your ass. What's the client going to think?"

"Who knows? He might like it."

"I do."

"But I'm not going home with you, am I?"

"No, but you should be," Kerry said, and he stepped forward. For a split second Mike thought Kerry was going to kiss him, but instead he just said, "Talk to you tomorrow." Then Kerry smiled and walked out.

The next day at 3:00 Mike made a point of not being in his room. He lingered at the clothing-optional pool, sprawled out naked in the sun, and managed to wait until 3:15 before wrapping a towel around his waist and returning to the room. When he called the front desk, he was relieved to find a message from Kerry, but forced himself to resist calling back. He sat down on the bed and turned on the television. He wanted the phone to ring again, wanted Kerry to be so intent on seeing him that he wouldn't give up after just one call. Ten more minutes went by. Mike was about to break down and call when the phone finally rang. It was Kerry.

"Hey there," Kerry said. "I thought I'd missed my chance."

"I was out." Although he was trying to sound indifferent, secretly Mike was thrilled.

"You're a busy man. Do you have time for coffee now?"

"I've got another job tonight. The driver's picking me up at seven."

"But we can meet now, can't we?"

"Okay."

They met at the Seascape Bar and Grill at Ocean Drive and 12th Street, right across from the beach. Mike was there first and was already sitting at a table drinking an iced tea when Kerry walked in. Mike's chest tightened. It hadn't entirely hit him the night before, how much more attractive Kerry was now, how much stronger his once-lean body had become. He'd actually improved with age, appeared more solid and steady, as though he'd become more fully himself.

Mike didn't stand. He just watched as Kerry came over and sat down at the table. He felt awkward, like some high school kid on a first date, not sure what to say.

When the waitress came over, Kerry pointed to Mike's iced tea and said, "I'll have what he's having," and then they sat in almost total silence until she brought it. They looked out toward the ocean. Mike was afraid they'd start fighting if they talked. Kerry's iced tea arrived and conversation started slowly, full of long pauses.

Kerry asked how Mike's tour was going, and Mike said fine.

Mike asked how Kerry had liked Paris, and Kerry said fine.

"My French got pretty good," Kerry said.

"Say something to me in French."

"Tu me fais fondre."

"What's that mean?"

"You make me melt."

Mike broke into a smile. "You learned how to be cheesy there too?"

"How's LA?" Kerry asked. "What are you doing?"

"Same as always. Working. Making movies. Seeing clients."

"Your movies are all over Europe. You're a big star."

"You never liked me doing porn."

"I'm over that now."

"What do you mean?"

Kerry shrugged. "I was a kept man for years. What right do I have to judge?"

"You must be mellowing in your old age."

"Maybe I am," Kerry said, laughing good-naturedly. "But you're as old as me."

"What are you doing now?" Mike asked. "For money?"

"You're not going to believe it."

"Try me."

"I sell real estate."

Mike almost choked on his iced tea. "No way."

"You're looking at a certified real estate agent. I just bought into this business here in South Beach. I had some money saved by the time Burt dumped me, so I did this course, got certified, and got set up here. I've been selling

Miami real estate for over a year and a half now." He smiled. "It's not so different from hustling."

"You've gone straight."

"So to speak."

"What's it like?"

"It's great. I've got these ads running now that have my picture. *Call Kerry.* The gay boys in Miami love it, and the housewives too. They all want me to be their agent."

"And you're selling stuff?"

"Left and right. Houses, little deco apartments. Miami's hot now. Everyone wants a place in South Beach. I'm socking the money away."

"Jesus. I never would have thought you'd be selling real estate." Mike played with the straw in his iced tea. "Do you miss hustling?"

"No. Not for a minute. The money's not as easy. But I feel like I own myself."

"I'm getting certified to be a personal trainer," Mike said.

"Really? Why? You want to quit porn?"

"I don't know. I'm just interested in learning what you need to know to be a trainer. I like the gym. I think I could do it."

"You could totally do it. Are you still living with Dale?"

"No."

"Good. He was bad news."

Mike gave Kerry a stern look. "He's still around. He's like my family." It was one thing for Mike to feel frustrated with Dale. It was an entirely different thing for anybody else to speak against him – especially Kerry, who had no right. "At least Dale has never disappeared on me."

"I'd tell you I made a mistake, but you told me not to say it again."

"I'm living with Nick now."

Kerry looked at him. "Nick?"

"Nick Demachio. Just some guy. Another hustler."

"So he's your roommate?"

"We fuck all the time," Mike said, in spite of the fact that it was no longer true.

Kerry glanced down at the table, and he seemed so disappointed that suddenly Mike felt sorry for having lied.

"But he's not my boyfriend, if that's what you mean."

Kerry's face brightened. "Good."

When they'd finished their drinks, Kerry suggested they walk down to the beach. Mike didn't want to leave yet, so he said okay.

There were people in lounge chairs and on towels in the sand, mostly men in Speedos, a few women in tiny bikinis. The waves rolled in. The smell of the ocean was everywhere. Mike took off his shirt and shoes, and Kerry did the same. They walked along and talked, passing by a pink and yellow beach patrol station that looked like a spaceship fallen from the sky, hunky lifeguards instead of aliens at the helm.

"There are so many hot muscle guys in South Beach," Mike said.

"And they all need a personal trainer." Kerry laughed. "You're still the hottest one on this beach. Anywhere you go. You have always been the hottest guy." Kerry reached out touched Mike's back.

Mike smiled. It was nice to feel Kerry's hand on his skin after so long.

"I'd like it if you were in South Beach more often," Kerry said.

Mike stopped walking and turned to look at him. Over Kerry's shoulder palm trees moved in the wind. A pale blue

403

building across Ocean Drive caught the sun. "Kerry, what are you doing?"

"What do you mean?"

"What's going on here?"

Kerry shrugged. "We're catching up."

"What do you care about me? I thought I was just another fuck to you."

Kerry winced. "You were never just a fuck to me."

"It didn't seem that way when you left."

"Listen, I fucked up. I really fucked up. I've spent a lot of time thinking about it, about you."

"You could have called, or sent a post card."

"I should have. You're right. I'm sorry. I didn't think you'd want to hear from me. I didn't think you'd respond."

"I probably wouldn't have."

"See, what good would it have done? But now here I am." Kerry stood there and held his arms out into the air like he was putting himself out on display, hoping to be chosen.

49
Couch Potato

DALE WAS SPRAWLED out on the couch, eating potato chips in front of the TV. There was a pile of laundry on the arm chair that needed to be folded. The floor was scattered with newspapers and magazines. Sitting on the coffee table were the dishes from this morning's breakfast, which he'd also eaten in front of the TV. It was early in the afternoon now. The only things on were children's shows and sports. He flipped through the channels and finally settled on a handsome park ranger who was talking to a group of kids about alligators. "Alligators are a kind of lizard," the man said.

Dale mumbled toward the television, "Oh, Mr. Ranger. Shut up and suck my dick." Then he shoved a handful of potato chips into his mouth, wiped his salty fingers on his shirt. He chewed and sighed. There was no way around it. He was miserable without Mike.

When the commercials came on he walked down the hallway, past Mike's closed door, and into his own bedroom. He looked at the calendar hanging on his fuchsia wall, where he'd marked September 15th with a star. Today was already September 29th. Mike would be in South Beach now. And he'd back in LA in just two more days. Things would be better then.

50
Hit Me

MIKE WATCHED AS Kerry unlocked his apartment door.

"Are you sure you've got time?" Kerry asked.

"I said the driver doesn't pick me up until seven. I've got time."

Kerry held the door open for Mike, and Mike walked in. As he closed the door behind them, Kerry said, "You seem a little prickly, sort of on edge."

"I don't really know why I'm here."

"You don't have to stay."

"No. I want to."

"I'm not sure you do."

They were in a small front hallway, painted pale green. Mike's back was to the apartment. He saw a black-and-white photograph of a sidewalk café on the wall to his left.

"That's my café in Paris," Kerry said. "It's in the seventh. I used to go there a lot. I had a lot of free time in Paris, when Burt wasn't there."

Mike looked at Kerry, at his new thickness, the old familiar blond of his hair. "Ever since I saw you in that changing room last night, I've been feeling like I want to hit you and hug you all at the same time."

Kerry stepped closer. "So just hit me and get that part over with."

Mike didn't move.

"Seriously," Kerry said. "Fair enough, too. I deserve it. Hit me."

Mike wanted desperately to do it, to punch him hard in the face, perhaps give him a black eye, something that would hurt and show. Kerry seemed completely vulnerable, open. He was honestly going to let Mike do it, wasn't going to dodge or block the blow. There was such a powerful tenderness in the way he stood there, waiting to be punched, that Mike felt something inside him change. The hard-edged fist in his imagination softened, melted. He reached out and touched Kerry's chin, pulled him close and hugged him.

Kerry leaned down, put his face down into the crook of Mike's neck, and breathed in. He moved his head up and kissed Mike gently on the mouth.

Mike remembered Burt saying that Kerry was such a tender fuck. *He doesn't fuck. He makes love.* And Mike felt a little edge of anger rise up again, but he pushed it away. He decided to pay close attention, as he opened his mouth and felt Kerry's tongue touch his, to see if what Kerry was doing was fake, if it was just a question of technique.

Kerry reached down and tugged lightly at Mike's T-shirt, and Mike raised his arms, allowing Kerry to pull the shirt up over his head. Kerry's mouth went down to Mike's chest and kissed his nipples. Mike looked up at the ceiling, at the photograph on the wall. He touched the back of Kerry's head.

When Kerry stood tall again, he took Mike's hand and walked through a doorway to the right and into the bedroom. He immediately undid Mike's shorts, pulled them down, got on his knees, and took Mike's dick in his mouth. Kerry was very good, there was no question. This was technique. For a moment Mike almost believed that this was all there ever had been between them. Two professionals having sex. It felt good. That was all. But then Kerry looked up, his lips still around Mike's dick, his head moving back and forth, and in his blue eyes Mike saw something else, something definitely *not* technique, something multi-layered and unstated but entirely sincere.

By the time they moved onto the bed, Mike had forgotten about trying to pay attention to Kerry's technique. He was just there. He climbed down between Kerry's legs and began sucking his dick. He watched the old familiar blue-green ankh come closer as he relaxed his throat and Kerry pushed slowly in, stroking the back of his head and moaning. It felt fantastic to have Kerry inside him this way. He let Kerry fuck his mouth for a long time. Then they rolled around together and kissed, felt the new contours of each other's body. It was like becoming reacquainted. Eventually, Kerry knelt over Mike and jacked off until his cum was running warm down Mike's chest.

Kerry looked down and smiled, tousled Mike's hair, and Mike smiled back. In that moment there was no doubt in his mind that Kerry was the most amazing man he'd ever been with, and not simply because of the physical pleasure, not because of the technique. There was an attachment that Mike had never felt with anybody else.

"What do you want me to do for you, to make you come?" Kerry said.

Mike looked up at him. How was it that after all these years here it was again, so suddenly, this feeling with this man – all connectedness and safety? Mike was overwhelmed by it. It had returned with such strength that it seemed it had never actually left him. It had somehow been lying dormant under the surface of his skin all this time, just waiting for Kerry to touch him again.

"Hold me," Mike said, and Kerry sat back and put out his arms. Mike leaned back on Kerry's chest, felt Kerry all around him, and then jacked off while Kerry stroked his sides, kissed his neck. When Mike came, it somehow all made perfect sense, as though Kerry had never really gone away at all, as though this was of course what they should be doing, as though they'd just woken up in their bed together after a long, comfortable sleep. Mike relaxed back into Kerry and felt an old, weightless joy return.

Kerry reached up and wiped off Mike's chest with his hands, rubbed it across his own chest, then pulled Mike down beside him and spooned him. They lay like that for a long time in silence, both of them still covered in each other, Kerry's dick slowly softening against Mike's ass, until they were almost dry.

"Move to South Beach," Kerry whispered.

Mike turned toward him. "What?"

"Move here. So I can be with you more."

"Jesus." Mike shook his head and turned away, but he pulled Kerry's arm around him again. "It's really good to see you, Kerry. But that doesn't mean I'm moving across the country for you."

"Don't you like it here?"

"That's not the point."

Kerry sat up. "What's the point then? You could get a job as a personal trainer. Or whatever. Keep making porn. I don't care. Just move here."

"You dumped me, remember? You left me in the worst possible way. I'm not moving here for you. And besides, it's been years. I hardly even know you anymore."

"Of course you know me. It's just me. But I'm smarter now. I know what's worth keeping." Kerry smiled.

"I've got my life in LA."

"What exactly do you have there?"

"You know. Movies. Clients." Mike thought about it for a moment. "Dale."

Kerry got up off the bed, walked out of the room, and came back with a warm washcloth. He wiped off Mike's chest, then his own. He took the washcloth back to the bathroom and then came in again, sitting down on the bed and stroking Mike's arm. "Burt told me something," he said. "Years ago. You should know. It's about Dale."

Mike closed his eyes. "What about him?"

"Remember that first night when Sasha showed up with Burt at Exposé?"

"Yeah. How could I forget? Burt ogled you the entire time."

"Well, Burt paid her to introduce us."

Mike pulled his arm away and sat up. "What are you saying?"

"It wasn't a coincidence that they showed up together that night. Burt was looking for someone to take to Paris. Sasha introduced him to me as a possible candidate. When it worked out, when I agreed to go to Paris with Burt, he paid her.

"You're saying she pimped you?"

"Well, yeah. Except I didn't know it. Not until years later, when Burt told me. She called it a finder's fee."

"Bullshit Kerry. Sasha knew how I felt about you."

"I think that's why she did it."

"Sasha would never do that to me. Burt's lying."

"Why would Burt lie about that? What benefit is it to him?"

"He's full of shit."

"Mike, she wanted you for herself. She wanted to get rid of me."

Mike looked through the open doorway and into the hall. He couldn't believe that he'd let his guard down, that he'd allowed himself to imagine he felt connected to Kerry again – this man who'd already left him once, who'd always hated Sasha. He should have punched him when he'd had the chance. "You're a fucking asshole, Kerry. You're making this up because you want me to hate her. You've always been jealous. I told you Dale's like my family. He's always been closer to me than you."

"Burt paid him a thousand bucks."

"Fuck you. Fuck you for saying that." Mike got up out of the bed and started putting on his underwear, then his shorts.

"What are you doing?" Kerry asked.

"I'm leaving. I'm sorry I ever laid eyes on you again."

"You're totally over-reacting. Don't go like this."

Mike pulled on his shirt and quickly sat down on the bed to put on his shoes. He said nothing.

Kerry looked upset. "Mike, you're too loyal for your own good. Look, I'm sorry. I forgot that in your book Dale is this holy man who can do no wrong."

He felt Kerry's hand on his shoulder, and he pulled away. When he'd tied his shoes, he simply stood and left. Kerry was still calling out to him from the bedroom, even as he slammed the apartment door.

51
I'll Take Care of You

DALE HAD BEEN boiling an orange for over two hours now, peel and all, and the kitchen had a bright, citrusy smell. He lifted the lid to the pot, saw that the water itself had turned a clear orange color, and he pushed a fork into the fruit. It was soft, as it should be. He drained the water and set the orange aside to cool.

Mike had called early that morning. Dale hadn't even gotten out of bed yet for work, and at first he'd been furious to hear the phone ring at such an hour, but when he heard Mike's voice coming from the answering machine down the hall, he jumped out of bed, ran to the front room, and answered immediately. Mike said he was calling from Fort Lauderdale, just before heading to the airport for his flight back to LA, and he was calling just to ask Dale if he could see him that evening. Dale's spirit lifted with that small request. Suddenly the early intrusion was charming.

"Of course," said Dale. "Of course you can come to dinner." He didn't care that it was actually Hump Night and he had to perform, or that he was supposed to work and wouldn't normally be home until after five – not enough time to make dinner between coming home and going out. It didn't matter. Mike had called. As soon as he hung up, he'd called Cougar to say he was home sick, and then he'd started boiling the orange.

Now he cut the orange in half and pulled out the little beige seeds, then dropped the entire unpeeled mess into the blender, along with six eggs. He was making a cake for Mike. He mixed the cocoa, sugar and ground almonds in a large silver bowl, folded in the orangey egg mixture and then poured it all into a springform pan. He put it into the oven right away. When it was done he would start the lasagna, making the tomato sauce himself, chopping the fresh vegetables. This entire meal would be from scratch. Only the best for his Mike.

Most of the day went by that way, cooking and cleaning, although he did run out once to buy some things he was missing, and to get a good bottle of wine. He wanted this night to be special.

By the time Mike rang the buzzer that evening, everything was ready. The citrus smell of the kitchen had faded, replaced by the fragrant oregano and basil and tomato of the lasagna now baking in the oven. The house was spotless, with the exception of his room, so he kept the door shut. The dining room table was set, the candles were lit, and Lotte Lenya was playing on the stereo – her gravelly German voice like incense hanging in the air. The chocolate orange cake was proudly displayed on a round cake platter on the kitchen counter, dark brown chocolate topped with powdered sugar and orange zest. It was lovely.

Mike walked in wearing a pair of ripped blue jeans and an old grey tank top. Small spots of skin showed along his thighs through the ripped denim. He was covered in muscle now, and tanned. He looked incredible, as he always did, no matter what he wore. He gave Dale a hug that was larger and longer than what Dale had expected. Lately Mike had been so distant, so to feel this hug now – it was heaven.

"Sit down with me and have a glass of wine," Dale said. They sat in the front room and Dale asked all about the

Bullfight tour, how it went. Mike said he'd liked Miami the best, but didn't exactly say why.

Seeing Mike sitting on the old leather couch – those patches of thigh showing, the tank top revealing just a little bit of his chest, graced by a small silver chain around his neck – Dale felt incredibly at peace. This was where Mike belonged, here, with him, dinner in the oven and wine in their hands. This was how it would be again, all the time, soon.

"I've missed you while you were gone," Dale said.

"I've missed you too," Mike said, but it was quick and Mike looked away. Dale wondered if it was really true.

It was over the starter course – rocket salad with crumbled feta and roasted pine nuts – that Mike said, "I saw Kerry in Miami."

Dale felt the words like a blow to his body. "Oh. Is that bad smell still around?" He picked at his salad. "I thought Kerry was still living off Burt's largesse in Paris."

"He's back. He's been in Miami a couple years. South Beach."

"Did you fuck?"

Mike shrugged.

"Damn, you're easy. You were probably down on your knees before he even said hello."

"Dale, listen. He told me something. Is it true that Burt paid you to introduce him to Kerry?"

Dale set his fork down. He couldn't believe Burt had told Kerry. Discretion was usually Burt's forte. "Mike, do you honestly think I would do that?"

"I don't *think* so."

"Look, it's no secret I never liked that Cory, or whatever his name is, but you were ga-ga for him. I wouldn't do that. More salad?"

414

"No, thank you. You've never liked any of my boyfriends. You absolutely hated Rafael."

"Ricardo had the brain of a retarded albino newt. I can't help it that you have astonishingly bad taste in men." Dale stood up to clear the salad plates. Mike stood to help, but Dale said, "No, you sit. You've been touring and working hard, dancing that little ass off. It's time somebody waited on you."

Mike sat back down. "Thanks."

"Now, we'll have no more talk of that Kerry, or that Burt." Dale walked into the kitchen.

Mike called out. "So you never got paid to introduce Burt to Kerry?"

Dale was already putting the salad plates in the sink. It dawned on him that that this was why Mike had come here tonight, to find out if this was true. He yelled back into the dining room. "Mike, please! Give me a little credit, will you? Are you ready for my out-of-this-world lasagna?" He stood by the oven and dished out the lasagna in enormous portions, accompanied by steamed broccoli drizzled in fennel-infused olive oil. He set the plate in front of Mike and poured him another glass of wine.

"That looks amazing," Mike said. "You take such good care of me." He took a forkful of lasagna.

"Well, I try. You know if anything ever happened to you, if you were sick or hurt, I'd take care of you. You know that, right?"

Mike smiled back at Dale. "Thank you. I know you would." His pager went off and he looked at it. "It's Nick," he said, and set the pager down on the table. "The lasagna's terrific, by the way."

Dale was glad that Mike didn't call Nick back until after they were done with the main course. Dale stood in the kitchen making coffee and trying to listen to Mike out in the front room on the phone. He couldn't quite make out the conversation.

Eventually Mike stepped into the kitchen. "Dale, Nick's having a sex party tonight and I don't really want to be there. Do you mind if I stay here tonight?"

Dale couldn't believe his good luck. "Stay? Of course you can stay. We can both come back here and crash after Hump Night." Dale looked at the clock. It was nearly nine o'clock. "I've got to be on stage at the Lucky Pony by ten. We have to hurry up and eat dessert."

"Shit," Mike said. "I forgot it was Wednesday. I'm still on tour time. I'm sorry, I'm pretty exhausted. Do you mind if I don't go tonight?"

Dale felt horrible. He'd wanted to show up with Mike on his arm. He'd wanted them to go together, like before. "But I'm doing Cher. You always like it when I do Cher."

"Oh, yeah, but I'm really not up for a night out tonight."

"Are you sure?" It was true, Dale thought. Mike did look tired. "Well, I guess you could just stay here, if you're really too beat. While you were away I, ah, I got some furniture for your old bedroom. You can sleep in there." Dale looked down at the cake and started to slice a large piece for Mike.

"Furniture?" Mike was already walking down the hall. Dale heard the door opening to Mike's old room, then Mike walking back. "I can't believe you got a bed, *and* a dresser, *and* a night stand," Mike said. "How'd you afford all that?"

"That's why the goddess invented credit cards."

"But no roommate yet?"

"No. I suppose I thought it would be easier to find one if I advertised that it was a furnished bedroom. In the meantime, you can sleep in there tonight." Dale held out a white plate with a piece of dark chocolate cake, and he saw the smile on Mike's face.

"The cake is beautiful. Did you buy it?"

"What! Serve you a store bought cake? I'd sooner have my dick fall off. I baked this for you this morning, after you called. It has an orange in it."

"An incredible meal, a bed for me in my old room, homemade chocolate cake. You're really too good to me."

"Yes," Dale answered. "I am."

52
In the Closet

THINGS GOT CRAZY after they finished dessert. Mike watched as Dale started running around, looking for his Cher dress.

"I was just mending it the other day!" Dale yelled. He ran off into his bedroom to see if it was there. Mike slowly cleared the table, stacked the rest of dishes in the sink, then wandered down the hall and looked into Dale's room.

It was a mess, as always. Dale was rummaging through his closet, flipping past dress after dress hanging on hangers. He pulled out things at random and threw them behind him. Dresses arced through the air, hangers leading a streamer of fabric as they fell and crumpled into lifeless heaps on the bed or across the floor.

"Don't just stand there," Dale said. "Help me find it. It's black and sequined with red metallic shoulder pads."

Mike laughed. "How do you misplace a dress with red metallic shoulder pads?"

"Shut up and look."

Mike walked out of Dale's room and into the bathroom. He looked behind the bathroom door and there it was on a hanger, hanging neatly, all black and red and very Cher.

He took the dress and stood in Dale's bedroom doorway. "Is this it?"

"Oh, my lucky angel!" Dale came running over. "Where the hell was it?"

"Back of the bathroom door."

"Oh, Jesus. If you hadn't been here I would have looked forever and ever and never thought to look there."

Dale zipped the Cher dress into a garment bag with two other dresses, and threw a bunch of makeup into his old train case. He grabbed several wigs and threw them into a bag. Then he picked up a black stiletto off the floor. "Where's the other one? Oh God." He started rummaging through the heap of shoes on the closet floor, scattering them everywhere. "Got it!" He threw the shoes into a handbag and turned to Mike. "You're sure you don't want to go?"

Mike was sorry to disappoint Dale, but he couldn't deal with the Lucky Pony tonight. He was exhausted. "I'm sure."

"Well then make yourself useful and help me carry this all down, would you?"

When they stepped out of the apartment and into the hallway, Dale said to him, "You'll need my key to get back in."

"I've still got my old one."

Suddenly, in the middle of all that flurry and scuttle, Dale stopped right there in the hallway. He looked at Mike and grinned, "It's like you never left."

Mike helped pack Dale into his car and waved him off, then went back up the stairs and inside. He looked around the kitchen, at the dishes piled in the sink, the lasagna still sitting on the stove top, the cake uncovered on the counter. He felt perfectly at ease, like he was home, even though he hadn't lived there in almost four months now. He put the lasagna in the refrigerator and covered the cake with plastic wrap. The entire time he was thinking that he was too hard on Dale, too easily annoyed. The incessant phone calls that had bothered him all summer long weren't really so bad. If they'd suddenly stopped, he probably would have missed them. He would have felt even more alone in the world. He put the stopper in the kitchen sink and filled it with hot soapy water. Then he washed every last dish, dried them, and put them all away.

When he was done, he walked down to Dale's bedroom and looked in. It looked worse than usual, as though a dress bomb had gone off. He started picking up the dresses and hanging them back in the closet. Almost every dress brought back some kind of memory of Sasha in it, singing on stage at the Lucky Pony or laughing in some club somewhere. When he began pushing the shoes back into their heap on the closet floor he noticed the safe again. There was a long red dress hanging down above it that had gotten shut in the metal door, so that the safe didn't seem entirely closed. He tried to gently tug at the fabric, but it was caught. He pulled at the door a little to see if he could release the captured dress, and the door swung open easily.

The edge of something sparkling inside the safe caught his eye. He pulled the door open wide then, just to have a quick look. He saw Sasha's tiny gold crown. He almost laughed out loud. It was a fake crown, he knew, something cheap she'd bought at a costume shop years ago. It was covered in plastic rubies and emeralds. Only Sasha would lock up her fake gold crown. He was about to shut the safe door when he noticed a brown plastic pill bottle with a white cap.

Mike reached into the safe and picked the pill bottle up. There was no label. He pushed down on the child-proof cap and turned. Inside there was a handful of dull green, oval shaped pills. He poured them into his hand and picked one up. There was a split-pill line on one side and on the other side was the number '542'. He put the pills back in the bottle and screwed on the lid.

There was one more thing in the safe – a simple black videotape. It, like the bottle, had no labels of any kind. The black plastic tab on the side of the videotape was punched out, protecting the contents from being recorded over by mistake. It looked rewound, ready to watch. He knew he shouldn't watch it, but he couldn't help himself.

Mike took the videotape out to the front room and put it in the VCR. He sat down on the floor in front of the television to watch.

The first thing he saw was someone's foot. It took a moment before he recognized it as his own. From there the camera trailed up his body, moving from ankle to calf to knee. It slowed at the crotch of the red gym shorts he was wearing, moved to his bare chest, and finally stopped on his face. He was napping on the fake leather couch, out in the front room. The camera panned back. The windows were open, and the curtains were blowing in. He rolled over, the camera jumbled, and the scene cut.

There were two other scenes of Mike sleeping before suddenly there was Earl, talking directly into the camera, mumbling. His hair was a mess and his eyes were red. "Yeah," he said to the camera. "Yeah, he's hot. I said I'd do it. I'll do him."

What Mike saw next confused him, made him feel like he was suddenly outside of himself and somehow watching from very far away. The wobbly, hand-held video camera panned back, and there he was, Mike, apparently passed out on the bed behind Earl, wearing nothing but the brilliant blue shirt he'd last worn the night of the Lessing party. The shirt was unbuttoned and lay open across his chest. His dick was flopped to the side.

421

Mike had no memory of this at all. He watched as Earl reached over to him and began caressing his body, playing with his dick. He was surprised to see himself turning his head, moving his arm, acting strangely compliant, as though he didn't even care.

Earl reached behind Mike's back and sat him up, and it seemed Mike was a rag doll, doing whatever Earl wanted. Earl slipped off Mike's shirt, then stood and took off his own clothes, lay back on the bed, and pulled Mike's face into his crotch. Eventually Earl pushed his dick into Mike's mouth, and Mike seemed almost to accept it, or at least he didn't fight it.

The scene cut then, and suddenly there was Earl's finger, pushing into Mike's ass, playing with it, one finger, and then two. "What a fucking great hole," Earl said clearly. The camera tilted and things shuffled around, then Earl was kneeling behind Mike on the bed. Mike was bent over on all fours, his face pushed down into the mattress. Earl's dick was hard. He slapped Mike's ass a couple times, then reached out to pick up a bottle of lube. He squirted some into his hand and applied it to his dick, then rubbed the rest onto Mike's asshole He moved his hips forward. He wasn't wearing a condom.

"That's it," a voice said from off camera. "That's it." The voice belonged to Dale. "Fuck him just like that." The camera jostled and Mike saw Sasha's hand move into the frame, wearing her sapphire ring. She pulled away a pillow, and the camera moved in and went steady again.

Mike watched in total disbelief as Earl's cock slid, bareback, into his ass. Earl pushed in deep, then slid out, pushed back in again. Mike heard himself mumble some-thing, but it sounded like somebody speaking out of the depths of a dream, a sleepwalker who wasn't really there in the room at all but far off someplace else instead, in another world. Nobody, neither Earl nor Sasha, paid any attention to what he was trying to say.

The camera panned back, and Earl started to thrust harder into Mike. His hands held Mike's hips in place. There was the slapping sound of Earl's body against Mike's ass, Earl saying, "Fuck yeah."

Mike watched, horrified, as he himself in that bed did nothing to stop it from happening, just let Earl fuck him that way.

When Earl said, "I'm gonna shoot my load," Mike's heart fell.

Dale's voice came through clearly now, cold and monotone. "Come inside him.'

Everybody knew Earl was HIV positive. Sitting there in front of the television, watching, totally helpless and unable to intervene, Mike began to cry.

Earl began shouting, "Aw, yeah, yeah." His hips quickened and then he pushed deeply into Mike, tipped back his head, and let out a long, deep moan.

Mike could barely see for the tears streaming down his face. He was only vaguely aware of the camera moving closer as Earl pulled out slowly, semen dripping, and then the screen went black. Mike curled up into a ball on the floor, and he sobbed.

He didn't know how long he lay there on the floor. Eventually he stood up and started shouting at the walls, not saying anything that really made any sense, just yelling. His hands were shaking as he took the videotape out of the VCR, picked up his car keys, and walked out the door.

He threw the videotape onto the passenger seat and started the engine, then pulled out into traffic. As he did, he felt small things inside him beginning to break. The Lessing party was in mid-June, over three months ago. He had to get tested. Driving down La Cienega Boulevard, he began crying all over again, the windows rolled up, inside the bubble of his car alone, surrounded by darkness. He wiped the tears off his face with the back of his arm, and then returned to yelling.

He went down Santa Monica Boulevard and parked not far from the Lucky Pony. He left the videotape in the car. He didn't want her to have it anymore. The bouncers didn't stop him as he walked into the bar. He barely even saw them as he passed them by.

Inside people were laughing, drinking, some were dancing. The stage was empty. It was almost eleven o'clock. Mike looked around, but Sasha was nowhere. The music was loud. Somebody turned to him and yelled, "Hey, Billy Knight! Nice to meet you." He turned away and went to the door at the side of the stage, opened it, and headed down the hallway toward Sasha's dressing room. There on the door was the star that she'd recently made herself – yellow cardboard, her name in gold glitter at the center. He threw the door open without knocking and stepped in.

"Billy!" Sasha looked up at him in the mirror, her back to him. "You gave me a fright, barging in here like that. But you're just in time. I'm about to do Cher. What made you change your mind?" She was wearing the long black Cher wig, the dress with the red metallic shoulder pads. There was an eyeliner pencil in her hand. She glanced up again, and then turned around. "What's wrong, baby? You look upset." She stood up, put her arm out and came toward him.

He lunged at her, pushed her hard, felt his hands sink into the padding of her bra as she stumbled backwards, landing half-seated against the vanity, the back of her head banging against the mirror. Her eyeliner pencil fell to the floor. She looked shocked, and suddenly frightened, and surprisingly frail.

He screamed. "God damn you!"

"Baby, what? What?!"

"You had him fuck me bareback! You did it!" He was nothing but rage and tears. He could barely see again.

She stood and moved toward him again, slowly, holding both arms out as though to hug him, whispering "No, no." He pushed her harder this time, and she tumbled down between the chair and the wall. He pushed the chair away, and she lay there looking up at him, one arm up, scared. He wanted to climb on top of her and choke her, wanted to kick her. She deserved it. But something stopped him. He stood over her crying. He didn't want to hurt her.

"Baby," she said, looking up at him from the floor. "I never did that." Her wig was crooked, the black sequined dress tangled around her legs.

He had to concentrate to push out the words. "I saw your videotape. I looked in your safe."

Her eyes opened wide. She shook her head violently, as though an electric shock was suddenly running through her.

He faced her vanity and leaned over it. In one large arc with both arms, he swept away everything there, pushed it so that it went flying into the air and onto the floor and on top of Sasha. Tubes of lipstick. Trays with small square colors of eye shadow. A compact and a hand-held mirror. Lotion. Cotton balls. Small glass bottles in different shapes. Little tiny pencils.

Sasha let out a strange noise from the floor – a low, mannish howl.

Mike turned toward the chrome rack that stood behind him, where dresses hung on hangers, and he pushed it over. It fell toward her, and she quickly pulled back her legs and shouted, huddled against the wall. "But I love you! I love you!"

He looked at her. "You *love* me?!"

"I did it because I love you." The high, affected voice of Sasha was gone. This was Dale. "I want to take care of you. I just want you to need me. You can live a long time on the drugs. I'll take care of you."

Mike stepped backwards. "You *want* me to get sick? You want to do that to me? You had Earl fuck me bareback for *that*?" He felt his face twisting into shapes he could not control. His eyes burned. He struggled to breathe. He wanted to get away from that small, dingy room, to get away from Dale, to go far. It was as though a room that had always seemed safe was suddenly lined with daggers and knives, landmines under the floor.

Carl was at the door. "What the hell's going on?"

Mike pushed past him and ran into the hallway. Carl tried to grab his arm, but Mike pulled away and ran down the hall, out into the bar and through the crowd gathering now at the foot of the stage, and then through the doors back outside, out onto Santa Monica Boulevard. One of the bouncers called out to him as he pushed past. "Yo, Billy! What's up?" Mike didn't stop, just ran down the street as fast as he could, past men wandering toward the Lucky Pony, past shops that were closed, a movie theatre, a young straight couple speaking Russian, past the Mexican cantina, a group of lesbians, a gallery, past a line of muscular men in Levis in front of the country-western bar, past the book store. And then he just kept going. He was almost all the way to La Cienega before he realized he'd passed his car. He stopped and looked around, breathing hard, a sweat breaking across his forehead and back. The streetlights turned everything yellowish-green, and cars were driving up and down the boulevard. He glanced ahead toward La Cienega and then back toward where he'd come. He had no place to go.

53
The Blackness

DALE HEARD THE sound of the street cleaner in the morning, but he didn't care. He'd barely slept. It was Monday morning. He knew his car was parked on the wrong side of the street, knew that if he didn't get up and move it quickly, he was going to get a ticket. He scratched at the stubble on his chin, rolled over, and went back to bed.

After several more hours of light and unsatisfying sleep, he opened his eyes and lay staring at the ceiling for a long time. Today would be the fourth day that he would not show up for work. Since calling in sick on Wednesday, he hadn't bothered calling in again. He just didn't show. It didn't matter. He felt as though his head and chest had been hollowed out. There was nothing left of him but the most minimal of necessities. Eat. Shit. Sleep. He hadn't showered in – he wasn't sure how many days.

Slowly he sat up, paused, eventually got out of the bed, and then walked down the hallway in his boxer shorts. It didn't matter if he put on his robe. He was alone. He pulled at the elastic waist, which curved down around his large belly. Standing in front of the phone, he picked up the receiver and dialed the number again. What came back was the familiar beep of Mike's pager. He slowly entered his number and hung up. He'd lost track of how many times he'd done this since Wednesday night. Maybe twenty or thirty times a day? Maybe more? He couldn't say.

Next he dialed Mike's home number. The machine clicked on. At least with this number he always heard Mike's voice. "Hey there, you've reached Mike and Nick. Leave a message."

Dale cleared his throat before the beep.

"Hi Mike. It's me again. Please, just call me back. I need to talk to you. Call me. Please." He hung up and started walking back toward his room.

Before he got there, the blackness came down again. It felt like a heavy wool blanket falling over him, shutting out all the light and sound, pushing him down with a horrible weight. He felt his back sliding down the wall outside the bathroom door, and he ended up sitting on the floor. Up above him, on the opposite wall, three of Mike looked out, smooth skin like marble against the dark background of the photos. He would never have any of those Mikes. That one would never call him back again. That one would never say hello on the street. That one would always despise him.

Dale balled both hands into fists, curled his body into a ball, and began to punch his head. His knuckles against his skull made a satisfying *thunk, thunk*, and white-sharp flashes of pain ran through him.

The blackness happened now from time to time, and when it was all gone, when it had run its course and lifted off him, he felt hollow again, and he could begin to move, to do the basic things. Finally he was able to put his hand on the wall and pull himself up. He stepped like an old, feeble man back to his bed.

Sasha never did Cher that night. Dale had thrown off the wig and stayed huddled in the corner of the dressing room, telling Carl to go away. Carl left and got one of the lesser queens to take over the show, but then came back as Dale was taking off the makeup and changing out of the dress. He kept asking Dale questions, wanting to know what had happened. *What was Mike saying about Earl fucking bareback?* Dale never answered, just said Mike was confused or having a bad trip, or something. Eventually Carl helped Dale slip out the back way.

Dale turned and looked over at the safe now. It was still wide open, had been since he came home and found it unlocked, his private videotape gone, his tiara on the floor, the bottle of Rohypnol lying nearby. It somehow seemed too final to shut that safe again, to lock it. Besides, the only thing that really mattered was gone.

The Rohypnol had been relatively easy to get. His old contact, Fabio, a drug dealer, had helped him. Dale hated it when Fabio called it the 'date rape' drug. He didn't like to think that was what he was doing. Fabio hadn't been able to get his hands on any of the old pills, the ones that dissolved clear in liquid, and so Dale had been forced to settle for the new pills – the ones with the blue core that dyed the liquid blue to make them easier to detect.

Dale climbed back out of bed, picked up the bottle of pills, and walked into the bathroom. He lifted the toilet lid, opened the bottle, and poured the pills into his hand. They were such a funny color green, so dull they were almost brown. He dropped one into the toilet and watched it dissolve, watched the water in the toilet bowl turn blue. If he wanted, he could drop them all in and flush them down, and they would go away. But it wouldn't make a difference. He couldn't undo what he'd done.

He wished he could blame Sasha, but he knew that was a lie.

If he could just get Mike to call him back, to talk to him, he would tell Mike how much he loved him, truly loved him, and not like a sister and not like a brother and not like a mother or a father. He would tell Mike how he'd wanted him with every cell in his body ever since first seeing him under the disco ball at the Lucky Pony, how that initial feeling had only grown into something more as they became closer, how deeply and intensely he had fallen in love with him, how much he wanted to take care of him.

Dale shook his head and sighed. He slid the pills back into the bottle and screwed the white plastic cap down tight. Back in the bedroom, he finally put everything back into the safe – the tiara and the pills. He shut the safe door firmly, checked it twice to make sure it was locked and then, pulling his tired body up, he climbed into bed again. He turned away from the closet, away from the safe, and he tried, once again, to sleep.

54
Looking for Change

MIKE FELT HIS pager go off, looked at the number on the tiny screen, recognized it as Dale's, and deleted the message. He looked out at the ocean. Over the past few days he'd been doing everything he could to avoid going places where Dale might be, and this morning he'd driven down the freeway to Santa Monica.

He walked through the palm-filled gardens that overlooked the beach, where homeless people were lying on benches next to grocery carts filled with stained blankets. Grey-haired couples wearing khaki shorts and expensive tennis shoes strolled by. He looked down the walking trail. If he walked a mile or so south, the trail would take him to Venice Beach. Sasha liked it there. He wouldn't go south.

He walked toward the pier. It was why he'd come here.

The Santa Monica Pier was somewhat rundown, but dotted with cafes and arcades. There was an old hand-carved carousel, even a small amusement park. It wouldn't be very crowded on a Monday morning, and he liked that idea. Besides, Dale never came here. Mike walked up along the pier, out over the water now, past a seafood restaurant that was just opening. Santa Monica Bay surrounded him. There were telescopes nearby. He put in some coins, looked north at the Santa Monica Mountains, then out at the sea.

The entire day lay empty in front of him. He'd cancelled all his appointments for the next two weeks. The agency was furious, but he didn't care. It was impossible to see clients now, the way he felt. He looked out at the water again. He hadn't been knocked this hard, felt this bad, since that night in the hotel across from the Spares 'n' Strikes, back in Cincinnati, just before he left.

Back then, when that guy had held him down, Mike had felt that it was his own fault. He'd been drinking. He'd shown poor judgment going with a guy he didn't know. But this time it was different. Yes, he'd been drinking at the Lessing party, but it was with Dale, someone he knew, someone he trusted. Yet even so, it had happened to him twice now. He wondered what he was doing wrong, what he was *still* doing wrong. He wondered what he had to change.

The day after he found the videotape, Steve Logan called, and immediately Mike wondered if he knew. Very quickly it became clear that Steve had no idea. He just wanted Mike to come in and talk about doing a new movie, but Mike didn't want to go to Cougar. Even if Sasha wasn't directing for them anymore, she still worked there. She would be around, in their studio, somewhere. He told Steve he'd call him back, but it was a lie.

Mike didn't want to do any more movies for Cougar. He didn't want to do any more movies for anyone. He tried to imagine his life without porn, without escort work, and it almost seemed possible. He'd never felt that way before. It could be something that he *used to do*.

He'd gotten tested that same day Steve called, at the old community health center on San Vicente that he always went to, because it was anonymous and free. He was terrified. The only way he was able to get there was by telling himself that it was just his usual test. There was nothing different about this one. Nothing bad had happened.

Standing alone on the pier, he calculated the days. He wouldn't get the results back until Thursday. That meant three more days of waiting.

He was standing in front of the amusement park entrance when his pager went off again, and he was ready to delete the number almost automatically. Then he noticed it was a 305 number. That was Miami. It was Kerry. They hadn't spoken since Mike had stormed out of Kerry's apartment and slammed the door.

Mike went back to the seafood restaurant and stepped inside. There was a pay phone near the door, but he had no change. A waitress was setting tables. He asked her for change and called Kerry. The restaurant was empty and silent, and the waitress could hear everything Mike said.

"Hey, it's Mike."

"Mike! Hello! I'm so glad you called me back. I was worried you weren't going to."

"Why wouldn't I?"

"I don't know. You know, the way you left. Who knows? Anyway, it's really good to hear your voice."

"It's good to hear yours, too."

"How are you?"

"I've been better." Mike looked over at the waitress, who was carrying a tray of silverware from table to table, arranging knives and forks and spoons. "I'm at a pay phone. Can't really talk."

"Is something wrong?"

"No. Well, sort of. I'll be okay. Don't worry about me."

"Wait. Tell me what's going on."

"Can I call you at home later?"

"Of course."

434

They agreed on a time, and Mike hung up and walked back out onto the pier. The ocean air hit him, and he wandered along again. He had no idea how he was going to fill his day.

Eventually he ate breakfast at a café overlooking the water, and then he drove back to West Hollywood and sat in his room for a while. Nick was home, in the kitchen doing something. Mike felt trapped. After a while he got up and went to the gym, thinking he could lose himself in a workout. He just hoped that he wouldn't see anybody he knew.

He was on the treadmill when he saw Earl on the rowing machine in the corner. It was so ordinary, so plain – just a guy on a rowing machine – but he felt everything inside him heave and churn. He hit the red 'STOP' button, and the treadmill slowed and came to rest. He stepped down, moving slowly, trying not to draw any attention to himself. The locker room wasn't far, but as soon as he turned from the treadmill to cross the floor, Earl looked up and saw him.

Mike looked away quickly, kept walking. He made it to the locker room, fumbled with his lock before finally getting it open and grabbing his gym bag. As he turned to leave, Earl was standing behind him.

"Hi Mike."

"Fuck you. Get away from me."

"I need to talk to you."

"*Talk* to me?" He paused, then walked around Earl, giving him a wide berth. He stepped out of the locker room.

"Hey, Mike." Earl was right behind him. "Wait up."

Mike kept walking. "Leave me the fuck alone."

There was a yellow hallway off the reception area that led to the parking garage next door. Mike moved quickly down that hallway and then out into the grey concrete of the garage, all the angled ramps. Earl was still following him when Mike got to his car.

"Mike wait. Sasha told me you wanted to do it."

Mike had just unlocked the driver side door. He stopped and looked at Earl, said nothing. They were standing close to each other now, there between the cars. Noises echoed around them – the occasional engine starting, tires on the ramps.

Earl actually looked upset. "Carl told me what happened at the Lucky Pony, how you and Sasha fought. And he told me you'd mentioned my name. Sasha wouldn't tell him what the fight was about. Carl came to me asking what happened."

Mike threw his gym bag in the car. He didn't want to hear any of this.

"She told me you wanted to make a bareback movie, Mike. She said she was paying you too."

"She *paid* you?"

How many people, Mike wondered, had Sasha paid to hurt him?

Earl nodded slowly. "She said you didn't want to talk about it. About making the movie. That's why I didn't mention it at the party beforehand."

Mike turned his body toward Earl. He could smell Earl's sweat. He could see the shadows under his eyes, the thin stretch of his face. "Wasn't it obvious to you that I was fucked up?"

"I was too, by then. I was totally drunk."

"You fucked me bareback. You're positive!"

Earl looked surprised. "Who told you I was positive?"

"Everyone knows you are."

"That's bullshit. I'm not positive."

"Fuck off. Sasha wanted to infect me. That's why she asked you."

"Whoa. If she wanted that, she never told me. I wouldn't have done it bareback if I were positive. Mike, I just wouldn't do that."

Mike wanted desperately to believe him. "You're lying."

"That was my first time bareback, and I'm negative. I only did it because I needed the money. I kept telling myself it's not as risky if you're a top. It's the bottoms who get infected easily."

Mike punched Earl then, hard, and Earl spun back and fell against a blue BMW. Earl looked up, his hand to his face, and Mike saw that he was bleeding.

"Stay the hell away from me," Mike said, then got in his car and drove away.

That night, when Mike called Kerry, he told him everything. Kerry listened in silence. Mike knew that Kerry had never liked Dale, and he expected Kerry would launch into some kind of 'I told you so,' but it never came. Instead Kerry just said, "When do you get your HIV results?"

"Thursday," Mike said. "9:00 a.m."

"Do you have someone to go with you?"

"No."

"I'll come to LA. I'll go with you."

"Don't be silly. They make you get your results alone anyway."

"I'll wait in the lobby."

"You don't have to do that."

"I know I don't have to. I want to."

"You'd fly all the way out here just to sit in some clinic and wait for me?"

"Of course I would. And I'm going to. I just have to cancel some appointments. I'll get there as soon as I can."

Mike picked up Kerry from LAX on Wednesday afternoon, and Kerry immediately insisted that Mike stay with him at his hotel. Mike was reluctant at first, but finally said yes. The entire time they never talked about why Kerry had come to LA. It was the terrible thing that hung in the air between them, but was never mentioned. That evening in the hotel room Mike's pager went off twice. Both times it was Dale. When they got in bed Kerry tried kissing Mike, put his hand on Mike's ass, but Mike pushed him quietly away.

"No. I don't want to," Mike said.

"Come on."

"What if I'm positive?"

"We'll be safe. I assume every guy is positive."

"You're still negative, right?"

"Yeah."

"I just can't. I can't have sex right now."

Kerry sighed. "I'm sorry. I'm an idiot." Kerry wrapped his arms around Mike and held him. "We'll talk instead. Let's talk about you moving to Miami."

"You won't want me there if I'm positive. It'll change everything."

"That's not true. It may come as a surprise to you but guess what, I really like you. I lost you once. I'm not making that same mistake again."

Mike put his head on Kerry's chest, and he fell asleep that way.

The next morning he was too nervous to eat, so he just lay in bed with Kerry, watching morning television and waiting until it was time to go. Kerry drove Mike's car to the health center, and then they sat side-by-side in the waiting room.

There was a skinny gay guy across the room who kept staring at Mike, and it made Mike uncomfortable. The guy must have recognized him, but he didn't want to be Billy Knight right then. He wanted the guy to stop staring.

Kerry realized what was happening and, in a loud voice across the waiting room, he said, "What you are you looking at?"

The guy turned away.

A woman in a white uniform came out. Mike had never seen her there before. She called Mike's anonymous number. Kerry squeezed his leg and said, "I'll be right here."

Mike stood up and followed the nurse. She sat down across from him in a small grey room and opened his file. She looked up at him. There was a mole on her left cheek, just to the left of her nose. "Now, I just need to confirm once more," she said. "You're DY67392, correct?" Her mole moved when she talked.

"Yes," Mike said.

"And your birth date is April 29th 1965, correct?"

"Yes."

"Good. Your test came back negative. Congratulations."

Mike stared at her blankly.

"Do you have any questions?" the nurse asked.

"No." Suddenly he couldn't stop smiling.

"Do you need any condoms?"

"Sure."

She reached into a basket and gave him a handful, talked to him about safe sex. He stuffed the condoms in his pocket and walked out.

In the hallway he felt his pager go off again. It was Dale's number. He immediately deleted it. He could not, would not, talk to Dale ever again.

As he stepped into the waiting room, Kerry glanced up and saw him, and suddenly the look on Kerry's face changed. He looked worried, almost panicked. He got up and came to Mike.

"No, I'm fine," Mike said. "I'm negative.

Kerry hugged him. "Thank God. Thank God."

"And I'm hungry."

"That's good. Let's go eat." They began walking toward the door.

"Over breakfast we can talk about how I'm thinking of moving to Miami," Mike said.

Kerry paused as they stepped out into the street together. "Really? Would you do that for me?"

"Maybe." Mike shrugged. "If I moved to Miami it just might be the end of Billy Knight. I could retire from porn, from hustling."

Kerry touched his arm. "I won't lie, Mike. I'd like it if you did. But you know you don't have to. Not for me. I figure Mike Dudley and Billy Knight are sort of a package deal."

Mike shook his head. "None of it would be for you. It would be for me. I want to do something different. I could be a personal trainer. I could train all the hot muscle guys of Miami."

"They'd love you. You could easily do that. You could do anything. But I just want to be around you. I don't care what you do for money. Seriously."

"Around me?"

"You know. *With* you."

Kerry put his arm around Mike, and they started walking toward the car. The day was bright and sunny, the sky perfectly clear. Mike looked up as a gentle breeze came by.

Although they were miles away from it, Mike swore he could smell the sea.

55
An Old Routine

SASHA TOOK HER place in the dark, quietly straightening a timeworn gingham dress. On her head she wore a faded red cowgirl hat and on her feet, her old red cowgirl boots. The costume was over sixteen years old now, but up on stage she was certain that nobody could tell.

Finally the lights came up, and she was alone on stage. She felt the warmth of the spotlight frame her face. When the music started she began to sing, in her own voice, words she'd either sung or pretended to sing many times before. It was Patsy Cline's "Crazy."

There were no melodramatic gestures this time. She no longer twirled her finger around her ear and rolled her eyes every time she said the word 'crazy.' She sounded incredibly sad. Her voice wrapped around the words and held them close. The old disco ball turned slow blue points of light around the room.

She did not feel like looking for a cute young man for the end of the song. She just sang. But then, by chance, she noticed somebody standing up in front, to the right. He had sandy brown hair, like her Billy did. She turned away from him and sang out to the crowd.

She reached her hand out, up toward the spotlight, then down, and she placed it on the side of her face. When she came to the last lines of the song, she turned quickly and looked at the one with the sandy brown hair. He was not her Billy but he was, she had to admit, very, very cute.

Could it work with this one? This time? Would it work if she tried it again? Should she? She pointed at him on the last word of the song and blew him a big, fat kiss.

Much to her delight, he looked up at her, and he smiled.

About the author

Ty Jacob is the pen name of author Jared Gulian. *The End of Billy Knight* is his first novel.

Jared's memoir, *Moon Over Martinborough*, was published by Random House New Zealand and became a #4 national best seller.

Visit Jared's website at JaredGulian.com.

You can also find him on Facebook, Instagram, Twitter, and YouTube.

Also by this author

If you enjoyed *The End of Billy Knight*, discover the truth behind the pen name. Read the author's endearing memoir about living on a tiny olive farm in New Zealand.

Moon Over Martinborough

From Michigan to the Wairarapa... How an American city boy became a Kiwi farmer

By Jared Gulian

Published by Random House New Zealand

The hilarious tale of how two American city boys learn to become olive farmers on a lifestyle block in New Zealand.

For Jared Gulian, leaving the United States and coming to tiny Wellington, New Zealand, was switch from the bright lights of big cities enough. So when his partner decided they just had to buy a rundown olive orchard in the Wairarapa, it was almost too much to cope with.

First they'd have to drive over the dangerous Rimutaka range road to get there, and he was terrified of heights. And second, they'd have to figure out what on earth you do with 500 olive trees that hadn't been pruned for years, a geriatric rooster, warring hens, an obese kunekune pig, cast sheep, marauding cattle and understanding your neighbors when they said 'yiece' but meant 'yes'.

In this endearing, hilarious, wry and warm-hearted book, Jared Gulian describes the first four years of their new life in the country, its disasters and small triumphs, its surprises and pleasures. But most of all he describes the warmth of the local community that welcomed him, saved him from certain peril, taught him how to cook, how to care for animals, and how to understand and love the land.

32572903R00269

Made in the USA
Middletown, DE
05 January 2019